TRUE PATH

Book 2 of the Timesplash series

Graham Storrs

First published Pan Macmillan Australia, 2014

This Edition, Copyright © 2018, Graham Storrs

ISBN: 978-0-9945899-8-9

Published by Canta Libre
Cover design by Graham Storrs
Edited by Tara Goedjen
Interior design by Write Into Print (writeintoprint.com)

This is a work of fiction. Names, characters, places, brands, media, and incidents are either the product of the author's imagination or are used fictitiously. The author acknowledges the trademarked status and trademark owners of various products referenced in this work of fiction, which have been used without permission. The publication/use of these trademarks is not authorised, associated with, or sponsored by the trademark owners.

Dedication

All the Timesplash novels are dedicated to the three brilliant and beautiful women who are at the heart of everything I am and everything I do; my mother, Audrey, my wife, Christine, and my daughter, Katherine.

Chapter 1

Splashfail

"Three, two, one…"

The big capacitor banks discharged with a bang, pouring their pent up energy into the coils. Within femtoseconds, the temporal displacement field bloomed around the three men on the platform, flinging them out of the spacetime we know and into the void beyond. To Isaac Callendro, team leader of this makeshift bunch of heroes, all he knew was that the lights went out.

The ruins of the Lyndon B. Johnson *Space Center* disappeared in a blink. He was in total darkness and silence, weightless and disoriented. In the void, he knew, there was no up or down, no light at the end of the tunnel. There was nothing but himself, the whole of Creation shrunk to the space within his own skull. Yet he also knew that, out there, beyond the stiff, inflated skin of his renovated shuttle-era space suit, his two companions were also with him, travelling in lonely isolation into the past. They had all been lobbed from the present, through the void, to splash down in the timestream forty-one years earlier, a time before dreams of space and exploration had died forever, before the certainties of religion had ripped apart the fragile network of science and reason upon which the greatest superpower the world had ever known had been built.

Just a single minute. That's all the lob would take. Callendro just needed to hold on to his sanity for one minute and not let the awful blackness suck it out of him. He worried about the others, though. Jacob was so young and brash. Callendro would need the young man's aggression and callousness at the other end of the lob, but he feared the boy was too unstable. Even if they pulled off the timesplash, it could unhinge a mind like Jacob's. If that happened, what kind of person would be returning with them to 2066? And Rebekka, with her poise and her old money manners, how would she respond when the madness began?

And yet, after six failed attempts—three crews fried at the lob site, two spat out of the field generator dead on their return, and another that had simply disappeared into the void—the project was running out of suitable volunteers. Callendro knew this would be their last attempt. They must succeed. Everything depended on it.

He tensed his body as they burst into light and weight and noise. Into a room full of shouting, frightened people. Callendro stumbled to his feet and quickly observed his surroundings. They had interrupted some kind of briefing. There was a big image projected on one wall, where a terrified-looking man was huddling, his features blurring as his face vibrated. Other people in the room were cowering in fear, backing up against the walls of the room. Callendro saw Jacob and Rebekka among the upended chairs and dropped tablets. Jacob wasn't moving. Not moving at all. He had somehow died in the void. Perhaps a leak had sprung in his ancient space suit. Rebekka climbed to her knees and pushed up her visor. She was clumsy in the fat white gauntlets and seemed stunned but OK. Beside her, a chair was bouncing against the floor, hitting the ground and springing back onto its legs, over and over, like a film repeatedly running forwards then backwards. Tiles fell from the ceiling as a crack ripped through the building. The men and women in the room cried out in fear. Callendro winced as the wailing sound shifted up into painfully high registers before grinding down into a deep bass growl. He had hoped that the room would be empty, that the splash would not begin until they were well clear of the origin. Now they would never make it. The splash would grow around them and they'd have to fight it for every inch of ground. It would be a miracle if they made it out of the building alive.

Callendro lurched toward Rebekka. He noticed everything in the room with a bitter detachment. He had landed badly. His helmet had hit a table corner and now his visor was a web of cracks around a tiny hole. If the whole crew had matching spacesuits, he might have been able to use Jacob's for the return trip. But their suits didn't match. Only the first few crews had had that luxury. Since then they'd had to make do and mend, refurbishing any suit from any era that they could get their hands on. He thought about trying to squeeze into Jacob's suit but the suit was defective. Jacob's frozen corpse was proof of that. With a sigh, Callendro pulled off his helmet. It would be two hours before the yankback pulled them all back to their own time. He had only two hours to find another suit, or he would die. The primary mission was shot. The operation had failed.

"Rebekka," he said. The woman looked at him with wild, half-panicked eyes. Whatever she had expected, Callendro could see that this was not it. "Becky!" he shouted. He felt the ground ripple beneath him. They needed to get out of that building at once. "Get to the exit. Get out of here."

Despite her fear, she understood and began stumbling towards the door, panicking the fleeing people jammed in the room even more.

Callendro hurried after Rebekka. A timesplash was unpredictable. Every person in this room might be affected by the sudden appearance of three astronauts. Witnessing the lob could change the rest of their lives. They might make a future decision in one way rather than another. They might fail to do something they should have done. They might drop dead of a heart attack. All of which could cause a temporal anomaly, creating an inconsistency between the future that might unfold and the present that Callendro came from. And if there was one thing the Universe hated, it was a temporal anomaly. As soon as an anomaly arose, massive forces began coercing the timeline back into shape. The bigger the anomaly, the bigger the forces involved. That was a splash: the unravelling of spacetime, the mangling of causality required to put the Universe right, to heal the wound, to return everything to how it was.

Callendro stomped along after Rebekka. The big windows on one wall of the room burst into a million fragments as the building warped. The fragments showered to the ground but stopped in mid-air, trembling. Callendro knew what it meant. Someone among the scattered occupants of this room had been a person who affected the future in important ways. Or perhaps it was the meeting itself. The bigger the effect, the bigger the splash would be. Maybe a space program employing thousands of people would not happen now. Maybe another program just as large would be started. It was impossible to know. But Callendro was sure of one thing: he had to find a suit or he was a dead man.

He saw Rebekka make it out through the door. There were still other people in the room, cowering away from him. Some seemed almost normal, no vibration, no jerky twitching.

"You." Callendro picked on a woman clutching at a table as if it were a life raft. "I need a spacesuit. Where should I look?"

She stared at him in terror. "Please don't kill me."

"I'm not going to kill anyone. I need to replace my suit. Where do you keep them?"

"I—I don't know. I work in IT. I've never…"

"Who are you?" The question came from behind him, from a balding man in a white collared shirt.

"I'm from the future. Look, I don't mean to scare you, but I really do need to get into a new suit."

But the man became incoherent, repeating the same syllable over and over, stammering out the beginning of a sentence he would never finish.

"Training," the woman said. "You should look in the training areas. Try Building 9."

Callendro nodded his appreciation and left the room. He was keen to get away before he did her and the others any more harm. He knew that everything would soon go back to how it was. After a while, the building would mend, the people would return, and the meeting would resume from the instant Callendro's crew had arrived. He knew all that, but the sight of the horrified people in that crumbling building still affected him at a level below rationality.

* * * *

Out in the corridor, Callendro reeled to a stop, unable to understand what he was seeing. Radiating lines seemed to stretch away for miles to a white dot at the centre. It was only when the corridor snapped back into shape that he finally realised it had been stretched away from him to a vast distance. The white dot was now Rebekka, standing just a few metres away with her back to him, staring into a gaping crack that ran right across the floor. He hurried over to her and put a hand on her shoulder. She turned towards him, her face white with shock.

"They fell in," she said, turning back to the crevasse.

"It doesn't matter, Bec. Nothing that happens here matters—except to us. It's the past. We've stirred it up a bit but it will settle back into place. No harm has been done."

Her expression was ragged. "I... I know. It's just..."

"Rebekka, I'm cancelling the primary mission." They were supposed to steal a car and drive ten miles to where Jacob's grandfather had once lived, but now Callendro had other priorities. "We'll never make it." He considered asking her to pursue the secondary mission—to reach the Director's office and shoot the man—while he went off on his quest for a new space suit. But the idea was ridiculous. Rebekka was barely functioning now. She wouldn't last five minutes on her own. "Come with me." He took her hand, leading her away from the hole in the floor.

"Jacob's dead," she said.

"I think he had a leak. We'll be fine." She looked quickly at his face, where his helmet should have been. He could almost hear her thinking that he wouldn't be fine, but she didn't say anything.

He saw an exit sign and followed it. He had studied maps of the building, walked around the future remains of it until he knew it well. Yet now he was disoriented and did not recognize that particular corridor. He tried not to panic. He kept reassuring himself that he was in a space centre at the dawn of the Orion Mars Mission—the ill-fated manned mission to Mars. If there was anywhere on Earth he could find a spacesuit, it was here.

They crashed through a fire exit and into the bright light of a Houston morning, frantically scanning the surrounding buildings for any that they recognized.

"There," Rebekka said, pointing. "That's Building 31. Building 9 is just beyond it on Avenue C."

Callendro wasn't sure. What if they made a mistake, wasted time going all that way? "We need to ask someone." There were people about but nobody close. The building they'd just left was shaking itself apart, yet no-one else seemed to notice. They would start to notice, eventually, if the splash spread to the adjacent buildings but, until then, the effect was localized, contained.

Callendro saw a van parked just a dozen meters ahead of them and he made for it. There was no way he or Rebekka could fit in the driver's seat wearing their space suits—the bulky environment packs they each wore made that impossible. But Callendro's suit was useless anyway and he could bundle Rebekka into the back.

"Help me out of this thing," he said when they reached the vehicle. He disconnected his gauntlets and Rebekka pulled them off. Tearing at the seal at his waist, he tried to remember what he could about internal combustion engines. He'd seen them in old vids, and knew there would be a key somewhere to start the engine.

It took an age to get out of the bulky, cumbersome suit. He knew it would take even longer to get into a new one, but if they could get the car working, they could cover so much more ground in the time that remained. Helping with the suit had seemed to calm Rebekka, restoring some of her usual poise. Yet, when a scream came from the building behind her, she flinched. He tried to comfort her but felt ridiculous trying to hug her in his underwear while she was in the bulky suit.

He went to the back of the van and pulled the door open. Inside there was painting equipment—cans, rollers, dust sheets. He pulled everything out and dumped it on the road before helping Rebekka climb inside. He slammed the doors after her and ran for the driver's seat.

"Hey! What the hell do you think you're doing?"

Callendro turned toward the shouting. Two men in overalls were approaching from across the road. Callendro quickly opened the driver's side door and looked inside. He could jump in now, but the chances of starting the vehicle in a hurry were zero. In frustration, he stepped away to face the men.

"I need to borrow your van," he said. "Just for a short while."

"Beat it, creep. And get some pants on."

The other man was staring at the road behind the van. "Hey! He pulled all our gear out. Look."

Callendro clenched his jaw hard in frustration. Couldn't anything go right?

"I'll put it all back," he lied, edging around the front of the van towards his discarded suit. "I just need it for an hour. It's a matter of life and death."

But the two men were watching him with a mixture of aggression and wariness. "Call the cops, Al," the first one said to his friend. "This guy's a freakin' whack job."

Callendro ran to his spacesuit. *It's all right*, he told himself. *Everything will put itself back the way it was.* He fumbled with the stiff white fabric, turning one legpiece until he found the pocket.

"What the hell is he doing?" Al asked.

"Just call the cops, OK?" The man hurried around the van to get a good look at Callendro and stopped dead. "Oh Jesus."

Callendro pointed the gun at his chest and squeezed the trigger. He missed. He fired again and missed again. The man turned and ran. Callendro fired again and this time blood splashed from the man's back and a red bloom coloured his white painter's overalls. The man stumbled one last pace, fell to his knees and then toppled forward to lie still. His companion, Al, didn't move. He just gaped at his friend with wide eyes. Then he looked at Callendro. The sight of a strange man in his underwear turning to face him, gun raised, seemed to snap him out of the trance he'd fallen into. He threw up his arms and said, "Take the van, all right? Take it. It's yours."

Callendro fired again, hitting Al in the shoulder. Then again. A miss. Then again and again until the clip was empty and Al was dead. The man's body did not lie still but twitched and shook on the ground, reliving its last few moments, over and over. From the body, small ripples fanned outward across the concrete. Bile rose in Callendro's throat. He threw away the gun and climbed into the van. In the back, Rebekka was sobbing. He wanted to shout at her to shut her up, but he didn't have the energy. Even without the suit, every movement he made was a struggle against the weight of his limbs. He looked for where the ignition should be but could find nothing. There were displays set into the dashboard but nothing that looked like a key or even a starter button. He looked around in desperation. Maybe there was an instruction manual.

"Isaac!"

He pulled his head up from under the dash at Rebekka's frightened call. She was staring through the back windows at a police cruiser that was pulling up behind them.

Callendro took a deep breath. "Stay quiet and keep out of sight," he told her. "You've still got your gun?" She looked horrified but pulled the weapon out of her suit and showed it to him.

He climbed out of the van and walked back towards the police car, acutely aware that he had no clothes on. The two policemen threw open their car doors and jumped out, crouching behind them with guns drawn. Callendro raised his arms and stopped walking. The bodies of the two painters were clearly visible on the ground.

"Get down on the floor and put your hands behind your head."

"Officer, I can explain everything."

"Get down on the floor and put your hands behind your head."

Emboldened by his obvious lack of any weapons, one of the cops came round the door and edged towards him.

Frustration welled up inside Callendro. He didn't have time for this. The minutes were ticking away on his life and these two fat cops were going to get him killed. With a jolt, he realized that everyone he had seen since arriving in 2025 was fat. Everybody. Living high on the hog, spending the energy from all that oil on making food to stuff their faces with, while just forty years into the future… And then he noticed that the police car's engine was still running. They had not turned it off. The incredible profligacy of burning petrol like that, without a thought, just because it might be a tiny bit inconvenient to stop the engine, hit him like a blow to the chest. This greedy world had destroyed his own, stolen his future, taken a world of peace and plenty and squandered it on fast food and air conditioning, cars and shrink wrap.

"Down on the floor. Now!"

He looked into the man's eyes. "All I want is to get a spacesuit and go away." The cop blinked and, apparently reassessing the situation, frowned. "Chuck, it looks like we've got ourselves some kind of crazy guy."

"No kidding?" said the other cop. "From the way he's dressed I thought he might be one of those NASA eggheads."

"Says he wants a spacesuit."

The other cop came out from behind the door and joined his partner. "We got great spacesuits back at the station, buddy. They got arms that tie up at the back and everything. Now get down on the floor like the man told you."

"I'm going to die if I don't get a spacesuit," he said, kneeling on the hard concrete, still managing to keep his anger under control. "I'm here from the future."

"Yeah? And there's me thinking you was an extraterrestrial." The cop stepped forward to cuff him but looked up sharply at the van.

The rear doors burst open and Rebekka began firing from inside. Callendro threw himself to the ground while the cops ducked and ran, returning fire as they went. The one called Chuck fell, dead or wounded, Callendro didn't care because the man had dropped his weapon.

Callendro got his legs under him and ran towards the gun, with Rebekka and the other cop still exchanging shots. He scooped up the gun and dropped behind Chuck's body. Taking careful aim, he fired maybe a dozen shots before the other cop fell down dead.

But the body didn't stay down. It bounced back up, sucking sprays of blood out of the air back into itself and then spurted them out again as it fell. Then it did it again, and again.

Callendro cursed and ran. Another splash had begun. A crack tore through the pavement and tripped him, sending him rolling across the ground towards the van, so close he could smell the oil and metal of its underside. The twitching body of the painter was nearby, the ground still rippling in concentric circles all around him. As Callendro scrabbled to get up, he saw one of the rear wheels. It had sunk to its axle in the concrete. He reached out a hand and touched the ground around the wheel. For all that it was rippling, the concrete felt completely solid. There was no way they could drive away the van now.

He got up and looked into the back of the van.

"Come on. We need to get you into the police car, somehow." Maybe she could take off the suit while they drove around looking for Building 9. On the other hand, maybe he should just leave her here. "Rebekka!"

She was leaning against the wall, staring at the ceiling of the van. *God damn the woman!* This was not a good time to be having a breakdown. "Rebekka, we need to get moving." He reached in and shook her. She toppled over and lay still on the floor of the van.

His heart thumped. Thumped again. Then he climbed into the van and lifted her head. She was big and awkward in the spacesuit, almost impossible to manoeuvre. He pushed her back up against the van wall and felt her neck for a pulse. Her skin was clammy and cold but she was still alive.

His relief lasted only a second or two before the realization struck him. Frantically, he felt around on her suit until he found it. The bullet hole. It had gone through the front at about waist height. He heaved her forward. The life support pack was positioned near where the bullet might have come out. The chances of it working properly with a bullet lodged in it were slim. And, even if he could mend the hole at the front somehow, the suit was almost certainly compromised at the back.

Now both of them were without a suit. Not that Rebekka would need one if he didn't find her medical care very soon. He could still use the police car. Its engine was running and it looked OK, even though mayhem was breaking out around the cop who was still flipping up and down. If Callendro was quick, he might get the cop car away from there before it too sank into the pavement, or a street light fell on it or whatever.

He lay Rebekka down as gently as he could and then sprinted for the cruiser. The ground was shaking as if gigantic animals were burrowing just below the surface. He leaped into the driver's seat and looked at the displays, all lit up to display an array of dials and buttons. There should have been pedals on the floor. He was pretty sure he'd heard about that. A gas pedal and a brake. But there were none. He scanned the displays again. He had never seen technology like this. It was far more advanced than what he was used to in 2066. The cop car might as well have been an alien spaceship for all the sense its controls made.

He pushed some buttons at random and the car spoke to him.

"Only authorized drivers may operate this vehicle. Please identify yourself and speak your security code."

He almost screamed in anger and frustration. "This is a medical emergency. A matter of life and death. Just give me control of the car."

"Only authorized drivers may operate this vehicle," the car repeated, without rancour. "Please identify yourself and speak your security code. Failure to comply will mean all systems will be locked down in twenty seconds and the authorities informed. You are advised that attempting to operate a police vehicle without permission is a crime punishable by up to three years imprisonment."

Callendro jumped out of the car. He was scared that a lock down might involve closing the doors too. After a few seconds the engine stopped. He walked back to the van over ground that was cracked and distorted, past the flapping cop and the twitching painter. He didn't go inside to sit with his dying companion but went to find his discarded spacesuit. In one of the document pockets was a small notebook and pencil. He moved away from the van, away from the shifting ground and the spreading splash. He found a shaded spot in a doorway at the other side of the street. Then he took the pencil and paper and wrote:

Tell him the mission was not a complete failure. We got back to 2025 and we started a splash. Just not the one we planned for. Tell him not to waste any more lives on trying to get this right. Tell him to go to Plan B. I don't know if he has a Plan B, or what it might be. All I know is that anything has to be better than this. Tell him goodbye from someone who never even met him but who would do it all again if he thought there was the slightest chance of it helping him get the job done.

Isaac Callendro

In the strange calm he now felt, an astonishing thought occurred to him. Even if he'd found a new space suit, it wouldn't have done him any good at all. He'd have left it behind like the rest of 2025 when the yankback pulled him home. He'd felt so rational and purposeful and yet he'd been in the grip of some kind of mind-numbing panic all along. For a while, he sat there laughing at his own stupidity. He laughed so much he ended up crying.

It was just fifteen minutes now until the yankback. No time to do much at all except wait. There was only one thing he needed to do, anyway. He got up and walked back towards the cop called Chuck. He didn't want to find himself in the void, almost naked, with no air and no heat. He picked up the gun he'd dropped earlier and checked the clip. There were three bullets left.

One would be enough.

Chapter 2

Embarkation

Leaving Boston in the summer of 2067 without the proper papers was no easy matter, but Zadrach Polanski had many friends who would give their lives to help him. One of his friends had introduced him to Captain Lee Xiangpo. Captain Lee—"Wayne" to his friends half a world away in Sydney—was Master of the handymax bulk carrier *Lucky Country*. And the *Lucky Country* was due to depart soon. With a Filipino crew and a cargo of fifty thousand tons of Montana corn bound for Liverpool, England, the *Lucky Country* was sailing with the morning tide. Meanwhile, she waited heavy and low in the Port of Boston's Black Falcon Terminal while the Massachusetts rain scrabbled against her superstructure and along her decks.

From an old customs shed, Polanski and his companions watched the docks through infrared binoculars. It was two in the morning and the wharf was quiet. Much farther away, floodlights lit up the container docks where ships were still being loaded and unloaded despite the late hour.

"I make it two on patrol at this end and two more in the hut." The speaker behind Polanski was a large and strong young man of eighteen, with fair hair and clear skin. He looked every inch the Kansas farm-boy he was, but his voice had the hard-bitten self-assurance of a man who had been fighting a guerrilla war since the age of twelve.

"Why so few?" Polanski asked, thinking out loud the way he often did. He turned to address a bulky, middle-aged man, crouched beside him in the cold, dark shed. "You did most of the recon work, David. Did you ever see just two SOBs patrolling this wharf?"

The big man shook his head, looking concerned.

Polanski turned back to the glistening wharf and peered again through his binoculars. "Could just be the rain, I suppose."

They waited in silence as the two Sons of Joshua trudged along the quayside. They hunched against the rain in their brown uniforms, their long cloaks slick and wet. They passed within a hundred meters of the abandoned customs shed, then turned and trudged back the way they had come.

"So it's a trap then?" the farm-boy asked.

"Looks like," said Polanski. "Do we call it off?"

"Nope. We just tread careful, that's all." He turned to the young man with a grin. "I promised you the flesh-pots of Europe, Peter, and I aim to make sure they're yours."

The young man grinned back. It was a private joke between them. No-one on this mission expected to have any time for pleasure.

"It's time for that distraction now, David," Polanski said. His taciturn companion nodded.

David was part of a local chapter of the sprawling, loose alliance of resistance groups of which Zadrach Polanski was the nominal leader. The reality was that that the local chapters pretty much led themselves. But Polanski was changing that.

In the past couple of years, he had coordinated several brilliant attacks on State and Federal Government facilities. He was making their presence felt. People were talking. For the first time in thirty-five years, the idea of taking America back from the Lord's True Path Party seemed like something more than a crazy pipe dream.

Polanski's new plan was as daring and original as his others—and every bit as risky. He listened with half an ear as David murmured through a compad to his team, keeping his eyes on the docks. Somewhere out there, Federal agents were in hiding, waiting for Polanski to make his move. He knew with the certainty that only a lifetime of evading the Feds could give a man. Someone had tipped them off. Someone had betrayed him. It had happened so often in his life, it didn't even hurt any more. He hoped it hadn't been David. He liked the big guy. Chances were it was someone in David's chapter—or maybe a spouse or sibling, even a child. There would be an investigation, and David would have to do whatever needed doing to protect the rest of his team.

"Sixty seconds," David said.

Polanski and the young man, Peter, put away their binoculars and adjusted their backpacks. They moved to the door. Polanski looked back at David. At the same time, David looked across at him. Even if things went well, Polanski might never see the Bostonian again. They exchanged a small nod, each acknowledging the other.

Then the sky brightened, lighting the side of David's face. Peering through the door, Polanski saw the patrolling militiamen stop and turn to look just as the thump of a large explosion shook the air. Pulling snub-nosed machine guns from under their cloaks, they began running away from Black Falcon Terminal. They were heading towards the Conley

Terminal container facility, where a fireball was rising among the cranes. The two guards in the hut burst out onto the quayside and joined their companions in a dash towards the containers. The rattle of machine-gun fire could be heard in the distance.

Polanski waited, a steadying hand on Peter's shoulder. Perhaps a full minute passed before David, still at the window with his infrared binoculars, said, "There."

Following the direction of David's gaze, Polanski saw a half-dozen black coated men. They emerged from whatever shadows had held them, cautious as cats on the hunt. They looked all around, but mostly at the container docks. Some of them held handguns in two-handed grips, pointing the muzzles at the ground. FBI for sure. Polanski watched as one of them spoke urgently into his compad. After a moment, he shouted at the others and they all ran off towards the fighting.

"Time to get your people out," Polanski said over his shoulder. Without looking back, he and Peter slipped out of the shed and ran at a crouch through the cold rain towards the *Lucky Country*.

* * * *

"That's far enough, mate."

Captain Lee was not a big man but the way he blocked the top of the gangplank left no doubt that the only way to get past him would be the hard way. Behind him, two men with machine guns stood ready to back him up.

"Can we come aboard and discuss this?" said Polanski, glancing pointedly at the commotion farther up the wharf.

"Not till I'm happy with your credentials."

Polanski reached into his jacket, causing the armed sailors

beside Captain Lee to stiffen. He pulled out a small black bag, weighed it in his hand for a moment, then handed it to Lee. The captain took a look inside. Polanski watched in silence. The bag held twenty carats of cut diamonds, the price of his and Peter's passage to Liverpool. Each stone had been donated by a supporter of the resistance, each taken from an engagement ring or brooch, each torn from the heart of someone who had clung to such mementos despite all the privations and necessities of life in modern America. Polanski had written each and every donor a personal IOU. He doubted that Captain Lee had the slightest notion what that bag of gems was really worth.

"Happy now?" he asked.

With a smile, the captain stood back and said, "Welcome aboard, Mr. Smith. These men will show you and your mate to your cabin. I'll be along in a while to explain the ground rules. Until we're under way, don't leave your cabin for any reason. Understood?"

Polanski nodded. "Sure."

"Not exactly friendly, is he?" Peter said as the Filipino sailors—one in front and one behind—led them into the bowels of the great ship.

"It's a business transaction, that's all. He's taking a big risk," Polanski said. "So is his crew. I don't expect any of them to be happy about it."

They were taken to a small cabin with bunk beds and very little else. They stowed their gear and lay on the hard mattresses. Neither of them were speaking nor sleeping, instead listening to the sound of water slopping against the steel hull, breathing air that smelled of oil.

After a long time, Polanski heard the boy's breathing deepen into a steady, regular rhythm. He gave it another half hour and then climbed out of his bed and crept out of the room. The ship was large and lightly crewed. Its five massive holds were forward. The bridge, engines, crew quarters, galley, and everything else, were crammed into a relatively small space aft. Polanski made his way up to the deck without challenge and climbed up into the superstructure. There he found a quiet place to hide, a place where he could keep an eye on the docks and the gangplank. He settled down to keep watch. The rain had stopped but the wind was chilly and the painted steel he sat on was wet and cold.

At about four AM, a military vehicle drove down the quayside from the direction of the container docks and pulled up alongside the *Lucky Country*. A couple of Feds with a squad of Sons of Joshua militiamen at their heels got out of the armored vehicle and marched purposefully to the gangplank. Polanski eased himself into a crouch, ready to do whatever needed doing. Floodlights from the ship snapped on and caught the Feds in the glare about halfway up the gangplank, where their troops were forced into single file with nowhere to run. On the deck, Polanski could just make out the captain and several of his crewmen. He relaxed a little.

For a while, no-one spoke and no-one moved.

"God be with you," the Fed at the front said. He waited for the reply but none came. He pulled a badge out of his coat pocket and held it up for Captain Lee to see. "I'm Special Agent Cartwell. This is Special Agent Drake." Drake also held up a badge. In the bright lights, Polanski could see the silver crucifixes on the two agents' coat lapels. The very sight made his jaw clench.

"And you are?" Cartwell asked and began walking up the gangplank again.

"Stop where you are!" The captain's command was loud

and sharp. It was accompanied by the sound of bolts being slid on several firearms. Cartwell obeyed immediately. "No-one comes aboard this ship without my permission, Agent Cartwell. What do you want?"

Polanski couldn't help but smile. The FBI was used to being met with fear and submission, not open hostility. It was good to see how angry it made them. Let the bastards fume, he thought. Boarding an Australian ship against the captain's wishes was the kind of thing that sparked international incidents. And, now that Australia was a member of the Chinese Pacific Alliance—effectively a vassal state of the ever-expanding Chinese hegemony—the excrement would come pouring from a great height onto any FBI agent stupid enough to stir up that kind of trouble.

"We believe there are terrorist traitors in the area," Cartwell said. "We would like your permission to search your ship in case any of them have stowed away with the intention of leaving the country. It's in your own interest that these dangerous men are captured as quickly as possible."

"There are no terrorists on my ship, Agent Cartwell."

"Nevertheless—"

Lee raised his voice. "I said..." But, seeing the Fed wasn't speaking any more, he let the point go. "I saw the fighting over there." The captain looked off towards the fires that were still smouldering. "My men and I have been armed and on alert since it started. No-one got aboard who shouldn't have. You can take my word for it."

Cartwell's sneer showed what he thought of the captain's word. "If you would just permit a quick search, I can assure my superiors that there is no need to hold your ship in dock until a more thorough investigation can be made."

It was an empty threat and the captain knew it. "Good

luck with that, mate. Here's what I reckon you should do. Take your pack of God-botherers and stick them back in that antiquated APC of yours, then drive into town and have a good night of burning gays and torturing old women and all the other fun things you get off on in the name of your fucking god, because I'd sooner send the lot of you to Hell this night than let any one of you set foot on my ship."

Cartwell was practically foaming at the mouth. Even Polanski was shocked at the Australian's blasphemous outburst.

"Atheist!" one of the militiamen said and spat into the black waters below him.

"Foreigner," grumbled another.

Polanski heard a quiet scrape beside him and turned to find Peter crossing the roof to join him. The young man scowled an accusation at him as he settled into the shadows. In the lad's hand, the blade of a hunting knife glistened.

Polanski looked back towards the drama unfolding on the gangplank. There was no way the Feds could storm the ship without being cut down by the captain and his men. All that Cartwell could do was to retreat and call for backup. Despite Cartwell's fury, he was unlikely to do anything of the kind. He'd tried bullying his way onto the ship. Beyond that there was nothing he could do apart from escalate the matter to levels so high he would need absolute certainty that Polanski was aboard even to contemplate it. Even so, there was always the possibility that Cartwell was a fool, or that Captain Lee would goad him into starting a firefight. The silence dragged out until Cartwell turned abruptly and shouted at his men to get back to the transport. With muttered complaints, they obeyed him.

Before Cartwell joined them, he turned again to Lee and

said, "I'll be praying that we meet again, Captain." He stalked down the gangplank and then posted the militiamen to guard the dock before driving away with the other Fed.

Polanski watched in silence for a while to make sure the SOBs were going to obey their orders, then tapped Peter on the shoulder and led him off the roof and back to their cabin.

"You won't need that," he told the young man, nodding towards the hunting knife still in his hand. "The Feds are more scared of disturbing their bosses than they are of letting us get past them. We're safe now."

Peter nodded and sheathed the knife. He looked into Polanski's eyes and said, "I'd die before I let them take you, Zak."

Polanski brushed his declaration aside with a laugh. "Save your passion for the girls in Liverpool." *And pray to God I never put you to the test.*

Later, he left the cabin again and found the captain on the bridge. "That was a brave thing you did," he told the Aussie.

"I hate those bastards," Lee said.

"All the same…"

"My mother always told me the only way to stop a bully is to stand up to him. Reckon she was right. Anyway, I know who you are. Anything I can do to help, you just name it."

Polanski said, "You could give me my diamonds back."

"Fuck off, mate!" The captain laughed loudly. "Now get back below decks like I told you, or I'll fucking shoot you myself."

Chapter 3

Sandra

The drone delivery vehicle sat on its four spindly legs on a raised platform about three meters square, looking tiny in the huge warehouse. Black and yellow stripes marked the edges of the platform. The words, "Danger. Authorized persons only beyond this line," were stencilled on its sides. Thick cables snaked away to banks of capacitors, humming softly in grey steel cabinets. Behind a Perspex wall, two women watched the readouts projected in their virtual displays. Their hands moved confidently within the sensor fields. Their focus on the task was absolute.

"DDV power-up," one of them said. The rotors on the little quadcopter drone began to whine.

"Counting down," said the other, and a clock, projected so that they both could see it, began running backward in hundredths of a second. "Power at ten percent. All nominal."

"DDV to operating height." The little quadcopter rose into the air and climbed to one meter where it hovered, rock steady.

"Thirty seconds."

"DDV to automatic." The quadcopter went through a

rapid series of manoeuvres, ending up exactly where it started. "Test cycle complete. All nominal."

"Twenty seconds. Field at fifty percent."

The two women exchanged glances. It was all going exactly as planned. They had worked for six months on the DDV and its precious cargo and in a few seconds, their baby would be on its way.

Sandra allowed herself a moment of triumph. Her friend and colleague, Dr. Olivia Bradley, turned back to the displays and said, "Field at eighty-five percent. Ten seconds."

Sandra checked her readouts. Everything had a green light. "All systems nominal."

"Five seconds."

"DDV main engines online."

They both shifted their gaze to the quadcopter. Rocket engines mounted in its stubby wings would eventually explode into life, but not for a good few minutes yet. The clock's digits raced down to a row of zeros and the DDV popped out of existence. The clock immediately reset for a one hour and twenty-seven minute countdown.

With a whoop, Sandra leapt into the air, skipped over to Olivia and high-fived her. For a while they danced and hugged among the desks and cables, Sandra did most of the leading while Olivia, looking bemused but happy, let herself be pulled about.

"Time to grab lunch before The Little Pig comes home," Sandra said, dragging Olivia to the door.

Olivia laughed at Sandra's pet name for the DDV.

"How can you think of eating while the DDV is out there on its first mission?"

"Oh, Piggy's OK, and there's not a thing we can do about it if it isn't."

"All the same," Olivia said, insisting, causing Sandra to halt. "There's a lot to do."

"All the more reason to grab lunch while we can. Once all that data gets back, neither of us is going to get a break for the next few weeks." Sandra let go of Olivia's arm and stepped back. She could see her friend would only fret the whole time they were away from the lab if she made her leave. "OK. I'll go and get lunch. I'm going to have something really nice to celebrate, and I'll bring you back a cheese sandwich, or something else horrible, because you're such a miserable old bugger." She headed for the door again.

"Don't be too long," Olivia called after her. Sandra grinned and gave her friend the finger over her shoulder on the way out.

Outside it was a bright autumn day. Sandra was almost skipping, so pleased that the DDV had launched successfully. She checked the time on her commplant. Right now The Little Pig would be hurtling back through time through the pseudospatial void. She had done the trip twice herself—the last time, sixteen years ago in London—so she could visualize the DDV tumbling through the icy blackness with nothing but its accelerometers to tell it that it wasn't perfectly still. Her own trips had been short, a couple of minutes each time, but the DDV was going much farther back in time than she ever had. Its flight-time was thirty-six minutes each way. Thirty-six minutes in that awful nothingness. It made Sandra shudder every time she thought about it. It made her remember that first time—with her boyfriend, Sniper—sucking on an empty air tank on the return trip, so scared she could barely think, and Sniper tearing off her helmet, pushing his snarling face against hers.

Sandra stopped, looking around at the bright sunshine, the

brick buildings and the little groups of students on the lawns. Her breathing was laboured and her heart was thumping. Even after all those years, the memory of that timesplash could still do that to her. She closed her eyes, then opened them again after a moment and continued walking.

Sniper is dead, she told herself. He died sixteen years ago in a backwash in Deptford, his body torn to pieces by machine-gun bullets, his creepy little teknik also dead. The police had no idea who had killed them, but Sandra always supposed it had been Sniper's colleague, Camilla Vergara. She seemed the sort who would get her revenge.

It was all another world, another life. Sandra had been just fifteen when it started and only seventeen when Sniper died. She'd called herself "Patty" back then. All timesplashers had tags. It had all seemed so cool. Now it just seemed silly. Even Olivia had once had a tag. She'd been "Nahrees." When Sandra first met her she was working as a teknik for MI5, helping them create their own timesplashing capability so they could fight Sniper and his kind.

Thinking of Olivia made Sandra smile. Olivia had never been cool by any stretch of the imagination. She was pure geek to the very core. Being Dr. Olivia Bradley, a lecturer in the Temporal Sciences Department of the University of East Anglia was much more her style.

A young man caught Sandra's eye. He was tall, well-built, fresh-faced. The right age to be a student—a freshman, anyway—but he didn't look right. His clothes were wrong. Was that all? She studied him. He stood outside the cafeteria building, now intently reading the menu, but when she first spotted him, he'd been staring straight at her.

Which wasn't so unusual. Sandra knew she was a beautiful woman. The kind of beautiful that made her stand out like a

swan in a flock of geese. Tall, athletic, with a natural grace
and elegance that made Siamese cats look gauche, she could
easily have made a living as a model, except that she had not
wanted her picture flashed around. As a teenager she had
caught the eye of Sniper, the most famous brick in the world,
and had been photographed on his arm at every fashionable
party in Europe. At thirty-three, her beauty had deepened and
matured and supposedly half the boys—and faculty—on
campus were secretly in love with her. Some not so secretly.
But everyone knew to keep their distance. She would let no-
one near her and had a well-honed repertoire of stinging
rejections. Besides, she had a black belt in karate—she was on
the university team—and there were rumours that she
secretly worked for the security services and that she had
killed people. The rumours weren't quite true. She did not
work for the security services. She wanted nothing to do with
that life at all. She had once killed a man, though.

The young man was still reading the menu. Sandra
suspected he was watching her reflection in the cafeteria
windows. Just a lust-struck teenager? Or something more
sinister?

She went inside and bought the first two sandwiches she
could grab, snatched a couple of random drinks from the
cabinet, and a couple of chocolate bars from the display next
to the checkout, bundled them all into a bag, the cafeteria
automatically deducting the cost from her commmplant. She
hurried back to the lab. She walked fast, waiting until she'd
travelled fifty meters on a straight stretch of footpath before
stopping suddenly and turning round.

The path behind her was clear. No-one took a sharp turn
into the shrubbery.

The young man was nowhere to be seen.

Stupid, she told herself. *Paranoid.* She carried on to the lab. It was all this reminiscing about the past. She thought she was over all that. She'd spent weeks in a loony bin—the Porringer Institute for Mental Well-Being, to give it its proper title—and ten years in therapy after the events of 2050. She bloody well should be over it.

But, of course, hunting down Sniper—with a little help from MI5 and Europol—and facing him in London in 1902, were not what her problems had been about. The real issues had been to do with why she'd become involved with a bastard like Sniper in the first place. Getting to the root of that had been why her therapy had been such a long and painful road.

Yet she'd made it. Sorted herself out. Made up for all the school she'd missed, gone to university, discovered an aptitude for engineering and maths, and been one of the first graduates of Exeter University's brand new Master of Science degrees in Temporal Engineering. Her therapist had worried about her attraction to the mechanics of time travel, but Sandra thought it only natural that she'd be fascinated by something that had so dramatically affected her life. And, when she started applying for teknik jobs, she found Nahrees, running her own Direct History team there at UEA.

"You were quick," Olivia said, looking up from her work.

"Was I? I suppose I just wanted to get back to stop you messing up all my calibrations."

Olivia pulled a tight smile. "Once. Once I turned the wrong knob." She sighed. "What did you get me?"

Sandra glanced at the flight time display and saw the DDV had been falling through the pseudospatial medium for over twenty-five minutes. She hoped it would come out the other end still functioning. They had tested The Little Pig in zero pressure at almost zero Kelvin for much longer periods. It would be OK.

She tipped the contents of her bag onto the desktop. "Er, ham and cheese, or..." Her heart sank. "Beef and horseradish." Olivia was a vegetarian.

"What happened out there?" Olivia asked, suddenly serious.

"I, em..."

"A brick?"

Sandra knew what Olivia was thinking. It was the same thing that had sprung to mind when she saw the young man watching her: old enemies. There were people from the old timesplashing scene who knew Sandra had played a part in taking down Sniper and his team. Most of the old timesplashers—the "bricks" as they were known back then—had moved out of the time travel business and into petty crime. Sometimes, not so petty. A couple of timesplashers were big names in organized crime now. It was always a possibility that one of them would decide it was time to settle an old score.

"I'm probably just being paranoid," Sandra said, trying to convince herself.

"Shit." Olivia sounded scared.

"It's nothing. Probably. Just some kid, ogling me."

"Did he follow you?" It struck Sandra that her friend had been employed by MI5, and would have undergone at least basic training, even though she had been on the technical staff. *So many years ago.* The idea of her slightly plump, rather matronly friend on a firing range, or practising tradecraft, seemed ludicrous.

"I don't think so. Look, it was probably nothing."

"Do you want to...? You know."

They'd spoken about it just once, on a boozy night out three years ago. Sandra had told Olivia about the bag she kept packed, the secret bank account with her emergency fund, the passports in false names. Yet Olivia had remembered.

"Are you kidding? With The Little Pig out there on its first mission? No way."

"Better safe than sorry."

Shocked that this was escalating into the realms of panic so quickly, Sandra decided to quash it, firmly. "I am not disappearing into the night to leave you to take the credit for all my hard work. For all I know, you planted that kid to spook me just so you could get all the glory."

Olivia's worried expression twitched into a smile. "It's no wonder there are people out there who want to kill you. I feel the urge myself, sometimes."

"Come on, let's get the nets up."

Olivia seemed reluctant to let go of her concern, but allowed herself be drawn into the work. They needed to fit fine, strong netting around the platform from which the DDV had been launched.

"I can't believe it's gone back two thousand years," Sandra said, although that wasn't strictly true. These days she fully understood the energy fields that would lob an object out of the present and into the past, through the nothingness in between. Even so, the sense of wonder at the achievement hadn't left her.

"You and Jay did pretty well," Olivia said, referring to the lob they'd made in London, sixteen years ago.

"We agreed not to mention that."

"Sorry, your stalker friend just stirred it all up again."

Sandra felt her stomach flip as she remembered what had happened. It had all started with Sniper. He and two other bricks had gone back 150 years to the British Museum Library to assassinate Pyotr Illyich Lenin, who had been visiting there on April 4th 1902. The idea of a timesplash was to create a paradox, to change as much as possible so that the past became incompatible with the present. That was the essence; lob a brick back into the timestream and make as big a disturbance as possible. For the brick it s the ride of a lifetime—if you're of a disposition that likes wild, deadly mayhem. And that was all that Sniper and his kind lived for. And the best part is that whatever damage you do to history sets itself straight. The past reassembles itself. The anomaly is removed. Even the bricks are yanked back to their own time, as if the Universe just spits them out. Yet the splash ripples forward through time, and when those ripples hit the present, the acausal chaos is felt again. Only this time, any destruction is not corrected. Make a big enough splash, far enough back in time, and the backwash hits the present with the force of a nuclear bomb.

Sandra shuddered. The willingness of crazy psychopaths like Sniper to go back and risk their lives for the thrill of making a bigger, messier splash had soon been exploited by every terrorist group and organized crime gang who could find a splashteam willing to hit the targets of their choice. Beijing had been all but wiped off the map. So had Mexico City. London had been saved from utter destruction only because Sandra Malone and her friend, Jay Kennedy, had persuaded Europol and MI5 to help them go after Sniper.

It was all like a dream to Sandra now. In fact, between her first timesplash in 2047 and her last one in 2050, she had been declared certifiably insane and had spent most of that time locked up by the courts in an institution. In Sandra's opinion, she had been insane all her life until she got to know

Jay. Just a sweet boy of nineteen at the time, he had sparked a tiny flame of self-respect in her that had grown steadily over the years.

My God, Jay. Where are you now?

She thought about him every day. Literally, every day. When they parted, with half of London in ruins, Jay heading to a new job in Brussels, and she on her way to the Porringer Institute—voluntarily, this time—she had known they might never meet again. When she decided she needed to keep away from him, to stay out of his world, she had been overcome with guilt. It was only survivable because someone else had come into her life. Someone who needed her more than he did.

"You're sure this stuff's strong enough?" Olivia asked, picking at the netting.

Sandra snapped out of her reverie. "The Air Force came and fired shotguns at it, remember? Then they blew up a grenade inside a tent made of it. It'll be fine."

"Those drones might be moving at fifty kilometres a second when they get back. That's a lot of momentum, even for little things."

"So you want to worry about this right now, when there's nothing you can do about it? I did the maths. I did the experiments. It'll hold."

"Yeah, I know. I just never touched the stuff before. It's so light."

"You think I'd let my Little Piglets come to harm?"

Olivia smiled. "Stupid of me."

The DDV was The Little Pig. In its belly were a hundred tiny drones—The Little Piglets. Once the DDV reached its destination time, two thousand years in the past, it would emerge into the empty fields of Iron Age East Anglia and orient itself in mid air with its four rotors. Then it would climb to a hundred meters and fire its rocket engines. Like a bat out of Hell, it would fly at full thrust for twelve seconds on a high, ballistic arc. Its trajectory would bring it down over the coastal town of Camelodenum, a Celtic town then occupied by the invading Romans and renamed as Colchester. As the DDV plummeted to earth, it would open its belly and let the piglets out. A hundred little self-steering ornithopter drones, no bigger than dragonflies and bristling with sensors, would spread wide and start recording, storing away petabytes of data in their pinhead brains.

And, if the archaeologists and historians were right, they would return with detailed high-quality recordings of the Celtic Queen Boudica leading her Iceni horde to defeat and massacre the Roman occupiers. It would be a triumph for the Direct History group and a record that would set the academic world buzzing for years to come. The DDV would land harmlessly in the sea. The drones would be almost indistinguishable from real insects. The chances of causing an anomaly—even a small splash—were infinitesimal.

Yet the chance was always there, a fact reflected in the oversight and scrutiny the project had endured over the long years of its inception and development. Olivia had steered it through all of that, spending endless days in committees and hearings. Everyone needed to be convinced that the DDV would not land right on Boudica's head and create a timesplash big enough to wipe out half of southern England. The only reason they had been allowed to proceed, Olivia had told Sandra in private, was that the military had seen so many interesting applications and wanted the technology.

Sandra had been shielded from most of the bureaucracy and allowed to work in peace on building the rig—one of the most powerful time displacement field generators in the world—and getting The Little Pig and her piglets ready. Of course, she had agreed to letting RAF flight engineers critique her designs and CERN tekniks check her rig, but that had turned out to be a lot of fun. Waiting for the final sign-off from the MoD and then the Home Office had not been so enjoyable, but that was all over now. The Little Pig was finally flying and nothing could stop it.

"It's on its way back," said Olivia, staring at the clock. Sandra regarded her friend without speaking. Olivia had been a rock throughout the whole project, but even rocks wear away in the end. The stress of this wait seemed like the final straw that might break her.

"There's still time for me to get you that sandwich," Sandra said. The ones she had bought earlier still lay uneaten on the desk. It felt wrong to eat one in front of Olivia, having stuffed up the order.

"You were right, I should have gone to lunch with you."

"Why don't you go for a walk around the campus? I'm probably capable of staring at the clock all on my own for a while. You should get out. It's a beautiful day."

Olivia fought an internal battle for a moment then nodded to herself. "You're right. If I stay here, I'll be a gibbering wreck before the drones get back. A ten minute walk won't hurt, will it?" She turned to leave but stopped at once. "We should check the cameras," she said.

Sandra threw a pencil at her. "Get out. The cameras are fine." She pointed to a display showing several views of the platform. "Everything's fine. Bugger off before you make me a gibbering wreck too."

Olivia scowled. "Bully."

"Out."

Sandra watched until Olivia was out the door then turned back to the displays. She settled down to wait the thirty minutes or so until the drones came back. A lob was like dropping something massive but buoyant from a height into deep water. It sank and sank but, eventually, its buoyancy overcame its downward momentum and pushed it back up to the surface. That was the so-called yankback. She had experienced it herself. One moment you're in the past, coping with the frenzy of a timesplash, the next you're hurtling back through the nothingness outside of time. If you're lucky, you have your helmet on, sealed and ready. If not…

According to the clock, The Little Pig and her piglets had already been yanked out of Boudica's time and were on their way back. They'd arrive where they stared from, no matter how far they had travelled at the other end. However, quantum uncertainties, and limits on the reversal of entropy, meant there would be slight spatial discrepancies. Nothing would arrive in quite the same place as when it started, nor with quite the same momentum. But the nets would catch the drones—even The Little Pig. The biggest problem would be the rocket exhaust. The rocket fuel burned at the other end would all come back too. It would have cooled, but it would still want to occupy a far greater volume than the original fuel. Their calculations suggested a percussive expansion as the exhaust gasses blasted out through the netting and into the surrounding air. That's why Sandra and Olivia needed to be behind a protective screen, with all the doors and windows open, and industrial-strength extractor fans running at full speed to suck the noxious fumes from the building.

And that's why no moron has ever sent a nuke back in time to cause a splash, she thought, with grim satisfaction.

This technology was lethal enough without that kind of capability.

The door opened behind her. "That wasn't ten minutes," she chided, swivelling in her chair.

Olivia walked towards her on unsteady legs. A dark, lean man with hard eyes walked close behind. Too close, Sandra realized. Behind him, the fresh-faced youth from the cafeteria came through the door. He looked back the way they had come and then shut the door after him.

Instinctively, Sandra measured the distances between herself and the men, checked angles and spaces, identified potential weapons, cover, escape routes. She was still numb with shock, but part of her mind remembered how this worked. She was on her feet, weight shifting. She could take these two, she was sure. The boy was big and strong but that wouldn't help him much. The older man looked tough and fast. He would be more of a problem. But she couldn't see his right hand, the one behind Olivia's back. If he had a gun in that hand, all bets were off.

"Don't try anything stupid," the man said. He had an American accent. "Just keep calm. We don't want anybody to get hurt." He stepped back a pace so that Sandra could see the pistol in his hand.

"Do I know you?" she asked. There might still be a chance to disarm him, if she could just get close enough. An American, though. Some of Sniper's lunatic, terrorist backers had been American. Was this some kind of payback?

"We'll have lots of time to get acquainted," the man said. "Why don't you sit down?" Sandra didn't move. In a flash he had the gun against the back of Olivia's head, holding the terrified physicist by the back of her collar. "Please, sit down." Still, Sandra hesitated. The man looked hard and he looked determined, but he didn't look cruel. She had seen cruel often enough to know it well. On top of that, he seemed completely in control of himself. If this man shot someone, it would be a deliberate, calculated act. It would not be in a passion of hatred or fear.

"Let her go," Sandra said. If she could stall this man another twenty minutes, the DDV would arrive with a bang and she might have a chance to overpower him.

"Sandra," the man said. "You are number one on a list of five possible targets. If you prove to be too much trouble, I will move on to number two. Do you understand me?"

Sandra understood all right. She stepped back to her chair and sat down. Instantly, the tension in the room eased. The man took Olivia to a chair and made her sit down too, his gun still against her head. Without any signal, the young man went over to Sandra and tied her hands behind her. He grabbed her upper arms from behind and lifted her to her feet. The older man put away his gun and tied Olivia to her chair. Olivia was so frightened she gave no resistance at all, for which Sandra was immensely grateful.

"Where are you taking me?" Sandra asked, since that was obviously the plan. The older man gave her a reproachful look. "I could tell you now if you like, but then I'd have to kill your friend."

"Olivia?" Sandra had to repeat her name to get her friend's attention. "I'm going to be OK. You just wait here until someone comes. Mike and Greg will be along at two to help with processing the drones. Remember? Then you should go and see Cara, she needs the first four Fibonacci numbers. You won't have to wait long. It's all going to be OK."

"That's enough," the older man said. The younger one moved her towards the door.

"No," she said. "There's something else. We're running an experiment here. There will be a release of toxic gasses in sixteen minutes. You need to turn on the fans before we go, or Olivia will be dead before they find her." He looked sceptical. "It's the switch on the display there. The one marked 'extractor fans'. Just flick it and I'll go with you with no trouble. If you don't, you'll have to drag me every inch of the way."

He studied her face for a long while, then strode over to the display, found the switch and flicked it. The big fans boomed into life. He looked again at Sandra.

"Thank you," she said.

"You're welcome. Can we go now?"

With Olivia watching in wide-eyed horror, the two men took Sandra away.

Chapter 4

Jay

"You know damned well the threat hasn't gone away."

Jay Kennedy paced the Superintendent's office, too agitated to stand still. As a Chief Inspector, he had no business speaking to his superior like that, but the news had rattled him—however much he had been expecting it—and he refused to accept it.

"Jay," Superintendent Kappelhoff spoke in a strong, German accent. "We have known each other a long time. You and I were in the original TCU team that Bauchet set up all those years ago."

Jay clenched his jaw to stop himself screaming. This was not the end of an era. It was not some fond farewell to a glorious past. This was a stupid, nearsighted bureaucracy shutting down his department to save a few euros, when they should be ramping it up.

He was high up in the Berlymont Building, Europol's headquarters in Brussels. Outside the floor-to-ceiling windows, the skies were grey and the city was a dismal mess of tangled highways and ageing highrise office blocks. Europe was having another prolonged recession, and Brussels, ever since the centre of European Government had switched to Berlin, appeared to be in terminal decline. All the same, Jay had come to love the place in the sixteen years he'd worked there.

"You're a victim of your own success, Jay," the Super went on. "The Temporal Crimes Unit, under Bauchet's leadership and then under yours, has been incredibly effective against the bricks. So effective that we really don't need a centralized unit to coordinate their eradication. To all intents and purposes, they're gone. We beat them. You won. There hasn't been a major timesplash attempt for five years now. It's time to wrap it up, Jay."

But Jay didn't see it that way. "The threat has changed, that's all. The bricks were a bunch of crazies, thrill seekers, psychos. They were born in a world of underground parties and young kids getting their kicks from drugs and weird tech. They just didn't know when to stop. They let themselves become a weapon for every cashed-up organisation on the planet with a grudge. But the bricks were a difficult and dangerous weapon to wield. Even the worst terror groups turned their backs on them in the end. The real threat now is government-sponsored temporal crime. Only last month, the Russian Federation took out a Chechen town with a splash."

"We don't know that."

"Yes, we do. And that's the kind of thing we need to be focusing on now."

The Superintendent's tone hardened. "No, it isn't. Government-sanctioned attacks are acts of war, or espionage, not criminal matters. Europol is a police organisation. It's the job of the European Secret Services and national counter espionage units to worry about what governments are doing."

The TCU had always sat uncomfortably within Europol.

There had been talk over the years of moving it into Interpol or the ESS, but they had each developed their own capabilities for dealing with timesplashing and no-one wanted it. By the time Jay got his promotion to Chief Inspector, the TCU had shrunk to a size where he could run the whole thing himself. It was a bittersweet moment when he took control of the unit he had devoted his professional life to.

"So you're just shutting it down? Just like that?" He realized he had just accepted the inevitable, and now he was merely whining. "What about my team? What about our ongoing operations?"

"People will be dispersed back to their national police forces. Operations will be passed to Interpol. I'll expect you to be able to do the handover and brief them in two weeks. The unit will close officially one month from today."

Jay sat down, defeated. "Yes, sir."

He stared at his feet but could feel the Superintendent watching him. "You haven't asked about yourself." Jay looked up at the Super. "If you want to stay in Europol," he continued, "I'd be glad to fit you in anywhere that takes your fancy. Organized Crime could use somebody with your drive." Jay said nothing, wondering if there was any drive left in him now. The Super pursed his lips. "You're still a young man, Jay. What? Thirty-five? Thirty-six? You've done incredibly well. If you hadn't insisted on sticking with the TCU, you might have done even better. Take a few days to think about where you want to go next and call my secretary. We'll have dinner and talk it over. You should see this as an opportunity. The TCU was a dead end. This could be just what your career needs."

* * * *

"This could be just what your career needs!" Jay's snarl surprised one of his sergeants. The woman was sitting in his office, apparently waiting for him, as he stomped inside and slammed the door after himself.

"Chief?"

"Never mind. What are you here for?"

"You asked me to come in and talk about vacation arrears."

"Right. Well that doesn't matter much now. I want you to call all the staff together, out there." He waved in the direction of the open-plan office. "No exceptions. Big announcement. Anyone who isn't here, patch them in on their commplants. I'll be out..." He glanced at the time. "...at ten past on the dot. Off you go."

The sergeant hesitated. "Can I tell them what it's about?"

"No, you can't. Just do it."

She hurried off and Jay threw himself into his chair, swivelling round to look out the window at the drab city, trying not to think about leaving it. Already he had begun putting together the phrases he would need in a few minutes time. "I want to personally thank you all for your dedicated service... This is no reflection on the quality of work we've done here, in fact... Each of you will be relocated. There will be no redundancies." Each new reassurance felt as if it stole a piece from his heart. Every last member of the TCU was as dedicated to their mission as Jay himself. He'd have them all in here, one by one over the coming days, each with that same feeling of having had their strings cut. Each looking to Jay to make some sense of it for them. The task of being encouraging and positive seemed overwhelming. He had no idea how he would do it. Even getting through this announcement seemed impossible.

He asked himself how his former boss, his friend and mentor, Jacques Bauchet, would handle it. And the thought of Bauchet made Jay long to go over to France right that minute to see him. *I will*, he promised himself. *As soon as I've got things in order here, I'm going to visit Jacques and Marie.* If anyone could advise him as to what to do next, Bauchet was the man.

The sergeant popped her head round the door and said, "They're ready for you, Chief."

He nodded and took a deep breath.

* * * *

"What will you do, Chief?"

The question and answer session after the announcement had been difficult and long but that question was the one that decided Jay to call a halt. There was a fine line between being fair to his staff and allowing the team to wallow in self pity. The fact that he increasingly felt the urge to wallow with them meant his judgement was probably not what it should be.

"First thing I'm going to do is to make sure we do a proper handover to Interpol. We're on the trail of some pretty nasty characters right now, and I don't want any of them getting out from under us just because we've moved their case to another department. In the longer term, like everyone else here, I'll be looking at what opportunities present themselves." He tried to sound buoyant. "I'm used to working with the best, so it's going to be hard finding somewhere else so good, but we've all got a chance now to find new directions, to reinvigorate our careers and re-inspire ourselves to do great things. The TCU was just the beginning. Thank you."

He turned away quickly and made it to his office before anyone could accost him. *Jesus Christ, Jay! When did you start talking like that?* Maybe the Super was right and this was a chance for Jay to re-evaluate his life. And the first thing he felt he needed was to re-connect with the real world and stop talking like a corporate drone. He felt soiled by the hypocrisy of sounding so positive when the reality for everyone in the unit was that this was a complete and utter disaster.

Or maybe that's just how it seemed to him. Maybe most of his staff would be glad of the chance to move on. Almost all of them were police officers from around Europe. Maybe they'd be glad to go back to their own cities and their families. The thought gave Jay pause. The idea of going back to London didn't fill him with any kind of pleasure. Sixteen years after the Big Splash the reconstruction was finally complete. A memorial park ran from the rebuilt British Museum to Charring Cross Station, a broad green scar that marked the site of so many deaths. The rail link from Charring Cross to Deptford crossed the delicate new Memorial Bridge and wound its way through a thousand acres of new development. London had bounced back, as it always did, but there was too much there to remind Jay of that dreadful day.

He also doubted that he would be welcomed back by any police or security force in the UK. MI5 had sacked him in a frenzy of finger pointing after Sniper's attack. The fact that— largely due to Jay and Sandra—the death toll had been thousands and not millions, cut no ice at all. The security services had failed to protect London from its worst disaster since the Blitz and heads had to roll.

"I'm going for a walk," he told Anna, the section admin officer, as he grabbed his coat and strode past her desk. "If anyone wants me, tell them I've gone out to reflect on the meaning of life." He stopped and went back. "That was a joke, of course. Tell them I'm in a meeting." Anna was a good administrator, but she had a tendency to take things literally.

"Are you all right?" she asked, big eyes full of sympathy. She was an attractive woman, a tall Nordic type in her early twenties. She had drunkenly confessed to him at the last Christmas party that she had a crush on him and he'd been terrified of showing her any kind of encouragement since then.

"I'm fine. How are you?"

She pulled a sad but brave face.

"You'll be all right," he told her. "You can count on a very good testimonial. Everyone can." She looked eager to talk about it but he drew back. "I'll be back in half an hour, probably."

The streets were as cold and miserable as they looked and a light drizzle began as he stepped out from under the massive entrance awning of the Berlymont Building. He had no destination in mind and didn't care where he went. Motion was what he needed, the illusion of doing something, of getting somewhere. Sitting in his office felt too much like his wheels were spinning while his spring wound down.

He had seen it coming, of course. He wasn't an idiot. The unit had slowly been losing budget and shrinking in size as it mopped up the last of the old bricks. But he had assumed the TCU would simply refocus, find a new mission, take on new enemies, and continue to fight the menace that time travel technology presented. He realized now what a pipe dream that had been. Hard times always saw governments pull in their horns, focus on domestic matters, become more myopic just when they needed to expand their vision. The world was in just as much danger from temporal crime as it had always been—perhaps more—and Jay could not see himself abandoning his life's work just because some idiot in Berlin had added the TCU as a line item in a budget balancing spreadsheet.

He caught the reflection of a young woman in a shop window, half a block behind him. Hadn't he seen the same woman a few minutes ago? He took the next left and walked a little faster. His MI5 training had saved his life several times in the years of his tenure at the TCU. However, it looked now as if a university degree or some other qualification might be more use in helping him find a new job. How did he get to be the world's leading expert on a bunch of ageing bricks and now facing redundancy? Maybe the truth was he deserved to be on the scrap heap, even at thirty-five. He'd become as obsolete as the people he had hunted to extinction.

He turned into a quiet alley and ducked into a doorway. Reaching into his shoulder holster, he drew his police issue stunner and waited. After a few seconds, he heard footsteps—a light step—hurrying to catch up. A moment later, a woman sped past without seeing him. Not a woman, he realized, but a girl. A teenage girl, tall and slender, her long legs in drainpipe jeans, her thick, black hair bouncing on her narrow shoulders. She stopped and looked side to side, realizing she had lost her quarry.

He stepped out behind her and raised his gun, placing the dot of the targeting laser in the centre of her back. When she turned, the dot ran across her back, round her arm and over her right breast to dance in the centre of her chest. He caught his breath. It wasn't that the girl was younger than he had supposed—no more than fifteen, he now saw—nor that she was a beauty—which she was, the kind to make older men act and feel foolish and ashamed—but because of the impossibility of what he was seeing.

His heart stopped. Time stopped. He let the hand holding the stunner fall to his side.

"Sandra?" he almost said, stupidly.

Wild surmises clamoured in his brain. She had found a way to come forward in time. She had come back from a future where she had been restored to the way she looked on the day he had first seen her. Time itself had fractured and fragmented. Past and present were mashed together. Ghosts walked the Earth.

She stared back at him, her initial alarm giving way to something like curiosity, an intense, questioning scrutiny. His heart beat again. He could see now that it wasn't her. This girl was similar, freakishly so, but there were differences. She was not quite so tall, not quite so beautiful. The hardness and strength that were always just below the surface in Sandra Malone were missing in this child. This girl had had an easy life, no old-before-her-time bitterness. She had been loved and cared for. She had grown up innocent and undamaged. And yet the resemblance was so strong.

"Why are you following me?" he asked in French, breaking the long silence.

"I…" she said, speaking English. "You're Jay Kennedy."

He switched to English. "Who are you?"

She seemed hesitant, nervous. He wondered if she might have information.

It wouldn't be the first time he'd been approached by a

stranger like this. "Are you Jay Kennedy?" she asked. "I need to know."

He holstered his gun and stepped towards her. He was fairly sure she was not armed. "Yes, I'm Jay Kennedy. Why were you following me?"

"I need..." The girl was breathing hard, as if strong emotions were seething inside her.

"Why don't you just calm down and say what you wanted to say?"

"Don't you recognize me?"

He studied her again for a moment. "I must say, you remind me of someone I knew once, but I don't think we've ever met."

"Who? Who do I remind you of?"

There was vehemence in her voice, a kind of pleading. It made Jay wary. Mentally, he took a step back. "Look, why don't we just stop pissing about? Who are you and what is it you want?"

The girl looked hurt. The open vulnerability that had been in her eyes disappeared, like a wild creature drawing back into its burrow. She took a breath and held herself upright. Jay could see she was preparing herself for some kind of pain but until she spoke, he had no idea what it might be she feared from him.

"My name is Cara," she said. "Cara Malone. I'm your daughter."

Chapter 5

Prisoner

Sandra woke to find two small children staring at her. As her eyes opened, their eyes widened. She squinted at them, trying to decide if they were a dream, and they ran off, slamming a door behind them.

She was on a wooden-framed bed, on a mattress that felt like a bag of loose springs. Her hands and feet were tied with plastic straps and her head felt like it contained a large burrowing animal trying to dig its way out through her temples. She closed her eyes against the harsh, strange light. It was hot. Her clothes were damp with sweat. The room smelled of fried food and unusual spices. *Not in Kansas any more*, she told herself. Yet, for all she knew, that's exactly where she was. How long she had been unconscious, she could not tell. Polanski and the other guy, Peter, had bundled her into a van and driven for what seemed like ages.

When they finally took her out, she was inside a hangar at a small airfield.

"We need you to be quiet for a while now," Polanski had said. He'd held a small disc in his fingers and reached out to press it against her head. She recognized it as a neural damper. Its carefully shaped magnetic fields would keep her unconscious for as long as it was near her skull. She began to protest and the next thing she knew she was airborne, curled up inside some kind of packing case, listening to the drone of a twin prop aircraft, flying straight and level.

When they opened the packing case, it was night time and she found herself inside another van. Polanski cursed the failed neural damper and apologised to her. "Tech's hard to come by," he said. "We take whatever rubbish we can." The boy, Peter, handed him a syringe. "This isn't so nice for you, but it's a lot more reliable." They both had to hold her down before Polanski could get the needle into her.

Now she was… where?

A small bedroom. Plastered walls. A single window with cheap curtains and faded wooden shutters. A dresser, with no personal effects and no mirror. A door. Closed. Bare wooden floorboards. It could have been a room anywhere, but it felt foreign. The smells, the heat, even the light, left her convinced she had been taken out of the UK, out of Europe too, unless she was in some sultry Mediterranean country. From the light, she suspected it was either just after dawn or just before sunset. From the heat, she guessed the latter.

She checked her commplant. She wanted to call Cara. Then she would call the police. But the commplant told her there was no service available. That wasn't too big a surprise if she had been taken out of the country. What was a surprise was that the device didn't offer her any alternatives. Where in the world could she be where there were no telecoms services at all? She'd just have to hope that Cara got her message and had gone to Jay.

She sat up and looked around for a way to remove her

ties. The bed springs clanked and groaned and her head swam. Whatever they had injected her with was not a modern, high-tech anaesthetic, but something crude and simple. Who the hell were these people?

She was grateful they'd tied her hands in front rather than behind her. It gave her a better chance of freeing herself. There was nothing sharp or obviously useful for cutting the ties, so she set that on the back burner and bunny-hopped to the window. The ties cut into her ankles and the wooden floorboards thudded with each hop, but finding out where they were holding her was high on her list of things she would really like to know. Besides, if she could climb out the window, maybe there would be something outside to cut her bindings with.

The window was on the ground floor, which was a good thing, but the view robbed the fact of any pleasure it might have given her. She seemed to be on a farm, a dirt-poor collection of single-storey buildings. The ground was sandy and an ancient flatbed truck without tyres was rusting in a clearing. A scrawny goat was tied to the truck's rear end. Beyond the fields the ground was dry and barren, broken and rough, rising gradually to distant hills with mountains far beyond. It could be the Middle East, she supposed, simultaneously praying that it wasn't. Since the Adjustment, the Kingdoms of Islam were no place for an infidel white woman.

Whatever it was, she didn't fancy her chances of crossing that endless desert. The temperature must be at least thirty degrees where she stood. Out there, in that treeless wilderness, the sun would burn her flesh and bake her dry. She hopped back to the bed and sat down. *So what's the plan?* she asked herself. *Hop across to the truck, get the goat to bite through your ties, and then leg it across fifty kilometres of burning desert?*

She looked at the door. She knew it was unlocked because the kids had run out through it... unless that really had been a dream. Polanski and his sidekick had brought her there in a vehicle of some sort and it was probably parked outside somewhere. She could climb out the window cut her ties on a rock—there seemed to be no shortage of rocks in this place—find the vehicle, steal it and drive off.

The fact that the vehicle would probably be biometrically keyed to particular drivers, Polanski and the kid, at least, didn't bother her too much. She had stolen plenty of cars in her misspent youth.

She was halfway through the window when Polanski walked in. "Hi. How're ya doin'?" he asked.

She heard him walking across the wooden floor behind her. Then a hand gripped the belt at the back of her jeans and she was yanked back inside and dumped on the bed. She struggled against the clanking mattress until she was sitting up with her back to the wall.

She snarled at the American, wishing her hands were free so she could beat the grin off his stupid face. "Who the hell are you, and what do you want?"

He went to the dresser and retrieved a tray he must have put there. It had a glass of water and a plate of food on it. Sandra's stomach reminded her how welcome that would be.

"If you want this, I'll untie your hands," he said. "But you've got to promise not to do anything stupid."

"I'll tell you what, why don't you just take me home and I'll forget all about breaking your neck?"

He pursed his lips and returned the tray to the dresser. "I guess you're just not in the mood. Shame, because the food's good here." It certainly smelled good and Sandra was already wishing she had eaten first and threatened later.

"Can we cut the bullshit and get on with it? If this is a kidnapping for ransom you're probably the most stupid criminal I've ever met. I'm an orphan on a research assistant's salary."

Polanski sat down on the end of the bed, which made Sandra think about kicking him in the face. "I know exactly who you are, Miss Malone. You used to be a timesplasher—a brick. You were part of a splashteam run by a guy named Sniper. You took out a small town in the Netherlands in 2047, but by 2050, you had switched sides and you helped the British cops bring Sniper down in London. Since then, you've done a whole load of menial jobs, working your way through college. You picked up a couple of degrees in physics and temporal engineering, and now you work for Dr. Olivia Bradley at the University of East Anglia, building time travel rigs for use in her research. In short, you went from brick to teknik. A very unusual career path."

"How do you know all—"

Without warning, she lashed out with her feet, delivering a fierce kick to the side of his head. Polanski didn't see it coming. His head snapped sideways and he fell off the bed. Sandra scrabbled after him. Although stunned and groggy, he was starting to lever himself off the floor. She dropped to her knees beside him, grabbed the front of his shirt and delivered the knockout blow by headbutting him on the bridge of his nose. He fell back heavily and Sandra began a rapid search of his pockets.

She found a bunch of plastic ties in his back pocket and a large penknife in front. With some effort, she dragged the penknife out of his jeans and opened it up. She had made a lot of noise so she kept her eyes fixed on the door as she struggled to cut the plastic strip that bound her wrists. It was awkward, but she managed it. She had just cut her ankles free when Peter came rushing in. He shouted something and charged straight for her. The boy was a fool. She could have ripped his throat open with the knife if she had wanted to. Instead, she nimbly sidestepped the heavy young man and managed to get in a blow to his ribs. By the time he got his balance, she was waiting, delivering two fast punches to his solar plexus and another to his throat. He slid down the wall choking and gasping for air, looking shocked. Stepping back, she raised one leg and shot a kick at his head, knocking it back against the wall. The young man slumped down, unconscious.

* * * *

By the time Polanski woke up, Sandra had searched the farmhouse, located the vehicle, and discovered a Latina woman, who allegedly spoke no English, and her four children. She had also learned something very interesting: she was in Mexico, near somewhere called Múrquiz Municipality, a couple of hundred kilometres from the Texas border. The woman and children seemed to be no threat, so Sandra went back inside to see her prisoners. She drank the water and ate the food while she waited for them to come round.

"You fight pretty rough for a girl," Polanski said once he'd opened his eyes. He massaged the side of his face, pulled at his ties, and then reached across to give his young friend a shake.

The boy groaned and looked up at her from the floor. Polanski kept his eyes on her while he wriggled himself into a sitting position, his back against the wall. There seemed to be no anger, or even reproach in his tone. It made Sandra wonder if he knew something she didn't. If she had any sense she'd have been on the road by now, heading for the nearest big town with a police station. Since this was a farm, there was probably a farmer out in the fields, maybe a bunch of farmhands too. Who knew? Hanging around was not a great idea. But she wanted to understand what was going on before she left these two behind.

"It's time you told me why you kidnapped me and dragged me halfway around the world."

Polanski smiled. "That's what I was trying to do when you started playing soccer with my head."

She smiled back. "OK. You've got the floor."

He chuckled at the joke. "It didn't say in your file that you were some kind of martial arts expert. Did MI5 teach you those moves?"

She snorted with derision. "You know a lot less than you think. Why don't you just get on with it?"

"I've got a project I'd like you to work on," he said, surprising her. "It requires your unique skill set. That's why you were top of my list."

"And you couldn't just offer me a contract, like anybody normal?"

"That's the problem. I ain't just anybody normal."

Beside him, Peter was struggling to sit up. "You're gonna be sorry for what you done, bitch," he said, glaring at Sandra.

"Peter!" Polanski's tone was harsh. "You apologize to Miss Malone. We're the ones in the wrong here. If you go around kidnapping folks, you can expect a bit of rough treatment from them if you let them get the upper hand. It's only reasonable."

Peter looked as if he'd been slapped in the face. He cast

down his eyes. "I was just sore, Zak. I didn't mean anything by it."

After a moment, he looked up at Sandra. "I'm sorry, Miss. I hope you don't take offence."

Sandra gaped at them in disbelief. What was wrong with these people? Maybe they were just crazy. Maybe there really wasn't any rational explanation for the kidnapping. "OK," she said, standing up. "It was nice meeting you guys, but I need to be on my way now. If you're ever in the UK again, don't call me, I'll call you."

"Don't you want to know what the project is?" Polanski asked. Before she could tell him just how little she wanted to know, he said, "We need to you run a timesplash for us. I want you to help me get back to Washington, 1735."

Again, she goggled. "You two must be the craziest pair of kidnapping arseholes on the planet. I can't begin to count the number of reasons why you picked the wrong girl for your harebrained scheme. Let me give you a few words of advice. Timesplashing isn't nearly as much fun as you might have heard. Sure, there's the buildings crumbling around you, and the streets are full of screaming people in pain, but, honestly, it takes a special kind of psychopath to enjoy watching a pavement turn to quicksand and swallow a baby in its pushchair, or a little girl screaming and dying a thousand times as a runaway truck smashes into her tiny body over and over again." She stopped, the memories overwhelming her as they always did. She looked angrily at Polanski. "If you want kicks, take up bareknuckle boxing. Timesplashing is for the seriously deranged."

She was about to go, but her anger was growing by the minute and she couldn't stop herself. "So you thought you'd just grab yourself a teknik and build a rig, did you? Jump back, shoot your grandmother, and have a wild ride? Was that the plan? To hell with all the people back at the lob site when the backwash comes to tear up their world and kill and maim them? What in God's name do you think would induce me ever to be a part of that kind of insanity ever again? Were you going to threaten me? Pay me? Seduce me? Because, I tell you, there is nothing you've got, nothing you could do to me, that would ever persuade me to help you. Nothing."

Even as she said it, she realized there was one thing. Just one thing. But if they had Cara, surely they would have said something by now. She turned to make her exit but didn't take a single step. There in the doorway, was the woman she had dismissed as harmless. Only now she had a double-barrelled shotgun pointing at Sandra's chest. How long the woman had been there, Sandra had no idea, but it would certainly explain Polanski's insouciance. Maybe there had never been a time she could have escaped from the moment she had walked back into the bedroom.

"Shit," she said, and sat down on the bed.

The woman threw a kitchen knife onto the floor by her feet and said something in Spanish.

"She'd like you to free us now," Polanski said.

Sandra considered her chances of throwing the knife at the woman and grabbing the gun while she was distracted. There was a slim chance it would work, but nothing she wanted to risk her life on. So she picked it up and cut Polanski's ties and then the boy's.

They got up and rubbed their wrists. Polanski went over to the woman and took the gun from her. They exchanged a few words in Spanish and she left. Sandra sat down again and waited, staring at the floor and silently calling herself every rude name she could think of.

"I'd like to think I could still persuade you to help us," Polanski said.

Sandra didn't even look at him. "Dream on, arsehole."

He was silent for a moment. Then he said, "What if I told you that by helping us, you could free my people and restore democracy to my country?"

Wanting to see his face, she looked up at him. He was not smiling. He was dead serious.

Chapter 6

Cara

Cara let Jay lead her through the busy streets of Brussels. He stopped at a quiet café where the manager seemed to know him. It was still mid-morning and there were few other customers. Jay ordered coffees and croissants and then turned his attention back to her to continue his questioning.

"When were you born? The exact date."

Irritated, she told him. She could see his brain clanking through the calculations. "I'm not lying," she said. "Anyway, I don't think this is the most important issue right now."

He seemed bewildered. Her mum had said that he could be a bit slow sometimes, that you had to spell things out, say things three times before he finally got it. She had seemed to think it was cute, but Cara was finding it infuriating.

"No, I think it's pretty damned important," Jay said. "Trust me, there's a lot going on in my life right now, but a fifteen-year-old girl turning up out of nowhere and claiming to be my daughter pretty much trumps everything."

"Not everything," she said. She could tell him why she was there if he'd just shut up for a minute. It had been non-stop questions ever since he sprang on her like some sort of mugger in that alley.

"How did you get here?" He was off again. "Does your mother know where you are? Where is she? Is she in Brussels too? How long have you been here? Where are you staying?" He kept asking question after question without even waiting for an answer.

"Dad," she said, wanting him to stop and listen.

The word hit him like a punch in the gut. For a moment he looked so stricken, so hurt, that Cara recoiled in alarm. His lips moved but he made no sound, as if the engine that had driven his endless stream of questions had slipped a cog and couldn't work his mouth any more. It was her chance to jump in and speak but now she couldn't. That look of pain in her father's face held her both fascinated and appalled.

Eventually he found his voice again but all he seemed able to manage was one word. "Why?"

"Why?"

"Why didn't she tell me? Why keep it—keep you—a secret all these years? Why...?" He seemed to struggle with his breathing and, to her horror, Cara saw tears in his eyes. "I thought she..."

Loved me.

Cara could hear the unspoken words as clearly as if he had shouted them. For a moment, she thought about getting out of there, just getting up and leaving. This was all too much. It wasn't what she expected. She didn't know what to do with this stranger's—her father's—heartbreak. Yet she had a message, something she had to do. Whatever else happened.

"Mum's been kidnapped." She watched her father stop and frown. He shook his head, like he was reeling from another blow...

"What?"

"Two men took her. Olivia saw it. She was there. They were Americans. They grabbed Olivia outside the lab and tied her up and then they took Mum."

Jay began floundering again. "The lab? Olivia? What?"

Cara had arrived home that day from school to find the police and Olivia waiting for her. She remembered the shock, and she remembered the nasty smell of the police woman's uniform. She remembered lots of stupid little details, but she couldn't remember what anybody said, or how it had come to be almost bedtime before Olivia found the chance to get her alone and say, "Your Mum said to tell you it's the first four numbers of the Fibonacci series."

Cara had known instantly what that meant. It was the combination to the safe, the safe that held her mum's instructions for what to do if bad things happened. She'd always thought her mum was an old drama queen, that nothing would ever happen to either of them in sleepy old Norwich, that they'd both grow old and die of boredom in that rural backwater. Her mother was always warning her to be careful about people she met, to stay clear of reporters, to avoid talking about her past to her friends. She made Cara report home all the time if she ever went anywhere. She'd tried and tried to get Cara to take karate lessons and made her carry pepper spray and an illegal stunner with her all the time. There were two bags in her mum's wardrobes, one bag for each of them with spare clothes, passport activation codes, and money. She thought her mum was mad, a crazy person, paranoid—probably from doing too many drugs in the 'Forties. But here it was, the bad thing, the one her mother had warned her about. It was real. It was happening.

She had run to the safe in her mother's bedroom and

tapped in the sequence. Inside were two envelopes. On one was written: "Read this if I'm dead." On the other: "Read this if I've gone missing."

She'd snatched up the "missing" envelope and torn it open. She tried to read it but it didn't make sense. She tried to focus harder, to look closer, but there was no information in it and the words were a grey blur. She gripped the paper tighter as if she could force it to make sense by sheer willpower. Then she realized she was crying. Her eyes were dripping tears. Her mother had been kidnapped. She was in danger. She might never see her again.

Cara couldn't breathe, couldn't stand up. The fear was unbearable, maddening. She couldn't lose her mother. It couldn't happen. She needed her. She wanted her so much it felt as if her insides were tearing apart. She fell to the ground, sitting on her mum's carpet, clutching at the quilt on her mum's bed, breathing her mum's scent. What if these were the last things of hers she would ever know? What if these *things* were all she had left?

Olivia came into the room and Cara shouted at her to go away. Olivia had let them take her mum. She'd been useless. She'd just let it happen. She didn't want to see Olivia ever again. She pulled the quilt from the bed and squeezed it to her, sobbing into it, all restraint gone.

* * * *

It was dark when Cara woke up. She was on the floor, the quilt under her and a blanket on top of her—put there by Olivia, she guessed. She crawled over to the bedside table and turned on a light. She remembered the letter from her mother and searched the bedclothes for it. The letter was on the floor, under the quilt, crumpled and torn. Frantically, she laid out the pieces on the bed, smoothed them down, tried not to drip any more tears on them. Angry at herself for being so useless, she wiped her eyes clear and read the letter.

Dear Cara,

The only reason you're reading this is because something terrible has happened—or you've added safe cracking to your many other accomplishments. I know you must be worried and frightened right now but it's going to be all right. There is someone who can help you—and me. I want you to go to your father. Take your running away bag and go now. The sooner you get to him, the sooner he will be able to help us. I know I promised you I'd take you to meet him when you were old enough and I know this isn't any way to say hello to your dad, but that can't be helped. He'll get over the shock soon enough and after that, I promise you, he will move Heaven and Earth to find me and to make sure you're safe. I've always told you he's a good man. The nicest man you'll ever meet. And it's true. He just does a dangerous job in a world I've always tried my hardest to keep you well away from.

Well, it looks like that world—the world of my misspent youth— has finally caught up with me. There isn't anyone else you can turn to except Jay to keep you safe and help find out where I am. The local police won't be any use. Don't waste your time with them. Jay has better resources and he's smarter than anyone they could put on the case.

Don't tell anyone where you're going—not even our friends. Anyone you tell could put you in danger, or you could be putting them in danger. Just slip away quietly and find your father.

I've never told you but I set it up so you can access my credit and my bank account. The passwords are attached. Program them into your commplant and then burn the piece of paper. Your father's work address is also attached, along with the home address of his friend, Jacques Bauchet, in case Jay isn't there any more for some reason. If you can't find him, come home and let Olivia look after you. I asked her if she would and she told me I need never worry about you being alone or uncared for.

That's all, darling. Be careful. Go to Jay. And remember that I love you more than anything in the world. I'm so sorry this has happened, but I know you will be strong and brave and that I'll be proud of you.

With all my love, Mum.

PS The other letter you found in the safe—the one you read when I'm dead—you can safely ignore. It's the one with all the smoochy stuff about how much I love you. Get to Jay and come and find me and I can slobber all over you in person, OK?

Cara called a taxi and went downstairs to the sitting room, carrying her bag. There she found Olivia asleep on the sofa, looking uncomfortable. A wave of gratitude washed through her for her mum's friend, but then she immediately felt guilty about what she would have to do. She opened the fridge and grabbed a carton of milk, taking a long drink before returning it.

She used her commmplant to write a note to Olivia.

Please don't worry. And don't come looking for me. I've gone to find Mum. It was her idea. Thanks for everything, Cara.

She set the message to send in one hour. By then, she would be far away.

She stepped outside and closed the door quietly behind her. The taxi she had called appeared within minutes and she climbed in. "Airport," she said and the driverless vehicle whined into motion, smoothly accelerating along the road. She looked back at her home and felt it being drawn away from her.

* * * *

Sitting in a café in Brussels talking to this strange man who was really her father was the end of a long journey. Cara was filled with sadness and anxiety and hope. Now, as she regarded Jay Kennedy while he floundered around trying to make sense of it all, she wondered what her mum had seen in him all those years ago. He wasn't bad looking, she supposed, in a tall, gangly, boyish sort of way, but she knew he wasn't her mum's type at all. And yet her mum always went on about how very *nice* Jay was. She made him sound like one of those blokes who ran the youth club in the Church annexe. And her mum and Jay had met when they were very young—not much older than Cara was now. They'd shared some big adventure back then, she knew. They'd been together during the Big Splash—although her mum had always been infuriatingly vague about just what had happened.

Maybe they were both caught up in some kind of adrenaline rush at the time. It was hard to see any other explanation for them getting together, in her opinion.

"All right," Jay said. He'd said "All right," about twenty times so far. "Let's start at the beginning." And then he stopped again with that bewildered look. For him the beginning was sixteen years ago, she supposed, and the thought of the road from there to here seemed to overwhelm him. With a sigh, Cara decided to take charge.

"Look, Mum told me all about you. She said you were some kind of cop and your life was dangerous. She said she wanted to keep me safe from all that so that I never got sucked into it, or something. She's completely paranoid about it. Said if you ever knew about me that you'd want us to move to Brussels, or you'd come to Norwich, and it would all start up again."

"Jesus," her dad muttered. He sounded angry. Cara pressed on.

"She always said her past had been stupid and reckless and there were people from back then who might want to hurt her—and you—and me. So she kept me quiet. She doesn't have many friends—just Olivia really—and we don't go out to places where anyone would know us. I only just realized that a couple of years ago. She just said it was better that way. And she freaks out if there's ever a hint that the press is onto us."

"Olivia's the one who saw the kidnapping?" Jay seemed to be getting over the shock at last.

"You know her, Mum told me. She used to call herself Nahrees."

Jay struggled with his memory for a couple of seconds before he remembered. "But she was... I thought your mum wanted to get away from all that."

It had always seemed odd to Cara too. "Yeah, that's the weird thing. She went off and got all these degrees and stuff and then she decides to work in a time travel lab with an ex-teknik."

"A time travel lab?"

"At the University of East Anglia. They do research on—"

"On remote sensing of historical events." Jay had either been running searches or he had a good knowledge of the field. "So Olivia is... Dr. Olivia Bradley, right? I never knew her real name. And Sandra works for her?"

"Mum's the teknik these days. She makes cute little insect probe things that go back to watch ancient battles and all that."

"Bloody hell."

There was a long silence while Jay digested this new information. Cara picked at her croissant. It seemed to be just plain bread. She looked about for some butter.

"All right," Jay said again. "So Sandra—your mum—and Olivia were in the lab and you say Olivia went out for a walk and two guys grabbed her and brought her back in. Then they tied her up and took your mum away. And there was no fighting and no struggle? She just went with them?"

Cara nodded. She could see what he meant. "Mum's on the uni karate team. You'd think she could have kicked their butts, right? But Olivia said Mum was trying to save her." It was good that her mum was so self-sacrificing and everything, but Cara wished she'd just kicked the bastards to death and let Olivia take her chances.

"And you've no idea where they took her?"

Cara shook her head. "Just that the guys were Americans. Do you think they've taken her to America?" She was beginning to think it was time Jay started doing something instead of just sitting there asking questions. But then, he didn't look like the kind of action man hero she'd been expecting. "Do you do karate too?" she asked, hopefully.

"What? No."

"Mum said you would save her. She said the Norwich cops were useless."

"Did she? And did she tell you I'm a cop?"

Cara couldn't help letting her disappointment show. "I got the impression you were in some kind of special ops unit, or something." Looking at this slender man in his business suit, she realized what a stupid notion that had been. Whatever her father was, he was definitely not a tough guy.

Jay looked dismayed. "Is that what she told you?"

Cara shook her head. "Not really. Mum's always a bit vague about what you do, probably so I don't go off trying to find you. She said you were in an anti-terrorist unit. I always supposed she meant you were in the SAS or MI5 or something. I didn't expect to find you in an office in Belgium. Look, shouldn't we be trying to find her, instead of just…?"

Jay regarded her steadily for a moment. "I'll try to find her. You are going home to Norwich. I'll call Olivia and have her meet you off the train."

She sat back and folded her arms. "No way. I'm staying with you. Mum said."

She saw him frown, not knowing what to do. "You can't stay with me. We don't know who's got her or what it will take to get her back."

"I'm not going. I'm staying with you."

He put his hand to his temple and rubbed his head, closing his eyes. Then he looked at her. "All right. Just for a while. You can go home tomorrow. Come on." He got up and led her out into the street. "We'll go to my office and I'll see if I can find anything out about what happened."

This was better. They were finally doing something. "Mum said you had resources."

He looked harassed. "Not for this. The UK police, Interpol, they've got resources for finding missing persons. I can't use my team for that."

"You've got a team."

"Yes. No. Not any more. Shit." He became flustered and tried to apologize for swearing. "I'm not used to dealing with kids."

Cara took umbrage. "Yeah, well, if I see any kids I'll warn them about you."

Which made him even more flustered. "I didn't mean to… You're obviously a…" He gestured for a while in lieu of finding the right words, then gave up and walked on in silence.

He had to sign her into the building. A security guard

scanned her and checked her bag. It was an old building, scruffy and musty. Jay took her up in the lift, along corridors, and through another security checkpoint that led to a big, open office. People looked up from their work to stare at her as she went by. It was a little intimidating, which made her straighten her back, tilt her chin up and walk with a bolder stride.

They passed a young woman at a desk who greeted Jay and told him about calls and appointments. She studied Cara with open curiosity but Jay did not enlighten her. "I do not want to be disturbed—for anything—until I say otherwise," he said. "Got that?"

The woman looked ready to protest. She cast a quick glance at Cara, opened her mouth and closed it again. "Yes, Chief."

They went into Jay's office and he closed the door behind them.

"All right," he said. That stupid phrase was beginning to grow irritating, but Cara let it pass. "You sit quietly and read a book, or whatever. I need to run some queries."

As long as things were happening, Cara was happy. She sat down on a beat-up old sofa and brought up a magazine on her commplant while Jay went to his desk and began popping up virtual displays. She watched for a while as he became engrossed in his searches and then began flicking through the pages.

It took Jay less than half an hour and a handful of phone calls before he sat back in his chair with a sigh and called Cara over. He did some quick gesturework in his desk's sensor field and suddenly Cara had access to his virtual displays. They appeared on a wall in front of them. Cool tech, she thought but didn't say anything.

"OK. This is the story," Jay said. He pulled a display forward, zooming it so it almost filled Cara's vision. It showed two still images of two men, one old and rugged, the other young and beefy. "These images are from campus security cameras. These two men were the only ones at the university that morning who are not in any European database. Which means they are probably our two Americans. There are no border security images from anywhere in the Union that match these shots, so we can safely assume they're here illegally. I've done a search of all passenger vehicles—aircraft, boats, cars, trains—leaving the Union within twelve hours of your mother's disappearance. These two have not crossed any border. Meaning they're either still here, or they left by some other means. So I searched for any non-passenger vehicle leaving the UK for the U.S. or any destination that could have made a connection to the U.S. There were quite a few that were suspicious-looking—but nothing obvious."

"So you drew a blank?"

"So I tried another approach. They had to have some kind of car or van to get Sandra away from the campus. Preferably something parked near the lab. I found it on the campus security recordings. In fact..." He pulled forward another display. It was a recording of two men—the same two—walking with Sandra between them. Her hands were tied. There was no other sign of coercion or rough treatment. They stopped at a van and Sandra climbed in the back with both of her kidnappers. After a while, the van pulled away. "I've got transponder hits of the van passing various checkpoints. It travels to an Airfield in Cambridgeshire, and doesn't move again."

"So they caught a plane?"

"Probably."

"Probably? Of course they caught a plane."

"There's no record of a plane taking off after they arrive, apart from a couple of flying school trainers, both two-seaters. There was also the scheduled shuttle to Stansted Airport—all passengers accounted for—and a robot freighter bound for Schipol in Amsterdam."

"So they're on the freighter?"

"We don't know. Record-keeping at the airfield is pretty lax and the freighter isn't licensed to carry passengers. It landed at Schipol about three hours after your mother was abducted. They have excellent record-keeping there, but it's one of the biggest airports in the world. If they were hiding in the freight, they could have been shipped on to any of hundreds of different destinations by now."

"Including America."

Jay nodded. "Yeah."

"So you've got to track every piece of freight from that plane and see where it went."

"I've already sent out the requests to do that but you shouldn't get your hopes up. If Sandra was in a box, they'd just need to have the box delivered to a warehouse, then swap her to another box and send it on to its next destination. There's still a chance we can find someone in the chain and make them talk, but this is looking well planned and well organized. They've gone to a lot of trouble to get hold of your mother and get her out of the country. I've put out a missing persons call to Interpol and I've sent pictures of the kidnappers to the FBI. Maybe they'll know who they are."

Cara didn't like the way this was going. She walked away from the desk, unable to stand still. "So you're just going to give up? You've done a few poxy computer searches and that's it? Now it's somebody else's problem?"

"I didn't say that."

"I can see it in your body language. It's in your voice. You've done all you can. That's what you think. My mum's just some woman from your past. Someone you had a fling with sixteen years ago. So why should you care what happens to her now?"

"Cara! You don't know what you're talking about." Jay was on his feet, looking mortified. But Cara didn't buy it.

"That's why you never came looking for her, isn't it? That's why you just left her to fend for herself? You didn't care how much we struggled. You didn't care how hard she had to work. The sacrifices she had to make." She saw the look of horror growing on his face. Well, it's about time he heard some home truths, she thought.

"It wasn't like that," he said, coming around the desk. "It wasn't anything like that. She insisted on going back to the Institute to sort herself out. I all but begged her not to go. I knew if she got herself together she wouldn't—" He stopped dead.

"Wouldn't what?"

He seemed to be in real pain, struggling to breathe. For a moment, Cara wondered if he was having a heart attack. But he pulled himself together and said, in a more even voice, "I thought she wouldn't want me any more." He looked away from her as if ashamed of himself. "She was supposed to join me in Brussels. I found us a place, furnished it, got everything ready. Then, just like that, she stopped answering my calls. I knew why, of course, but I went to the Institute to see her. I wanted her to tell me to my face that she didn't love me."

He walked over to the window and looked out, a dark figure against the grey skyline. "She'd gone. Left. Her doctor wouldn't tell me anything. Wouldn't even give me her number. He said I should respect her wishes. That she'd get in touch when she was ready. I could have tracked her. I wanted to, even though it would have cost me my job. But what would have been the point?"

He turned back to Cara. "The thing is, I really did love her, and I thought, 'If she's happier without me, then that's what I want for her.' So I came back here and got on with the job of putting away every scumbag splashteam in Europe. And I did it with such a vengeance that I ended up running the place. But there was never anyone else. For a long, long time, I waited for her to call. After that… Well, I stopped waiting. If I'd known about you, it would have been different."

He fell silent. Cara could feel her heart thumping in her chest. She hadn't meant to say those things to him—about him neglecting her mum and all that—they'd just come pouring out. She realized she had never really believed her mum when she'd said what a nice man her father was. She'd always wondered why, if he was so bloody nice, had he made no move to find them and help them for all those years? Now he was standing there looking crumpled and beaten and saying it was all her mum's fault for dumping him and hiding his child away from him.

She thought about going to him and giving him a hug, but he was still a stranger and every second that passed made it harder. Besides, it didn't matter how he felt, or how she felt. Her mother was still out there and they had to do something to find her.

She took a breath and tried to keep her voice steady. "We still have to find her. You have to find her. She trusts you. She told me to trust you. I can't do this on my own." She found herself crying again. Not the deep racking sobs of last night, but a quiet trickle of tears that hardly did justice to the wild turmoil of misery that filled her up.

He took a step towards her. "I'm sorry. I can't imagine how bad this is for you."

"Then find her, please. Just find her."

He looked like he might come and hug her. He actually swayed where he stood. But she didn't want that. That would be too much on top of everything else. She turned away and put her head in her hands, feeling the wetness of her cheeks, feeling tears slide between her fingers. She stood there a long time and, when she looked again, he was back at his desk, his long-fingered hands doing their silent dance within the sensor field.

Chapter 7

The Border

Four of them set off for Texas the next morning in a rugged, Kenyan Jeep knock-off, the seats configured for manual driving. They drove through countless miles of hot scrubby desert. The few towns they passed looked abandoned.

Polanski and Sandra rode up front, with Peter and another man in the back. The plan was to cross the border and let the fourth man take the Jeep back to the farm. Others would meet them in Texas and take them farther.

"Couldn't you just take these things off while we drive?" Sandra asked, holding up her tethered wrists.

"Sure," Polanski said, not taking his eyes from the road. "But if I did, you'd be tempted to make a run for it, and, if you made it, you would most certainly die out in that desert. So I think it's best we just keep you trussed up. For your own safety."

"I suppose that's what passes for humour where you come from."

"Hell, yes. I'm considered a regular wit and raconteur back home in Baker. Ain't that right, Peter?"

The young man laughed, at some kind of inside joke,

Sandra assumed. "So is that where we're going?" she asked. "Baker?" Again Peter laughed, but this time the laugh was cut short as the Jeep swerved to avoid a pothole that could have swallowed the entire vehicle.

"Gets worse every damned year," Polanski grumbled. The fourth man grunted his agreement and rattled off a long complaint in Spanish.

"So where are we going?" Sandra asked. "Isn't it about time you told me what the hell is going on? You said something about restoring democracy to your country. Maybe you'd like to expand on that."

"You don't even know who he is, do you?" Peter asked. He sounded angry. "This is Zadrach Polanski."

Sandra turned to give the boy a cold stare. "Yeah, we did the introductions. Zadrach Polanski: legend in his own lunchtime. And you must be Robin, the Boy Wonder."

The young man lunged at her, shouting, "You fucking atheist whore!" His fist struck at her, clumsily in the confined space of the car's interior. Sandra dodged it easily and grabbed his arm. She intended to pull down on it over the back of her seat and maybe break his elbow, but she didn't get the chance. Polanski slammed on the brakes and everybody was thrown forward. The Jeep slewed sideways on the sandy road and Polanski was out before it had rocked to a stop. He threw open the door next to Peter and dragged the boy out of the car and then kept on dragging him away across the scrubland.

Sandra watched as Polanski harangued the young man, clearly furious. She couldn't hear what was said, but the older man was doing all the shouting. Peter looked so obviously shocked and horrified at this treatment by his mentor that Sandra half expected him to burst into tears. Despite the younger man's size, she had no doubt that there was some element of physical fear behind the boy's reaction to Polanski's anger.

After an age, Polanski stopped shouting, but carried on speaking to his protégé. Peter began nodding and shaking his head, clearly responding to questions. Then he was allowed to talk. Eventually, Polanski nodded, satisfied. He smiled and slapped the young man's upper arm. Then he put his arm around the lad's shoulder and led him back to the car. Peter climbed in, subdued, avoiding Sandra's eyes. Polanski got in and started up the car.

"Peter didn't mean what he said," he told Sandra. "It won't happen again."

They drove in silence for a while before Polanski spoke up again. "Are you a good teknik, Sandra?"

"Fuck do you care?" She wasn't in the mood for polite conversation with this bunch of crazies.

"I care a great deal," Polanski said and something in his tone made Sandra's jaw clench.

"No," she said, shaking her head. "No way." Polanski said nothing. "You want to make a big splash? You grabbed me so I could build you a rig?" Again no reply. "Well fuck you, Mr. Charismatic Leader of The Cult of One Deranged Kid. If you're recruiting for your splashteam, you picked the wrong woman. You might as well let me out right here, because there is no way in hell that I'm going to help you kill innocent people. I would rather die in your fucking desert."

Polanski sighed but kept his eyes on the road. "I'm sorry, Sandra, but you're it. We don't have the resources to go all the way back there and kidnap someone else. Heads up! There's the border."

In the back, Peter and the fourth guy reached under their

seats and pulled out machine guns. Ahead, Sandra could see
nothing but more desert. The car lurched as Polanski drove
off the road and along a winding track that he seemed able to
pick out from the rugged desert by some kind of magic sense
that Sandra did not possess. She put both hands on the dash
and hung on as best she could as the Jeep bounced and
lurched across the rocky ground, heading about forty-five
degrees away from the road. They kept it up for ten or fifteen
minutes that felt like twice as long, grinding through low
gears, the car's electric engines straining under the demand.
When they rounded a ragged outcrop of rock, they stopped.

Beyond a level overgrown strip of land, Sandra saw a
fence. It was easily five meters high and topped with razor
wire. Massive steel posts held it in place. Far to her right,
where the road should be, Sandra could make out a guard
tower rising another five meters above the fence. The sinking
sun glared from one of the tower's windows. She looked back
along the fence in the opposite direction and thought she
could make out another tower shimmering in the heat haze.

Big signs on the fence advertised various dangers. The
fence was electrified, the sign said, and she should look out
for dog patrols, land mines, and automated gun
emplacements. Beyond the fence was a thirty-meter strip of
scrub with landmine signs planted in it like grave markers.
Beyond that was another fence, just like the first.

Polanski gave a nod to Peter and he and the fourth man
got out. They ran to the fence and, heedless of the warnings,
grabbed it and pulled. A small cut-out section came away, just
big enough for the Jeep to get through. They set the piece of
fence aside and ran on, through the supposed minefield to
the second fence.

"They don't electrify it any more," Polanski said. "Not

since Texas broke away from the United States. They don't patrol it much worth talking about, either. Part of the secession deal was that they keep the border strong, and they did, for a while, but Texas ain't got no particular beef with Mexico. And it ain't like a lot of Mexicans want to get into the States no more."

Sandra realized she knew almost nothing about American politics. She hadn't even heard that Texas had left the Union. For all she knew, other states had seceded too. All she knew was that, when the Adjustment hit in the mid Thirties—the biggest global recession ever—the U.S. had suffered badly, worse than almost any other country. She remembered a teacher telling her about it at one of the many schools she had been thrown out of as a kid. "While Europe turned left," the woman had said, "America turned right." Meaning that, while socialist, even communist governments were being elected all over Europe, the U.S. had voted in a hard-right Christian fundamentalist coalition—the Lord's True Path Party. The new government had almost immediately declared a state of emergency and then suspended the Constitution. The move had saved America from going under. Other nations had been far less fortunate. What once had been Russia was now an anarchic mess of tribal warlords. Africa and the Middle East had gone the same way. Parts of India had hung on to democracy. China had stayed strong and had annexed dozens of countries in South-east Asia—including Australia and New Zealand—most of which had welcomed the move.

But, while the Lord's True Path Party had kept America together and mitigated the worst of the decade of starvation and chaos that had characterized the Adjustment, it had been reluctant to return to an open and free democracy. A number of constitutional amendments ensured that Lord's True Path Party became the only legitimate political party. Soon, its extreme brand of Christianity became the official State Religion. The FBI became the new government's feared enforcers, and religious and political dissent became capital crimes.

All in all, it wasn't the holiday destination of Sandra's choice.

"So you guys are, what, CIA? Some kind of special ops team?" The Jeep crossed the minefield between the fences. They passed the other two men running back to close up the gap behind them.

Polanski laughed. "No, nothing like that."

"Then what?"

"We're the good guys."

"Right. The good guys who kidnap people and sneak across borders."

"We're the resistance."

"The what?"

He sighed and climbed out to help the others cover their tracks.

The resistance? It was about as bad as Sandra could imagine. She'd been kidnapped by self-righteous jerks who wanted to overthrow the government, or whatever, and they wanted her to help them create a timesplash to do it. It was crazy on so many levels.

"Look," she said when they all got back in the car. "I'm sure you're all terribly oppressed and you want the good ol' US of A back like it was in the glory days and all that, but a timesplash is not the way to get it. A timesplash is not the way to get anything. Shit. Do you even know what a timesplash is?"

Polanski didn't reply, which she took to mean that he didn't have much of an idea.

"It doesn't change things. You know that don't you? If you go back and shoot... whoever the hell is in charge now... when he was a baby, it doesn't mean he's gone. You create an anomaly, sure, and all hell breaks loose, but the timeline restructures itself. Think of it like this." She paused, wondering if they'd get it. "Every event is a ball connected by elastic strings to every event that led to it and that leads from it. Everything's pulling on everything else and it all holds itself taut and firm. You can go back in time and kick those balls around, even break a few links here and there by shooting your own grandmother, or whatever, but no matter how much you distort it, everything soon snaps back into place. You can't change the past. It's happened. It's done."

"We don't want to change the past," Polanski said. "Just the future."

"Well that's easy enough. You make a big enough splash, far enough back, and you'll change the future all right, but not in a good way. The backwash from a big splash ripples forward like a tsunami until it hits the present, and then it breaks. And all you've got left of your future are smashed cities and piles of dead bodies. Trust me. I've been there and seen it. It's not the future you want."

Polanski glanced at her, his expression grim. "Why don't I show you a bit of the present before you start telling me what kind of future I want?"

Chapter 8

Shit Storm

"So what was your tag?"

"What?" Jay was staring into his fridge wondering what on earth he could give his daughter for breakfast. It wasn't a problem he'd had in mind when he last went shopping.

"In the old days, when you and Mum were cool dudes in the splash scene." Cara grinned and made a funny voice when she said it, as if the very idea were a joke. "So what was your tag? I know Mum's was Patty—after Patty Hearst, some brainwashed terrorist chick. What was yours?"

"Luke. After Luke Skywalker."

"Never heard of him."

"Yeah, well, it's really old now. Was old then. But we were all into the late twentieth century, because that's where most of the bricks went to make their splashes, I suppose. It sort of made sense at the time. What do you usually eat for breakfast?"

She shrugged. "I dunno."

He shut the fridge. "We could go and find a café."

"Can't we just get on with finding Mum? Do we have to

go traipsing round in the rain looking for food? I'm not even hungry."

OK, so no breakfast. "Did you sleep all right?"

She looked at him, seeming vaguely irritated. "Is this some kind of bonding thing? 'Cos if it's for my sake, you don't need to bother. I'd rather just get on."

He wanted to snap at her. Having a fifteen-year-old daughter you never knew existed just turn up out of the blue was a hell of a big deal. The least they could do was exchange a few pleasantries. But he kept his mouth shut and got himself ready to go out. He noticed her staring as he strapped on his shoulder holster with the Department-issue stunner. "No, you can't have one," he said.

She gave him a startled look. "How did you know…?"

"Because I saw one of your mother's expressions on your face. The one that goes, 'Me want big gun!'"

For an instant she tried to look affronted, but then cracked a grin. "That's Mum all right. But, really, wouldn't it be better if I had one too, just in case?"

"You're perfectly safe with me." And she'd be safer still after he sent her back to the UK.

* * * *

They reached his office as Cara was explaining for the third time, and just as vaguely, what she thought it was her mother did at work. Sandra's job was the only reason Jay could think of as motive for kidnapping her. Yet archaeological experiments were hardly a reason for international kidnap dramas. It's true, Dr. Bradley had made breakthroughs and was operating at energies hardly ever used before—he'd spent half the night researching her and the whole field of direct history—but the technology for lobbing a couple of kilograms back two thousand years wasn't unique to her research group. And why pick on Sandra, the lab technician, when they could have had Dr. Bradley herself?

Cara's knowledge of her mother's work was dismally incomplete. It was as if the girl just wasn't interested. Yes, she thought it was vaguely cool, but she'd have been much more impressed if Sandra had been a pop star or a footballer. So Jay had been making phone calls at two in the morning, waking people up, demanding answers.

He'd spoken to Dr. Bradley herself.

"If they'd wanted to use our rig, they had access to it right there and then," she said. "We had a payload being yanked back when they grabbed me. Everything was fired up and ready to go. They might not have made two thousand years, but they could have sent a man back five hundred or so. It would only have been open countryside back then, but if they'd managed to find even a stray farm worker to shoot out in the fields, the splash could have been enormous."

"So it wasn't just mayhem for the sake of it, then," Jay said, rubbing tired eyes. "If they're planning a lob, it's something specific, somewhere important to them."

Or not.

The people who took Sandra could still be leftover relics from the glory days of timesplashing, planning the big one, the party to end all parties. In many ways, he hoped he was dealing with the egomaniacal bricks he knew so well. The idea that these might be government agents planning an act of war terrified him.

"Nahrees—I mean—Dr. Bradley—"

"Call me Olivia," the woman at the other end of the line said.

"Right. Olivia, I'm sending Cara back in the morning. She says you're a family friend. Will you be able to look after her until…?"

"Of course. Do you really think you can find Sandra?"

"Honestly? It's not looking good. But I'll try."

Afterwards, he had looked in on Cara, sleeping soundly in his bed. He didn't know what to feel about this beautiful young woman being his own child. She was so much like her mother that she'd brought back all the pain of losing her. And yet, in her vulnerability, her childlike innocence, she was also so unlike the woman he had fallen in love with. Long before she'd reached Cara's age, all the innocence, all the trust, had been knocked out of Sandra.

It hurt to think about Sandra, even after all those years. And now he was angry with her. Fuming that Cara had been kept a secret. He felt his anger surging inside him. He was shaken to the core, as if the pillars that held his world in place were toppling and everything would soon come crashing down around him. But he was also awed and amazed by this gift that Life had given him. His child. His daughter, Cara. Right here, real, and wonderful.

"So, what do we do now?" Cara asked, standing in the middle of his office with her arms spread, deliberately breaking his reverie.

He sat down at his desk. "First I check my—"

At the top of his prioritized messages, an urgent communication from the FBI was blinking, followed by two others from Interpol and one from his own boss.

Cara hurried round to see what had startled him but his displays were all virtual and she did not have the necessary security access to see them. "What is it?" she demanded. "Let me see."

He grunted a response, scanning quickly through the messages. The first was the FBI responding to a request for information on the older of the two men who had kidnapped Sandra. His image seemed to have set alarm bells ringing all over Washington. The man had been identified as Zadrach Polanski, Public Enemy Number One, a terrorist of such importance Jay could almost hear the U.S. authorities slavering in their eagerness to get their hands on him.

The second message was a report from Interpol. The freight from the Cambridge flight had been scattered to various locations. Every box and bag had been found and opened by the Amsterdam police, but there was no sign of the missing Englishwoman. They were currently following a possible lead. Security footage of two men moving a crate from the general vicinity of the Cambridge flight towards another part of the airport, possibly towards an Argentinian aircraft bound for Mexico. The recording was low resolution—no faces recognized, no licence plates from the van they used—and the Mexico flight had already departed and landed before the police had flagged it as suspicious. It was a long shot and also a dead end. The trail had gone cold.

After that was a request for clarification from Interpol concerning the involvement of a high-profile U.S. terrorist in the Sandra Malone kidnapping case.

Finally, there was the message from Superintendent Kappelhoff, asking Jay to report to his office immediately to explain why the Commissioner and the British Home Office had been on the phone asking him about an international incident that was brewing.

"I've got to go," he told Cara. "You stay here and don't touch anything. If you want a coffee or something, go ask the constable outside. I'll be a little while."

"Hey!" He stopped halfway to the door. "You can't just run off and not tell me anything. It's about Mum, isn't it?"

He almost made some wisecrack about how the sheer scale of the shit storm would definitely suggest Sandra's involvement, until he saw the anxiety in the girl's face.

"Yes," he said. "The Americans may know who kidnapped her. I need to go and talk to some people about it. Until then, I don't really know much." It didn't seem to settle Cara's anxiety at all. "I'll be right back as soon as the meeting is over."

He hurried away, knowing he couldn't ease her mind until he knew more and, probably, not even then.

* * * *

"You know this woman?" The Commissioner seemed to be taking Jay's reluctant confession as a personal affront.

Superintendent Kappelhoff stepped in, as he had done several times already in the past few minutes. "Ms. Malone assisted the Temporal Crimes Unit in bringing down the splashteam that attacked London in 2050. Chief Inspector Kennedy was working for MI5 at the time and they formed a relationship."

"Did they indeed!"

"Yes, sir. We fell in love." Jay felt like a complete idiot saying it in that room. The two senior officers stared at him as if he'd just put on a silly hat.

"They were both very young," the superintendent explained.

"And you still have a relationship with this woman?" It was clear that the fact that one of his subordinates was tied up in a case of such career-threatening proportions did not sit well with the commissioner.

"No, sir, not since after the London attack."

"So how come this case landed in your lap instead of being handled by the British police?"

Jay grimaced, not wanting to say the words. "Ms. Malone's daughter came here to seek my help."

The commissioner stared at him angrily while the superintendent sighed. "Why would that be, Jay?"

"Because, sir, she appears to be my daughter as well."

"Appears to be?"

"Is, sir. She's my daughter. I only found out yesterday."

"Congratulations," the commissioner said, his face set. Jay could see a vein throbbing in the man's temple. "Are you running a police department, Kappelhoff, or a soap opera?"

Kappelhoff did not react. He turned to Jay and said, evenly, "Chief Inspector, please tell us the whole story, from the beginning."

Jay did, leaving nothing out. As he told it, the commissioner grunted and huffed but did not interrupt.

"And you're convinced this man Polanski has taken Ms. Malone back to the U.S.?" Kappelhoff asked.

"No, sir, not convinced. It just seems like the only possibility. They may have flown to Mexico from Amsterdam. We know the Texas-Mexico border is one of the easiest ways to smuggle people in and out of the U.S. It just... adds up."

The commissioner was doing sums on his fingers. "It's more than twenty-four hours since the woman was grabbed. They could easily be in Texas by now—in the U.S. even, if they had transport at the other end. How could Interpol just let them slip out of the Union like that?"

"The question that puzzles me," said Kappelhoff, "is why

this girlfriend of yours is so important to Zadrach Polanski."

Jay found it hard to think with these two staring at him, demanding explanations. "I just don't know, sir. I haven't spoken to her for sixteen years, remember."

"But you must have some idea," the commissioner insisted, no doubt anticipating the same question from his political masters.

Jay took a stab at it. "Well, she's a capable teknik these days, I gather. Works for a UK university, building rigs for very long range lobs. I don't think there's anything special about the project she's working on, although it no doubt has plenty of military applications. Dr. Bradley, Ms. Malone's boss, tells me her work would need years of additional research to develop it as a weapon. I got the impression that's exactly what the Ministry of Defence is planning, but terrorists wouldn't kidnap someone to help them run a research program, they'd steal a completed weapon, or at least someone who could build one. Besides, there are other groups with similar capabilities all over Europe—all over the Chinese Hegemony too—why pick someone as obscure as Sandra Malone?"

He was thinking aloud, going over the same ground he'd covered again and again during his sleepless night, but his two bosses seemed happy to let him ramble. "It must be either purely for her skill in building long range rigs—which would suggest they're planning a major timesplash, probably in the U.S.—or it's connected with Sandra's past. My past, too." He realized he'd made a gaffe in calling her Sandra but stumbled on. "She was involved with several splashteams back then. She was Sniper's girlfriend for a while and she worked with Flash in the UK."

"Sniper? Flash?" The commissioner turned to Kappelhoff

for clarification.

"Big name bricks who were operating when the TCU started up. Go on, Jay."

Jay had no idea where he was going with this train of thought but he went on.

"The point is, she knew every important brick back then. Many of them swore to kill her when she helped us take Sniper down. But it all blew over. Many of the people who might have borne a grudge are either dead or behind bars." He made a mental note to check whether any of them had been released recently. "It could be that something she knew then would be worth grabbing her for. It could be that someone she knew then is taking his revenge. We don't have much to go on, sir."

Meaning, can I go now and get on with tracking her down, and will you stop asking me to speculate in a vacuum, please? Jay was getting antsy. Kappelhoff seemed to take the hint.

"Thank you, Jay. If that is all, Commissioner?"

But the commissioner had other ideas. "No, that is not all, Superintendent." He turned his scowl on Jay. "Chief Inspector Kennedy, I'm sending you to Washington. The FBI has asked for our cooperation in capturing this Polanski fellow. More importantly, the Chair of the European Parliament's Standing Committee on Civil Liberties, Justice and Home Affairs has told them we will do everything we can to help. So we're going to give them you. You know the victim, you're familiar with all the details of the case. You know more about timesplashing than any man in Europol. I want you on the next available flight." He stood and picked up his hat, a gesture that seemed to block the option for any objection. To Kappelhoff he said, "Charge it all to Special Projects. If you want to send more people, I'll leave that to your discretion. Let my office know the flight times and such. The UK's Department of Foreign Affairs will be all over this, as well as our own standing committee. I'll appoint one of my people to liaise. I'm sure Interpol and MI5 will want a finger in the pie too. Let me sort that out. The rest of the details I'll leave to you."

When he left the room, Jay finally found his voice. "I'd be better off coordinating things from here. I don't see what I can achieve in Washington."

Kappelhoff kept his face blank. "I'll just call the commissioner back and explain that to him, shall I?"

Jay subsided. "There's no point sending anyone with me. It would just add to the waste of time and money."

It was a *fait accomplis*. There was nothing he could do about it except resign. And if he resigned, he could do nothing at all. Even so, he felt anger bubbling up inside him. He stood and took two paces away from the superintendent. "This is ridiculous. Doesn't he know how important this is?" Kappelhoff raised an eyebrow. "To me, I mean. This is someone I care about, not just some random victim. She's…" The woman I love, he was about to say, but he switched it to, "…the mother of my daughter. What am I going to tell Cara? Sorry but I can't save your mother, I have to go on some bloody useless flag-waving trip to Washington. What does he care what the Americans want? Why does the Standing Committee care for that matter?"

Kappelhoff shrugged. "You haven't been reading the newsfeeds?" Jay's heart sank.

"The feeds?"

"They're predicting a very bad harvest this year in Europe. You know how the Gulf Stream has been shifting about since the Forties."

Jay blinked. What the hell did all that climate change legacy crap have to do with Sandra? Everyone knew the temperatures in Europe were still falling since the melting Arctic ice had moved the ocean currents around.

"I don't understand."

"Two years ago, the U.S. became self-sufficient in wheat again for the first time since the Adjustment. This year, they're going to have a surplus. And Europe is going to need it. In case you haven't noticed, we're in another recession. If we have to pay the Yanks too much for their wheat, things could get ugly. You remember the bread riots in 2061."

"But... But... we've been sending them aid since the Forties. No-one's done more for them than us. Surely they wouldn't..."

"Shaft us? Just because they can? Don't be naïve, Jay. Business is business."

"So we're pandering to that bunch of despots just so we can save a few cents on a loaf of bread? You know what kind of government they have over there?" Jay could see that Kappelhoff was beginning to grow impatient with him.

"You also know what kind of government our close friends and allies the Chinese have. It doesn't stop us pandering to them now, does it?"

"But the Lord's True Path Party makes the Chinese Communist Party look like a bunch of benevolent—"

"Jay!"

Jay closed his mouth and drew a deep breath. Venting at Kappelhoff was absolutely pointless. The decision had been made. All he could do now was make the best of it.

"I'm sorry, sir. It's just... I'll go and get things organized. Pack a bag."

And get Cara on a plane back to the UK.

Chapter 9

Texas

"Roadblock," Polanski said as they drove through the endless night.

"Official?"

Sandra opened her eyes in time to see Polanski shake his head.

"Let me handle it," the big guy at the wheel said. "You all just stay calm now and let me do the talking."

Sandra heard a bolt slide as the nozzle of a pistol poked into the small of her back through the car seat. "You heard the man." Polanski spoke softly. He reached forward and spread his jacket across her lap, hiding the tied wrists.

They were in an old Ford Greenie, one of the last Fords to be produced in the States before the company moved all its production to Africa and its corporate HQ to Berlin. The Greenie had been the Ford Popular of its day, offering affordable, petrol-free driving for the masses. But, when the Americans couldn't even afford the Chinese-built, barebones Greenie, Ford, like all the other U.S. car manufacturers before it, took its business elsewhere.

The driver had joined them just north of the border, waiting on a side road in his thirty-year-old rattle trap. Sandra was sorry to see the large, comfortable Jeep knock-off turn around and head back to Mexico without them. Their new driver took the meaning of taciturn to a whole new level. After the initial "Howdy," he hadn't spoken a word until that very minute.

For an unofficial roadblock, the structure ahead of them had a disturbingly solid appearance. Built of sandbags, it featured gun emplacements on either side of the road, and thick walls to channel traffic through a narrow, twisting passage between armed men in ragtag uniforms. Big floodlights came on as they approached.

"How many?" Polanski asked.

"I make it ten," the big guy said, slowing to a stop beside a young man with one arm raised and the other holding a snub-nosed machine gun. Sandra guessed the guard could be seventeen or eighteen.

"Bit late for a drive," the young guard said, bending to look into the car through the open driver's side window. His big, dark eyes wandered lazily across the occupants of the car. When they reached Sandra, they lingered for a long while.

"We're visiting folks up in San Antonio," the big guy said. "Big family get-together."

The young man nodded. "Open the trunk."

"Sure," the big guy said and reached down to pull the lever.

The young man stayed where he was and another man went to look. "You got papers?" he asked, and held out a hand.

"Sure," said the big guy again and pulled a small bundle from the glove box.

The young man took it, pulled off an elastic band and began idly flicking through the papers, glancing now and then at the silent passengers of the car.

Sandra watched him carefully. It was a surprise that their IDs were recorded on paper. She wondered what it said about the level to which Texan civilization had fallen. One quick scan from a modern reader would pick up her ID from her commplant and this whole trip could end in a bloodbath. If things went badly, she would have to get out of the car and make a run for it, take her chances in the black moonless night and hope neither Polanski nor the roadblock guys got a good shot at her before she was out of range. She heard the boot close. The other guard walked back to join the kid at the window.

"Travelling mighty light," the man said. She felt the muzzle of Polanski's gun move away from her back and imagined him training it on the men outside.

"That's OK," the young man said, smiling. She saw him take a wad of paper from the bundle of ID documents and put it in his shirt pocket. Then he handed the IDs back to the big guy. Could that have been money? Paper money?

"You folks have a nice trip now, ya hear? *Via con Dios.*" He stepped back from the car and shouted something in Spanish to the other men.

The big guy thanked him, started up the engine, and drove slowly through the sandbag passage.

* * * *

The next time Sandra woke, it was morning and Polanski was at the wheel. She looked around. The big guy was in the back and so was Peter. They were both dozing.

"Where are we?" she asked. It was a town, dusty and run down.

"Houston. We're a bit behind schedule. Batteries ran dry in the night and we had to wait for sunup to get moving again."

"We've got a schedule?"

"Sure. What kind of evil master plan do you think I'm running here?"

"For a wannabe mass murderer, you seem very pleased with yourself."

"I guess I'm just a morning person."

She turned away from Polanski's annoying smile to stare at the crappy town they were passing through. It was a poor town, full of poor people. There were few cars and no-one seemed to have anywhere urgent to get to. She called up a map on her commplant without thinking and got the usual "No network" message.

"Shit. Don't you have comms networks at all over here?" she asked. How was anybody supposed to function without even basic network services?

"Sure. In the cities up north. Not so much elsewhere. You want to make a phone call?"

"Yeah. To the local police."

His cheerful mood seemed unshakeable. He actually chuckled. "Boy, would that make the sheriff's day!"

Sandra decided she preferred Polanski grim and silent. This new jolly version made her want to scream. "So what's making you so fucking cheerful? Did the boy wonder give you a blow job while I was sleeping?"

The smile fell from Polanski's face. At the edge of her vision, she saw the young man sit up in the back.

"Peter," Polanski said, his voice even and calm. "You

remember what I said, now."

He turned to Sandra and studied her for a moment, then looked back at the road. In the same, steady voice, he said, "I know you must feel aggrieved, Sandra, and I apologize if you found my cheerfulness offensive under the circumstances. But my friends and me, we're not used to a woman speaking with such a foul mouth. Do you think that maybe, despite the provocation you're under, you could try to speak civilly?"

Sandra looked from Polanski to the two in the back. It was not a joke. They were all taking this very seriously. What kind of terrorist killers had she fallen in with, here? She'd heard that the U.S. had tough public morality laws. She'd also heard they had pretty much abolished women's rights, trying to turn the clocks back to some mythical heyday when nuclear families were the source of all happiness, and the husband was God's representative in the home. That phrase Polanski had used, "we're not used to a woman speaking with such a foul mouth," was strangely chilling. It had never occurred to her to wonder what life was like in America for ordinary women. Something like life in the Middle East now, she supposed.

"Well?" Polanski asked.

"Go fuck yourself, you misogynist creep," she answered, as politely as she could.

The big guy put the barrel of his gun against her head and she froze. "You people are seriously fucked up," she said through gritted teeth. "If you ever untie my hands, I'm going to stick your guns so far up your arses you'll be coughing bullets for a month."

Polanski pulled over to the curb and took a length of cloth out of the glove box. He handed it to Peter. "Would you gag her, please." The young man grinned, obviously happy to oblige. "Last chance, Sandra. Can you mind your tongue or do you want to wear a gag the rest of the way?"

"Fuck you," she said.

Immediately, the big guy's arm went round her throat and Polanski leaned over to hold her arms down. She struggled like a wild animal but, in the end, Peter got the gag in her mouth and tied it tight. But that did not stop her kicking and fighting and doing the best she could to shout for help. "Peter," Polanski said. "Get the dope out of my bag in the trunk. We're going to have to—"

A rapping at the driver's-side window made everybody, even Sandra, stop dead and look. A policeman was visible from mid-thigh to mid-chest. Easy to see that he had a hand resting on the butt of his sidearm. The cop bent down to peer inside the car window. He was looking at Polanski and hadn't yet noticed Sandra. "Would you mind winding down your window, sir?" the cop said. As Polanski complied, he scanned the inside of the car, his gaze finally resting on Sandra. The sight of a woman bound and gagged in a car full of men did not seem to alarm him unduly. He straightened up and stepped back a pace. "Would you mind stepping out of the vehicle, please, sir?"

As soon as the cop's face was out of sight, Sandra saw the big guy slip a gun into Polanski's hand. As Polanski got out of the car, he pushed the gun in the back of his jeans and let his shirt fall over it. Sandra tried shouting to the cop that Polanski was armed, but couldn't make herself understood. The policeman leaned in through the open door and looked at her. Even as he did so, she felt the big guy shove another gun into the small of her back. She stopped shouting. Meanwhile, the cop was taking a long hard look at Sandra, taking in the long legs in tight jeans, the trim waist and large breasts under her snug T-shirt.

"I'll get to you in a moment, ma'am," he said and ducked back out to talk to Polanski.

She heard their murmuring voices for a while. Then Polanski leaned in to grab the documents from the glove box. Sandra wondered if there would be another bribe involved. Surely the policeman would have to take them in for questioning. Surely he'd call for backup and arrest everybody. The conversation continued inaudibly outside the car for a minute longer and then Polanski climbed back in. He stared up the engine and drove away up the street, the cop standing watching them, not doing a damned thing.

Peter and the big guy let out whoops of relief and amazement, slapping Polanski's back and congratulating him.

"How'd you do it, Zak?" Peter asked for the third time.

Polanski turned briefly to Sandra and winked. "Told him Sandra here was my runaway sister, that's all. Said she left her husband for some city-slicker from Austin and we'd just been down there to beat the guy's brains out and bring li'l sis back home to her two heartbroke baby boys."

The others thought that was the funniest thing they'd ever heard, judging by the howls of laughter and Peter's shout, "Shame on you, you hussy!"

Sandra added the Houston police department to the list of people who were going to come out of this badly when she got her arms free, and hunched down in her seat to fume in silence.

* * * *

They crossed the Texas-U.S. border with Sandra unconscious in the boot of the car. Promising not to make a fuss didn't persuade Polanski to let her sit up front with the gag off.

"Those ain't small-town cops at the border crossing, darlin'," the big guy explained as he carried her back to where Peter was waiting with a syringe. "One false move and they'll shoot the whole danged lot of us just to keep up their quota for the month."

As far-fetched as that seemed, she could feel the tension in the air. These men were scared. Crossing the border would be dangerous for them and they didn't want a loose canon like Sandra to worry about.

She let Peter inject her, hoping he could see the contempt in her eyes.

When she woke up, she was in Louisiana, in the United States of America. She was lying at the side of a dirt road with Polanski and his sidekick sitting beside her. The tail lights she could see in the distance belonged to the Greenie that the big guy was driving back towards Texas. It was night-time and Sandra was cold, hungry and hungover from the drugs. With a shudder of revulsion, she realized her jeans were wet from having peed herself.

Chapter 10

Mid-Air

Jay pondered the view from the Airbus electroprop. Below him was an endless plain of bright white cloud that had looked so grey and dismal on the ground. It was a crowded flight and the aisle seat beside him was occupied by a chinless young man in a business suit who was on his way to sell bibles to the Americans. They'd exchanged a dozen words before lapsing into a silence that would probably last the rest of the Atlantic crossing.

Jay's flight was from Schipol to Mexico City. None of the major airlines flew direct to the U.S. mainland these days. Not after a series of incidents in which planes had been shot at and a couple even brought down. The U.S. Government had blamed anti-European extremist factions but had failed in the course of thirty years to bring a single one of them to justice. It was widely held in the intelligence community that some of the more radical States were funding and arming these extremist groups, with the Church of the Lord's True Path's tacit approval, to further their agenda of keeping America free from corrupting external influences. Nevertheless, small aircraft from South America were hardly ever attacked—

possibly because they were indistinguishable from typical domestic air traffic to a man on the ground with a surface-to-air missile on his shoulder.

Jay had never really imagined travelling to the United States. He'd never seen a reason to. From time to time, he'd sat in on briefings by the CIA. He knew that Interpol and other agencies still went through the motions of sharing intelligence as if the Adjustment had never happened and the U.S. had not become a nuclear-armed theocracy. It definitely wasn't a place Jay would ever choose to visit.

His old boss, Jacques Bauchet, had often said the Americans would wake up one day, throw religion right out of the Whitehouse, and reclaim their freedom. Jay wasn't so sure. After two generations of oppression and religious fundamentalism, it seemed to him that the people of America were now less able than ever to throw off their shackles. Most Americans had grown up learning nothing except what their religious schools told them. The universities had been burnt down or had become theological colleges. Anti-science fervour in the early days had seen mass executions and the razing of laboratories, museums and libraries all over the country. Intellectuals and liberals, Jews and gays had fled to Europe in droves—almost an exact mirror of the process that had so benefited the U.S. in the 1930s.

"Hello."

Cara was standing in the aisle and smiling sweetly. Jay did a double-take and was about to express his shock when he saw that she wasn't addressing him but the young bible salesman sitting next to him.

"I wonder," she said, looking tragically apologetic, "but could I ask you to do me a huge favour?" Under the sunshine of that beautiful smile, the young man was visibly melting.

When she explained about the mix-up at the check-in and how she and her father had been put miles apart, he almost literally fell over himself in his haste to swap seats with her. Jay's scowl did nothing to curb either Cara's simpering performance or the young man's drooling gallantry.

"There, that's better," she said, dropping into the newly-vacated seat.

"What the hell are you doing here? I put you on a plane for Gatwick."

"Well, obviously not. You left me at the check-in, remember, then hurried off. All I had to do was follow you and see which plane you were catching, grab a ticket, and here I am."

"This plane's going to Mexico! What do you think you're playing at?"

"I'm coming with you to the States."

"What? No, you're not. We had all this out in my office. I'm going to Washington on official police business. It's not a family vacation."

She looked away, clearly irritated. "Yeah, yeah. Whatever."

For a moment, Jay was speechless. He glared at the back of her head. She couldn't just follow him around. Surely she could see that? Why wouldn't she just do as she was told?

She turned back, suddenly, putting them nose to nose and Jay had to pull away. "Look," she said. "Mum said you would help me. She didn't say you'd pack me off home and pat me on the head saying, 'There, there, don't worry, little girl.'"

"I never said any such—" He stopped himself. This was a time for calm authority, not to be bickering about who said what. He drew a settling breath. "Your mother would not want you travelling to America. According to you, she's done all she could to keep you a secret all these years just so you didn't have to face the kind of danger that comes with my line of work."

"Things are different now."

"Really? She loves you less now? She worries less about your safety?"

Cara frowned, which Jay took to mean he'd won his point. When her face brightened, he almost flinched.

"But I'll be safe with you, Daddy. You're an important man in Interpol. You'll be able to protect me."

"It's Europol, not Interpol. Very different." He sat back in his seat, tired of sparring already. Was Cara like this at home? Wilful, argumentative, devious, willing to use any kind of emotional leverage to get what she wanted?

"Have you ever wondered if your mother faked her own kidnapping? I would if I had to put up with this kind of brattish behaviour for long."

She looked cross and threw herself back into her seat, no doubt to plan her next tactic. He let her stew for a while. Calling him "Daddy" had stung. Far from endearing her to him, it had shown a callousness, a contempt for his feelings that upset him more than he expected. Yet why should she respect him—or have any feelings for him at all? He was a stranger, her absent father who, he had to suppose, had not turned out to be the hero she was hoping for.

And, if he were honest, did he love her? Yesterday he hadn't known she existed. And there she was, fully grown, her own person, a complete stranger who had literally stepped out of a crowd on the street and said, "I'm your daughter." He felt he should love her. He felt some kind of instinct should have kicked in. But there was nothing there except an irrational guilt, and a massive resentment. And yet… Every time he looked at her, he saw Sandra, and with every word she spoke, he heard Sandra's voice. Even her stubbornness, her determination, were Sandra's. If ever there were a time when he should love a stranger, this would be it.

He turned to look at his miraculous daughter and found her looking at him. "I'm not going home," she said. "If you get armed guards and drag me onto a plane, all I'd do at the other end is get right on the next flight to the States. You can't get rid of me, not while Mum's over there. I know you're going to Washington. I'll just search until I find you again. If America is so dangerous, isn't it better that you keep me with you? Do you want me out there alone, trying to find you?"

Jay simply did not know what to do. For Cara's sake, he should take her back to the UK, deliver her directly into the hands of social services and let them take care of her. But that would consume another whole day and Sandra was still out there in god-knows-what kind of danger. And even if he did take Cara home, he knew it wouldn't take her long to escape whatever kind of watch they put on her and make her way back to the U.S. And she was right, it was better by far if he could keep an eye on her. She couldn't be alone out there.

"Well?" she said. "Say something."

"All right. You can stay with me. But you have to do as you're told when we get there."

She burst into smiles and bounced in her seat.

"I'm not kidding. Promise me you'll do as I tell you."

"Anything you say."

"No. Promise me. I don't know what you get away with at home but when we're there, you will have to be the model of obedience. The government, the FBI, these are deeply religious people. Fundamentalists. Fanatics. They have very particular views on how children should behave towards their parents and towards authority. Do you understand?"

"Yeah, yeah, bunch of loonies. No swearing in church. No running in the corridors."

Jay rounded on her angrily. "You're not listening. The FBI is one of the most feared state police organizations ever. Federal agents have the power to summarily try and execute citizens for crimes such as blasphemy, adultery and witchcraft."

"Witchcraft?"

"Yes, witchcraft. These are not policemen in the sense that you and I know it. The FBI is like a cross between the KGB and the Spanish Inquisition. Every field agent is an ordained minister in the Church of The Lord's True Path. The Director of the Bureau, the Reverend Matthew Jones, who wants to see me when we get there by the way, is arguably the most powerful man in America. He's a man with so much blood on his hands, it would fill the Great Lakes. Am I scaring you?"

Cara had stopped smiling and was looking uneasy. "A bit."

"Good. I hope so. Because I'm scared shitless at the thought of the kind of trouble a careless, cocky teenager could get herself into over there. So when I say 'do as you're told' I mean do exactly what I say, don't ever argue with me, or even think about it. That way we might both avoid a major international incident and get back home alive."

She nodded, watching him warily. She was deep in thought and he reckoned it best to leave her to absorb what he'd said. He settled back in his seat and popped up a folder of briefing papers on his commplant. There were masses of documents to absorb on European-American relations, various inter-agency protocols, and lists of topics to avoid. As hard as he tried, he could not focus for long. He closed his eyes and tried to think how he might explain to his superintendent why he'd let his daughter tag along on this delicate mission. It was a good thing his unit was closing down because this was just the kind of thing that could get him fired.

He felt a hand touch his arm and turned to see Cara looking at him with tears in her eyes. For a moment, he wondered if this was some new ploy.

"Is she all right, do you think?" The question was put so simply and bravely that his heart went out to her. She was a child, after all, and his child, frightened for her mother's safety.

"Your mother is the strongest woman I have ever known. She's clever, she's resourceful, and she's been known to beat up men twice my size. I'd say it's the kidnappers you should be worried about. They're the ones in real danger." A hint of a smile crossed Cara's face. "I had a cat once—well, my parents did—called Cleopatra. She was beautiful and sleek and elegant and all she wanted to do all day was sleep in front of the fire and have people admire her. Yet she was fierce and fast when she needed to be. She ripped up a big dog's muzzle one time, and another time she woke us all up in the night to find she had a fox cornered in the garden. She could get up on the roof of our house—no-one knew how—and get down again. Dad even had to fit locks to the windows because she worked out how to lift the catches and get out when she felt like it."

He hadn't thought about Cleopatra the cat for donkey's years, and now he wondered if the pride and admiration he'd felt for his childhood pet had anything to do with why he had fallen in love with Cara's mother so easily.

"Anyway, the point is, your mum's that kind of combination badass-escapologist-tightrope-walker, and I have every confidence that she'll be just fine."

Although, the fact was, he had no idea at all. They had still received no demands, so they had no idea what the motive for the kidnapping might be. The involvement of the United States' most wanted terrorist made Jay's stomach tighten every time he thought about it.

"You really loved her, didn't you?" Cara asked, bringing him back.

"She was a great cat."

Cara slapped at his arm. "No! Mum."

"Yes, I did." *More than she loved me, it seems.* Even after sixteen years, it hurt so much. "We'll get her back. I promise."

Chapter 11

Railroad

What do you do when crude oil is worth five thousand dollars a barrel and your currency is so weak that even buying cheap fusion reactors from India is a huge extravagance? Well, for one thing, it seemed to Sandra, as she rattled along in the shabby railway carriage, you refit all your old diesel engines with boilers and revert to the Age of Steam.

They'd caught the train at a town called Lake Charles, after being dropped near the station by yet another anonymous helper, this time with a woman in tow. The woman had brought clothes for Sandra to change into—a loose, floor-length smock dress in plain grey cotton, a matching headscarf, round-toed, low-heeled shoes, white ankle socks, and underwear that a Victorian peasant would have been proud to own. Sandra had argued, even when they pulled their guns on her, even when the woman whispered in her ear that if she did not dress "modestly" she would be a spectacle everywhere she went, and that there would be trouble, that they might lynch her for being a whore. In the end, her own desire to get out of the soiled clothes she'd been travelling in had changed her mind.

"There now, don't you look pretty?" Polanski had said when he saw her in the new outfit. In response, she explained, in fluent Anglo-Saxon, just how little she cared about his opinion of her appearance.

It bothered her that the yards of material around her legs would hamper her if she needed to run or fight, but she had to admit that, dressed as she had been, she would have stood out on the streets of Lake Charles like a showgirl in a nunnery. For all her bravado and determination to be free, walking through the town on the way to the train station had intimidated her.

It was like another world, not just another country. The women—even the little girls—wore long dresses with long sleeves. Every one of them also wore a headscarf or bonnet. Nobody wore makeup. The men wore jeans and plaid shirts and a good many of them wore cowboy hats. They were all clean shaven and short haired. It looked for all the world as if they'd been issued outfits by Central Casting for a historical vid about the Old West. More strange than the clothing, stranger even than the bizarre collection of rusty trucks that clanked up and down Ryan Street, dodging the potholes and the cyclists, was the way people behaved. All the women had their eyes cast down, as if they were frightened by some constant threat. The men seemed completely normal by comparison, except for two things. One was that they seemed to feel free to stare at Sandra as much as they pleased, and to glare angrily if she stared back. The other was that, whenever they passed members of the Sons of Joshua—brown-shirted men with crucifixes sewn on their left sleeves, who carried sidearms and night sticks and strolled about the town as if they owned it—the men of the town also adopted the flinching attitude of the women.

Sandra noticed that Polanski and the others would cross the street rather than pass close to these swaggering, uniformed men. Instinctively, she rejected the thought of turning herself in to the Sons of Joshua. Something about them told her to stay away.

"Are they the police?" she asked Polanski.

"Keep your eyes down," he snapped. "People are looking." Her wrist and leg bindings were off but Peter and the two newcomers walked behind her and she knew they were armed. "They're not police. They're the Church militia. The police just do detective work these days. Even then, only where the crime doesn't involve Church ordinances. The SOBs keep order."

"Why is everyone so scared of them?"

"Get yourself noticed and you'll find out."

"What's wrong with this place?"

"Lake Charles? What do you mean?"

"It's so… derelict, poor, run down. It's a dump and everyone looks like they're frightened of something."

"Lake Charles is a good place. Doing well. You'll see a lot worse where we're going."

"And where's that?"

"Washington, DC."

* * * *

The train rattled along at a slow but steady pace, passing through desolate suburbs, then broad farmland, in an endless, monotonous ride. Every farmhouse they passed sagged with age and neglect, every town was a core of decay surrounded by shanties and slums. Barefoot children stared stupidly at the passing train. Some of them had sores on their faces. Quite a few were lame. Polanski told Sandra it was polio. "Been real bad lately."

But the big cities were the worst. They passed through New Orleans and Atlanta, Charlotte and Richmond. In every one, the downtown skyscrapers had crumbled to jagged stumps. Some of them lay in heaps beside the railway. In the city of Greensboro, she saw a gang of workmen digging through the rubble.

"Recovering metals and plastics," Polanski told her. "Lot of steel in them old office buildings." She looked at him hard, but he did not seem to be joking.

They travelled all day, then slept in their seats. Whenever Sandra wanted to go to the toilet, two of her guards accompanied her. Despite the bulky dress, she could have taken them in the narrow swaying corridors, grabbed a gun and leapt from the train. But the unbroken miles of poverty and decay had left her shaken and unnerved. She didn't want to be out there any more than she wanted to be Polanski's prisoner. It was a strange and alien land. Not quite the Stone Age desolation of the Arab Peninsula, or the lawless Steppes of Eastern Europe, but still the too-quiet orderliness of the place filled her with unease. People were going about their business in the ruins of this once-great country with a lethargic acquiescence that made her skin crawl. It seemed as if everybody was too scared to admit that they could see what was happening to their home towns.

All that day and the next they travelled the line. At Charlottesville, a hundred and twenty kilometres from Washington, just as night began to fall, a boy got on the train. He was selling the local newspaper—a real, paper newspaper. It had happened many times along the route. A squadron of Sons of Joshua were also on the platform and they too boarded the train. They moved up and down the carriages in pairs, demanding papers and asking questions. Sandra felt Polanski and his people tense up as the militiamen approached. The three men drew their weapons but kept them concealed. Sitting in the window seat with Polanski and the boy Peter beside her and the other two men opposite, Sandra felt trapped and vulnerable. If any trouble started, she would be exposed and almost helpless.

"Papers." The big man stood facing them with his booted feet in a wide stance and one hand resting on his night stick. He looked sternly at the five of them as if he already had them pegged as troublemakers. His sidekick was a smaller man who stood gazing around the carriage as if bored.

Polanski and the other men began fetching out paper documents. Sandra took in the embroidered crucifix and the colourful "Sons of Joshua" arm patch on the SOBs' shirts. She also noticed the two militiamen were carrying other equipment on their thick leather belts. Primitive communications gear, perhaps, along with scanners, handcuffs, and what might have been an overly large stunner... She was sure the militiamen she'd seen farther out from the capital didn't have that kind of equipment.

"What do you think you're looking at, woman?"

Without thinking, Sandra looked up at his face, ready to snap back a reply. She saw his eyes widen with surprise.

"No need to take offence, sir," Polanski said, half rising to obscure Sandra's view of the man—and his of her. "My wife doesn't always know her p—"

"Sit down!"

Polanski hesitated but sat. "I just wanted to exp—"

"Shut up!"

Sandra could see the man now had his hand on his gun,

and so did his partner. Her pulse raced. If she pushed the SOBs to start a fight—something that seemed disturbingly easy—there was a good chance she could get away in the confusion. Or get shot. Or get everybody in the carriage shot. She'd seen at least four more of these guys board the train, but who knew how many more were nearby? If she got off the train, at least she'd stand some chance of getting clear, but then what? This whole society seemed insane, a throwback to the Middle Ages but with turn-of-the-century technology.

In her mind, she saw the moves she would make, choreographing it the way she would a complex katana in a karate bout. She would step up to the big guy. A quick blow with the heel of her hand under his nose would incapacitate him—or kill him. Then step to the side of him before he had time to fall, so he would be between her and the second SOB who would have drawn his gun by then. But Polanski and the others would have drawn too. They would take him out while he was distracted by his partner, and Sandra would sprint along the corridor to where the other SOBs had gone. She would yell, "Help, the terrorists just killed a man," to stop Polanski's crew from following her.

She also saw how it could go wrong. The floor between the seats was full of legs and feet. She could easily misstep and stumble. If she missed hitting the SOB just right on her first try, he could grab her. Even if he didn't, if the second SOB were faster than he looked, or if Polanski were slower, the militiaman might get off a couple of shots before they took him down. Two shots that could end up in her back, or someone else's.

It was too big a risk. Keeping her eyes down, she said, "I'm sorry, sir. I was startled. I didn't mean to be rude." She didn't look up, willing Polanski to take the ball and play it from there.

"As you can tell by the accent, sir," Polanski said, not missing a beat, "my wife is a foreigner and is still learning our ways. But she's a good Christian and she's keen to be instructed."

"She'd learn a mite quicker if you took the strap to her more often," the SOB said. He seemed to have relaxed a fraction. "I've seen this kind of thing before. A man takes a pretty wife and he lets her get away with too much. A man's gotta take responsibility for his wife's salvation and not let her fall into error. It ain't a kindness to put a woman's soul in peril."

"Thank you, sir. That's good advice. I mean to chastise her as soon as I get her home. I think you're right, I've been lax in my duty."

* * * *

The train picked up speed as it left Charlottesville, the last leg of their journey. Sandra stared out of the window at the procession of towns and farms sliding by. On the whole, things seemed a lot more prosperous than they did in the South.

Polanski leaned close and said, "Thank you. We could have been in big trouble back there."

She turned abruptly, making him flinch. "Even if you don't care whether innocent people get hurt, I do."

He seemed to want to retort but restrained himself. She turned away and gazed at the scenery again but she wasn't taking anything in. When she looked back at him, she found him still watching her.

"Tell me about the timesplash," she said, full of anger she

needed to dump somewhere. "You and your friends aren't crazies who live for kicks. You're... organized, steady, conspirators..." She nodded towards the man and woman sitting opposite. "All these people working for you all over the country, helping you smuggle me in... You're not some kind of lone gunman, or even an isolated domestic terror cell. Why do you want to make a splash?"

Polanski thought about it for a second and then drew a deep breath. "OK. The first thing you should know is that none of the people you've met work for me, except Peter here. The rest are part of another organisation altogether, an underground railroad. A group of brave people who risk their lives, day after day, to help smuggle people out of the country into South America or Canada."

"I can see why people would want to leave," she said. "Especially women."

"You ain't seen nothing. You've had the smallest glimpse of what's going on here. You've met the Sons of Joshua." He shook his head. "Well, you just wait till you meet the FBI. You've seen some poor folk out in the country, but just wait till you see the Alley Shanty, or the Great Lakes Marshall Law Zone, or the labour camps, or the Manhattan Ghetto..." He paused, as if reluctant to let himself get worked up about it, but then continued with even more passion. "You think women have it bad because some preaching fool from the SOBs tells me to slap you around more? Down in Alabama they have witch trials in permanent session. In Seattle, they just changed the city ordinances so that a man can kill his wife or daughter if he suspects her of immoral conduct. He doesn't have to prove it, mind you. Just the suspicion will do. In Atlanta, they—"

"You don't have to convince me the place is a shithole. I

agree, you guys make the Middle East look civilised. Just tell me about the splash."

He narrowed his eyes. She thought he was probably thinking how nice it would be to knock her teeth out. Then he looked away, as if the sight of her staring him down was too much to bear. When he looked back, he seemed to have himself under some semblance of control again.

"You talk like we're all part of some big, half-assed cult but it ain't like that. Nothing like that at all. We took a wrong turn, that's all. Thirty-some years ago, people were desperate. People were starving. Millions died. The economic system had collapsed. Just gone. Things kept going in a patchy, hit-and-miss kind of way, God alone knows how. Criminal gangs moved in to fill the vacuum left by Government agencies that were closing down. The only people to stand up and offer any kind of leadership was the Lord's True Path Party which came out of the old Republican Party, but by then it was just another radical fundamentalist Christian party that wasn't getting a lot of votes any more. They said they had a plan and people listened. They got elected and that's when the real trouble started.

"Sure, they got people organized again, they got the gangs off the streets, they got the trains running and the airports open, they got the food distributed and they re-opened the hospitals. But they also changed the Constitution so that nobody could get them out of power. When the schools came back, they weren't teaching the old curriculum, they had new faith-based lessons. I didn't go to school much myself until I was ten, but when I did, all I got was Bible Studies, Christian Morality classes, and propaganda for the new government. Teachers—the good ones who were brave enough to slip in a bit of science or geography—had a habit of disappearing overnight. And you know who was turning them in? Us. The kids. And that became a pattern for the whole country. Everybody was scared of the FBI and the SOBs and the Church. People knew that if they had information about a blasphemer, or an atheist, or some other kind of subversive, they'd be arrested as an accomplice if the authorities ever found out. It was safer by far to turn in your neighbour or your workmate in order to protect yourself and your family.

"I've heard it told that it was like that in Communist Russia, and East Germany. Well it's like that here, now. And there don't seem no way to stop it. The resistance is up against a massive and powerful organisation. And we never know when someone we trust—a wife, a child, a best friend—might say the wrong thing to the wrong person, or might give you up to save themselves or someone else they love."

"So now what?" she asked. The picture he painted was more-or-less what she'd heard about the U.S., only he seemed to think his people were the victims, rather than willing participants in their glorious theocracy. "You plan to take back the power? You're building up to some kind of armed rebellion? Another War of Independence?" Which, of course, must be exactly what he was planning, and the ability to run timesplashes was going to be his secret weapon. She saw the hard determination in his expression and knew she had it right.

"Oh shit," she said.

Chapter 12

FBI

At Miguel Hidalgo y Costilla International Airport in Guadalajara, Mexico, Jay called Kapellhof and told him he would be travelling with his daughter. The superintendent's first reaction was to order Jay to send Cara home. When Jay explained that it wasn't an option and that the only way she was going back to the UK was if Jay accompanied her, Kapellhof fell silent for a long, worrisome time. Then he said, "The girl is Malone's only living relative. You took her with you to help with identification."

"You'll inform the Americans?"

"No. I'll inform the commissioner's office. He can liaise with the Standing Committee and then they can talk to the Americans. You say she just got on the plane on her own initiative?"

"Yes, sir." Jay supposed he sounded as glum as he felt.

"Sounds like her mother's daughter. I've been re-reading the files from the Sniper affair. Sandra Malone ran rings around all of us back then, wouldn't you say?"

"Definitely, sir."

"Especially you, Chief Inspector."

121

"Point taken, sir. Thank you, sir."

The plane from Guadalajara landed at Jesus Our Redeemer Airport, Washington in a cold and gusty dawn. A black, Ford SUV drove onto the tarmac as they taxied to a halt. Jay and Cara were among just a dozen bleary-eyed, exhausted people who filed from the plane into the chilly bluster of that autumn morning in DC. No-one spoke. Everyone was wrapped up in their private struggle to stay awake, fight the cold, and keep up their steady shuffle towards the heat and light of the terminal building. They all loathed the prospect of still having to wait for their luggage to appear, then drag it off to wait in line at customs, and then wait for a taxi, all before they might finally reach somewhere comfortable.

So, when a cheerful young man in shiny shoes, leather gloves, and smart wool overcoat strode from the black SUV and called out, "Chief Inspector Kennedy! Very pleased to meet you," Jay received several resentful looks from his fellow passengers.

The young man, oblivious and smiling, scooped Jay and Cara out of the line to the terminal and led them to the car. He shook Jay's hand and Jay noticed the small silver crucifix on his lapel.

"I'm Special Agent Simmons but you should just call me Zeke. Short for Ezekiel. Always hated the name. I'll be your liaison while you're here." He grinned and winked. "That means I get to drive you around, make sure you've got what you need, run any errands. That kind of thing. And this," turning to Cara, "must be your lovely daughter." Without breaking pace, he swept up Cara's hand and kissed it, saying, "Absolutely beautiful." Addressing Jay, he added, "Don't worry about suitable clothing, I'll arrange to have something sent to your hotel."

The car was a modern, driverless vehicle with a plush, roomy interior. As they wound through the quiet streets, Agent Simmons kept up a non-stop stream of pleasantries, interspersed with commentary and anecdotes about the city and its sights. It took Jay several minutes to notice that he wasn't getting any useful information at all from his garrulous companion.

"Where are we going?" he asked, breaking Simmons' stream of Washington trivia.

If the man minded his interruption, it didn't show. "To your hotel first. You might like a nap, or at least to freshen up. Your meeting with the Director is at ten AM, so there's plenty of time. We've booked you into the Hilton and I absolutely recommend the breakfast menu. The eggs Benedict is to die for."

"Good, I'm starving," Cara said.

Simmons' smile wavered. "Little girls should not speak unless spoken to," he said, pleasantly but firmly.

Cara's mouth fell open and Jay could see that only her surprise had so far prevented the angry retort that was building. Into the silence, he said, "We do things differently where we come from, Agent Simmons. Do I need to remind you that we are guests of your government and that we expect our customs to be respected? Please do not chastise my daughter again, for any reason whatsoever. If you do, I will make my displeasure known to the Director."

Simmons' eyes widened and his skin paled. Jay felt Cara turn to goggle at him but he kept his gaze on the FBI man. No doubt they had chosen Simmons for this job because he was considered smooth and urbane. To upset his charge enough to receive a complaint even before they reached the hotel would not reflect well on Simmons—nor on whomever had chosen him for the job.

"Of course," Jay went on, briefly turning to Cara, "we will also try to respect your customs while we are here. With a little effort, I'm sure we'll all get along fine."

Simmons' smile flickered back to life. "Of course. A minor misunderstanding." He regarded Jay with a new wariness, perhaps beginning to see that this might not be the simple assignment it had seemed.

Jay regarded the man. In all likelihood, Zeke Simmons really was one of the more worldly and open-minded people he would meet here. Simmons had probably been selected to chaperone them because he was considered less likely than most to create an international incident. Now he worried that Cara had, with her very first utterance, provoked him into correcting her behaviour. Having her with him in the presence of people he could not browbeat, like the Director of the FBI, would be like walking about with a ticking bomb. He needed to keep Cara out of sight and away from anybody important. The best thing would be to lock her in her hotel room. Failing that, he needed to keep her in the hotel.

"Zeke," he said. "Will there be a female agent to look after my daughter while I'm working?" He felt Cara stir beside him, but she didn't protest. Maybe she had understood something of the dangers of the situation. Maybe she just wanted to hear what he was going to say.

"A female agent?" Simmons sounded as if the idea was incomprehensible. "In the CIA, maybe. Not in the FBI."

"Someone else then? I need a woman to take care of my daughter when I'm not around, someone to keep her out of trouble and to keep her entertained."

"I assumed she would accompany y—"

"She won't."

"Oh yes she will," Cara said, her face set and angry. "If you think you're palming me off on some flunky while you swan around finding Mum, you can think again. That's not why I came all this way."

Simmons looked nervous and unsure about what to do. Jay ignored his discomfort and focused an angry glare on Cara. He needed to make her understand. "Cara, these people—the FBI, the Church, the people I'll be working with—don't like women. To them, you are something less than a person. Not quite an animal, but definitely not as exalted as a man."

Simmons spoke out. "I assure you, we—"

"Please don't interrupt me. No, wait. Let me ask you a few questions for my daughter's benefit. Why are there no women in the FBI?"

"Well, for a start, all ranks from Special Agent upwards are only open to ordained ministers of the Lord's True Path Church."

"And can't a woman be ordained?"

Simmons seemed to think Jay was pulling his leg. "Not in any church I've ever heard of!"

"Are you married, Zeke?"

"Sure. With two kids and another on the way."

"What does your wife do?"

"Do? You mean like housework and such?"

"I mean what's her profession or trade?"

Jay could see his questions were beginning to needle the young man. Simmons looked suspicious, as if he thought Jay was trying to trick him. "I'd like to think no wife of mine would ever need to earn a living, sir. If a man can't provide for his family... Well, he isn't much of a man, is he?"

"I didn't mean to imply anything, Zeke. I'm just exploring our cultural differences for my daughter's education. Tell me, did you ever have sex before you were married?"

Simmons' eyes widened. "I don't think that's a topic for discussion with a young lady present."

"What about your wife? Did she have sex before she was married?"

The agent's expression hardened, anger was written in his whole posture. "That is a filthy suggestion. I don't care where you're from or who you tell, you take that back right now."

Jay raised his hands in submission. "I'm sorry, Zeke. I didn't mean to offend you. I certainly didn't mean to imply anything about your wife. But, can I just get this straight? The kind of women who would have sex before marriage—?"

"Whores and sluts!"

Even Jay was surprised at the young man's vehemence. "Er, right. So, if men had sex outside of marriage, it would have to be with these, er…"

"Whores, sure. What's your point, Chief Inspector? That American society isn't perfect?" Simmons was frowning heavily. "Sure, boys sow their wild oats. It's only natural. As long as there are fallen women, men will be tempted to stray. At least if a man sticks to whores, he isn't in danger of corrupting a decent woman and condemning his own soul. What are you getting at?"

Jay took a breath. "It's this. What if my daughter here was out on the street, with no chaperone, and she smiled at a good-looking boy? What if she started up a conversation, flirted a little? What would people think?"

Again, Simmons was flustered. "I… I wouldn't like to say."

"They'd assume she had loose morals, don't you think?"

"I guess so, yes."

"So what if the boy, quite reasonably, assumed she was one of these 'fallen women' you mentioned and tried to kiss her? What would he do if she hit him in the face for it and called him names—as well she might?"

"Why… er…"

"Do you think he might get violent? After all, she came on to him, didn't she?"

Simmons nodded.

"He might even drag her off to the police, or the militiamen, and denounce her, might he not?"

"He'd be within his rights," Simmons said, guardedly. "Some might consider it a public duty."

"And the authorities might impose punishments?"

Simmons didn't want to be drawn any farther. "I'll see what I can do about arranging a chaperone for the young lady, sir."

Cara had listened to all of this in shocked silence. "But I'm not going to go off flirting with boys."

"Maybe not," Jay said. "What about swearing at someone who bumped into you? Blasphemy can get you into just as much trouble here as soliciting for sex." She opened her mouth to protest and Jay raised a finger. "You weren't just about to take the Lord's name in vain now, were you?" From the way she shut her mouth and swallowed, Jay saw he had guessed correctly. "Honestly, Cara. It's a minefield over here. Zeke, tell my daughter what the penalties are for blasphemy."

"It depends on how large the offence is. For something small you might only get a fine or a beating. For something major, the punishment is death. It's really at the discretion of the arresting officer."

"Not the judge?"

Simmons gave a wan smile. "For offences like blasphemy, law enforcement officers are authorized to impose summary judgements." He paused, looking at Cara, who was open-mouthed with astonishment. "I'll make sure I find you a chaperone," he assured her. "It's probably for the best."

* * * *

"Chief Inspector Kennedy, how nice to meet you."

The first thing that struck Jay about the Director of the FBI was his immense size. Matthew Jones was a giant—not just tall but massively overweight. Even from across the wide expanse of the man's office, Jay felt physically intimidated. As he walked across the deep pile carpet to shake hands with Jones, Jay had the sensation that he was shrinking and the FBI Director was growing.

The second thing he noticed was that Jones wore a dog collar. His briefing materials had given the Director's full title as "Reverend Doctor Matthew Jones, Director, FBI." Now Jay wondered quite how he should address the man.

"I'm very pleased to be here, Reverend Doctor," he said, hazarding something that at least showed he wasn't ignorant of the Director's status in the Church.

For his part, Jones feigned surprise and touched his collar with a polite laugh. "Ah yes, this. It must seem strange to your European eyes, but we are warrior priests in the Bureau. The Church and the State are one, you see, and we are its guardians." He waved Jay towards a group of uncomfortable looking leather armchairs and sat in one himself. "I won't take up too much of your time, Chief Inspector. I merely wanted to tell you that the case of this missing female is of great importance to us."

"Sandra Malone, sir."

"Yes, yes. The man who has taken her is a most dangerous terrorist. An insane, deranged man. He is responsible for many atrocities and he does not scruple at killing and maiming innocents. The fact that he has kidnapped a specialist in the diabolical arts of time travel is of great concern to us."

The diabolical arts of time travel? Jay tried not to look amazed. "If done correctly, a timesplash can be a terrible weapon," Jay said. "Do you believe your enemies are attempting to acquire the capability to create a major splash?"

"My enemies, Chief Inspector?"

"This man, Polanski, and his followers."

Jones's eyes narrowed. "Polanski is a rogue terrorist, Chief Inspector. He has no agenda other than anarchy and destruction. Within our borders, the United States of America has only one enemy—the Old Enemy, Satan himself. We have established the Kingdom of God here on Earth, Chief Inspector. You can imagine how wild with rage that makes the Devil and what he would do to drive this nation back into sin and error."

Jay nodded, not trusting himself to say anything. The Director's eyes seemed to pierce through Jay's silent acquiescence and lay bare the moral turpitude within.

With a look almost of disgust, Jones said, "Trade relations with Europe have become important to us. We are pleased to find that we have something Europe wants after having been treated as the poor relation for so many years. Help us bring Polanski to justice and you will have served the cause of international accord as well as having brought God's judgement on an evil man."

He stood up and walked to his desk. Jay stood up too.

"That will be all," the Director said, picking up a file and flicking it open. "God be with you."

"Er, thank you, sir." Dismissed, Jay hurried to the door.

Outside, Agent Simmons was waiting. "Everything go well?" he asked in his usual cheery tone.

Jay studied him. "Have you ever met the Director?"

"I'm afraid not. It's quite a privilege."

"It was certainly something. What's next?"

"Deputy Director English is waiting for you."

"When do we start work?"

Simmons looked confused.

"I'm eager to bring God's judgement on an evil man," Jay said.

"Ah, of course. Deputy Director English is in charge of the investigation. I'm sure he will assign someone to bring you up to speed."

* * * *

Cara Malone regarded her reflection in the mirror. So did Eve, the lady from the clothes shop.

"Now doesn't that look pretty!" Eve exclaimed, as she had exclaimed over every hideous outfit Cara had tried on. "That is definitely your colour, and we have a full range of matching accessories."

Cara thought the floor length grey skirt, high-collared white blouse and grey cardigan looked awful. The only good thing about the whole ensemble was that the skirt was so ridiculously long and full that it completely hid the vomit-making round-toed shoes and white ankle socks they'd found for her.

"I know it's a little bit risqué," Eve said, standing back.

"It's from our young ladies range, not our children's range, but you're just so tall, my dear."

Cara glanced over at her chaperone, Mrs. Mueller, a beefy woman in her mid-thirties with arms as thick as drainpipes and brown eyes that scowled at her resentfully. Simmons had dug her up from somewhere—Cara suspected her usual job was laying out bodies at the morgue—and dumped her at the hotel that morning. With her long black dress and black headscarf tightly tied under her chin she looked like an Italian peasant woman from the 1950s. If she had any expression other than that resentful scowl, Cara had yet to see it. Right now, Mueller was slumped in one of the shop's uncomfortable chairs and reading a little black book—a paper book no less, like ones Cara had seen in museums—that she kept tucked away in her dress most of the time. It was a Bible, of course. Everybody in America seemed obsessed with religion.

Beyond Mueller, standing by the door, was a young man in a dark suit. He was Cara's own, personal, FBI bodyguard. Simmons had seemed very pleased with himself when he told her that Special Agent Lowry would accompany her everywhere to make sure she didn't get into any trouble.

"Don't you like it, honey?" Eve asked. "It really is what all the best young ladies are wearing. I really don't know what else I can show you."

With a sigh, Cara yielded. "Oh, what the hell. It's only for a few days."

Eve gasped and Mueller was on her feet. "Young lady! You will behave with decorum or I will take you straight back to your hotel room where you will stay for the remainder of your visit."

Mueller hadn't strung together so many words since they

met. It took Cara a moment to realize what all the fuss was about. When she realized what it was, Cara then had to bite down hard on her first reaction, which was to say, "Oh, bugger!" Instead she apologized through gritted teeth.

The truth was, she was a bit scared of Mrs. Mueller and her FBI enforcer. Between them, they had complete power over her and neither seemed to like her one little bit.

She turned to Eve and smiled. "The outfit's fine," she said. "I'll take it—and all the accessories you think it needs." Her father was paying, after all, and, as long as he didn't mind her throwing everything in the nearest bin when they got back to the UK, it was no skin off her nose. At least none of her friends would see her looking like a complete twonk and no-one here seemed to care what they looked like.

She checked her commplant for messages without thinking and almost screamed when it gave her the same "no service" message it had given her the last five hundred times she had tried to use it. As Eve went to select belts and headscarves, and to find a bag to put her old clothes in, Cara said to Mueller, "I'd like to talk to my father, please. How do I do that?"

"Have you got a compad?"

"You mean a commplant?"

"No, I mean a compad." She pulled a small black tablet out of a hidden pocket.

"Is that how you talk to each other? Where can I get one?"

"Does your father have one?"

"Why would he have one of those? He's got a commplant, like everybody." Mueller sighed and shook her head, heaving herself to her feet as though she were exhausted from having to sit there. "Are we finished here? Can we go now?"

"Yes, but…"

"There's no point trying to call your father if he doesn't have a compad."

"Well how am I going to talk to him then?"

"I'm sure you'll see him at the hotel tonight."

"Tonight? That's no good. I need to talk to him now. You don't understand. My mother has been kidnapped by some evil creep named Polanski and my father's here to find her. I'm here to help him. And I'm stuck here wasting my time buying Halloween costumes with matching accessories."

"Polanski?" the woman said, as if none of the rest mattered. She glanced across at the FBI man by the door, which made Cara look too. The agent was watching them. Hastily, Mueller looked away. "Come on," she said, flustered. "We are going to see the sights."

"What?"

"That is our schedule. Those are my instructions. Once you are properly dressed, I can show you the monuments and the museums. Unless you would rather return to your hotel."

Cara couldn't understand what was happening. Mueller seemed to have dismissed her request to speak to Jay and now she wanted to drag Cara off on a sightseeing tour. But she wasn't acting like her old, phlegmatic self. Now she was agitated and bustling. She called to the shop assistant to hurry up and then took Cara by the arm and almost shoved her out of the shop.

"You know this Polanski, don't you?" Cara asked as they crossed the street to the black government car.

"I certainly do not," Mueller said, loudly. "But I've heard of him, of course. Who hasn't? Such an evil, terrible man." She looked around nervously. "Now hush. All this talk is making me sick. I've never known such a talkative, rude child."

Cara, who, in her own opinion, had been extremely forbearing, scowled at the woman in silent resentment. Something funny was going on here and none of it made sense. She looked across at the FBI man to find him still watching her. Some instinct for self-preservation kept her from asking what the hell he thought he was staring at. Deep in thought, she subsided into the car's plush upholstery.

Chapter 13

Alley Shanty

In 2039, Government forces bulldozed the Washington suburb of Alexandria. The Lord's True Path Party had a firm grip on the nation by then and the existence of rebel-infested enclaves like Alexandria was an embarrassment. They'd shelled it and raided it for two years beforehand, but after each assault, the rebels would just crawl out of their hiding places like rats from the sewers and begin their campaign of rocket attacks and sabotage all over again. After a rebel rocket took out the West Wing of the White House, killing twenty-seven people, then-President Carpenter ordered the whole area levelled. Troops and tanks cleared out the residents, and the wrecking crews and the bulldozers followed behind. By the end of that week, Alexandria was a nine thousand acre car park, devoid of all life.

Two years later, every square inch of that wasteland was covered with makeshift housing and the population was three times what the old suburb of Alexandria had been. The Alley Shanty seemed to spring up overnight. Tens of thousands of displaced and homeless people from devastated cities like New York and Chicago found their way there. If they didn't have food, or jobs, or running water, at least they had a corrugated tin roof over their heads and a packing case wall to keep out the winter snow.

Things were better now that the City had installed stand-pipes in the streets so people could get clean water, but, to Sandra—as Polanski led her down the noisy, cramped, rubbish-filled streets—the Alley Shanty looked like something Bosch might have painted. If a party of winged devils had appeared to devour some of the squabbling, screeching children, or their listless, sullen parents, the picture would be complete. As it was, the stench of untreated sewage, mixed with the aroma of greasy, fried foods, added a dimension of disgust no mere painter could ever adequately represent.

"Where the hell are we going?" she asked.

"Not far," Polanski said.

They passed a block of two- and three-story buildings that had collapsed, spilling mattresses and clothing, chairs and crockery into the muddy streets. It seemed to be a recent catastrophe because men and women and half-naked children were swarming among the ruins, salvaging boards and wooden beams, and dragging them off to begin life anew as parts of other homes.

Two blocks up, they stopped outside a door in a plain plywood wall. Two men sat outside the door on rickety wooden chairs nursing machine guns in their laps. Polanski greeted the men by name and they grinned and hugged him and welcomed him back. They eyed Sandra with curiosity but asked no questions and were given no explanations.

It was the same inside. More armed men, more happy reunions. They passed from one room to another as they burrowed into the shanty, sometimes crossing an alley that let in a little light from above, sometimes encountering women and children, or a family eating a meal, or a couple having a screaming match—more happy to see Polanski than they were concerned to have been caught in the act. Finally, Sandra and Polanski reached another door with another brace of guards. A handful of people came running up, calling greetings as they arrived. No-one seemed to dispute Polanski's absolute right to walk through their homes as he pleased.

"This is terrorist HQ, isn't it?" Sandra said. "And this bunch of half-starved desperadoes is your rebel army. Am I right?" She saw one of the guards clench his fist and step forwards but Polanski stopped him with a gesture.

"Feisty little thing, ain't she?" Polanski said, grinning at her would-be assailant. "Peter and I only managed to get her back here by watching each other's backs all the way. I thought for sure one of us was gonna wake up with a knife in his ribs."

Everyone relaxed.

"You'll get used to her ways and her foul mouth after a while. But don't let that pretty face fool you. This little lady is one vicious little hell-cat. Let your guard down for a minute and she'll be out of here. And you'll be left trying to explain to me how your arm got broken."

People laughed but Sandra saw them studying her with a new uncertainty. They also seemed to hear Polanski's unspoken message: anyone who failed in their duty to keep her a prisoner would have to answer to him personally.

It irritated Sandra to think that Polanski was closing down her options for escape. She said, "And behind that door is the hardware you want me to assemble, right? The displacement rig."

Polanski's expression hardened. His followers stopped smiling.

She looked from face to face. "Do you know what will happen if we ever run that thing in there? This whole rat-infested cesspit you live in will come down like a house of cards. Everything for miles around will be destroyed. People will die. Lots of people. The backwash from a timesplash doesn't discriminate between men and women, good and bad, old and young. Nobody will be safe. Not your children, not your lovers, no-one. It'll be like a nuke going off right here. This room will be ground zero."

She was pleased to see anxiety creeping into a few of the faces around her. Polanski shook his head. To the crowd, he said, "She doesn't understand. Even though she's seen a little, she hasn't seen enough yet. She hasn't had to live here. She hasn't had to bring up her kids here, to watch them die of dysentery, or cholera, or measles. In her whole life she hasn't had to go without food. She hasn't had to live in fear of the SOBs and the Feds. She hasn't had her parents dragged away in the night, never to be heard of again."

He looked Sandra in the eye. "If you knew what these people lived with, you'd appreciate their willingness to do anything, to take any risk, to lay down their lives if need be, so that the people of this country can be free again."

She opened her mouth to reply, but the people around her were shouting their approval and slapping Polanski on the back, looking at her with contempt and defiance. She shut her mouth again.

"OK," said Polanski, bringing everybody to order. "Open her up."

The anticipation in the small group told Sandra she was expected to be impressed. Polanski stood back and let her walk in alone.

The room was large. For a roofed space in the middle of a

labyrinth of lean-to shacks, it was palatial. And, mostly, it was empty. Near the middle of the room was a group of electronics racks—all different makes, models and generations, and all stuffed with boards. Beyond them were big, boxy devices that she recognized immediately as focus fusion generators. Again they ranged from fairly modern, Indian-built units, about the size of a compact car, to older units of uncertain provenance, some as big as a garden shed. One or two looked as if they might be hand-built. If even half of them worked, there was enough power generation capability in that room to light up a small city. She spotted displacement field coils, high-voltage power switches, heavy-duty cables and a table piled high with screens and keyboards. The whole collection looked as if it had been salvaged from junkyards and landfills—and perhaps it had—but all the pieces were there to build a lob site. It wouldn't be the kind of site she knew from her work at the university. It would be the kind of site that brilliant, enthusiastic kids used to lash together in the bad old days of the splashparties.

"It all works," said Polanski, standing beside her. "We've had it down in Houston running trials."

Her eyes kept moving over the equipment, assessing and inventorying it. "Don't tell me, lots of people died."

"Good people," he said. "Friends." There was a long silence before he added, "We planned to go back twenty or thirty years, travel to the target, and make a splash. It seemed simple enough but…"

"But you couldn't control the splash, could you?"

A new voice said, "In the end, that's what finished us."

She looked around. The voice belonged to a man about the same age as Polanski. He was short, mousy, unprepossessing. The kind of person you'd see standing around the edges of a nightclub, holding a drink, hugging the shadows. The trace of an English accent made her search her memory, but she couldn't place him.

"At first," the man went on, "we couldn't get the calibration right. The lob itself killed them. Then there were problems with equipment, the suits, even targeting accuracy. The thing was, if we couldn't land them somewhere quiet at the far end, they never had a chance of making it to the splashtarget. And we just never had the accuracy."

He held out a hand to her, which she ignored. "We have met before," he said. "When you used to work for Flash. When you were hunting Sniper. My tag was Jean Luc. I was on Flash's team. One of the tekniks."

She eyed him coldly. "I never worked for Flash. We had a mutual enemy, that's all." As for having met him, tekniks were just part of the furniture in those days. It was the bricks that mattered.

He looked a little deflated. "You don't remember me, then? But I remember you. You were on the Ommen splash in the Netherlands, and then on the London splash when Sniper died. I read about it in the papers."

She felt anger boiling up inside as the man spoke.

"Even though I had to get out of Europe when they started rounding up all the players from the old days, I kept tabs on you," he said. "I couldn't believe it when you became a teknik. When Zak asked who I knew who could help with this project, you were the obvious choice. You were perfect."

So it was this little shit who had set Polanski onto her, who had dragged her into this nightmare and left her daughter at home probably going crazy with worry. Before she had even completed the thought, her fist shot out and hit the man in the face. His eyes boggled and he brought his hands up, blood bubbling between his fingers. His eyes rolled back but before he fell, she hit him twice more in the ribs, happy to feel one yield and crack.

Reacting far too late to do anything, a couple of Polanski's men grabbed her arms and she let them. Polanski organized someone to get the injured man to a doctor and then turned to Sandra. She could see he was angry but also perplexed. This wasn't part of his plan. He probably intended Sandra to work with the creep she'd just put down. Just so that he had no illusions on that score, she said, "If he comes near me again, I'll kill him."

Polanski tensed as if he might hit her, but she saw him fight the urge and slowly relax. It was an impressive display of self-control. Even so, when he spoke, he was almost snorting with rage. "I've made a lot of allowances for you, because I need you on this project. But you need to consider this: the day I decide you're not going to be of any use to us, is the day your body is found floating in the Potomac." His face jerked into a snarl and he looked away from her. Perhaps it was to hide his self-disgust at having let himself off the leash, or maybe for letting the desperation show in his eyes.

He took two long, deep breaths. When he looked back, he was calm again. "I was hoping you'd get some sense of how this nation is suffering under the present government. I was hoping that you'd feel some sympathy for our cause, despite what we had to do to get you here. But maybe you can't see past your own hurt feelings, your own sense of injustice at the inconvenient situation we've put you in." He stepped away from her, on his way out. "They'll give you a cot and someone will bring you food. You'll sleep here until the job is done. There will be an armed guard with you at all times." He raised his voice to a shout and looked around the room. "No-one goes close enough to her to let her take his damned gun away from him. Do you hear me?"

* * * *

They left her to brood alone for a couple of hours. Alone, that is, except for the guy who brought in a chair, placed it close to the door, and sat watching her with a gun in his lap. After a while, she almost forgot he was there. She had more important things to worry about.

It was clear to her that she could not help them build a lob site and kill half of Washington. Whatever the government was like, whatever crimes they had committed—or were still committing every day for all she knew—a timesplash in a crowded city could never be the right solution. Two million had died in Beijing and over a million in Mexico City. Even in London, where the splash had been relatively small and the city centre partially evacuated ahead of time, thousands had died. Polanski and his people had to be fanatics even to consider such a monstrous action.

Yet Polanski didn't seem fanatical. He didn't rant or yell. He seemed pretty normal for someone who went about kidnapping people. A little bit intense maybe... In fact, despite everything, she'd grown to quite like him. He'd taken a fair bit of crap from her and had only lost his temper with her one time, just then, when she'd beaten up his slimeball teknik. Mostly, he'd been apologetic for snatching her and dragging her halfway around the world. It didn't make sense that he was willing to put millions of lives at risk. On the other hand, she couldn't deny that he seemed genuinely committed to his cause. Maybe he wasn't quite as sane as he looked. Maybe "freeing his people" was an ideology that justified anything for him, the way his enemies' theology seemed to justify anything for them.

Whatever made him tick, she could not doubt that he meant to make her help him and, if she wouldn't, that he'd have her killed. Well, that wasn't going to happen. She had a daughter at home who needed her mother to come back alive.

Sandra wondered how Cara was getting on with Jay. It was a hell of a way for her to meet her father. A hell of a way for Jay to discover he had a daughter. But that couldn't be helped. She'd followed Jay's career over the past sixteen years. She knew he was a big-shot cop now, running the whole show at the Temporal Crimes Unit. He could look after Cara and keep her safe until Sandra got back. Meanwhile, he'd be going all out to rescue her. She knew he would, even if he was furious with her for keeping Cara a secret. Jay was like that. He couldn't help himself.

One thing—the only thing, in fact—she felt good about was having been cautious enough to keep Cara out of sight for all those years. Olivia was the only one at the university who knew Sandra had a daughter. She was really the only person who knew Sandra, and who also knew about Cara. Olivia had claimed that Sandra was being paranoid. She said her behaviour worried her. But now Sandra felt completely vindicated. If Polanski and his thugs had known that she had a daughter, they'd have taken her too and used her as leverage. It was exactly this kind of scenario that had plagued Sandra from the day she first learned she was pregnant.

While she pondered, people brought in a makeshift bed with a musty old mattress and a couple of blankets that Sandra wouldn't have given to a dog. They were poor people, with stooped shoulders and rickety legs, bad teeth and bad skin. She felt a vague anger that, even here among the revolutionaries, it was the women who did all the work while the men held guns and acted important. She hoped their revolution would bring these women a better life, but she wouldn't help them if it involved committing mass murder. Besides, she had only one priority: to get home to her daughter.

They brought her a bowl of stew and a hunk of gritty bread. She ate the food quickly and climbed into the bed, keeping her clothes on. She had been famished and now she was exhausted. Tomorrow she would watch them and talk to them and find out how to break out of the rat's nest they held her in. If she could sabotage the time travel equipment along the way, she'd do that too.

Chapter 14

Mueller

Jay brooded in the limo on the way back to the hotel. Sitting opposite him, the ever-present Simmons stared out of the window, having learned, at last, not to start idle conversations. Jay regarded him under hooded eyes as the day's resentments projected onto his FBI minder.

"You guys will never find Polanski," Jay said, breaking the long silence.

"You should have more faith, Chief Inspector."

"In God?"

"In Deputy Director English."

"Well, I don't. His only tactic seems to be rounding up Polanski's suspected associates and torturing them."

"It will work. It always does."

"Really? That's not the impression I'm getting. The more I speak to people, the more I realize that Polanski has a huge organisation spread across the whole country."

Simmons smiled. "They like to make out they're heroic freedom fighters but they're just petty crooks and terrorists. If we crack enough heads together, somebody will give up Polanski. He's got them all pretty scared of him, so we just

145

need to make sure they're more scared of us."

Jay wasn't very sure about that. He'd sat in on as many "interviews" as he could stomach and had spoken separately to half-a-dozen prisoners. Simmons was wrong. These people did not sound like self-aggrandizing criminals to him, they sounded like ordinary people swept up in a police dragnet so broad that he believed most of them to be completely innocent. As much as he wanted the FBI to find Polanski in time to save Sandra, there had to be a better way than this.

"Deputy Director English seems to think we're on the wrong track," said Jay. "He told me not to worry about a timesplash. He said the real danger was a dirty bomb."

"Really?" Simmons looked shifty.

"He said that there was a slight possibility that 'atheistic elements' had acquired quite a lot of weapons-grade plutonium."

"I'm surprised he mentioned that," said Simmons, who seemed to be making an effort to act nonchalant. "It's really just a rumour and most likely completely explained by an accounting anomaly. The Deputy Director worked on the efforts to clear up the confusion. I expect he was discussing worst-case scenarios."

Jay nodded, not wanting to pursue it. Whatever the state of the world's largest nuclear arsenal was these days, he imagined that many American lawmen had plenty of sleepless nights about it. He would probably have a few himself after today's revelation.

"What about the route into the States? Any more news on that side of the investigation?"

"Dead end," Simmons said, reflecting a widespread indifference to good procedure that was driving Jay crazy. "The Mexicans drew a blank. They could have arrived at a dozen airports on scores of flights. Once they're in Mexico, the Texas border is wide open. No way to say where they might have crossed."

"And the Texan police? Any leads from them?"

Simmons gave him a look that said, "You're kidding!", which turned up Jay's frustration another notch.

All day long he had been biting his tongue, making helpful suggestions, trying to get lines of investigation going that might actually lead somewhere. All day long he had been rebuffed, put down, even ridiculed by arrogant, opinionated agents who told him that he didn't understand the way "these people" thought, that he didn't understand how the law worked in the U.S., and that he wasn't in Europe now "with AIs and implants and God-knows-what kind of infernal technology." One of them even told him that, if he wanted to be really useful, there was a chapel down the corridor and he might try praying to God for help.

Jay had told the Deputy Director that he had been a first-rate analyst in his day and, if he could just sit down with the data mining team, he might be able to add some value. The man had looked at him oddly and said, "All the files are in the archives, Chief Inspector. Feel free to take a look." The archives turned out to be a set of rooms in a lower basement containing countless cabinets full of paper files. Standing down there and staring at that useless mass of information was probably the low point of Jay's day.

"Science is a dirty word, here, isn't it?" he said to Simmons.

"Jesus didn't need science," came the rote answer. "Science won't get you into Heaven."

"Do you really believe that? I mean, that science has no value? Not even just for the sake of material comforts, healthcare, engineering…? Just practical stuff?"

Simmons shrugged. "Of course, it would be nice to have polio vaccines and virtual TVs as big as a cinema screen, and all that tech you guys have over there… but it's really just a snare to trap the unwary and lead them into error."

"How does a polio vaccine lead anyone into error?" It was hard not to sound tetchy.

If Simmons heard his tone, he magnanimously overlooked it. "Well, it starts with medicines and healing and people seem to think that's all good, but it ends with announcing that people are just biological machines, programmed by their DNA. It starts with understanding human anatomy and great new surgical techniques that save lives, but it ends with comparing human anatomy to chimps and concluding that we all evolved from monkeys. You see where I'm going with this? You look at the stars and ask how the universe works and pretty soon you're trying to convince people that it all came from a big bang, billions of years ago. Heck, the Bible tells us as plainly as it can that the Universe is six thousand years old, but even harmless-looking sciences like geology and archaeology get people declaring the Earth is billions of years old and that human beings have been around for hundreds of thousands of years!" He looked pleased that he had made his point. "If God chooses to take a few children to his bosom early with polio, isn't that better than the whole nation going to Hell with their arms full of vaccine?"

Jay didn't know what to say. He had to remind himself that everyone he had met in the FBI was ordained or was taking holy orders. It was a prerequisite of the job. This was not a typical group of people. So he nodded as if Simmons had made an interesting point.

"You're a man of strong beliefs, Zeke."

* * * *

Simmons said goodnight to him in the foyer and went off to speak to another FBI agent who seemed to be there for the night shift. Jay tried his commplant again but there was no signal. He had been issued with a compad, the kind of thing that might have been used back home fifteen or twenty years ago, but he didn't want to use it to call his office. The device was almost certainly bugged. So was the limo he'd just been in, and so was his hotel room, he was sure. What the FBI made of his conversations, he had no idea, and he cared even less. How they reconciled their use of surveillance technology with their general anti-science stance was another mystery he couldn't be bothered to ponder. Probably some guff about the lesser of two evils, he supposed.

He took the lift up to his floor and was anxious over meeting Cara again. She'd be grumpy and frustrated by her day just as he was. He cringed at the thought of facing her complaints. Long-lost daughter or not, he was too miserable to face a whining teenager right now. Which immediately added guilt to the list of the day's woes. Here was a child whose mother was in mortal danger, who had been forced to run for help to a father she didn't know, and who was now in a foreign country—foreign in so many ways—and being watched by strangers. It was a miracle she wasn't in pieces. She was Sandra's daughter all right: beautiful and tough. But she was still only a child and he—as strange as it still seemed—was her father. He needed to be the grown-up. He needed to be strong for her.

All the same…

Taking a deep breath, he opened the door and went inside.

Cara was on the sofa, her long legs hidden by voluminous skirts, as she read from what looked like an ancient tablet device. The minder, Mrs. Mueller, sat across the room in an armchair, watching some kind of entertainment on a wall-mounted display. Cara turned to him and smiled, giving him a cheerful hello. Mrs. Mueller switched off the display and stood up, black dress rustling. She collected her bag and her headscarf.

"May I have a word, Chief Inspector Kennedy?" she said, tying the scarf tightly under her chin. "About our arrangements for tomorrow?" She headed for the door and he was forced to follow.

"I assume I should arrive at the same time tomorrow morning," she said, opening the door and stepping into the hallway. Jay followed her out. "And can I expect you to be home at the same time tomorrow evening?"

She kept walking down the corridor, towards the lift. Jay stayed with her, odd as it seemed. She reached the lifts and stopped, stepping around Jay to stand behind him, making him turn right round in order to face her.

"Please don't say anything," she said. "And don't look up. There's a security camera over my left shoulder. No doubt they will have lip-reading software."

Jay almost shook with the effort not to look.

"That's fascinating," he said, trying to look relaxed. His brain was suddenly fizzing as he tried to guess what might be going on.

"Your daughter said you are looking for Polanski."

"Yes," he said, as if the woman's statement was not pregnant with possibilities. "That's right."

"Reach across me and press the lift button. I'm going to give you an address."

Casually, he did as he was asked and felt her slip something into his jacket pocket.

"Good night, then, Chief Inspector. I will see you tomorrow."

"Good night."

He walked back down the corridor to his room. As he went, the lift arrived and the doors opened. He did not look back but went inside and locked the door.

Cara was still on the sofa, watching him. "Did you have a nice day?" she asked, pleasantly.

"Yes, thank you. Did you?"

"We saw the Lincoln Memorial," she said. "Why don't we go down to dinner and I'll tell you all about it?"

So Cara was in on whatever the hell was going on. Which was why she was being all "Stepford Wives" with him. She jumped up and went to her bedroom.

"I'll get my shoes. Can we go out? There were some lovely little restaurants just down the street."

"Of course. I love the new outfit by the way."

She reappeared, smiling tautly. "It's the latest fashion for the Washington young set. I have a matching headscarf. Very chic. I think I'll wear it next time I'm in London. I think it might just turn a few heads."

They went down to the lobby and out onto the street. Their FBI man fell in discretely behind them.

"OK, what the hell is going on?" Jay asked when they were out and moving on the busy street. It was possible the Feds were listening with parabolic mikes or had microdrones in the air around them, but he couldn't see why they'd go to so much trouble. He was supposed to be on their side, after all.

"Mueller stared acting funny as soon as I mentioned

Polanski," Cara said. "While we were out sightseeing, she took off her brooch and dropped it. She said they'd had her wired but we could talk now."

"What did she say?"

"She said Polanski is a bad man, an evil man, a godless atheist, all that kind of stuff, and that Mum is in great danger if he has hold of her."

"We pretty much knew that already. What's Mueller's angle?"

"She says her friends can help us rescue Mum, but not if the Feds are involved. She hates the FBI as much as she hates Polanski."

"Seems reasonable. Who are these friends of hers?"

"She said she'd give you a name and you should go see him—without the cops. He'll explain everything."

"I don't see how I can shake the FBI. They're keeping a close watch on both of us." Jay didn't like the sound of things. How could he trust some stray childminder the FBI had arranged for them? He would be putting Cara and Sandra at risk. What if it was all some kind of trap? Although, if it was, he had no clue as to why they'd do anything so bizarre.

"I knew you'd fuss," Cara said, giving Jay a stab of hurt. She stopped and he wondered what kind of a scene she was about to make but she just nodded towards a doorway and said, "This place looks OK."

They went into a small Italian restaurant. It was nearly full. Half the men in the place had either dog collars or silver crucifix lapel pins, or both. Several people noticed the FBI minder who came in with them and then proceeded to study them with interest. The minder took a seat by the door while a waiter showed them to a table. Although he was sitting within a couple of meters of several FBI agents, Jay realized the general hubbub was enough to mask their conversation from all but the most determined listeners.

"It's not possible," Jay said, smiling and pretending to talk about the menu. The menu was printed on paper and bound into a stiff, padded folder. If he hadn't seen such things in old vids, he wouldn't have had a clue how to order.

"Of course it is. We go tonight."

"Tonight?" Yet, even as he said it, he realized it was the best option. There was an agent in the foyer but there were none on Jay's floor, and earlier he'd noticed the door to the service stairs, no doubt as Cara had done. "What about the surveillance? In the room. In the corridors. Probably on the service stairs too?"

But the biggest problem wasn't circumventing the security. The biggest problem was Cara. He wanted to meet Mueller's contact. He had to. Yet he couldn't unnecessarily expose a young girl to dangers like that. He had no idea what Mueller's friends might be like. Worse than that, he had no idea what the FBI might do if they caught the two of them sneaking around meeting unsavoury characters. A waiter came and Jay ordered, picking dishes at random. At the very least, they'd deport them—and that meant he'd be off the case and would have no chance of finding Sandra.

"It's a bad idea," he told Cara. "Don't even think about it."

Cara pursed her lips and glared at him. "OK. Tell me what leads you've got that are better than this?"

And, right there, was another problem. The FBI was getting nowhere. He was getting nowhere. And the clock was ticking. "For all we know this is an FBI trap to…" To what? Provoke an incident and get Jay off the case? Having gone to the trouble of making him come all the way to Washington, it hardly seemed likely they'd want to send him home now. Besides, if they wanted rid of him, they only had to say the word and he'd be gone. "All right, it's not an FBI trap, but it's still too dangerous."

"For me, you mean, don't you? You're thinking you'll go off on your own and find these people and leave me to my sightseeing."

It was certainly a good idea, Jay thought. He could give Simmons the slip somehow and go off on his own, meet the contact, and be back at the J. Edgar Hoover Building claiming he had been lost before he was missed too much.

The meal arrived and they sat back while it was served, then began to eat in silence.

"Well you can't leave me out. I'm the one who got this lead, remember? Without me, you'd be nowhere."

"What part of 'too dangerous' didn't you understand? I'm trained for this stuff. I've had more secret rendezvous with shady characters than you've had secret trysts with pimply boyfriends." He felt mean as soon as he said it.

She continued to scowl at him. "They're not pimply. Well, one of them was. Anyway, who says 'trysts' any more?"

She grinned and so did Jay. Silently, they agreed between them that dads were supposed to be a bit old-fashioned and daughters were supposed to think it was quaint and endearing. But the moment of bonding was soon over.

"You're not leaving me behind," she said, but even that piece of defiance was an admission that Jay had the power to do so if he chose.

"It's really for the best. You have to trust me, Cara. It's why your mother sent you to me, wasn't it? Because I know how to do these things and you don't? And shouldn't? What do you think she'd say about it?"

Cara looked down at her plate and pushed a couple of meatballs around for a while.

Sensing victory, Jay pressed his advantage. "She wants you safe. She'd be worried sick if she even knew you were over here." He reached out and laid a hand over hers, briefly stunned by the awareness that it was the first time he had ever touched his daughter. "I want to keep you safe too. I've only just found out you exist. You can't expect me to risk losing you now, can you?"

She looked up at him. "That's emotional blackmail."

"Maybe, but it's true." And it was. Among all the confusion about having Cara suddenly turn up, he was certain he wanted the time to get to know her and work out what it all meant to him. He took his hand off hers and said, "Eat your meatballs. They'll get cold."

Her mouth twisted up on one side into a wry grin, so reminiscent of her mother. "I'm a vegetarian," she said.

He looked down at the mozzarella and tomato salad he had barely touched. "I'm not," he said, and they both laughed.

* * * *

The next morning, Simmons took Jay to the FBI offices as usual. Jay put in an hour's work before deciding the day would be as much of a waste of time as the previous one had been. Feeling his heartbeat quickening, he came to the conclusion that Mueller's contact was the only way forward. He said he wanted some air and left the building with Simmons in tow. They crossed Pennsylvania Avenue and went south towards the National Mall. Strolling into it, they headed west, away from the Capitol and towards the Lincoln

Memorial, just like a pair of tourists. By the time they'd been walking for fifteen minutes, Simmons was beginning to look anxious.

"You can go back if you like," Jay told him, trying to sound casual. "I'm enjoying this. And, let's face it, I'm not being much help in there. I think I'll take in the sights. I always wanted to see the monuments and the White House. I think I'll make a morning of it."

"We should probably get back to work," said Simmons.

"Surely this is your work, isn't it? Keeping me happy? Keeping an eye on me?"

The FBI agent looked uncomfortable. "I'm just here to smooth the way, Chief Inspector. To make sure your time here is spent as efficiently as possible."

"Well, look at it this way. If I have to watch one more poor bastard being beaten with a rubber hose, I'll be on the next flight back to Brussels."

Simmons' brows came down in a scowl. "Those 'poor bastards' are known terrorist sympathizers."

"My arse! And, if they are, I'm beginning to think that if you throw a rock anywhere in this city, you'd hit two terrorist sympathisers every time."

Simmons was getting worked up now. "With all due respect, you don't know the situation here and you're in no position to judge."

Jay veered towards a knot of people and increased his pace.

"I know a bunch of scared people when I see them," Jay said. "And I know when I see a bunch of thugs picking on women and minorities when they're supposed to be protecting them. And I'll tell you this, I know when I need to get away from what's going on back there to get the stench of oppression out of my nostrils."

"You don't know anything about what's going on here. There have been bombings, assassinations. These people are not the simple innocents you think they are. Hey!"

Jay ducked into the crowd and ran at a tangent to his previous route, keeping low and heading for the nearest shop doorway. He could hear Simmons behind him shouting, "What are you doing? Come back here." Then, "FBI. Out of my way!" Then there came screams from the crowd that told Jay Simmons had drawn his gun.

He reached a door—a gift shop of some kind—and slipped inside. There was a counter with a bald man behind it. A handful of customers dotted the shop. Without glancing back, Jay strode up to the shopkeeper and in a low voice said, "I'm Special Agent Simmons, FBI." He saw the man's eyes widen and flick to Jay's lapel, looking for the crucifix. "I'm undercover. Is there a back way out?" Without speaking the man pointed and Jay hurried past, through a door, along a corridor, through another door and into an alley.

He queried his commplant. He may have no network services, but he still had the street maps of Washington he had uploaded before the trip, and he still had the global positioning signal from the Galileo 2 satellites. He grabbed the scrap of paper Mueller had slipped him last night and read the address. The route from the alley to his destination lit up on the map. It wasn't too far. He switched to augmented reality and large green arrows appeared as if they were drawn on the pavement. They lead him out of the alley and around the corner. He pushed the slip of paper in his mouth and chewed it as he ran.

Making the best speed he could without drawing attention to himself or using the main roads, it took him most of an hour to reach the address. It was along a side street in one of the smarter neighbourhoods. He didn't go straight to the door, but walked past the end of the street and checked out the house first. Then he walked up the opposite side of the street, past the house a couple of times. He could see no-one watching, no-one waiting in ambush. The house had a wrought iron fence behind which a short flight of steps ran up to an impressively large front door. Finally, he crossed over to the house and put his hand on the metal gate.

A sound behind him made him turn. Three men emerged from a van parked nearby and were on him before he could decide what to do. He let them take him without a fight and they pushed him into the van, climbed in behind him, and closed the doors.

"You took your time. I thought you weren't coming."

He blinked in amazement at his daughter, sitting at the back of the van, regarding him reproachfully. Her hands and feet were tied but she seemed unharmed and quite comfortable.

"Are you all right?"

She lifted her bound wrists and pulled a wry face. "The lovely Mrs Mueller took me out for a walk and straight into the hands of these guys. I was pretty sure they'd pick you up too, since it was all a setup."

His captors bundled him into a seat and the van set off with a smooth, gentle acceleration that meant it was a robot vehicle. They tied Jay's legs and hands. "Would someone tell me who you are and why you've kidnapped me and my daughter?"

"Don't worry, cop. No-one's gonna hurt no-one."

Jay did not feel much consoled. "Where are we going?"

"You'll see when we get there. Now shut up or I'll gag you."

Jay reluctantly closed his mouth. He looked across at Cara and shook his head in exasperation.

"Sorry," she said, and his only consolation was that she looked genuinely ashamed of herself.

Chapter 15

Breakfast

"Are you going to kill him?"

Polanski stood with the teknik behind him, the one who used to call himself Jean Luc. His sidekick, Peter, and two burly tough guys stood nearby.

Sandra craned her neck to peer round Polanski. The injured man had a plaster on his nose and stood slightly twisted from the pain in his ribs. He looked scared and clearly didn't want to be there. She looked back at Polanski.

"Nah, that's enough for now. I like it that he's suffering."

"Good. He's going to help you put this rig together. I've got guys to do the grunt work. As many as you need. Can you do it by tomorrow?"

Sandra laughed. "Give me a week. Maybe two." Polanski wasn't amused. "A day. Maybe two."

"Or else what?"

"Or else Peter and I go back to Europe and grab another teknik. I hope you're not thinking of putting us to all that trouble."

Sandra didn't want to bring on a full-scale confrontation, just enough to make it look like she needed to be pushed into cooperating. "Two days is impossible."

He smiled. "I said one day."

"One day is twice as impossible."

"Matthew?" It was clearly the name the teknik was now going by. Perhaps it was his real name. Sandra had finally twigged that everybody here had biblical names.

Matthew addressed her warily. "It's not like we're starting from scratch. This rig was running in Houston just a few weeks ago. It got a bit messed up but we've repaired everything. It just needs to be put back together." From the way he kept shifting his eyes towards Polanski, she could see Matthew was nervous as hell about the rebel leader believing him. Perhaps the failures of past lobs had left the teknik's credentials a little tarnished.

She walked a few paces away from them, as if she were grappling with her conscience. "All right," she announced after a suitable interval. "Two days. You," she nodded towards Matthew. "Get your crew in here and start assembling it. Right now. And you," she switched her focus to Polanski. "You can tell me all about your stupid plan."

Nobody moved until Polanski gave them the nod. Then the place erupted into frantic activity, with the teknik shouting out instructions and more guys coming in from outside to provide the muscle.

Polanski took her by the arm and Peter moved into place behind her. "You know Peter has a gun aimed at your back, right? So why don't we go for a walk? We'll get breakfast and I'll fill you in on what you need to know."

"I thought I was confined to this place until the lob was over."

He gave a shrug. "That was before you started cooperating. Put your headscarf on."

He led her out into the maze of corridors, through people's living spaces, and out into a part of the shanty she hadn't seen when they brought her in. She winced as a gust of sewage-laden air hit her. He must have noticed because he said, "No-one here chooses to live like this. Try and remember that. A lot of people who should know better talk about 'shanty rats' and 'slum dogs' but they're only one wrong word, one corrupt official, one SOB with a chip on his shoulder away from ending up here themselves—or places like it."

"They might not choose it, but you do, don't you? Some kind of statement?"

He laughed. "Sure. If you like. The thing is, I live on the charity of these people. They help me out because they believe that one day, I'll set them free. I want people to remember that I didn't take their faith and squander it on living in a big house or riding around in a smart car. I want them to know I was with them in every way possible, to the very end."

They came to a café, a bunch of trestle tables and benches with a sagging tarpaulin stretched above. A couple of women were ladling a kind of thick broth out of tureens into some chipped bowls on another trestle table. The kitchen behind them was basically a handful of brick barbecues with large pans steaming on top. It was a setup that made most soup kitchens Sandra had seen look like five star catering.

"It's not your university canteen," said Polanski, "but the food's good and it's cheap."

As soon as he appeared, people greeted him. One of the women serving food shouted that she'd send breakfast over right away. A minute later a couple of women from the back appeared carrying bowls filled to the brim and hunks of bread

162

to his table. It was all on the house and he thanked them profusely, even though they must have fed him a hundred times before.

Sandra was surprised to find the food smelled good and she dipped a spoon in to try it.

"You don't say grace?" Polanski asked.

She looked up at him. His own food was untouched and he had his hands clasped in front of him.

"You do?" She realized she had not sat down to a meal with this man in all the days they'd been travelling together. "You believe all that crap, even after you've seen what it's done here?"

She felt Peter stir behind her but a quick shake of the head from Polanski made the lad subside again.

"Nothing that's happening here is because of God, Sandra. It's men that are doing this. Narrow-minded bigoted men. Greedy, selfish men. Hard, cruel men who love power more than they love their neighbours. I'm more than happy to thank God for this food, for my health, for the hope in my heart, because He's doing all that for me despite everything that men are doing to my country."

"Shit. I thought you were crazy, but I didn't think you were that kind of crazy."

Peter started to say something but Polanski shut him up again. "What kind of crazy do you think I am, Sandra?"

"The same kind as those SOB creeps and the other good Christian folk who think it's right to turn women into domestic slaves. I almost believed all your pompous crap about freedom for a while there, but the reality is you just want to change one brand of vicious, god-worshiping bully for another."

Polanski sighed but he didn't look annoyed. "You know,

the United States was run by decent, religious people for over two hundred and fifty years before the Lord's True Path Party came to power. In all that time, we were a liberal democracy, a pluralist society, where freedom of religion was pretty much taken for granted. Religion isn't the problem here any more than atheism was the problem with the Soviet Union. People are the problem. Events arose at the start of the Adjustment that scared people into voting for the one group that stood up and told us it knew exactly what to do to save us all. You know, if I'd been old enough at the time, maybe I'd have voted True Path myself, given the situation. People voted for Adolf Hitler, you know. And it wasn't because they wanted to burn Jews and conquer Europe. It's because they were in a bad situation that looked like it was getting worse all the time and a man came along who looked like he might be able to make it all better. Once they gave him the power, of course, it was too late. Look at Lenin and Stalin. Look at Mao Tse-tung."

"So you're going to restore democracy?"

"I'm sure going to try. And I'm going to disestablish the Church of the Lord's True Path, 'cause I'm going to bring back the old separation of church and state. I'm going to abolish the Sons of Joshua and curtail all the summary judgement powers that various law enforcement agencies have been given. I may have to rebuild the FBI from scratch. Now, if you'll excuse me a moment. My food's getting cold."

He mumbled a quick prayer and began eating. Sandra was feeling somewhat deflated. It was easy to hate him when he was a crazy terrorist, easier still when she thought he was a crazy, religious terrorist, but not so easy when he talked sense and sounded like he might just be a good guy after all.

Then she remembered the timesplash.

"OK. So you're not quite as evil as I thought you were. Maybe. Why don't you tell me about how you plan to kill all these people we're having breakfast with?"

He thought for a moment and then asked, "If you wanted to get rid of an oppressive government that has murdered millions of your people—possibly tens of millions—and controls your country with fear and violence while plunging it ever deeper into poverty and ignorance in the name of a bizarre and twisted theology that maybe no-one at the top of government even believes in these days, except as an expedient, how would you go about it?"

"I don't know. Why don't you tell me?"

"No, seriously. Think about it. You can't hold an election. You can't just ask the evil, bloodsucking scum to hand back their power. What can you do? You could wait, maybe, until this generation of rulers dies off, and maybe the next, and the next, until things just start drifting back to some kind of normality. It might happen. But could you risk it? Could you stake the lives of hundreds of millions of people on that possibility? And if it takes twenty more years, or fifty, or a hundred, how do you justify all those generations of murder and oppression?"

"All right, all right, so you have some kind of revolution. Is that what you want me to say?"

"Yes. A revolution. The people rise up and take back the country. But we're in a bad way here. Worse than any oppressed people in history, I'd say. The Government not only has the usual tools of repression—the state police, its militias and armies, its courts and its punitive laws—but it also has a twenty-first century technology making it almost invincible. Technology that isn't shared with the rest of us.

"When this government took over, the U.S. was a

superpower. The arsenal includes everything from non-lethal riot control weapons, to ICBMs and cruise missiles with nuclear warheads. And that means no other country would risk supporting a resistance movement. Would you want to start a war with a nuclear power that could wipe you out at the flick of a switch? No, of course not. That's why Europe and China are happy to sit back and wait until things just sort themselves out over here. Trust me. I've spoken to their foreign ministers and I've gotten it from them first hand. The only way they would be willing to help us is if we could deal a decisive blow at the heart of the Government and it looked like we were a cinch to win."

"Hence the timesplash."

He sat back in his seat. "Give the lady a coconut."

"Wouldn't it be easier to steal a nuke or something?"

"Not really. It's easier to steal old F2 generators and computers—and kidnap pretty young hell-cats to plug the pieces together."

"You've got Matthew for that. What do you need me for?"

"For Plan B, that's what." He leaned forward, speaking more softly. "I told you about Plan A. We were going to go back to 2025. The idea was to steal a car, drive over to the Capitol and shoot Isaiah Douglass, the founder of the Church of the Lord's True Path. He was a nobody then, and he visited the Capitol on September 17 that year at ten AM to take a tour, just like anybody else. If we timed it right, we could have done the lob while the whole House was sitting. The backwash would have brought down everything within a two mile radius." He leaned in farther. "That would have gotten the White House too."

"But you couldn't get the accuracy."

"And we didn't have any confirmation of what was here at

the lob site back in September 2025. We lost a lot of people and we never once achieved the objective."

"And you think I can improve the accuracy?"

Polanski shook his head. "Maybe, but we still wouldn't know what the bricks would find when we lobbed them back there. The plan's useless without that."

"So?"

"So we need Plan B. A complete rethink. Even though a short lob with little travel at the far end is the best way to control the situation and gives us the best chance of success, a lot of the information we need was lost during the Adjustment. It's like all the fine detail just got wiped from the record. Sadly, the information people held back then was on computers, and when companies collapsed in their thousands and the power went off almost everywhere, no-one thought to put the computers somewhere safe so they could be resurrected one day. People were too busy starving and dying, I guess. So it's all gone."

Sandra was already thinking ahead of him. If a short, controlled lob was no good, maybe something more radical would serve better. Something Sandra was a world expert in.

"You want to do a long lob, back into deep time! That's why that little shit teknik of yours said I was perfect for the job."

He winced and leaned into her again. "If you could try not shouting that out loud, I'd appreciate it. Most of these folks are friends, but you never know."

"It's crazy. No-one's ever sent anything but small discrete packages of scientific instruments back more than a hundred and fifty years. No-one would dare." A squadron of British SAS soldiers still held the record for the longest manned lob, and all but one of them died doing it. Sandra was there and had seen the bodies. "What's your target?"

He pointed down at the table. "Right here, 1735. There was a cabin in these parts. Early settlers. Family farmed this land for a hundred years before their property was bought up and they moved west to Oregon. But the youngest son stayed behind and made his living as a lawyer in New York. His son, another lawyer, was there in Philadelphia in 1787 when the country was founded. That gentleman gave rise to a long line of patriots and liberal thinkers. One of them, my grandma, married Wacslev Polanski, an immigrant teacher from Warsaw, and she passed the family story down to her son, Stefan, who passed it down to me."

Sandra blinked at him for a moment, stunned. "You want to do this yourself, don't you, to make sure of the paradox?"

Polanski nodded. "Is there a better way?"

"You'll die. You can't imagine how sensitive the timestream is to intrusions that far back."

He shrugged. "I think it's better that the people who lead revolutions stand aside when their work is done. Don't you? That way they don't get tempted to become monsters. I'm always thinking about Stalin and Mao, you know, and Fidel Castro, and Adolf Hitler. The kind of person it takes to lead a revolution isn't the kind you want running the country afterwards."

What kind of new nonsense was this? "You're not Adolf Hitler."

A smile twitched on his lips. "That's kind of you to say so, but if I go back three hundred years and kill my fifteen-times great granddaddy, I might as well set off a nuke in this town. What kind of a man does that? And if I did survive it, what would I have to become to live with what I'd done? What kind of lies would I need to tell myself? What kind of delusions would I need to keep from drowning in that much innocent blood?"

"So why are you doing this?"

"Because it has to be done and no-one else can do it. I'm not just blowing up Washington and hoping for the best. There are people all over the country waiting for the signal. People elsewhere too. When Washington falls, the whole country will rise up."

"And what about me? How am I supposed to live with it if I help you?" The crazy thing was that, in the moment, she was caught up in his madness enough that it seemed like a question she needed to ask.

He shook his head and looked away. He looked tired. "You'll tell yourself I made you do it. You'll tell yourself you came to believe in my dream. You'll tell yourself it was the right thing to do in a world where the people in power have raised the stakes so high that only rivers of blood can keep you in the game."

"I'm sorry," she said.

He looked up at her.

"I think maybe you're the right man for the peace and the wrong man for the war. You can't justify this, even to yourself. This talk about dying in the act that brings the future you want isn't noble martyrdom, it's just a coward's way of not having to face what he's done."

She could see the anger build up in him like an engine being revved to full power. "Get up," he said. "And get to work. That rig had better be assembled, programmed and ready to run in forty-eight hours." He was snarling, a different man now. "Let's go."

Chapter 16

Duvalle

The van brought Jay and Cara to another large house in an expensive-looking neighbourhood. This time, it pulled into the drive and parked at the back. The three men hustled them into the house.

It was a beautiful house, with high ceilings and polished wood floors. They entered through a spacious hallway with a sweeping staircase, and then went through a heavy panelled door into a library. Along one wall were tall, arched windows, along the others were shelves from floor to ceiling divided by a balcony halfway up with a wrought iron spiral staircase. Several reading tables and green leather armchairs were placed near the light from the windows. On the shelves were books—real, paper books—some so old they were bound in leather. It was a collection so astonishing that Jay gaped in wonder at that vast array of precious antiques, despite his predicament.

"Good morning, Chief Inspector. Welcome to my home."

Jay saw a man rising from one of the leather chairs. A big man, meaty and solid, wearing a black suit and a clerical collar. He glanced at the man's lapel but there was no silver crucifix.

"Yeah, it's… big," Jay said.

The man smiled. "Yes, it is. Perhaps I should introduce myself?" His accent was a Southern drawl and Jay could see he fancied himself as a man of culture and distinction.

"Perhaps you should just tell us where Polanski is and let us go."

A frown ruffled the big man's brow. "Let you go? Do you suppose you are my prisoner? Far from it. You are my guest. Please, take a seat and I will tell you everything you need to know. Your daughter may wait outside."

"My daughter stays with me."

The big man gave a quick look of disappointment and said, "Very well." He looked past them to the three heavies and thanked them. "Send Mary in with some coffee and refreshments and then see that we are not disturbed." He resumed his seat and gestured for Jay to sit down. Reluctantly, Jay complied. Cara took the chair beside him.

"Look, whoever you are, I didn't come here to play out some kind of costume drama, or practice my etiquette. I got a message that suggested you could help me find Polanski. So, can you?"

"I am the Reverend Simon Duvalle," the big man said, as though Jay had not spoken. "You may have heard of me."

"No, I haven't heard of you. But I'm a police officer with Europol. If you're someone involved in criminal activities in Europe, I would be glad to add you to our database." He wished he had his commplant online so he could run a search on the name. Something told him he would probably find it.

Duvalle laughed as if Jay had made a big joke. "Well, you may have heard of my church, The Measurers of the Temple?

Yes, I see you have."

Jay certainly had. It had never been proven, but The Measurers of the Temple had been suspected of funding the timesplash that had destroyed parts of London sixteen years ago. The one Jay and Sandra had prevented from destroying the entire city. The church had been implicated in sponsoring several other attacks around the world, all aimed at what they termed "decadent, atheist governments." They were rich and influential in the U.S., one of the few fundamentalist sects allowed to operate under the umbrella of the Lord's True Path as an affiliated church.

"I know the Measurers, all right," Jay said. "You sponsor foreign terror groups. You provide money, weapons, training, and—we suspect—your 'missionary program' supplies skills and personnel as required to terrorist cells that need a helping hand. The Government here allows you to operate—in fact, encourages you—because you're doing a lot of things they'd like to but can't do openly themselves. A kind of deniable, black ops unit for stuff even the CIA can't touch. Did I leave anything out?"

Duvalle kept smiling. "My, my. You really don't like us much do you?"

"I liked it better when churches stuck to saving souls and left the politics to less dogmatic minds."

Again, Duvalle laughed. "There never was such a time, Chief Inspector. Sometimes the churches have less power, as they do in Europe right now. Sometimes they have more, as in the days when the Popes commanded armies over there. But we're always around, sleeves rolled up, doing what we can. You see, salvation isn't just a matter of singing songs on a Sunday. It's about creating a world where sinning is against the laws of man as well as the laws of God. And for that, the churches need power."

"And, for that, your church needs the Lord's True Path."

"And that's where Mr. Polanski comes in."

A maid entered with a tray of coffee and cakes and set it down between them.

She seemed confused as she glanced around the table. "Shall I pour, sir?"

"I'm sure Miss Malone here will do us the honour," Duvalle said.

Jay put a hand on Cara's arm to stop her from erupting and said, "My daughter is not your servant, Duvalle."

With a sigh, Duvalle gestured at the maid to proceed. When the woman left, Duvalle picked up his fine china cup and saucer and sat back in his chair. "You know I could have you shot, Chief Inspector. It would be very easy for me. A single command. You've absconded from the FBI's care, I suppose, and rich foreigners so often fall prey to the riff-raff that infest this fair city."

Jay knew it was all true, but he also knew Duvalle was simply irritated about Cara.

"All right then, have us shot. Oh wait, you're not going to do that, are you? What could it be that's holding you back? Oh yes, you still want something."

"Are all the British so ill-mannered and brutish these days? I do hope not. I like to maintain the illusion that you are a genteel and polite people. But perhaps the corrupting influence of a secular government slowly eats away at the souls of its citizens and leaves them debased and degraded."

Jay was growing angry. Only the slim hope that Duvalle might actually help him find Sandra kept him in his seat. "If you want to see ill-mannered and brutish, I'd be very happy to oblige. Meanwhile, can we cut the crap and get down to business?"

Duvalle looked pained. He took a sip of his coffee and set the cup back in its saucer. He drew a deep breath before shifting his dark gaze to rest on Jay. "Polanski is a meddling fool who fancies himself as some kind of hero of the people, like a Polak Che Guevara, or somesuch. I want him out of my way."

"Your way?"

Duvalle ignored him. "The man is an imbecile but he is gaining public support all the time. Now he's kidnapped a teknik and he's clearly planning a timesplash that he's going to unleash any day now. That is, I clearly see his plan, and no doubt you do too, but my friends at the FBI seem to think that they have all the time in the world. They think Polanski will make demands, that he'll try to blackmail them. They think he's one of us, a player, a power-broker. They think he wants to get his nose in the trough, but they're wrong. Polanski is a true believer, a fanatic. He won't be happy until he has burned down the whole farm and everyone in it."

"So tell me where he is."

"He's here, in Washington."

Jay's heart skipped a beat. If Polanski was here, so was Sandra. "Well?"

"Not so fast. First, we need to agree terms."

"Terms? You know that if Polanski creates a timesplash, he could take out the whole city?"

Duvalle sipped his coffee as if they were merely exchanging social pleasantries. Jay was developing a strong dislike for the man.

"Nevertheless, you and I want quite different things, Chief Inspector. Why should I help you achieve your goals without you helping me achieve mine?"

"Just tell me what you want."

The church leader lowered his cup and smiled. "I want Polanski's head on a platter."

Jay gaped. Did he mean it literally? "I suppose you know the story better than I do, but I seem to remember it ended rather badly for Salome when she provided a similar service."

"You talk as if you had any choice. I will tell you where to find this… unmarried mother you care so much about, and you will bring me proof of Polanski's death."

"I'm not a murderer. Polanski is wanted by the FBI. I'll do my best to bring him in if I can."

"You still don't understand, Chief Inspector. You will do exactly what I tell you to."

An uneasy feeling crept over Jay. Duvalle was not the kind to threaten him without being able to back it up. He had to get Cara out of there—and himself for that matter. He reached across to take Cara's arm, saying, "Come on, we're leaving," and froze. Cara was slumped in the big chair, her head lolling to one side, her arms loose at her sides. For a terrible moment, he froze, watching her. Then, at last, her chest rose and fell. She was still alive.

He turned to face Duvalle, eyes blazing. "What did you do?"

Duvalle had a weapon in his hand, aimed at Jay. "See that little gadget in the ceiling?" Jay kept his eyes on Duvalle, wondering whether he could shove the coffee table into the smug bastard's shins before Duvalle took him down. It might be worth a try. "It's a neural damper, just like the kind they use in hospitals—I believe your police use them to immobilize criminals during arrests—only this one projects a very tight beam. I control it from my commplant. I suppose you thought we were all too primitive over here to have such technology." Jay was thinking no such thing. His mind was overwhelmed with relief that Cara hadn't been hurt. "Well, I'm sure we would be if our friends in the Church of the Lord's True Path had their way. Fortunately some of us have the power to stand above their ridiculous anti-technology edicts."

"You just zapped my daughter and now you want to lecture me on politics?" If Jay could have got his hands on that thick throat, he would gladly have strangled the man.

"Shut up and listen. The Lord's True Path has shown itself incapable of sustaining a modern economy—or even a Mediaeval one. While their moral principles are sound, they apply them too rigidly. This country is going to the dogs. The South American Alliance is psyching itself up to invade us. Did you know that? Brazil, Argentina, Mexico, countries we wouldn't have stooped to wipe our boots on a few years ago, are seriously thinking about 'restoring democracy' to their neighbour. How do you like the indignity of that? They're gambling on our nuclear arsenal being so run down and neglected that we couldn't strike back. And they're not so wrong. I have people everywhere, you understand, and I know what's going on."

"Will you get to the fucking point?"

"I said shut up and listen." He fired his weapon and Jay's world exploded into pain—hot, searing pain that shook his body and blinded him with jagged lightning. He heard the coffee service crash to the floor, felt his body fall against the chair and table. He found himself on the floor at Cara's feet, gasping for breath, tensing against the unbearable, scorching pain, not daring to believe it had stopped.

"Get up," Duvalle said. "Come on, get up."

Jay hurried to obey. The churchman was watching him, still covering him with the gun. He waved it towards the chair and Jay climbed into it, limbs trembling.

"What the hell was that?" Jay said, but, of course, he knew.

"I like to think of it as a foretaste of what you atheists are in for on Judgement Day. The Korean police use it, I believe. Don't ask me how it works. Now, where was I?"

Jay noticed his trousers were wet and hoped it was just spilled coffee. He clenched his teeth against the slowly-subsiding pain. Duvalle relaxed into his armchair. He looked solid and heavy and completely confident in his domination of Jay.

"Ah yes, the South American Alliance, waiting down there, ready to pounce. And what they're waiting for has something to do with what Polanski is planning. He's made several trips across the border in the past few years—probably several more than we're aware of. And now they have fleets on manoeuvres in the Atlantic and the Pacific. A very unlikely coincidence, don't you think?"

To Jay it sounded like paranoid ravings from a man who had spent too many years scheming and conniving in secret and now saw plots everywhere he looked. Besides, an invasion from the south to restore democracy sounded like a pretty good idea. Maybe he would have to revise his opinion of Polanski upward by a notch or two.

"Why don't you just go to the Government with all this?" Jay asked. His limbs felt weak and his chest felt as if someone large had been sitting on it. He should probably find a doctor, he thought, or at least lie down for a week.

"People who can deny the evidence of a crumbling economy and a population on the edge of uprising are hardly likely to listen to evidence of a foreign invasion. You fail to grasp the essential nature of the Lord's True Path Party. God has given them this country. He gave them the Adjustment to cleanse the nation of sin. He speaks directly to the President and directs his domestic and foreign policies. The party is not prepared to accept that the God who did all this for them would abandon them now and let their Paradise on Earth be destroyed. That would imply that they had lost His favour. It would mean He had turned His smile away from them despite all their devotion, and had bestowed His grace upon the idolaters from the south and the atheists and doubters within their gates."

"I thought you were supposed to be one of the believers."

"Oh, I am. Don't mistake me. But the Measurers of the Temple are rather pragmatic. We believe that God helps those who help themselves."

Jay certainly didn't want to argue theology with this man, but he needed time to get over that damned pain ray he'd been zapped with, and he needed time to work out what to do next. "You know that's not actually in the Bible, don't you?"

"You've got a smart mouth, Chief Inspector. If you want a real Bible quote, how about this one? Suffer the little children... something, something." He swung his gun towards Cara.

Jay was on his feet and standing between them in a moment. "All right, all right. You've got my full attention. Tell me what you want."

Duvalle shook his head in bewilderment; real or feigned, Jay could not tell. "You know, I've often wondered what it is that makes a godless man behave with moral integrity. I mean, what's in it for him? Just look at you now, ready to take another taste of hellfire to spare your daughter pain. Just like a regular Christian father.”

The weakness and trembling was seeping back into Jay's body as the adrenaline surge faded. He sat down again and gave in to his weariness. “Can we stop playing games now?”

Duvalle rested the gun in his lap and sat back. “Of course. How rude of me.” Jay closed his eyes as the man continued. “You will go to Polanski's nest in the Shanty. You will kill him. You will bring back proof of his death. I will then hand you your daughter. If you can free your... What should we call her? Whore? Fornicator? Jezebel? Never mind. If you can free her, then by all means do so. But, remember, this pretty little lady is counting on you coming back for her.”

“You think killing Polanski will make everything all right again?”

“It will help.”

“And what makes you think Polanski's people will let me get close to him?”

“Don't worry. That's all taken care of.”

“I'll need a gun.” *And if you hand me one now, I'll shoot you where you sit, you evil bastard.*

“All taken care of.” He made no movement but the library door opened and two armed men came in. Jay rose on wobbly legs. “You've got twenty-four hours, Chief Inspector. Try not to be late.”

Chapter 17

Convergence

Sandra had to admit that Matthew and his team worked hard and fast. It was only early afternoon and the basic structure of the lob site was already in place.

She had taken over the assembly of the computer systems that constituted the control desk, and that too was coming along nicely. Of course, there had been a few unpleasant surprises when she booted up the systems and took a look inside. The basic field generation circuits were making so much high frequency electronic noise that it was no wonder the lobs had been dangerously inaccurate. It was probably because of the cheap and ancient parts that had been used to construct the systems, so there wasn't much she could do about it except try to use software filters to tame the worst of it. The motley collection of old fusion generators was certainly putting out enough power for a lob into deep time, but that too was dirty. She should strip down the generators, replace the most decayed parts and tune each one. As it stood, the power spiked unpredictably to levels she wouldn't trust to keep a probe in one piece let alone a human being.

But that would not be a problem. No-one was doing a

long lob with this equipment. Not if she could help it.

Polanski looked in once to see how things were getting on, but he didn't speak and he didn't appear again. She doubted that he had any clue as to what progress was being made, but the general air of industry and order must have been reassuring enough.

One of the fusion generators, number seven in the array, was making a loud hum—nothing too serious, she decided, probably a fractionally misaligned magnetic field. But she made a point of clucking over it, taking off a side panel and shaking her head. In the end, Matthew came over and asked her what the problem was.

"I don't know. I don't like the readings from this one. It's pretty unstable."

Matthew looked concerned. "It's always made that noise. I thought it was just a bit of field misalignment."

"Did you look inside?"

"Focus fusion isn't really my thing. I looked, but I didn't touch anything. I'd probably have made it worse."

Which was just what Sandra was hoping to hear. "Second generation Indian crap. This model was always dodgy. I should take it apart. If it's the primary laser, we could be in big trouble."

"We don't have time. That could take a day all on its own."

She put on a worried face. "How long's it been making that noise?"

"Since we got it. Months now. We've used it on eight different lobs."

"Well, I suppose it only has to last for one more."

She went back to the control desk, leaving Matthew anxiously studying the suspect generator. She needed maybe a couple more hours to sort out the software and set up the parameters for the lob. The power train was all in place, the displacement field coils were almost set up, and some preliminary calibration work was already underway. She smiled to think of what her university's health and safety people would think of the spider web of wiring and jerry-rigged equipment, or the workers clambering around inside that live, high-voltage junk pile.

To do the lob properly should take weeks. Not just weeks of careful construction, but of careful calibration and testing. Doing it this way was suicide.

But then, that seemed to be what Polanski wanted.

* * * *

The van pulled up in a rough neighbourhood. of abandoned industrial buildings and empty lots. Two men got out of the back with Jay. They were Duvalle's men but they were dressed in the brown shirts and long coats of the Sons of Joshua militia. Jay had been held in a scruffy house by other men for hours while Duvalle's people made their arrangements. Now he was painfully aware that his twenty-four hour allotment had shrunk to something less than twenty and Cara was still back there at Duvalle's mansion.

"There's the Shanty," one of the men said, pointing across a rubble-strewn expanse of concrete to where a chain-link fence rose high into the grey DC sky. Beyond the fence was an insane tumble of shacks and lean-tos that might have been dropped from a plane for all the order and solidity they had. Windows, roughly cut into plywood walls, faced them through the fence.

"This way," said the man and pushed Jay towards a low

office block with no glass in its windows and a sign outside so faded it was impossible to read. It was dark when they went inside but Jay's captors seemed to know the layout. They took him to an office door, one of the few still hanging, and unlocked it. Inside was a small room with a rectangular hole in the middle of its concrete floor.

"Down there," the man said.

Jay saw there were wooden steps leading down into subterranean darkness. He hesitated, not trusting the deep blackness below, or the two thugs behind him.

"It's just a tunnel," his guard said and flicked on a flashlight. "Go on."

Jay counted twenty-five steps before his feet touched the dirt floor of the tunnel. The ground was squishy and wet and he heard things slither and scramble through the muck. His guard's flashlight barely lit up more than three meters ahead but even that was enough to convince Jay this was not a safe place to be. He studied the rough-hewn ceiling for signs of imminent collapse and found far too many of them.

"Keep moving," the guard said, shoving him forward. "This place gives me the creeps."

In all, they walked maybe forty or fifty paces through the dark, damp tunnel, driving a small army of rats and other, less savoury creatures, ahead of them. At the other end of the tunnel was another staircase. They emerged through a trap door into a wooden box barely large enough for the three of them to stand in. It was lit only by the gaps in its ill-fitting joints and panels.

"You know what you got to do?" one of Jay's guards asked him.

He nodded. Realizing the man probably couldn't see him well enough to tell, he added, "Yeah."

The guard unlocked the only door and they stepped out into a small alley, a shoulder-wide gap between sagging, teetering shanties. Sheets of decayed polythene flapped in a breeze ripe with the smell of raw sewage. Jay gagged and the man behind him sniggered.

"Welcome to the Shit Hole," the guard said.

"Dear God," Jay could hardly believe the squalor of the place. "Why doesn't the city do something about this?"

"They did," the guard said. "Didn't you see the big fence around the place?" He turned to share a grin with his companion then turned back to Jay, all business. "Head that way. Once we get out into the street, we'll turn left. You go right. Remember the route?"

"It's in my commplant."

"In your what?"

"Yes, I remember the route."

"Then let's go." He handed Jay a small, snub-nosed revolver. Jay checked that the six chambers were all full and pushed it into his pocket. With a gun like that, you'd need to be standing right in front of someone in order to hit them.

They squeezed their way along the alley and came out into a broader street that had people in it and even a couple of cyclists. The group turned left. The fake Sons of Joshua had their riot sticks in hand and held Jay firmly between them. It took a moment for the people on the street to start noticing the trio, but soon every eye was on them.

"Hey, what'd he do?" an old man shouted from his perch on a wooden chair beside a furnished hole between two multicoloured, board-built homes.

"Stay out of it, Granddad. This is a dangerous terrorist."

On cue, Jay shook off the fake SOBs, turned on his heel and ran back up the street. Behind him, he heard them shouting. Then he heard them shooting. People screamed and yelled and ran for cover. He wanted to duck down and hide too. He didn't trust Duvalle's men not to shoot him in the back. After a minute, the shooting stopped and he glanced over his shoulder. The fake SOBs were chasing him now but they'd given him a thirty meter lead and he knew they'd let him keep it until they pretended to give up and let him escape. He switched his commplant to aug, and green arrows marked his route along the ground. He felt tired and was already struggling for breath. Duvalle's pain ray had left him weak and aching, but he kept running. There was no other choice.

* * * *

The software was running and the generators were as steady as they'd ever be. The capacitors weren't charged but that wouldn't matter. On her display, every circuit check she ran came up green.

"I'm going to run the generators up to twenty-five percent," she called. "Everybody off the rig. All non-essential crew please leave the room."

Matthew came to stand beside her. People downed tools and most of them shuffled out through the door, glad of a break. She waited until they were all clear then stood back to give Matthew access to the controls.

"Why don't you do the honours?" she said.

Looking sheepish, he pushed the slider across to the twenty-five percent mark. Immediately the generators began to respond. The power climbed steadily, the status indicators for the various subsystems lit up in green and held steady. The hum of the reactors rose as tens of megawatts of power

185

became available. He turned to Sandra with a grin. Everything was going great.

Then an alarm sounded. On the displays, a schematic of the generator array popped up with one generator flashing red, the words "Overload Imminent" flashing with it. Matthew gawped at the message, open-mouthed.

"It's number seven!" Sandra shouted over the racket. "Evacuate the building! The fusion reactor's going to blow!"

Already scared, the people remaining in the room panicked and ran for the door.

"But I don't understand," Matthew said, no doubt because in all his years working on displacement field rigs, he'd never heard of such a thing. Focus fusion reactors were one of the safest electricity generating technologies ever invented. They just didn't blow up.

"It's the magnetic containment bottle," Sandra shouted, talking nonsense. "It's causing a flux build-up in the reactor chamber." She grabbed him by the shoulders. "Get out of here now. There's one thing I can try. Maybe there's still hope." She shoved Matthew towards the door. For a couple of paces, he stumbled uncertainly, then he ran. Turning back to the desk, she hit the "Lob" button and a timer sprang to life. Ten seconds, nine...

She grabbed the length of angle iron she had stashed beside the console, then ran to the platform above the displacement field coils and leapt up onto it. In a few seconds the power of the perfectly stable generators would surge through the coils and the field would bloom, throwing her out of spacetime and back through the pseudospatial void.

She had no suit on, no air to breathe, and only her stupid cotton dress to insulate her from the cold. She breathed out as hard as she could, emptying her lungs so that the vacuum would not force them to decompress explosively. She bent her knees, screwed her eyes shut, and buried her face in her hands.

* * * *

Jay rounded a corner into a long street of mud and shanties. There were few people about. But up ahead, where the green arrows of his augmented reality route-finder turned to point at Polanski's headquarters, two men sitting quietly with machine guns on their laps stood up as he raced towards them. They half raised their weapons, not sure how to respond. He slowed down and put his hands up. Behind him, he heard the two fake SOBs clatter round the corner, shouting for him to stop.

Now Polanski's guards knew what to do. They aimed their weapons past Jay at his pursuers. Jay threw himself to the ground just as the fake SOBs fired at the guards. The guards ran for cover, firing back, and the SOBs beat a quick retreat into the nearest side street. Hearing the shots, more armed men came rushing out of Polanski's HQ, they exchanged shouted questions and answers with the first guards and set of after the fake SOBs.

"Who the hell are you?"

Jay lifted his head from the foul-smelling mud and looked up into the barrel of gun. The man behind it turned out to be a skinny teenager with the wispy beginnings of a moustache.

OK. So far, so good. Now he had to intrigue Polanski's men enough so that they'd take him in for questioning. "I… er… I'm nobody. I…" He climbed slowly to his feet, trying not to alarm or threaten any of the three men pointing guns at him. The mud sucked and squelched unpleasantly as he separated himself from the road. "I just got into some trouble with those Sons of Joshua people. I think you chaps saved my life."

"What do you reckon, Jed?" asked the first.

Jed sucked his teeth and said, "I reckon the SOBs don't chase nobody into the Shanty unless they're real important."

The third one added, "Looks like you ruined a real nice suit there, Mister Nobody. Now why don't you tell us what got them brownshirts so riled up against you?"

"Oh, you know what it's like with those chaps; say one wrong thing and they take offence."

"You sure talk funny," said the first. "Like a foreigner," said Jed.

The third rubbed his jaw. "A foreigner in a fancy suit and the SOBs want him so bad they'd risk coming in here after him."

"Think we should take him to the boss?" said the first.

"I'll have him if you don't want him."

Jay turned to see a fourth man approaching, a short, round man in clean clothes and a cowboy hat. He felt the sudden tension in Polanski's men, saw them firm up their grips on their weapons, slide fingers onto triggers. This new guy was trouble and these armed terrorists were scared of him. He scanned the street and found two men with rifles watching from a spot that afforded plenty of cover if they were to need it.

"With all due respect, this ain't none of your business, Mr. O'Dell," said Jed. "Take him inside," he told his companions.

"Not so fast," O'Dell said. "I'm curious as to what this fella did to get himself in so much trouble."

Jay did not want the distraction of being caught up in some kind of gang war between rival slum lords, or whatever was going on. To the new man he said, "All I did was to comment that I knew a man called Joshua once who claimed to have slept with every whore in Washington, and maybe that's why he seemed to have so many sons in this city."

O'Dell opened his mouth in surprise and then started to chuckle.

"If you'll excuse me," Jay said. "I have an appointment with these gentlemen." He headed towards the entrance to Polanski's labyrinth and the three guards fell in step with him. Behind him, O'Dell's chuckle turned into a laugh.

"Hey, Limey," O'Dell shouted after him. "Come and see me when they let you out. I like a good laugh."

"Who was that guy?" Jay asked as they led him inside.

"O'Dell? You want to stay away from him," said Jed. "Runs the rackets round here—drugs, whores, protection. We don't mess with him and he don't mess with us. Where you from anyway?"

"Out of town." He gave the wall a poke and it wobbled. "Is this place safe?" Very few of the walls looked vertical and most of them gave the impression they'd topple over if he leaned on them.

"Sure, nothing's fallen down since the last big storm. Come on, I want to see the boss's face when you tell him what you said to them SOBs."

* * * *

Sandra was in the void for exactly four tenths of a second. She had not even had time to feel the cold and vacuum start to burn her exposed skin before she arrived and fell a meter to the ground, taking the impact with knees bent like a parachutist and rolling the way her years of martial arts training made almost instinctive. The metal bar clanged to the ground behind her.

"Holy crap," Sandra said from the bed. The guard almost fell off his chair with surprise. She had gone back just 12 hours, to the evening of her arrival, when she'd been alone with her guard and had just climbed into bed.

"It's my brilliant escape plan," she told her shocked and amazed past-self who was staring at her open mouthed from the bed. "We need to fix him." Meaning the guard.

She grabbed up the iron bar and was on her feet and sprinting towards the stunned watchman in an instant. Nevertheless, he had the time and the presence of mind to raise his gun and take aim. But, unfortunately for him, the other Sandra was on him before he had the chance to fire. She laid him out with two solid blows to the temple.

The two Sandras stood and stared at each other for a moment. "Nice dress," they both said, and grinned.

"I've always wanted to do this," Sandra said.

"Sometimes you meet yourself on the road before you have a chance to learn the appropriate greeting," her past-self misquoted. She looked at the meter-long iron bar in future Sandra's hand. "You weren't..."

"Planning to kill myself?" Sandra grinned again. Despite the dangers of the situation, she couldn't help thinking that this was so cool. She couldn't wait to tell Olivia when she got back. "I'd have thought you knew me better than that."

"Ha! What then?"

"The F2 reactors. I need to smash them. If they're broken, I can't use them to send myself back to break them, can I?"

"Anomaly. Then what, you escape during the backwash?"

"It should bring half the block down."

"A stiff breeze would do that."

"I don't want to hurt anybody."

Her past-self frowned. "It's a damned shame I won't remember any of this. I don't, do I?"

"Sorry, them's the rules. Everything back to how it was before the lob." She sighed. "Come on then, let's start smashing things."

Her past-self picked up the past edition of the iron bar Sandra held and they began breaking up the focus fusion reactors, which were still stacked in a bunch waiting to be assembled. They worked fast and systematically. Sandra undid the access panels and her past-self leaned in with the iron bar and pulverized the delicate photonic circuits. When they got to the very last one, her past-self removed the panel but stood in front of it, blocking her doppelgänger.

"We haven't made a splash yet," said Sandra.

But her twin refused to move. "I reckoned we'd be OK until the last one. Your lob was so short you could have done it with a car battery. One of these things would have been enough."

"Damn, you're right. I could probably have done it off the mains. Especially if I charged up the capacitors." She did some sums in her head. "No, I'm pretty sure I'd need the capacitors. Besides, you've seen the wiring in this place. Trying to power a D-field generator off this junk might start a fire but it wouldn't give me enough impetus even for a twelve-hour lob. We'll need to smash the capacitor racks too. Just the controller boards would be enough." She raised her bar to smash the final generator.

"Just in case," said her past-self, still blocking her. "Just in case smashing this causes the splash, and I… Well, you know. I just wanted to take a minute."

Sandra at last saw the fear in her past-self's eyes. "I don't want to die," her past-self said.

"You don't. You live. Look." She opened her arms to display the proof.

"That's easy for you to say. You've never been me, not this me. We're in a potential future that never happened to you—at the time."

"It's one that won't have happened to you, either—soon. None of this will ever have happened, except to me. That is, to you, in the future."

"I know the theory as well as you do, remember? But that doesn't help when I think that, in a while, I'm going to start that hideous vibrating as causality starts to unwind, to unravel my life. What do you suppose that feels like?"

An empathic wave of horror ran through Sandra. She remembered the nightmares—all down to post-traumatic stress disorder her shrink had said—after the timesplashes she'd been through sixteen years ago. No doubt her past-self was remembering them too.

"Oh God, I'm sorry," Sandra said and hugged her copy, pulling her close and sharing her distress. How would she feel knowing she was living a brief, impermanent, stolen fragment of life, one that should never have happened and that would soon be erased from the universe?

"We should never have messed with this stuff," her past-self said, pulling away.

"What?"

"You and me. Time travel. It's a kind of sickness. The same old sickness. I see it so clearly now. It's like I needed to learn to control this thing that I feared so much."

"We don't really have time for—"

"No, listen. This is important. When you get back home, I

want you to promise you'll get out of the time travel business."

"But it's my job. How will I look after Cara?"

Her past-self smiled. "You're a bright girl. You'll work it out."

"But I can't just—"

"Trust me. I know what I'm talking about. You'll see it yourself one day, maybe. What I've been doing is wrong, playing with fire because it fascinates and scares me. Because, deep down, I knew one day it would kill me."

Sandra stared helplessly at her past-self. How could she not believe her insight? How could she doubt what she could feel, on some deeply buried level, to be true? And yet...

"No," her past-self said, perhaps seeing the rebellion in her eyes. "Just promise me. It's my dying wish."

Sandra felt as if she'd been punched in the gut. She responded with anger. This whole conversation was insane. She pushed her past-self aside and tore into the reactor's innards. When she re-emerged, her past-self was standing there, watching her with an expression that might have been pity. Well, screw that!

Sandra went over to the capacitor racks and began furiously pulling out the controller boards and smashing them to fragments. She'd done most of them when the board she smashed flew back together again, then flew apart, and then together again. It had begun. She whirled around to look at her past-self, suddenly appalled that she had not said goodbye.

The other Sandra was standing still, watching her, but there was a shimmering aura around her now and her features were indistinct as her whole body vibrated at an impossible speed.

Sandra gasped in anguish. It was too late. She'd let her past-self stand there waiting for her inevitable death, frightened and alone, probably fighting the urge to stop her, and Sandra hadn't even said goodbye.

A chunk of ceiling fell down and hung in the air, never to hit the ground. One of the reactors groaned and slumped, as if it's own weight had become too much to bear.

Sandra ran to the door. The splash was building. It would never be the kind of acausal anarchy she saw in London or Ommen, but she could still get crushed under a falling wall if she didn't get out of there. She jumped across a crack that ripped through the floor, flung open the door, and ran.

Chapter 18

Backwash

Before they could bring Jay to Polanski, a commotion broke out in the depths of the ramshackle building. People ran through the corridors, some towards the disturbance, some away from it, mixing up the chaos until it seemed to be all around them.

"Keep him here," the one called Jed shouted and ran off, taking the kid with the facial hair with him. Jay and his impromptu captor kept back against the wall as men, women and children hurried past them in both directions.

"Shee-it," his companion said. "I should be in there. Just listen to it."

"Don't mind me," said Jay. "You do what you think is best. But, you know what that sounds like to me?"

"Yeah? Whaaaaaaa…" The man's voice slowed and deepened to a bass rumble as his movements slowed to stop.

"A backwash," Jay said. Either Jay himself was now moving at super-high speed, or time had slowed for the man beside him. Regardless, he took the opportunity to unburden the man of his machine gun, remove the clip, and empty the chamber.

"Nice knowing you." Jay set off in the same direction Jed had taken, figuring that was most likely to lead him to the source of the trouble—which would be Sandra, if he were not mistaken.

He squinted down a corridor that stretched as far as he could see. Out of it came a dozen panicked people, racing towards him at frightening speeds. He flung himself against the wall and the wall yielded like thin rubber. He stumbled and fell, scrambling back to his feet only to fall again as the ground heaved beneath him. A small backwash could be quite fun—it was trippy and crazy outside, in an open field, especially if you were smashed out of your head on splashparty drugs. But inside a building, stone cold sober, it was just dangerous and frightening. He called Sandra's name. His voice echoed around him. He called again, still trying to get to his feet. It was like a fairground cakewalk with the added pleasure of knowing that the roof might fall on you at any minute.

People reeled and staggered past him, all going in one direction now, away from the centre of this mayhem.

"Sandra!" he bellowed, and pushed against the fleeing people, making little headway. He reached a junction and, as he clung to the corner, a big section of wall buckled and crumpled. The ceiling above it fell, trapping a dozen or so people beneath it. But because the materials from which this house of cards was built were lightweight—plywood, corrugated iron, plastic sheeting, even cardboard—he doubted that anyone was seriously hurt. All the same, he hurried over to help pull people clear of the wreckage. When he looked up through the hole above him, he saw another layer of occupation. He kept shouting for Sandra but, in that cacophony of rending, tearing, and screaming, there was little hope that she'd hear him.

Then he heard shooting, a few shots from a handgun, followed by the burp, burp of machine gun fire. He dropped everything and ran towards it.

But the building was a maze. No corridor seemed to lead in the right direction. He charged through people's homes, trying to keep to the direction of the shots, sometimes having to kick down sections of wall when he hit a dead end. The air was full of dust. In one place, the dust shimmered in rainbow hues, in another the particles were almost immovable, filling the corridor he needed to pass through like a steel wool fog that scoured his palms when he tried to shift it.

He was almost weeping with frustration when he broke through a wall into yet another shuddering corridor and saw her. She seemed to be miles ahead of him, running towards a door that opened into sunlight. He yelled her name and she stopped, turning to look at him. The surprise on her face was almost comical. He saw her mouth his name but heard no sound. He sprinted towards her, but his legs moved too slowly and the corridor seemed to stretch out even longer, taking her farther away. He saw her shout something again and then wave her arm, urging him to follow her. She ran out through the door into the blinding sunlight.

"No, wait for me," he shouted, pushing himself with fierce determination against whatever bizarre corruption of time and distance was slowing his body, but he couldn't fight it. He screamed in frustration but couldn't go any faster than a slow walk down that endless corridor.

The corridor snapped back to its proper length, his legs moved at their proper speed, and Jay, suddenly released, went sprawling across the floor. He picked himself up and ran, bursting through the open door into the light and skidding to a halt in the muddy street.

Sandra was at the other side of the road. She was being held at gunpoint by two of O'Dell's men. The little gangster in the cowboy hat stood to one side of them, watching Polanski's building slowly demolish itself. Jay still had the revolver in his belt and weighed up his chances of hitting anything smaller than a warehouse with it from that distance. He decided it was safer not to shoot, but he couldn't leave Sandra like that. He decided to charge at O'Dell's men and take his chances. The moment he moved, his arms were grabbed from behind by a big, beefy young man who looked like he'd just arrived from a country pig-throwing contest.

"Don't hurt him, Peter," said a dark, moody man, stepping up beside Jay. Despite the chaos behind him, the newcomer focused all his attention on Sandra.

"O'Dell," he shouted. "You've got something of mine."

The rotund gangster glanced at Sandra. "What, this? I just found it in the street. These are my streets, remember."

Jay saw Polanski's eyes flick along the buildings opposite. He looked himself and saw armed men standing in the shadows. Polanski said, "Don't make me come over there, O'Dell."

"You know what, Polanski?" O'Dell waved an arm at the disintegrating buildings. "I think you've got bigger problems than one little stray. What in God's name have you been doing in there?"

Fascinating as this was, Jay had a much bigger problem than either of these men. Things were definitely not going to plan and the way things were now, he might not get back to Cara in time.

"Sandra," he shouted and the boy, Peter, nearly broke his arms to shut him up. "Sandra, Cara's here. She's being held by a thug called Duvalle."

Sandra goggled back at him in disbelief. Both Polanski and O'Dell turned to him and said, "Duvalle?" and in that instant, Sandra whirled into action. She took down one of her captors with a single kick to the head. Before the man fell, she had grabbed his gun and fired two shots into the other man. Everybody dropped to the ground or ran for cover. Sandra took off into the rabbit warren of the Shanty without a backward glance.

Only O'Dell, Polanski, Jay, and the muscular Peter were left standing in the street. O'Dell whooped and danced a little step. "Man oh man! She's a feisty one." The death and injury of his men didn't seem to worry him at all. Around them, people began to stand up again. "I sure wish you'd tell me what's going on with you guys today."

"You done spying on my place, O'Dell? Or do I need to call the Sanitation Department to come clean up the street?"

O'Dell was still chuckling over Sandra's surprise exit. He waved a dismissive hand at Polanski and walked away. "See you in Hell, buddy," he called over his shoulder.

Polanski watched him go without a word. After a while, he turned back to his headquarters, still shimmering and folding in on itself. "How long will it keep doing that?" he asked.

It was a question clearly meant for Jay. "Not long now. It's not a big backwash. Sandra probably didn't mean for it to kill anyone, just distract you while she got out."

Polanski turned to Jay for the first time since he'd emerged into the street. "You and me got to talk," he said. "Can Peter let you go without you trying to escape?"

"What makes you think I couldn't just break free any time I like?"

Polanski almost broke into a smile. "Gets your goat that

your lady friend's tougher than you, huh?"

Jay realized that Polanski was almost right. Sandra had floored two guys like some kind of Amish ninja. What irked him was that Polanski didn't credit him with the same skills.

"OK, call off your gorilla and we'll talk. I did come here to see you. Thing is, I need your help."

* * * *

Polanski left instructions with his lieutenants about how to prioritise the reconstruction. First thing was to get someone called Matthew on the job of getting the "time machine" back up and running. Then he and Polanski left to find a café. They walked a long way. The boy, Peter, and two other armed men followed close behind as they passed through the big main gates of the Shanty and into a far more salubrious suburb—one that didn't smell of excrement. A few blocks into the rows of brick houses and concrete roads, they found a small diner that smelled of roasted coffee beans and had large Italian sausages festooned behind the counter. Polanski took Jay inside while his men loitered by the door.

Although Polanski was outside his own turf, the proprietor greeted the rebel leader like a national celebrity, which, Jay supposed, he probably was. The man brought them coffee and plates of food and cakes, all unasked for. He beamed happily at Polanski all the while, chattering away about the food, his family, the weather, with Polanski nodding and smiling and asking by name after various relatives. It was quite a performance and while it went on nobody else in the place got any attention whatsoever. Eventually, Polanski called a halt by saying, "Joseph, my old friend, I need to talk business to this gentleman here."

"Of course! Of course! And here am I jibber-jabbering about my Mary. Hey…" He leaned close to Jay, with a hand on his shoulder, and spoke into his ear in a lowered voice. "This man here is going to save us all. He's going to bring back the old days, like it used to be. So you treat him with respect, OK? OK?" Jay gave back a weak smile and nodded. "OK," said Joseph, his point made, and left them alone.

"Who are you and what's your relationship to Duvalle?" Polanski asked—the first words he'd spoken to Jay since they left the Shanty.

Jay had already decided that the whole truth was his only possible play. So he told him who he was, who he worked for, and how he'd become tangled up with Duvalle.

Polanski listened in silence. "And the girl?"

"Cara?"

"Sandra," Polanski said.

"That's… a long story."

"I've got time, and Joseph is going to keep filling up our coffee cups whether we want him to or not. So let's hear it."

"No, we don't really have time at all. Duvalle is holding my daughter hostage to make me come here and kill you."

Polanski took the news with remarkable calm. "The Reverend Jeremiah Duvalle? Head of the Measurers of the Temple?" Jay nodded. "So why haven't you done it yet? You're armed. You've had plenty of opportunity."

"Because I'm a cop, not a murderer. Besides, I don't have any reason to want you dead—except that you brought all this down on —" he almost said, "my family," but that wasn't quite true. So he said, "—the people I love," instead, which also wasn't quite true. "I just want to get Sandra and Cara out of this mess and get them home. The only people who want you dead are your Government, the FBI, and Duvalle. Oh, and that guy in the cowboy hat we met in the street. He doesn't seem to like you much, either."

Polanski nodded. "It's a long list."

"Maybe you ought to stop kidnapping people and plotting mass murder."

Polanski seemed to consider making such a career move for a moment, and then said, "What do you know about building lob sites?"

"Nothing, I'm happy to say. I've devoted my working life to putting people with such dangerous knowledge in prison."

"Do you want to put Sandra in prison, then? I thought you just said you loved her."

"It's complicated."

They both fell silent for a moment until Polanski said, "Here's the thing, Chief Inspector..."

"Please, call me Jay. I find such formality coming from people holding me prisoner just a bit creepy, you know?"

"OK, Jay. The thing is, I'm going to create a timesplash."

Jay's heart sank. There was no way Polanski could let him go now.

"When?" The chances of getting back to Duvalle within the twenty-four hour period looked vanishingly small.

"When? Tomorrow, I hope, if Sandra didn't destroy my equipment completely. I've got a guy who can screw the pieces together but he doesn't have the skills to set up a rig to do what I want. I need Sandra for that."

"She won't help you."

"She has to."

"She won't. She's not the kind. It wouldn't matter what you threatened her with."

"You sure about that?"

"Yes."

Polanski continued to study him with his dark, steady eyes and Jay tried to keep the thought from his mind that there might just be one threat that would do it.

"What about the girl?" Polanski asked.

"Sandra?"

"Cara."

A switch inside Jay's head flipped to overload. Just as a dog that has been driven back and back until it is cringing in a corner sometimes flips from flight to fight, so Jay's mood changed in an instant from desperate hope to furious anger. His lips pulled back into a snarl and his eyes narrowed. "You so much as touch that child and I will make it my life's work to hunt you down and destroy you."

Polanski blinked in surprise but did not look the least bit frightened. Which made Jay even more angry. "So," Polanski said, still watching Jay's eyes. "You think Sandra might do it to save the girl?"

With an eruption of rage, Jay shoved the table. It hit Polanski in the stomach and knocked him back. His chair toppled and he flailed as he fell to the ground. The table, with Jay still pushing against it, toppled after him, hitting Polanski in the stomach once again as it landed knocking the breath out of him.

Jay yanked his revolver free of his belt and knelt down beside the gasping rebel leader. He pushed the stubby barrel into his face. "You and I are leaving here, now," he said, still snarling. "Get on your feet."

He grabbed Polanski's shirt to heave him up. There was a quick footstep to one side and Jay looked up just in time to see the proprietor, Joseph, swinging a gigantic salami down onto his head.

Chapter 19

Revolutionaries

Sandra walked and walked. The day became cloudy and cold and she was glad of the exercise. She walked with her eyes cast down and spoke to no-one. When she left the Shanty and moved into the more fragrant suburbs, she did not entirely break clear of the poverty that she had seen since she first reached the Americas. Paint peeled on doors and window frames, the grey wood beneath revealing decades of neglect. Despite the cold, children played in bare feet, or if they had them, scuffed old boots. There were few vehicles around of any kind except bicycles. Horse-drawn carts were not uncommon, making deliveries alongside battered electric trucks.

She had noticed that few women went anywhere on their own. After the third incident of a young lout shouting out to her as she passed, she tried to walk close to small groups, pretending to be walking with them. Early on in her travels, she stole a shopping bag from a shop and used it to hide her gun. She also picked up a headscarf the same way, and supplied herself with enough cash for a few meals and maybe a room for the night by mugging a very surprised cleric who had offered her money for sex in a quiet alley.

There seemed to be no way to find Duvalle except to ask the people she passed, but every time she did so, she got the same polite but confused response: "What does he do? What's his full name? What does he look like? If you could just give me a bit more to go on…"

She did learn that there was a public database of contact details available through the compad system—but nobody she spoke to had a compad. "Advanced electronics" as one woman described the compad, were expensive, imported devices that ordinary people couldn't afford, and, besides, the Church frowned on their use by anybody who didn't need them for their job.

An old woman—grey hair, overweight, missing teeth, walking with a stick—tried to keep Sandra talking, telling her tales of the old days when she was young, "before all this One Church stuff started up." It shocked Sandra that the woman was only sixty. No age to be so decrepit, yet old enough to know that in pre-Adjustment America things could have been very different for her.

"My name's Ruth," she said and pulled Sandra close as she whispered that her name used to be Charlene. "But we all had to change our names back in the Fifties when they brought in the baptism laws. Damn fool laws if you ask me. I was perfectly well baptized the first time. So was everybody else I knew. Didn't make no sense then and it don't make no sense now. Used to be a Baptist back then, before all the churches joined into one. Why'd they go and do that? That's what I want to know."

Sandra tried to sound sympathetic as she extricated herself from the conversation.

"I suppose you've got a fella to meet," the woman

complained, shaking her head wearily. "All the trouble in the world is down to men, girl. Women used to be free back then. Now we're no better'n slaves, but the fellas is doing just fine. Made themselves a real cosy little world now they have. And young things like you, you don't even fight it. Born to it, I guess, and don't know no better. But some of us still remember how it used to be."

On impulse, Sandra asked her if maybe Polanski might make things right again. The old woman looked at her sharply with her rheumy eyes. "I don't know nothing about Polanski. What are you doing, coming around here spying? Everybody spying on everybody else. What kind of a world is that? You should be ashamed." Painfully, she limped away, looking back at Sandra with fear in her eyes.

As the afternoon wore on, Sandra began to feel desperate. She found herself walking down a busy street lined with shops and offices, and considered which one she might go into, brandish her gun, demand that somebody look up Duvalle on their compad for her.

Then she saw the offices of The New Church Times, est. 2051, and claiming to offer "All the news that's right to print." She might have missed it altogether except it had headlines, hand-written on paper, clipped to boards outside the entrance, and one of those said, "Duvalle Slams Defense Cuts."

She went inside. A dimly lit reception area with a wooden counter greeted her. Behind the counter an empty chair seemed to reproach her for her haste. A glass-panelled door beside the counter led to a much larger, brighter room in which men in shirtsleeves occupied desks cluttered with paper.

In a shadowy corner of the reception area, a smartly-dressed man watched her. "He went out for something," he said.

"The receptionist?"

"Why don't you sit down here and wait with me?" There was a self-confident arrogance about the man that Sandra liked.

Danger, Will Robinson! she told herself. Not only were men like that the bane of her life, but out here anybody who dressed that well was either Government, or Church—or maybe something just as bad. "How long will he be?"

"Search me. What's the rush? You got some breaking news that just can't wait?"

She gave him a tight smile and turned away. She didn't want to hang around with this nosy official poking and probing, but she had wasted so much time already and needed a lead on Duvalle right now. She considered bursting into the back office and just asking someone, but who knew what kind of reception she'd get? She'd certainly get more attention than she wanted.

"I came to ask about someone they've just done a story on," she said. It was a risk, but then everything she did was a risk. "Duvalle. Do you know him?"

He stood up. He was tall and broad and smelled of cologne—surely some kind of deadly sin around those parts. "I know of him," he said. He sounded cautious, as if just talking about Duvalle could bring down trouble on them.

"I don't," she said. "I'm a stranger here. I saw the headline outside and wondered, so I thought I'd ask. I know a Duvalle family back in London. They'd be thrilled if they had a famous relative out here." Lame, she thought. Now he knows I'm lying to him.

He certainly looked more suspicious than ever. He leaned

on the counter, too close to her, and said, "The Reverend Jeremiah Duvalle is one of our leading churchmen. A very influential man."

"Does he live here in Washington?"

The stranger broke into a lewd grin. "Let me give you some advice," he said, and Sandra could have hit him for the patronizing tone alone. "You're a beautiful woman. Quite possibly the most beautiful woman I've ever seen. I can understand why a rich and powerful man like Duvalle would single you out for... special attention. And I dare say he led you on and maybe you did some things you now regret." Sandra opened her mouth to set him right but he raised a hand. "I know you must have felt angry and foolish when he dumped you—although, if you ask me, he was the fool in this instance. You're probably feeling plenty ashamed of yourself too. So you're down here thinking you'll spill the beans on Reverend High-and-Mighty Duvalle and show him he messed with the wrong little lady this time. Well, honey, Duvalle would never let a story like that get into print and he is well known for being a man who knows how to bear a grudge when it comes to people trying to hurt his public image."

"And you made all that up on the strength of me asking one little question? That's quite a talent. You should write for the newspapers."

He looked amused, but sad too. "The only other explanation I can think of is that you want Duvalle's address so that you can go to his home and shoot him with that gun you're carrying in your bag."

"Who are you? A cop?"

He ignored the question but went on studying her. "Why don't you come for a little stroll? We can talk more freely in the street."

"Seems to me you've been talking pretty freely since I met you."

"I'm wrong about you, aren't I? You're not a fallen woman at all. You're… something else." He offered her his arm, as if they were old friends. "Let my buy you a coffee. If you do, I'll tell you everything you want to know about Duvalle."

"And what do you get out of it?"

"I get to be seen around town with the most beautiful woman in Washington on my arm."

She looked him in the eye but that told her nothing at all. The cocksure smile and the charming manner warned her to run a mile. But she didn't.

She took his arm and let him lead her out into the street.

* * * *

He took her to a smart little restaurant and ordered for her. By then, she knew not to protest. He said his name was John. She said hers was Susan. He asked her questions about herself and she lied or evaded until he grew tired of it.

With a sigh and a small smile he finally said, "OK. I admit defeat. There's no way I'll ever find out anything about you unless I tied you up and whipped it out of you." There was something in his manner that suggested he might just like to give that a go. "So why don't you ask me what you want to know and I'll see if I can do a better job of telling the truth?"

She was glad that the game-playing was over. Every minute was precious. "I need to get to Duvalle. He's got something of mine and I want it back."

"I can give you his address and you can go storming in there, guns blazing, or you could explain to me what he took and I'll give you my professional opinion on how to go about retrieving it without getting yourself killed." He handed her a small rectangle of paper. She had never seen a business card before except in old vids. The card had his name, John Vargas, and beneath it said "Attorney at Law".

"You're an ambulance chaser?"

"I prefer the term 'shyster'."

It hadn't occurred to Sandra that, in such a repressive regime, there would still be courts, but of course there would be. Even so, she couldn't believe they would be anything but a sham, or that the court officials would be anything but corrupt.

"I don't think legal representation is what I need right now," she said. What she needed was surveillance equipment, lock picks, maps, a moonless night, and spare clips for her gun. After that, she'd need a helicopter and suppressing fire from a special forces unit. "Thanks for the offer. Maybe you could just give me Duvalle's address and directions how to get there?"

He pulled a small notepad and pen from his jacket, and wrote down an address. "It's his home and also the headquarters of his church. If he's anywhere, that'll be it. You want to tell me what this is about?"

"Not really."

He leaned back in his chair and pushed his hands into his trouser pockets. "A woman of mystery," he said.

"What kind of lawyer are you?"

"The kind who'd like to take you to dinner. I'll pick you up at your hotel. It'll be fun. You can tell me all about how many of Duvalle's bodyguards it took to throw you out."

"His place is heavily guarded then?"

He frowned. "You're really serious, aren't you?"

"He's holding my daughter."

"Shit."

They fell silent for a while. Sandra could see Vargas revising his previous assumptions. "What were you doing at the newspaper office?" she asked.

"I had an appointment with the owner. I have an injunction I need to serve. I'm a defence attorney. Nothing religious, just plain old-fashioned crime."

"You don't like the Church, do you?"

Vargas smiled, leant back, and casually looked around him before leaning close and saying, "You're not from round here, are you?"

"I live in England. I was brought here against my will. It's a long story. My daughter and... her father came out looking for me and now she's in Duvalle's clutches and he's in Polanski's. And I've got to get them both out."

For the first time, his self-composure fell apart and he looked at her with genuine alarm. He dropped some money on the table and hustled her out into the street again.

"Polanski? As in Zadrach Polanski, the resistance leader?"

"Don't you mean 'terrorist'?"

"One man's terrorist is another man's freedom fighter, right?" She said nothing, wondering what Polanski was to this man.

"And you've met him?" He asked, before the obvious thought hit him. "Of course, he's the one who brought you here against your will. But why? Why would he do that?"

"Perhaps he likes to be seen around town with the most beautiful woman in Washington on his arm."

Vargas winced. "OK, I'm an asshole, but I thought I was picking up a cute honey with an exotic accent, not the most dangerous woman in the country. I don't think I should even be seen talking to you."

"You can always tell them I forced you at gunpoint."

"I'm not kidding. Polanski's public enemy number one. Multiple murder counts, extortion, racketeering, blasphemy, sodomy, you name it. They've also charged him with worshipping false gods, corrupting minors, and plotting against the State."

"Like Socrates. Someone's got a sense of humour."

He looked as if he hadn't heard of Socrates but didn't pursue it. "If you've been helping him, even unwillingly, I wouldn't fancy your chances of getting out of prison before the end of the century."

She held out a hand. "Well, thanks for all your help. And the coffee. I'll be fine on my own now."

He looked around nervously and wouldn't take her hand. "No, wait," he said. He seemed to be in some kind of turmoil of indecision. "Don't go. I want you to meet some people. They may be able to help."

"Lawyers?"

"Well, one or two are—oh, right. No, I don't mean that kind of help. I mean something more… direct."

Sandra could hardly believe where this was going. "You mean you're also part of some kind of underground resistance cell? You?"

He seemed too agitated to take offence, but he managed it anyway. "What do you think, that we're all just going to sit around waiting for this government to hand us our rights back? This is America. Land of the free. Or it should be. And it will be. Let me make some calls. I know people who can help you."

Sandra was reluctant to be blown off course by the first breeze she encountered. Vargas did not strike her as the kind of man who could help her in any way that she needed. On the other hand, his friends might be more useful, and she could certainly use some help from somebody. "And what would make your friends so keen to assist me?"

"Information."

"About Polanski? I thought you were on the same side?"

"My friends and I don't like his methods."

Well, that makes two of us. "All right, you've got an hour to set up the meeting. I can't wait any longer than that. And if this is a waste of time and the delay gets my daughter hurt, I'll take it out of your hide, lover boy."

Vargas swallowed and nodded. Then he pulled out his compad.

* * * *

The extraordinary meeting of the Friends of Democracy Society took place in the kitchen of a small apartment in the Washington suburb of Crystal City. Six people were in attendance plus Sandra, the guest of honour. Together they crowded out the little room so that Judith, the wife of the man running the meeting, could barely squeeze by them to fetch coffee and sandwiches.

The society members were all men. John Vargas was the youngest at thirty-something with the rest being in their fifties and sixties, Sandra guessed. The chairman was the oldest, with a bushy grey beard and a mane of white hair. As the latest member to arrive settled down, he said, "Very well, we are quorate. The meeting is called to order."

As the chatter died away, the chairman scowled at "Brother Vargas" and demanded to know what he thought he was doing dragging everybody away from work. No-one was in a good mood. Each had shied like a startled horse when arriving to find Sandra there. They muttered and grumbled about exposing their society to outsiders and putting people's lives and families at risk.

"Brothers," Vargas began. "This lady is Sandra Malone, a foreigner from the United Kingdom. She has recently been a prisoner of our friend Zadrach Polanski. Her husband is still a captive of the so-called resistance." Sandra didn't bother to put him right about the husband part. "Her daughter, meanwhile, is being held by the Reverend Duvalle." Everyone seemed suitably shocked. In fact, he had to raise his voice over the growing rumble of excitement from his fellow Friends of Democracy. "On the basis of what she has told me, I believe Polanski is planning direct action in the near future. Obviously this is a matter of great importance for our society."

"Agreed," the chairman said in a strong voice that silenced the room. "Now, young lady. Tell us what you know about Polanski's plans and what your involvement has been."

Sandra looked around the table at the stern, earnest faces and then said to Vargas, "What the fuck is all this? You told me there were people here who could help. I don't see anybody here who looks like they command a small army of assault troops. In fact, with all due respect to your secret society chums, it looks more like a debating society than a revolutionary council."

Pandemonium erupted in the little room and the chairman had to hammer on the table with his fist before the noise subsided.

"If I may, Mr. Chairman," Vargas said.

"Mr. Vargas has the floor," the chairman growled.

"Sandra, I assure you, you are in the presence of a serious and dedicated group of men who are working at great risk to themselves and their families to provide leadership and guidance to the coming revolution. These are well-respected men who wield considerable influence in our society. The Friends of Democracy are the intellectual vanguard of the freedom movement in this country and, if anybody can help you, we can. All I ask is that you cooperate with us—and, perhaps, show a little respect and decorum."

"OK," Sandra said, addressing the group. "Here's the thing. Some arsehole called Duvalle is holding my daughter hostage—no doubt to make her idiot father do something he doesn't want to do. Tell me how quickly you can break her free, and I'll be as cooperative as a… You know, something very cooperative." She watched them huffing and blustering for a count of five then stood up. She addressed herself to the chairman. "I thought so. All talk. Well, I'm sorry, Santa, but Polanski's crazy fanatics have got you blokes beaten by a mile when it comes to revolutions. In fact, if you want to pursue your intellectual masturbation—sorry, vanguarding— past tomorrow, you should probably be on the next train out of town because I reckon Polanski is about to make his move, with or without me, and this place is going to be a bloodbath."

She took a step towards the door as the meeting erupted once more. Vargas stood up and moved to intercept her.

"Don't," she said.

He reached out to take hold of her. "Please, just wait. We really need to know what Pol—oof!"

A lightning-fast jab to the solar plexus knocked the air out of him and he sank to his knees, looking like he might vomit on her feet. She grabbed him by the shoulder and heaved him aside. She could feel a powerful anger bubbling up inside. If she didn't get away from this bunch of time-wasters soon, she'd waste another five minutes beating each of their red and outraged faces to a pulp.

How could she have let herself believe that a self-important fool like Vargas could possibly help her? Right now he was just staring at her in disbelief. It was a measure of her own fear and desperation that she would listen to such a man. Well, she'd paid for it in lost time and with the knowledge that Cara had been in Duvalle's hands for yet another hour. Furious with herself, and the Friends of Democracy Society, and with every goddamned puffed-up, stupid, self-aggrandizing man who ever thought for one second that his own power and prestige were more important than her daughter's well being, she grabbed the nearest of the brethren by the collar and drew back her fist for the sheer pleasure of spreading someone's nose across their face.

At that moment, the door burst open and a small, round man in a cowboy hat came rushing in saying, "Sorry I'm late everybody, I—"

The meeting froze in a tableau of shock and violence. A grin slowly spread across the little man's face.

Sandra dropped her intended victim and straightened up. She too was smiling. "Mr. O'Dell," she said. "You are just the person I need to talk to."

Chapter 20

Preparations

Jay woke up with a new respect for the humble salami. In the right hands, it made a very respectable cudgel. So much so that he now felt as if his head had been crushed beneath a large rock for the past couple of hours. He attempted to rub his wrenched neck and discovered his hands and feet were tied.

"Zak," someone said, and Polanski's voice said, "Sit him up."

Jay's neck sent spikes of pain through his skull as Polanski's sidekick, Peter, heaved him into a sitting position. He discovered he was on the floor in a small room—some kind of office. Polanski sat at a desk a few meters away. Peter settled into an armchair, watching Jay with an expression that said the young man would rather be stomping on him.

"Got any aspirin?" Jay asked.

Polanski smiled. "My friend Joseph was a bit enthusiastic. I thought he'd killed you."

"I hope you didn't leave a tip."

Polanski turned back to his paperwork, no longer amused.

"Tax returns?" Jay asked. He couldn't think of anything

better to do under the circumstances than bait the man.

Slowly, Polanski turned back to face him. "Plans. From your reaction in the café, I take it that Sandra Malone might help me if Cara's safety was at stake. Well, that's good to know but it gives us the problem of how to get the child away from Duvalle and into my custody."

"You're talking about a fifteen-year-old girl, Polanski, not some piece in a board game."

"I'm sorry, but I can't worry about the suffering of one person. I'm trying to free millions of people—hundreds of millions. If you weren't so close to this child, you'd probably understand my position."

"I understand all right. You're so caught up in your fantasies of saving the world that you've lost sight of what an inhuman bastard you've become."

Polanski raised a hand. "No, Peter." Jay glanced at the boy, who had jumped out of his seat and was now glaring down at Jay, fists clenched and lips drawn back. Polanski spoke to the lad in a calm, gentle voice. "Peter, why don't you go and check on progress. Do the rounds. Make sure nobody's slacking." Without a word, Peter turned and left the room.

"Quite a boy you've got there. You must be proud."

Polanski looked nettled. "You're pretty quick to judge people. Let me tell you about Peter. His parents were farmers out West. They were raided by the FBI six years ago in one of their spot checks. They were both put against the wall of their house and executed by firing squad for possessing seditious, atheistic literature. The fact is, they found a stash of science books that the boy's grandmother had hidden away in the loft. His parents didn't even know they were there. Grandma had been a teacher at the local school before the Lord's True

Path took control, and she just couldn't bear to part with them. They were just high school science books but she insisted they were full of knowledge that people had worked hard for hundreds of years to wrestle from Nature, and it wasn't right to let them burn.

"Peter hid in the fields and watched his parents die. He buried them himself and the next day he buried his grandma too after she took her own life over the guilt of what had happened. After that, he joined the local resistance and dedicated his life to killing as many government people as he could find. He was twelve years old when I found him—practically a wild animal. The Feds had him in a compound with other undesirable types, ready to move them to one of their labour camps. After I liberated him, he started following me around and I kinda took to having him nearby. He's been a faithful comrade in arms and he's very devoted. You should try not to insult me too much while he's around."

"I'll try to remember. And if you think I feel bad about what a crap life your pet rottweiler had, well, you're not completely wrong. The thing is, how many wrongs add up to a right, Polanski? They shoot his parents. He shoots them. They shoot him. You shoot them. Where does it end?" Jay leaned back against the wall and closed his eyes to ease the pain in his head. "What the hell? You know all that and you do it anyway, 'cause you think there's no alternative."

"There isn't. What was the alternative to Stalin? What was the alternative to Pol Pot? You think we can talk our way out of this situation? The country is run by evil men. They surround themselves with evil men. They make sure only evil can prosper so that every position of power is filled with evil men."

"Stalin's gone. Pol Pot's gone."

"And Hitler's gone too. And you know why? Because, eventually, people stood up and fought his regime. Stalin ruled the Soviet Union for thirty years. During that time his secret police murdered twenty million people. How long should we wait for the Lord's True Path Party to fade away? How many people should we let suffer and die while we wait?" He stood up and began to pace in front of Jay. "You're a fool and you think like a child. The world doesn't change unless people make it change." He seemed to be warming himself up for a full-blown rant. "This is why Europe has sat on its hands for the past thirty years and done nothing. It's people like you. People who don't give a damn how we suffer. People who want to sweep it under the carpet and wait for it all to blow over. Imbeciles and hypocrites who think that freedom and democracy are your birthright, that people didn't have to fight and win them for you with blood and sacrifice."

Jay's head was throbbing. "Can I say something?" With a growl, Polanski turned away from him.

"I'm just a cop. I put away bad guys. At least, I was. Now I'm not so sure. I don't speak for all mankind—or even Europe. I've got enough problems without involving myself in everybody else's. So just gimme a break. All I want is to get my daughter and Sandra and go home."

Polanski didn't move, didn't react.

"Don't you have family? Aren't there people you care about? Not just nations and ideas? Surely you understand?"

Polanski went to sit down at his desk. He seemed weary and spent. "You want to hear about my family? Which ones? The dead ones in mass graves? Or the live ones in prisons and labour camps?"

He studied the papers on his desk as if they might contain

the answers. Then he sighed. "Tomorrow, I will do the only thing I know that might end this nightmare. God will judge whether it was the right thing or the wrong thing. But tonight, I will bring your daughter here and hope your friend Sandra loves her enough to save her life. I'm tired of arguing. I'm tired of trying to convince the timid and the selfish. I've spent years talking—to men in bars, to groups in people's homes, to crowds in barns and fields and town halls—and I'm sick of words. I'm sick of kindling that look of hope and excitement in people's eyes and telling them, 'Soon. Just have patience. Your day is coming.' Well, the day has come. Tomorrow I say, 'Enough. No more. This is the day.'"

"I want to come." Polanski no longer seemed to be listening, so Jay said it louder. "I want to go with you tonight to get my daughter."

"No."

"Are those the plans, on your desk? Is that what you're working on?"

"Yes, but you're staying here."

"I was trained by MI5. I've served sixteen years with Europol, a lot of that on active service. I'll be more use to you than a bunch of untrained zealots." Polanski ignored him. "Duvalle's a technology freak. Did you know that? I'm betting his headquarters is packed to the rafters with high-tech security, stuff you've never even seen before, stuff I know about." Still no response. "For God's sake, man. My daughter's in there. She'll be frightened and confused. She'll need to see someone she knows and trusts, not a bunch of armed thugs in ski masks. And don't give me another story about how emotionally damaged all your thugs are because, somehow, that's just not reassuring."

"Shut up, or I'll gag you."

Jay subsided, trying to think of a new approach, some way to appeal to the man, but he hadn't found it by the time Peter returned and reported that things were going well.

"Matthew says if they work through the night they'll get it all back together. There was something, some technical thing that got bent and they're having to make a new one from scratch, and some of the computers got broke, stuff like that, but he's got spares and backups and he says it'll be ready on time."

"And the building?"

"They've roofed over the lob site and put tarps and boards over the sleeping and cooking areas. If we don't get rain tonight, there won't be nothing that can't be fixed up soon enough."

Polanski nodded. He looked again at the papers on his desk and put a hand on Peter's shoulder. "I need a dozen good men. Go round 'em up for me. We're doing a job tonight. Is the big dining room still usable?"

"Sure."

"Tell them I'll be there in ten minutes."

"You haven't told anybody, have you?" Jay asked when he was alone again with Polanski. "You haven't told them you're planning a deep splash that will destroy the whole city."

Polanski was very still. "I can't. They'd want to evacuate their friends and families. Word would spread. There would be a panic. The Feds would find out. I can't risk it."

"What the hell makes you think you're any better than the people you're fighting? From here I can't see any difference at all."

Polanski raised his head and looked at Jay and his eyes were black pits. "There is none. You're right. Theology, ideology, it's all just fancy dressing on top of the ugly blackness in men's souls. I want freedom and peace for my people. I want to abolish fear in this nation and restore dignity. I want a government of the people, by the people, for the people. But it's not going to happen unless a lot of people die tomorrow. And, whatever happens afterwards, no-one is going to forgive me for what I did. But that's OK. Let me be the villain. Let me be the monster they write about in the history books. That's OK. Someone's got to blow that dam and set the river of history moving in a new direction. Someone has to take that on his conscience, and I don't see anyone else stepping up to the plate."

He opened a drawer and pulled out some rags. He balled up one and pushed it in Jay's mouth, tying it in place with another. Then he grabbed up the papers from his desk and left, locking the door behind him.

The filthy rag in his mouth made Jay want to vomit but that wasn't what bothered him most. He had to get free and get away, get help, and get back before the morning. Polanski was clearly hell-bent on martyrdom, a martyrdom that would finish off all of Washington DC—Sandra, Cara and himself included.

* * * *

Sandra drove with O'Dell through the dilapidated streets of the capital. His limo had a human driver. "I've heard the Feds can commandeer robot cars and make them drive you straight to the DC Jail if they want to," he told her.

She hadn't yet got a straight answer out of him as to why he was part of the Friends of Democracy Society. "Democracy's good for business," he said the first time she asked. Then, "What? Just 'cause I'm a crook, I can't be a patriot?" Finally, he said, "I'd rather those creeps got to be the Government one day than Holier-Than-Thou-Polanski. Those guys I can work with."

"OK, here's the deal," she told him as he sipped a double malt and ogled her in the back of the car. "I'll tell you everything that Polanski is planning if you help me get my daughter away from Duvalle."

He'd almost laughed his hat off. Sandra had to wait silently for him to settle down again. "Trust me, you want to know what Polanski is up to. It affects you and your business interests directly."

"Yeah? So why don't I just get some guys to make you talk? Then I don't have to do nothing."

"Oh, I don't know. Why don't I just stick a gun in your face and make you help me?"

He'd laughed at that one too. "You should go take a look at Duvalle's place. It's like a fucking fortress. If you can tell me how to get in, maybe I'll consider if it's in my interests to go up against one of the most powerful assholes in the country."

So they drove across town as night fell, heading northwest to where the one percent lived in big houses that were well spaced, with iron gates set into high walls. As they crawled past, Sandra glimpsed a brightly-lit mansion beyond smooth lawns. She also saw something about the size of a dustbin on wheels rolling along the drive—probably an automated sentry, the kind of little killing machine that would pack several lethal and non-lethal weapons and would patrol the grounds tirelessly all night. What she didn't see were the other kill-bots, the multi-spectrum cameras, the human guards, or the dogs, but she was sure they would all be there. O'Dell was right. The place was a fortress. Only a madman would attack it without a small army.

"Maybe I could sneak in," she said, thinking aloud.

"Yeah? Good luck with that."

"I'd need a diversion."

"You'd need a tank."

"Have you got one?"

"Nope. Oh, wait a minute." He patted his pockets. "No. No. I must have left it at home."

"Well, what do you suggest?"

He shrugged. "Why don't you and me go have a nice meal and talk it over. I know a great place, good food, good wine... We could get to know each other, chill a little, mellow out. Afterwards, go back to my place, put on some music... Who knows?"

"Right. But seriously, what kind of diversion can you provide?"

He grinned. "You don't find me diverting?"

"Yes, like a mosquito. I keep wanting to squish you against the window. Look, you don't even have to put your men at risk. Just set up something like a few little explosions. Give me a remote detonator, I'll do the rest."

"So, tell me what Saint Polanski has planned, 'cause, you know, if I wait till after Duvalle's buried your bullet-riddled corpse, I might never find out."

"When the diversion's all set up and I'm ready to go in. Then I'll tell you. Not before."

"A few explosives and a remote detonator. That's all you want?"

"That's all. No problem for a man of your resources, I'm sure. And another drive around the neighbourhood, just so I'm not going in totally blind."

"Sure," he said. "Knock yourself out." He gave the driver

the instruction, leaned back in his seat, and took another sip of his whisky. "You know, I've got an establishment on M Street. Nice, up-market kind of set-up, clean girls, top drawer clientèle. I could use a classy dame like you to run the place, someone with balls, if you know what I mean. What do you say?"

She smiled, amused despite herself. "I say that's about as interesting as your last proposition—the one with the wine and the mellowing. Now listen, this is what I'm going to need for tonight."

* * * *

Polanski stood in a room adjoining the lob site that Sandra had not seen. It had survived the backwash quite well and was now repaired and secure once more. In it were three transparent plastic spheres, each a couple of meters in diameter. They looked for all the world like giant beach balls, constructed from multiple plastic sheets, laid over a flimsy wire frame and glued together. Little plastic legs stopped them from rolling around. Inside each was a cylindrical, padded seat, stuck to the bottom of the sphere, and each had an oval hatch cut into its side—a piece of clear plastic, on plastic hinges, with a black rubber seal. Of the three spheres, one was crushed and had a gash in its side where a roof strut had fallen onto it.

"But the other two are OK?" Polanski asked, going over to inspect them.

"They're both fine," said Matthew. "We could fix up the other one if you like. It's not as bad as it looks."

Polanski shook his head. "I only need one."

He pushed the hatch on the closest sphere and it swung

inwards. There was no catch and no handle. The design was optimized for keeping the sphere's weight to a minimum. There was a vent in the side of the padded seat with a coloured ribbon tied to its grille. "You've tested them?"

"Yeah, don't worry. Air, heating, CO_2 scrubber, they're all working in both bubbles. There's an hour and twenty minutes' supply of each. More than enough to get the job done."

Polanski stared at the bubble for a long time. It was a scarily flimsy contraption to risk his life in. Yet the people who built it for him swore it would hold together. The plastics, the glues, the door seal, they would all withstand the pressure and the temperature. He'd asked them for a kind of bathysphere, imagining an impregnable steel shell, and they'd given him this. Lighter by far than the old spacesuits they had been using, the bubble could carry a man safely through the void to times as yet unreached by human travellers.

"And the weapon?"

Matthew squirmed and looked uneasy. "It's in the safe." He pointed to a big, old-fashioned iron safe. Only he and Polanski knew the combination. "You don't want me to open it, do you? We've put the real shell in there now and that thing gives me the creeps."

"I'll get it out when the time comes. The trials went well, I hear."

"Yeah, no problem. Dispersal over half a square mile. Pretty good accuracy for something that's basically a spud gun."

"And how is the shell?"

Again, Matthew squirmed. "It's fine. I'll be bloody glad when we're all well away from it. Imagine if that backwash had damaged it. Peter opened the safe to check, you know, not me. I was too scared to do it."

Polanski put a hand on Matthew's shoulder. "We all do what we're able to. None of us can do more. Come on, let's take a look at the rig."

He pushed back a sliding partition, big enough to roll one of the spheres through, and they walked over to where the lob site was being rebuilt. There was debris all around that no-one had cleaned up yet. The old roof boards and timbers had been roughly pushed aside along with the smashed computers and other rubbish. It hadn't been a big backwash, obviously.

"I suppose she just went back to yesterday and shot her past self," Matthew said. "Big anomaly but so recent it didn't disrupt things much. To do real damage, you've got to go a long way back. Then things have exponentially spreading ramifications."

Polanski glanced at Matthew. The teknik knew that Polanski knew all this. Yet the man was babbling away as if he were running a tour of the facility. He let it go for the moment.

"Will it be ready in, say, twelve hours?" he asked.

Matthew nodded. "You know, we might not even have to get that crazy bitch back. Just the few improvements she made while she was here made the targeting miles better."

"We can't afford to miss."

"I know, but it's not like you need to be very accurate."

"I get twelve minutes at the other end, right? So I need to be able to find a firing point in three minutes. The terrain back then could be slow going and the weapon is heavy, even the disassembled parts are heavy. I probably need to find somewhere within a hundred yards. The best time I ever made assembling it is eight minutes. Will the software improvements keep me from drifting more than, say, a hundred yards over the range of this lob?"

The teknik chewed his lip. "They might."

"Might isn't good enough. You know that. We only get one shot at this."

Matthew nodded and looked around. "We were lucky she didn't do more damage. She could have, easily. It's like she didn't want to hurt anybody. Can you believe that? And it's hard to control a splash. Did I tell you she went back without a suit? Zero pressure, zero Kelvin, worse than interstellar space for crying out loud. I can't believe she did that."

"What's bugging you, Matthew?"

"What?"

"There's something on your mind. Let's hear it."

The teknik looked hunted, as if Polanski had used some trick to get inside his head and expose him. He looked around at the people working on the rig and drew Polanski aside so no-one could hear them.

"You're doing the lob in twelve hours?" Polanski said nothing. "The thing is, I think I might be the only other person except you who knows how big a splash you're planning. The rest, they just know something big and bad is happening. They know there's about an hour from the start of the lob till the backwash hits us. They think an hour is plenty of time to get clear. I hear them talking. They're moving out to stay with friends in the area. Some are talking about going up to Fort Reno Park to get a good view of the event. But it's going to be worse than they imagine, isn't it? It's going to be worse than anyone can imagine. You can walk four miles in an hour, if you've got a clear road, but to get away from the splash you're planning, they'd need to be at least ten miles out, probably fifteen. A fit man on a bike could maybe get clear, but not the women and the children."

"You've known about the parameters of the lob for a long time now," Polanski said.

"And I've been waiting all day for you to give the order to evacuate." Matthew grew more agitated, more nervous. His voice took on a pleading tone. "If we told people to start moving now, they could get clear, no problem. They could catch buses or trains, get to another town."

Polanski kept his expression under control despite the turmoil inside. "No. I can't risk it. If I evacuate all these people, word will spread. The trains will be packed, the roads will be filled. The Government will notice. I can't leave them any chance to stop me."

He could see the confusion in his teknik's face as Matthew tried to marshal an argument against murdering all his friends. The teknik tried to speak several times and stopped himself. Slowly, his silent confusion turned to horror. Polanski saw it and quailed. What he saw in Matthew's eyes was what everyone would be feeling soon when they heard what Polanski had done.

"Matthew, it has to be this way. You're a smart guy, work it out."

"But I don't want to go down in some fucking blaze of glory. You think I'm going to stand there and push the button that brings the apocalypse down on my own head?"

"It's all right, Matthew. I've made preparations." He called for Peter to join them. The young man's solid presence made Matthew look unusually skinny and feeble. "OK, Matthew. I need you to be there to run the lob. Peter, I need you to keep an eye on Matthew and to make sure he does his job. Don't let him out of your sight and don't let him talk to anyone about anything except the work. If he gives you any trouble, break another one of his ribs. If that doesn't work, break his legs."

"What the fuck?" Matthew cast about as if he were about to bolt for freedom. Polanski had seen men scared before and this one was on the cusp of blind panic. "When you see me safely lobbed," Polanski went on, talking now to Peter, "show Matthew to the car and take him with you to Philadelphia to join our people there. After that, he's free to do what he likes."

Matthew's breathing was still shallow, but the wildness was fading from his eyes. "A car?" he said. "I don't know. Can we be clear in time, even in a car?" His brow creased as he did the sums. He nodded to himself. "Yeah, maybe. Probably." He nodded again.

"It's the only offer you'll get," Polanski told him. "Can I count on you to do the job now?"

The teknik stammered in his readiness to accede. "Of course. Yes. Of course."

Polanski turned to Peter. "Don't let me down. Get him to Philly as fast as you safely can."

Peter assured him he would and Polanski left them, feeling worse than ever. No matter how much he told himself there was no-one he could rely on more than Peter, he knew that he had just committed another act of monstrosity: selfishly saving his friend and protégé while leaving the rest to die. The burden of guilt was like a weight in his chest. This act alone might be enough to drag him down and down.

* * * *

Sandra took advantage of the time O'Dell needed to set up his diversion to reconnoitre the grounds of Duvalle's house.

She slipped quietly through neighbouring properties, climbed up trees and walls. By the time O'Dell returned, she knew just where to tell his men to place their charges.

She climbed into the back of his limo. "You brought the stuff I asked for?"

"On the seat there."

She grabbed the bag and pulled it towards her. It was gratifyingly heavy.

"Before you open it…" he said and she turned to see what he wanted. He had a nine millimetre Glock in his hand, pointing straight at her. The gun looked very large in his little hand but its barrel did not waver.

"What's this?" She was already weighing the odds of disarming him and pistol whipping the little bastard. They weren't good.

"It's just that, you know, I don't really know you very well yet, and there's some serious hardware in that bag. This is just so it don't give you no funny ideas when you get your hands on it."

She relaxed. Not perfidy but paranoia. "Yeah, whatever," she said and rummaged in the bag. There was a snub-nosed sub-machine gun—some model she'd never seen before, but it looked pretty standard—four spare clips, a handful of grenades, a hunting knife, a Glock like the one O'Dell was holding, spare clips for that too, and a shoulder holster. At the bottom of the bag was a garrotte. All present and correct. There was also a bundle of clothing. She pulled it out onto the seat and examined it. "Perfect," she said, flashing O'Dell a grin. She started taking off her dress.

"Hey, whoa!" O'Dell seemed genuinely shocked. "Don't you want to go behind a bush or something?"

"It's freezing out there. If the sight of my body offends

your delicate sensitivities, why don't you go behind a bush?"

He cleared his throat, looking embarrassed by his own reaction. "Yeah, well, if it's OK with you, I sure ain't gonna complain."

She stripped off the dress and the voluminous petticoat, and replaced them with the men's trousers and the black turtleneck O'Dell had brought. He'd packed some workman's boots, too, and she swapped those for her round-toed shoes. The fit was pretty good. She beamed at the little gangster and said, "That's better."

He gave a nervous giggle, his face flushed. "I thought you'd look like a guy in that outfit but you definitely do not."

Sandra had heard clumsier compliments. "Where will you be when I get out with Cara?"

He snapped back to business. "I'll be across town in a bar among plenty of witnesses. That's where I'll be. I'll leave a guy with a van, right here, to pick you up. He'll take you to somewhere we can talk." She nodded. It would do. "And this dope you got on Polanski better be good. That hardware's worth a lot of money." She put on the shoulder holster and pushed the handgun into it. She was already feeling better. The sub-machine gun was on a lanyard that she hung over her shoulder. The spare clips went back into the bag, along with the grenades and everything else. "Detonator switches?"

"Oh yeah." He handed her a small plastic tablet about the size of a compad, which turned out to be an actual compad. She touched the stud and it came to life. On its little screen were six green buttons labelled "1" to "6".

"Range?" she asked.

"How the fuck would I know? The guy just said you push the buttons and the bombs go boom."

She switched it off again and put it in her trouser pocket. "Enjoy your drink," she said and climbed out into the night.

Chapter 21

At the Mansion

Cara woke from a dreamless sleep to find a man filling her whole field of vision. Crying out in fright, she scrabbled away from him. She didn't get very far. She was on her back, on a bed, and her head hit the headboard with a crack. A meaty hand came down over her mouth.

"Shut up," the man said. "I've come to get you out of here."

She goggled at him, her heart racing. Where was here? Why was she on a bed? As if he understood, he held up a small silver disc, the size of a coin and said, "This is a neural damper. They've kept you under for twelve hours. Look, I'm not going to hurt you. If I take my hand away you won't scream?"

She shook her head. She'd been in some weird library out of a Dickens novel with her father talking to… "Duvalle? He did this?"

The man shushed her. "Yeah. You're still in his house."

"My dad? Is he here too?"

"No. Duvalle's got him out on some errand. You're the insurance to make sure he does as he's told."

"Jesus!"

"Don't blaspheme, child."

She looked at the stranger more carefully. "Who are you?"

"My name's Tonker, Jonah Tonker."

"Really?"

"What, you got a problem with my name?"

"No. I just… Can I get up?"

"Just so you don't do anything stupid, all right? If they hear us, we're both dead."

He moved back and let Cara swing her legs off the bed and sit up. She still had all her clothes on and the realization that she might not have been so lucky disturbed her powerfully. Another thought came to her. "Why are you helping me?" She was whispering now, finally comprehending the dangers of the situation.

"I'm FBI. Undercover. I know who you and your father are but I sure didn't expect you to turn up in this house. I'm here to watch Duvalle is all. I called it in and got a Deputy Director telling me to get you out of here, even if it blows my cover." He didn't seem resentful about it, just surprised.

"Why don't they just come and get me? I mean, they're the law, right? And, even here, you're not supposed to kidnap people, are you?"

"Even here?"

"It hasn't been a really good experience for me, so far."

"Sure." He seemed to understand. "Of course, if you hadn't run away from your protection detail this morning, it might have gone a little bit better."

"Yeah. Not my best move ever. Have they found my mum yet?" He shook his head. "Sorry, kid. Shall we get moving?"

"You've got a plan?"

"Sure." He went to the door and put his ear against it.

236

"So, what is it?" She got up and joined him.

"What's what?"

"Your plan? Tell me."

He frowned. "How about I worry about the plan and you just do what I tell you?"

Cara stepped back from him. "How about you tell me what this plan is so I can decide whether I think it's good enough to risk my life on?"

He studied her for a moment, his face unreadable. Finally, he said, "You know, that's a real sensible attitude. Of course, you've got to weigh up that, if you stay here, you're dead for sure. Either your dad delivers and Duvalle kills you both, or he don't and Duvalle just kills you. At least with me, you got a chance."

"All right, all right. Don't tell me your stupid plan. At least tell me if you've got backup or something."

He screwed up his face as if it pained him to break the bad news. "Yeah, that's a bit tricky. Thing is, Duvalle's a bit of a big cheese around here. No-one wants to be the guy that ordered an FBI raid on the Measurers HQ. That kind of thing has a habit of getting you noticed. But don't worry. We'll get out OK. Trust me."

With that, he put his ear back to the door and listened. Cara appraised him as she waited. On the one hand, he was big, and he looked tough. On the other hand, he didn't seem overly bright. On the one hand, he must have had some FBI training. On the other hand she didn't know how much of that was in hand-to-hand combat and how much was in theology.

Did she trust him with her life? Definitely not. Did she think going with him was better than staying put? Oh yeah.

So, when he said, "OK, it sounds clear. I'll step out first

and then you come after me when I give the signal," she took a deep breath and nodded.

"OK," he said, again, sounding nervous, and reached for the door handle.

There was a flash and a blast like thunder that rattled the windows and shook the house. Cara and Jonah looked at one another and then at the window. They rushed over to it and peered through the curtains. Across the lawns, from beyond the shrubs, a mushroom cloud of flame was rising on a skinny black stalk.

"What in the world is that?" Jonah said.

Cara wasn't sure. "I think it must be my dad." But, if she hadn't known better, she'd have sworn it was her mum.

* * * *

In the silence of the night, the explosion seemed to tear the fabric of the sky. O'Dell had certainly been generous with his charges. The two men on Duvalle's broad, balustraded verandah, turned towards it, red light flickering over their faces. Guards, or occupants, she couldn't tell, but they were looking the other way and that's what mattered. She raised herself from the ground and ran. There was a tree halfway across the lawn and that was her next stop on the way to the house. Almost as soon as she moved, a spotlight came on and swept with mechanical swiftness across the grass to find her. She jinked out of its beam and ran at right angles to her previous path, but it was on her again in moments. She cursed and kept running. The house systems must be tracking her with radar and guiding the spotlight automatically. Which meant that, any moment now…

Two robot sentries appeared, rolling around from the back

of the house. Their guns, no doubt synced into the radar sensors, were already pointing straight at her. She still had fifty meters to cover before she reached the relative shelter of the house but it might as well have been five hundred. The robots would start shooting long before she got there.

She pulled a grenade from the bag and tore the pin out with her teeth. She dug in her heels and skidded to a halt. The spotlight tracked on past her. In the moment of darkness, she lobbed the grenade at the killbots, grabbed up the submachine gun, and fell to the ground, spraying the robots with gunfire. The little killbots reacted by shutting away their sensors behind armour. Sandra's bullets pinged harmlessly off metal plating but she kept up the fire until the grenade went off.

Springing up again, every muscle tensed against the return fire she was expecting, she ran on towards the house. She risked a glance at the bots and saw that one was lying on its side and the other had rolled off in the wrong direction. She could only hope that it was due to some kind of mechanical damage. Cheap African knock-offs, she told herself. She ejected the clip and slapped in another, then ducked for cover alongside the brick wall of some kind of outhouse. Panting hard, she stood for a moment with the cool brick against her back. She looked around and listened. She heard voices to her left, so she ran right.

Straight into a man who had been sneaking up on her in the shadows. He threw his arms around her in a bear hug. He had the size and strength to make that a dangerous hold. Sandra had been gripping the short-barrelled machine gun in both hands and now her gun and hands were pressed against the man's stomach.

"Hey!" he shouted. "I got her!"

With all her strength, she pushed the barrel away from her. It barely moved, but she squeezed the trigger anyway. Pain flashed through her like a lightning strike as the gun went off, tearing a hole in her opponent's side and burning her arm and waist with the muzzle flash. The man let her go at once, screaming in pain as they staggered apart. A second burst of fire from the gun shut him up. Sandra fell back against the wall, nauseous and weak. Her flesh felt as if the flames were still searing it. Blackness crept in around the edges of her vision but a shout from nearby snapped her back.

It's just a burn. Worry about it later.

She stepped over the fallen man and ran unsteadily away from the shout. She didn't want to face anyone else. Not for a minute or two, anyway. She made for one of the back entrances. She was fairly sure that the radar couldn't track her this close to the house, but she kept an eye out for more robots just the same. They had their own sensors and didn't need to rely on external guidance.

A horse whinnied nearby. A stable block? The possibilities for cover and escape flashed through her mind. The idea of trying to mount a horse and gallop away made her smile, despite the pain in her side.

She saw a man standing guard at the door she was heading towards. No doubt every entrance was covered by now. Pushing the hunting knife into her belt behind her back, she stepped out of the shadows as close to the guard as she could get and raised her hands in surrender. It was almost comical to watch him jump out of his skin and then fumble to get his gun pointed the right way. She stepped towards him, hands high, dragging one leg.

"I'm injured," she said and saw his eyes flick towards her side. "I need a doctor." Which was the truth for sure.

"Stay there," he said. "Stop!" She stopped but she was already close enough. "Don't move." He fumbled with his gun again and put a finger to his ear.

Sandra had the compad in her hand. She touched one of the buttons on its screen and an explosion blasted out from the boundary wall. The guard almost dropped his gun as he jumped and turned towards the noise. Sandra stepped forward, grabbing the knife out of her belt and plunging it to the hilt in the man's neck.

He was still alive, but dying fast as she dragged him away from the door and into the shadows.

* * * *

"Hey!"

Jonah and Cara froze. Slowly they turned to find a suited man in the hallway behind them. Another explosion shattered the windows at the end of the corridor and all three of them ducked. It was the third explosion. To Cara, it felt as if a whole army was fighting its way into the house.

"Simon," Jonah said to the newcomer. "Give me a hand. I'm supposed to get this brat down to the basement."

To Cara, it sounded completely convincing, but Simon seemed uncertain. "Says who? It's arma-fucking-geddon out there. What I heard was every man to his post." His expression turned even more suspicious. "You know the boss said nobody touches her?" He began walking towards them. "She's just a fucking kid, Jonah."

"Looks grown up enough to me," Jonah said and Cara could only hope the FBI man was going along with his friend's suspicions as part of some brilliant ruse.

"What, so you thought you'd go somewhere quiet for a bit

of fun while the rest of us get our asses blown off?"

"Come on, Simon. It's not like that. This won't take more'n a couple of minutes. Who's gonna know?"

Simon was close now and he looked angry. "You know, I never had you pegged for this kind of sleaze bag." He turned to Cara. "Come on, kid. Let's get you back to your—"

The blow was so fast and hard, it made Cara jump. Jonah's hand lashed out, the butt of his automatic hit Simon on the temple, and the man's eyes rolled as he fell with a soft thud onto the thick carpet.

"Come on," Jonah said and took Cara's arm. "We need to keep moving."

"You might have killed him." She staggered into motion, impelled by the FBI man, but she couldn't tear her eyes away from Simon. She felt as if her chest were being squeezed. A trembling started up in her limbs. She wanted to see Simon draw a breath, just one, so she'd know he was all right. "No, wait," she said, resisting Jonah as he tried to pull her around a corner.

"He'll be fine," said the agent, almost yanking her off her feet. "It was just a tap."

Tears sprang to Cara's eyes and she didn't know why. She stumbled along with Jonah, half-blinded by them. Even though Simon was a thug who worked for Duvalle, he had tried to help her, and now he was just a heap of nothing lying on the floor. But why would she cry about that? He was going to lock her up again. He was going to go outside and fight her father, or whoever it was.

"It's all right," Jonah said. "I'll get you out of this."

She was mortified that he'd seen her crying. He thought she was just some stupid child who was feeling sorry for herself. A dumb kid who was scared and going to pieces.

Machine gun fire broke out somewhere in the house. She flinched and her heart fluttered against her ribs like a panicking bird.

Well, all right, maybe she was scared. And maybe seeing that man smashed in the face with a gun was more shocking and brutal than she could ever have imagined. It was no wonder she felt sick and weepy and resented the man who did it.

"Stop pulling me!" she cried, feeling dizzy and off-balance. Her legs were going to give up soon and the walls of the corridor had become a blur as they ran by. When they barged through a door onto a concrete staircase, she had to grab the cold metal banister with both hands and hang on hard, lest she tumble all the way down.

"That gunfire, it must have been my father. We need to get to him. He'll be looking for me."

Jonah shook his head. "That's the worst place to go. That's where the maximum danger is. He thinks you're locked up somewhere, remember? He doesn't know you've got a chance to escape. Trust me, he'd want you to get away if you could, not go barging into a gunfight."

Was he right? He sounded so certain. She thought about Jay trying to fight his way to her. If it had been her mother instead, it would be different. Nothing would stop Cara from going to find her. But, even though Jay was risking his life for her, what if she went to him and they both got killed? Her mother would never let that happen, she knew… but Jay? She didn't know him. She didn't love him. She couldn't trust him to save her.

Jonah didn't hurry her along but let her hang on the banister a moment. She felt the world steady and straighten. Anger welled up inside her—mostly directed at herself for the weakness she'd shown, but there was plenty left over. She turned her face to her would-be rescuer, her eyes hard, lips pursed. "Do you even know where we're going?"

"You're welcome," the FBI man said with that unnatural, unflappable, infuriating manner. "All right, this is the plan. We're going down these stairs to the ground floor. Then we get out and cross the yard to the garage block. Then we steal a car and I drive like a bat out of Hell, dodging the bullets that are going to rain down on us as sure as fire and brimstone rained down on Gomorrah. Then we're going to crash the gates, and, if that doesn't kill us, keep on going until we reach the J. Edgar Hoover Building. How does that sound?"

She looked into his steady eyes. Her anger drained away and she found herself smiling. "It sounds like the most stupid plan I've ever heard."

"Good. It's agreed then," he said, starting down the steps. "Let's go, kid. Those gates won't crash themselves."

* * * *

Sandra stood over the fallen man. A row of bloody holes perforated his chest. She knelt down and frisked him quickly for some kind of communication device—a radio, a compad, anything. It seemed unlikely that the guards here would have comms implants, since she hadn't seen that level of tech anywhere else. In the man's left ear she found what she was looking for: a tiny pink plastic lump. She pulled it out and stuck it in her own ear. She could hear people giving orders, confirming positions, announcing the results of sweeps and searches. It was better organized than she was hoping for, but at least she had some idea what her opposition was up to.

When she heard, "Man down. Top floor, east wing. It's Simon," she ducked into an alcove to listen. "Check the girl's room." Sandra's heart skipped.

Another voice said, "How could they be up there already?"

"I don't know, sir. Perhaps there are more than we think."

Whoever was on the top floor took his time checking Cara's room. "The room's clear," he finally said. "The girl's gone."

"Gone? Gone where?" The voice was angry and commanding. It had to be Duvalle. "Find her!"

Another voice, "Simon was killed by a blow to the temple, sir. A single, clean blow. The killer hit him from the front, I'd say, with something heavy."

Cara didn't do that, Sandra thought. Somebody's helping her. She wondered if it might be Jay. Or could O'Dell have sent someone in here without Sandra knowing? It didn't matter. Cara had a friend. She might get out of here alive.

"What are the exits from there?" Duvalle was asking.

"Service stairs at the far end of corridor B and corridor C. Main staircase. And the windows at the back of the west wing open onto the roofs below. You might be able to jump or climb that way."

"I want people on those staircases. I want people outside. Get people behind the west wing now!"

Sandra sprang into a fast run, ignoring the sudden flaring of pain from the burns across her waist and arm. She retraced her steps to the back entrance. If she were helping Cara escape, she'd head for the nearest motor vehicle. That meant finding the garage. She stepped out of the shadows to get her bearings and two men almost fell over her as they came sprinting along the path.

"Holy crap," the closer one had time to say just before Sandra hit him in the face with the stock of her machine gun. The other jerked his pistol up and fired. The bullet zinged over Sandra's head as she kicked out, fast and low, at the shooter's knee. He fell sideways with a cry of pain and his second shot went wild. Sandra rolled across the ground, glancing back to check on the first guy. He was rising from his knees and reaching for the gun he'd dropped. She kept rolling, caught up the sub-machine gun and fired. The man went down screaming and a bullet ricocheted off the wall beside her. She turned her gun towards the second man. He was down on one knee, with his gun pointing at her and his hands shaking. As soon as he saw her gun swing his way, he threw down his own and put up his hands, begging her not to shoot him.

She climbed to her feet. The pain in her side was screeching in her brain. She had to tense up that half of her body against it, or else let it consume her. She should just shoot this bastard and get on with things. She didn't have time for this. But she couldn't.

"Give me your communication device."

"My what?"

"From your fucking ear, arsehole!"

Quickly, he reached up and pulled it out. "I think you broke my leg," he whined as he handed it to her. She took it, dropped it on the floor, and ground it under her boot.

"Where's the garage?" she asked. "The garage?"

She pushed the barrel of her gun in his face. He pointed with a trembling arm. "It's round there. The low building at the end of the house."

In her ear she could hear people talking about the shots they'd just heard, organizing themselves to come and investigate. "Where's the other bot?" someone asked.

"Nearly there."

Shit!

She ran. The end of the house seemed a long way off but she had to reach it and be out of sight before the killbot appeared. She was almost there when the little machine came rolling around the corner right in front of her. She came to a skidding, heart-thumping stop, almost running into it. The bot, travelling at top speed, targeted her with its four main weapons, then suddenly turned them away as it swerved around her and rolled past. Astonished by her luck, she stood like a dummy and watched it sprint along the path towards the man she had left behind her. When it was about ten meters from him, it opened fire, almost tearing him in half with its heavy machine gun.

Sandra backed away, but the bot did not turn and pursue her. *It's the earpiece*, she thought. *You have one. He didn't. The robot's using them as friend or foe transponders.* She kept moving until she was round the corner, finally picking up speed. Ahead, she could see the back of what must be the garage block.

In her ear, Duvalle's men were crowing, believing the bot had just killed her.

* * * *

Cara and Jonah stood at the bottom of the stairwell, listening. far above them, they heard a door open and footsteps clatter down the steps. Even so, Jonah took his time opening the outside door and peering out.

"OK, we're good," he whispered. They crept out into the floodlit night, closing the door quietly behind them. "This way," he hissed, and they ran like eloping lovers from the big house towards the garage block.

The front of the block was a series of six up-and-over doors, all closed. They entered the garage through a side door. Enough light poured in through the windows to reveal a double row of cars and vans. The vans were dark green with the Temple of the Measurers' logo on them. The cars were a mixture of anonymous black SUVs and brightly-coloured muscle cars. Jonah ignored them all and made straight for a large, silver-grey antique, so old, it must be petrol-driven, Cara thought. She noticed the badge on the tall, chrome grille at the front of the car. It said "Rolls Royce", which meant nothing to her. Jonah opened the driver's door and leaned inside, burrowing down under the dash.

"Why this pile of old junk?" she asked. Surely one of the muscle cars would be faster.

"It's the heaviest pile of old junk in here," he said. "We're gonna need that. Also…" The engine purred into life and he pulled himself out from under the steering wheel. "It's got the kind of engine I can start without a digital security bypass kit."

"Jesus," she said, wrinkling her nose. The old car was stinking up the place. "Please don't use the Lord's name in vain," Jonah said. "Can you drive?" There was a burst of machine gun fire from outside. It seemed far away.

Cara shook her head. "Not that old thing." She didn't bother explaining that, where she came from, nobody "drove" cars any more. They just went where you told them to go.

Jonah looked unhappy. "OK, then. You're going to have to open the door so I can drive it out of here."

She felt the fear tightening her chest again. They could be

out there, waiting. She looked at the big, awkward, garage door. It would make a lot of noise when she pushed it up. People would hear. People would come running.

"I don't know," she said.

"Just lift it a crack at first and take a look. If it's clear, push it all the way. I'll drive out, you jump in, and we're away. It'll be over in a few seconds." He sat in the driver's seat and fiddled with something inside. "OK, Cara. Take a look."

She looked at the levers and wires on the inside of the door and then turned the handle. It slid a couple of bars out of their housings in the door frame. Then she got down on the floor and pushed the base of the door forwards. It moved easily and almost silently—for which she was immensely grateful—rising a handspan from the ground. Outside, she could see part of the house and the drive. There was no-one there. No voices, no gunshots.

"Is it clear?" Jonah whispered. She looked back at him. His face was starting to look strained, she thought. She felt her stomach knot.

"I—I can't see everywhere," she said. "I don't know."

"That's OK," he said. "As long as you can't see anyone. Open the door, Cara. We need to get moving."

She stood up. There was a rubber ball on a blue rope that she hadn't noticed before. It dangled from near the top of the door. She could see that, if she pulled it, the door would swing up and open. She took a breath, grasped the ball, and pulled. The door shuddered and rattled but was wide open in a moment. She stepped out of the garage so she could see the parts of the house she had been unable to see from the inside, and stopped dead. Four men were standing there. Three of them had guns raised and aimed at her. The fourth was Duvalle, who smiled.

* * * *

Sandra kept close to the house as she neared the garage block. She could see the front of the garages now—a row of big doors, one of them not quite closed. There was a gentle purring in the air, like some kind of engine was running. Had someone in the garage started a car? She saw the garage block had a side entrance. She could be there in a few seconds. It was open ground, but if she was fast...

Voices from the front of the house made her jam herself back against the wall with just a drainpipe for concealment. Four men came into view. They noticed the garage and its part-open door immediately.

"Beiden's down," someone said into the comm. The man sounded shaken and Sandra could imagine his horror at finding the bisected body behind the house. "And Samuel. I – I think the robot shot Beiden."

"Someone got his earpiece," one of the four men in front of her said. She recognized the speaker as Duvalle. "Somebody switch the robot off," he ordered. "Everybody else switch off your earpieces. They're listening in."

Duvalle and his men advanced a couple of paces until they were standing so close to Sandra that she dared not breathe in case they heard her. With a rattle, the garage door began to open wide. The men shouldered their weapons. Sandra expected a car to come charging out of the garage but instead a tall, slender young woman stepped out, peering towards the house. Sandra recognized her daughter immediately, even in her long skirt.

She watched Cara stop, frozen with fear when she caught sight of Duvalle and his gunmen. She could have ducked back inside the garage, she could have been safe, but she just stood there, her mouth open in a little O of surprise.

"Shoot the little bitch," Duvalle said.

Sandra stepped out from the wall and raised her gun, but she was too slow. All the gunmen had to do was squeeze the triggers on weapons they were already pointing. Fire erupted from three nozzles simultaneously. The noise hit Sandra like a fist.

In the corner of her eye, she saw a blur of movement where Cara stood. Something fast and incongruous. She squeezed her own trigger and emptied a full clip into Duvalle and his men. It took several seconds and she screamed as the gun roared and the people who had shot her daughter were torn to pieces. She wanted it to be her hands, her nails, her teeth, tearing up their flesh.

When the gun was empty, she let it fall on its lanyard and went to stand over the bloody, mangled corpses. She wished she could kill them all over again.

"Mummy?"

She twitched her head, trying to find the voice. But there was no Cara. That is… there was something. Something large and dark on the ground.

"Mummy!" It was almost a scream.

The dark figure on the ground was moving, splitting into two; a large man in a black suit, wet with blood, and Cara struggling out from under him.

Sandra ran to her daughter and dragged the dead man off her legs. She pulled Cara to her feet and they grasped one another in a bone-crushing embrace. Cara was babbling and crying, and Sandra felt herself sobbing too. Her mind was half numb with the shock and relief.

"Why did he do that?"

"Who, darling?" The wild emotions were loosening their grip and Sandra began to consider their predicament again. They should get into the garage. People would be coming.

"Jonah. Him," Cara wailed. "He didn't have to do that."

Sandra took a grip of Cara's shoulders. She saw the car in the garage with its engine running and a shot of hope pulsed in her veins. "Come on."

She dragged Cara into motion and got her into the car. Frantically, she studied the controls. Two pedals: accelerator and brake. Where the arcane knowledge came from she didn't know or care. She pressed her foot down on the accelerator and the engine raced. The car didn't move. She glanced over at Cara and saw her daughter watching her.

"Here," she said, pushing the remote detonator into Cara's hand. "When I say so, press all the green buttons."

Sandra studied the instruments again. A dim recollection about gears and shifting gears and automatic gears. There was a gear stick, a gear lever, something like that. She found something that might serve and moved it. The car rolled forward. She pushed down the accelerator again and the car surged forward, out of the garage and towards the lawn. She grabbed the wheel and turned it. The car lurched to the side. She heard shots and a squeal of terror from Cara.

"Push the buttons!" she shouted, but dared not take her eyes away from the road. explosions shook the air and flames leapt up around the mansion. The car bounced up onto the grass. Sandra kept her foot down on the pedal and swerved the car across the lawn and back onto the drive, off the drive and back onto it, all the while going faster and faster.

There was a needle twitching in a dial but she couldn't take a close look. It was all she could do to keep the lurching, rolling antique pointing down the drive towards the gate.

Bullets rattled off the bodywork as she drove. The back window shattered. "Get down!" Sandra shouted, but Cara was already cowering low. "We're going to hit the gate!"

The car was going fast now, so fast that if the gate did not break open, they'd surely be killed. It looked solid, but the car was heavy.

The old Rolls Royce hit the gates with a crash that ripped them from their hinges and wrapped them around the front of the car. The windscreen shattered and Sandra found herself slapped back against the seat, ears ringing, with the bizarre impression she had bounced off a big white balloon. The car was still racing along the road, showers of sparks and a banshee wail coming from the gate it was dragging. The Rolls spun around once, twice, and came to a juddering halt. Half-stunned, Sandra reached over to Cara to check if she was OK. Cara stirred, her eyelids fluttering open. Only then did Sandra take a look outside. The car was side-on to the mansion. Through the shattered gate, she saw men running up the drive towards them. She struggled to get her gun to ward them off, only then remembering it was empty. The spare clips were in her bag and her bag was… Back in the garage. The men slowed as they approached, probably calculating that Sandra should be shooting at them by now. Her only option was to get herself and Cara out the other side of the car and run for it.

Gunfire broke out all around them. Too close to be from Duvalle's men. She instinctively threw herself across Cara, but no bullets were hitting the car. Then she heard the door open behind her. She twisted to face it, knife in hand.

"Whoah. Steady girl." She blinked in astonishment at Polanski's smiling face. "The cavalry's arrived."

Chapter 22

Parameters

With a sinking heart, Sandra looked over the resurrected lob site. "I was hoping I'd done more damage," she said.

No-one commented. The woman bandaging her burns kept her head down and worked steadily. Sandra had been relieved when the woman fetched a military first aid kit instead of the old rags and Vaseline she had imagined. The kit had high quality burn repair patches and sterile bandages. When the woman applied a local anaesthetic spray, Sandra could have kissed her.

"I'll fetch you some clothes," her nurse said when she'd finished. "Just a jumper would be fine," Sandra called after her.

Polanski entered the room a few seconds later.

"Where's Cara?" she asked, standing up to face him. They had been separated and taken back to the Shanty in separate cars.

"She's with her father. She's fine."

"What the hell were you doing outside Duvalle's place with a platoon of guerillas?"

"We went to get Cara."

Sandra's dismay deepened at this confirmation of her worst fears. "I killed Duvalle."

Polanski's eyebrows went up, but all he said was, "A minor complication. They'll blame me. But then, they would have done anyway. It won't matter in a few hours' time."

Her fingers curled into fists. She felt like smashing him in the face. "All right. So you've got Cara, and that means you've got me. You want me to set up your lob, but we both know that will kill me and Cara and Jay anyway. So what's my incentive?"

He gave a tight smile. "Right to the heart of it as usual. You know, you're a fascinating woman. If we'd met under different circumstances…"

"Cut the bullshit. However we'd met, you'd still be a low-life creep with delusions of adequacy. Give me the deal or get out of my face."

He looked like he wanted to hit her. She checked to see where Peter was, just in case she had to lay out the boy's hero. "All right," Polanski said. "The deal. You make sure this contraption delivers me just where I want it to, and you and your daughter can leave as soon as the lob is activated."

"And Jay."

"Of course, Jay too."

"Not good enough."

"What?"

"We'll need a car."

"Fine. Take a car. Better yet, Peter is driving to Philadelphia straight after the lob. You can go with him."

"No."

"No?"

"We want our own car. I don't trust the Boy Wonder as far as I could throw him."

He was growing impatient. Clearly it didn't matter to him much either way. His planning stopped at the lob. "All right, you get your own car."

"Good. I want Cara and Jay waiting in it and ready to go. You'll need to get someone to show Jay how to drive it." Her eyes held his, steady and fierce. "You know how easily I could sabotage this whole thing if I wanted to, don't you, once you let me loose on that software?"

"I'll set it up. Anything else?"

"Yes, you're a fool. You don't have to do it this way. Have your revolution. I'm all for it. I'll cheer you on. But not like this. You destroy the whole city and it'll leave a stain of blood you'll never wash off."

"The whole city?"

They both turned to find Sandra's nurse standing there with a bundle of clothes in her arms.

"She means the city centre," Polanski said. "Here, let me take those." He smiled. "Thank you. That's all for now."

When the woman went away, frowning to herself, Sandra said, "She'll die too. Does she have children?"

Polanski's reply was savage. "How many people did you kill tonight? And for what? To get one single child out of the clutches of these people. One." He made a cutting gesture with his hand. His expression was pure contempt. "You have your deal. Get on with your work."

Sandra watched him stride out of the room. *I didn't kill one person who wasn't trying to hurt my daughter*, she thought. *Not one of them was innocent.* Yet his condemnation had upset her more than she could explain. "I wouldn't even be here if it wasn't for you, you bastard," she shouted to the empty doorway.

* * * *

After Cara had finished crying, Jay got her to tell him what had happened at Duvalle's mansion. He listened in amazement, remembering that feeling of awe and astonishment from the first time he had worked with Sandra.

"So she's here, in the building?" Jay asked, finding his heartbeat quickening. Polanski had removed his gag so that he could talk to Cara, but he and she were tied hand and foot.

Cara nodded, miserable and exhausted. "Polanski's got us all now."

"He's planning a timesplash. A big one."

"Like London?"

Jay shook his head. "Like Beijing. Like Mexico City."

Cara's eyes widened. To her generation those names tolled just like Hiroshima and Nagasaki had to her great grandparents. "Mum would never help them do that."

Jay smiled. "That's what I told them."

Cara started to smile too but then her face fell. "That's why they came for me, isn't it?"

Jay said nothing, but Cara was insistent. "She still won't help them. She knows I wouldn't want her to. She wouldn't, even for me, would she?"

Jay wasn't so sure. "I know one thing, whatever she does, she'll make sure you're safe."

Cara fell silent. "You should have seen her at the house. She was like a superhero or something. She was covered in blood and her clothes were torn and she was wounded and it was like nothing could stop her."

She looked at him with wonder shining from her eyes, and Jay recognized that feeling, too.

* * * *

Cara fell asleep soon after and Jay propped himself against the wall and watched her. He'd known her just a few days but he would have given anything to get her out of there, back to her own life, back to her childhood. Sandra had been right to keep her hidden. This was his life, a world of criminals and terrorists, where children were tied up and thrown in dingy little rooms to be used as leverage. And yet... He wondered what this beautiful young woman had been like as a toddler. Had she laughed a lot, or had she been the serious, thoughtful type? Had she been always grazing her knees, dressing up in Mummy's clothes, trying to do things beyond her years and understanding? A sharp pang of regret twisted inside him. It was a lot to take away from someone. It was a hard, cruel thing to deny him the joy of being there to watch his daughter grow up.

He worked at his bindings as he thought about Cara. He'd been working at them since the minute they'd been tied. The stinging soreness of his wrists merged with his newfound pain of loss and betrayal, sharpening it and focusing it.

Sandra had been right to want to save Cara, to hide her, to keep her away from the cesspit of greed and hatred that Jay worked within. He could see that. He could see how she would want to protect that precious child at whatever cost. But to hide her from Jay only showed how little she trusted him. How little she knew him. Because he would have felt the same way. He would have wanted Cara safe from her parents' past. He would have done anything, gone anywhere, to ensure that his daughter grew up free from any danger haunting their lives.

And yet...

How seriously would he have taken the threat? When he thought of the preparations Sandra had made, the lengths she had gone to, to keep herself and Cara off the radar of the kind of people she had once known… He had to admit that he probably would have said she was being paranoid, overprotective, a crazy woman. But everything had happened the way she feared it might. Somehow, the past had reached through time and space and plucked her out of her obscurity, thrusting her—and Cara—back into the nightmare.

Could he have been trusted to take the threat seriously? Could he have given up the Temporal Crimes Unit and gone off to live a quiet life—the life he might have led if a timesplash hadn't killed his best friend that infamous night, eighteen years ago? If he had never joined MI5? If he had never met Sandra?

The questions bubbled like a simmering stew in his mind as he watched Cara, strained at his bindings, and slipped in and out of a fitful sleep. They were the questions he and his colleagues at the TCU would discuss on late night stakeouts. What if you jumped back into your own past and changed some crucial incident? How big a splash would it make? Was his friend's death and Jay's reaction to it a big deal, or would the world have gone on much the same either way?

Well, he knew the answer now. If he had never become involved with Sandra, hunted Sniper with her, fallen in love with her, then Cara would never have been born, Sandra's life would have been very different, and she would probably not be here now helping a crazy man kill a million people. Changing his own past at that splashparty in Ommen might well have created a bigger timesplash than anyone could have imagined.

* * * *

Not far away, Sandra was also deep in thought. She had all the splash parameters now. Matthew had shown her the plastic spheres and explained how they worked. The lob would be three hundred and thirty years into the past, all the way back to 1736. One other man would be travelling with Polanski in the sphere. Matthew gave her the mass of the occupants.

"Guns?" Sandra asked. They would need guns if they were to do any killing. On such a long lob, the weight of even handguns would add hugely to the energy requirements. As it was, sending two people back was pushing the capacity of the rig to its limit.

Matthew stood there with his mouth open. *He's thinking up a lie,* she realized.

"One gun," said Peter. Peter was her constant companion now. He watched her like a cat watching a rodent.

She looked from one to the other. "What the hell is going on here?"

"He's right," said Matthew. "There's just one gun."

"Mass?"

"Eight hundred and fifty grams, loaded."

That would be heavy for a handgun but not excessively so, Sandra thought, yet too light for a shotgun or a semi-automatic rifle. "So he's just taking one handgun?"

"So what?" Peter asked.

"That's why the spatial accuracy is so important," Matthew said, and she could see it was another lie.

"Two men," she said. "Two big men and one handgun. And they're going back three hundred and thirty years to shoot one man on a remote farm." Again she studied their faces. "So what's really going on here?"

"Just do as you're told, woman." Peter stepped close,

standing over her like a slab of meat.

She was so sick of this kid throwing his weight around. The great bullying, misogynist lout summed up so much of what was wrong with this whole set-up. Maybe it was time for a little revolution of her own. First she had to give Peter what he had coming.

She looked into his eyes and said, "What is it about me that bugs you so much, Sidekick? Do I get your hormones all stirred up? Have you got a secret crush on me that you're fighting for the sake of the cause? Or are you worried that Polanski fancies me? He does, you know." She put a hand to her mouth in mock surprise. "Oh, I'm so sorry. All this time you were hoping he fancied boys but he likes women after all."

The young man was almost trembling with rage. Words came belching out of him in minor eruptions. "Foul-mouthed. Disgusting. Filthy. Whore!" His fist came swinging at her head like a sledgehammer but she ducked under it easily and landed a fast, hard punch in his right kidney before skipping back, balanced and ready. Roaring, he threw himself at her but she stepped back again, deflecting the remains of his lunge with a solid forearm block and again jabbed him in the kidney as he stumbled past. He found a few more insults to yell as he came at her again. Again she sidestepped his lunge, shooting out a kick to the back of his leg that brought him down. He knelt on the floor, glaring at her. She almost hesitated at the sight of so much hatred, but then took a step forward and delivered a flying kick to his head. Peter dropped to the ground as if his strings had been cut.

Sandra turned at the sound of booted feet running into the room. Two men with guns advanced on her, weapons raised.

Sandra was still in the mood for a fight. She squared off against them.

"What do you think you're going to do, arseholes, ugly me to death? Oh look, it's the Great Leader himself."

Polanski came to a stop at the sight of Sandra and his fallen friend. Sandra pointed at Peter. "You need to get a muzzle for that thing."

"If he's dead, I'll…"

"You'll what?" It was time for step two. In a blur of speed, she threw herself at Matthew, kicking and punching him in a furious attack that left him lying on the ground too, bleeding. She got off him. Polanski had stepped forward, perhaps to try to intervene, but it had all been over so fast, he didn't have a chance. The guns were still pointing at her.

"This one's alive," she said, panting from her exertions. "But I doubt he'll be much use to anyone for a few weeks yet. I'm pretty sure I felt his jaw break, and both arms. So now what are you going to do, Monster? I'm the only one who can run your fucking lob. If you want to destroy Washington and everybody in it, I'm your only option."

Polanski looked stunned. His eyes went from Matthew to Peter and then to Sandra. His face was grey and his breathing was shallow. "I've still got your daughter," he said, his voice a croak.

"And you're going to bring her to me. And Jay while you're at it."

He seemed to come out of his shocked state. He shouted at his men to get Peter and Matthew out of there and get them some medical help. Then he turned his attention back to Sandra.

"You think the tables have turned, don't you? But nothing has changed. Not really." Sandra was pretty sure things were very different now, yet Polanski sounded sure of himself. He even managed a taut smile when he said, "It's all a question of who needs what the most, isn't it?" He began walking around Sandra, easing his way into his theme. "I really need this lob to happen right now. Today. Groups all over the country have been given the signal. Allies outside the country have been assured we're about to act. If we don't go today, my leadership loses a lot of credibility. It could take years to get everybody to this peak of readiness again. It would be a disaster for me and my cause."

Sandra kept her eye on him as he moved around, not because she suspected an attack, but so she could watch his face. "On the other hand," he went on. "Bad as it would be, we'd recover. We'd reorganize—with a new leader, perhaps— but we'd try again. We will be free. We will take back our country."

The people around them grunted their affirmation, people that Sandra hadn't noticed gathering until that moment. Polanski moved closer until he stood at Sandra's shoulder. "You, on the other hand, could lose your daughter. It could happen like that." He snapped his fingers in Sandra's face and her fists clenched. "And once you've lost her, there's no recovering from it, there's just living with it for the rest of your life, knowing she died because of your stubbornness, or pride, or whatever passes for principles in your Godless morality."

There was no arguing with his logic. Sandra knew full well she had more to lose. She fought down a rising panic and tried to stay calm. Whatever the perceived inequalities here, Polanski gained nothing by hurting Cara, and lost a great deal instead. For him, it would be a last resort. She still had lots to bargain with.

A couple of men picked up Matthew. The teknik cried out in pain. Sandra had not forgotten it had been Matthew's idea to bring her there. She hoped the pain lasted a long time. As for Peter, two men struggled to lift him and called in a third to help. The boy was still out cold and Sandra thought it was probably best he stayed that way.

"Bring Cara and Jay here," she told Polanski. "Once I know they're OK, we'll talk again about going on with the lob."

Polanski's lips twitched into a smile, making her heart labour at the sight. He knew she was stalling, looking for some way out. He knew she couldn't risk losing Cara, no matter what.

If she killed him now, it would all be over. There would be no lob, no timesplash, all those people would go on living. Yet, if she killed him, the people around her would tear her to shreds. *It might be worth it.* The idea echoed in her mind. It was mesmerising. She saw the blow that would do it, felt her muscles tensing for the sequence of swift actions it would require. *Just one punch.* She could almost feel her knuckles driving into his throat, his windpipe collapsing…

"Fetch the prisoners," Polanski said, and walked away, breaking the spell.

* * * *

Jay snapped awake at the sound of boots outside the room. Cara was still asleep. He was still sitting with his back to the wall. He tugged frantically at the bindings on his wrists. When a coil of rope slipped loose and his wrists jerked farther apart, he was so surprised he stopped struggling for a moment. Then he redoubled his efforts. In seconds, the footsteps came to a halt outside and a key rattled in the lock. No time for his feet. He freed his hands but kept them behind his back. As the door opened, he dropped his head, pretending to be asleep.

Two men entered the room. One went to Cara and the other to Jay. An arm reached down and shook his shoulder. "OK, buddy. On your feet." Jay looked up, pretending to be thick with sleep.

The man's pistol was in his trouser waistband. Jay reached out and grabbed it before his jailer had time to react. The man jumped back as if Jay had stung him. Which was fortunate, because, to Jay's horror, the gun tumbled out of his hand onto the floor. His fingers were almost useless. Numb, weak and unresponsive, he might as well have had wooden sticks attached to his hands, and the pain in his shoulders made sweat spring out on his forehead. In a near panic, he fumbled up the heavy firearm using both hands and managed to get it pointing the right way just as its owner realized what was going on and came charging back.

Jay fired. The bullet took the man in the hip, and he swerved and fell beside Jay. The second man shouted, "Drop it!" and Jay looked to see him standing beside Cara, his gun aimed at Jay's chest. There was no chance of swivelling around to fire at the man. He clenched his teeth in frustration and was about to drop the gun when Cara, her feet still tied, kicked out at the gunman's knee. The gun went off and Jay heard the round zip past his ear. He took aim as the man staggered to regain his balance. "Don't even think about it," Jay said. The man froze. "Put the gun down and untie my legs." The man did as he was told and knelt down at Jay's feet. "Make it fast, or I'll shoot you and do it myself."

With his legs free, Jay told his captive to untie Cara. He

stood up slowly and carefully, shaking the blood back into his legs. The untying was going too slowly. There must be people on their way by now to see what the shooting was about. He didn't have time. He went to the door to quickly look out into the corridor. When he looked back, the man had dived across the floor to retrieve his gun. Caught off-balance, Jay just made it out the door again before a shot put a hole in the wall beside him. His only thought was to get back in there and get Cara free, but even as he swung himself back to the doorway, people came running round the corner into the corridor. He fired at them and they ducked as best they could. There was no rescuing Cara now. With a yell of frustration, he took off along the corridor just as the first bullets came after him.

It was a miracle that Jay made it out of there alive. Bullets ripped through walls and plastic sheeting all around him as he careered through gaps and rooms and corridors, trampling people's beds—with sleeping people in them—toppling makeshift tables, smashing down flimsy doors, knocking down anyone who couldn't get out of his way fast enough. He had no idea where he was going and no sense of the ramshackle architecture of the place, so he went in as straight a line as he could, praying there would be an end to it all soon. Dogs barked at him or yelped as they fled, and he almost broke his neck dodging and skidding and splashing his way through a set of buckets set to catch the rain as it dripped through the ceiling. His pursuers thinned out and fell behind as his reckless sprint took him into dangers any sane person would avoid. When he saw a wall ahead with a window opening onto a grey, wet dawn, he dived straight through it, hitting the muddy ground outside in a roll from which he was up and running again in a single fluid motion.

He would worry about the pain in his shoulder later, along with the many cuts and bruises he'd picked up during his escape. Right now, all he could focus on was keeping moving and not slipping in the mud.

Chapter 23

Target

Cara's hands were still tied when they brought her to Sandra, but they had freed her legs. Her mother looked awful—exhausted and filthy—still wearing the same torn and blood-smeared clothes as when she had last seen her. There were bandages on her left arm and around her middle beneath the ragged jumper, but blood had soaked through them. Cara wanted to hug and comfort her mother so badly it was an ache inside her.

Yet, when Sandra beamed her wide, beautiful smile and rushed forward to embrace her, Cara found herself crying helplessly on her mother's shoulder, overwhelmed with self-pity and wallowing in the delicious comfort of her mother's strong arms. When Sandra murmured in her ear that it would be all right, that everything would be fine now, Cara believed it with every fibre of her being, felt the comfort with a certainty that came from the very roots of their relationship.

As Cara's tears subsided, Sandra pulled back and looked into her eyes. "Are you all right? Have they hurt you?"

The look in her mother's eyes made her a little frightened

about what she might do. "I'm fine. Don't worry, Mum. But Jay—"

"That stupid man! What ever made him think it was a good idea to bring you here? When I see him, I'm going to–"

"It was all my fault, Mum. I made him. He didn't want to."

"Made him? How do you make a grown man take a child anywhere near a lob site? What kind of man lets himself be pushed around by a teenage—" She stopped, closed her eyes and visibly calmed herself, perhaps remembering her own time with Cara's father.

Cara moved in closer and whispered in Sandra's ear, "He got away, Mum. He'll bring help, won't he?"

"That's enough," Polanski said. Cara felt her mother stiffen. She hadn't noticed him when she came in, but now she looked at the revolutionary leader. He wasn't especially tall, but he looked tough and strong. He had a rugged face, but, though Cara looked hard, she saw little sign of meanness or cruelty. Instead she saw only sadness and a kind of stubbornness that might once have been determination. When he looked her way, she made sure that all he saw in her face was hatred.

"Sit over there, darling," Sandra told her, indicating a chair near the console. "And can we have her hands untied, please?"

Cara glanced nervously at the faces around her but no-one seemed angry at her mother's bossy tone. In fact, Polanski gave someone the nod and the man came over and removed the rope. Pins and needles built up quickly in her hands to the point where she felt they were swelling like blown-up rubber gloves. They looked normal, however, apart from the red welts on her wrists. She tucked them under her armpits and tried not to let the pain show.

Her mother saw, though, and led her over to the chair and sat her down. Then Sandra turned to Polanski and said, "OK, I've had the bullshit version. Why don't you tell me exactly what the lob is, what the target is, and who's going? Then I can program this thing so that you don't get shredded to atoms by tidal forces when the field kicks in."

Polanski nodded then shooed everybody out of the room except a single guard with a semi-automatic rifle. "If she tries anything, shoot the girl," he told the guard, who then pointed his weapon straight at Cara. It made it hard to concentrate on what her mother and Polanski were saying, knowing she was just a twitch of a finger away from death.

"Here," Polanski said, and went into the adjoining room where could see the two big plastic spheres. "Help me with this." Together, he and Sandra rolled one of the oversized beach balls across the floor and up a ramp onto a broad platform with heavy coils under it. They settled it on its little plastic legs, the white marshmallow seat at the bottom. They turned it so that the oval hatch faced the console.

Polanski led Sandra back to the other room and tapped a sequence into the lock of a big, black safe—the kind they had in cartoons and old westerns, Cara thought. He swung open the heavy door and reached inside. She couldn't really see what was going on but she heard her mother say, "A mortar? What the hell?"

"Give me a hand," he said again. He took a long, heavy tube from the safe and slung it over his shoulder. Sandra reached in and picked up what seemed like a meter-long pair of dividers. It took Cara a moment to realize it was a pair of legs for the mortar tube. They carried these to the sphere with Polanski talking all the while.

"This is an eighty-one millimetre, Venezuelan copy of a

European Defence Force K29 mortar." He gently eased it through the hatch and set it down inside the sphere, careful to keep the ball's balance. Sandra did the same with the legs as he went on. "It fires a range of shells, from simple, high-explosive rounds, which it can lob up to seven miles, to sophisticated, radio-guided, rocket-assisted rounds, that can go fifteen miles."

"So, you're going to lob a mortar bomb at the White House? Had it even been built three hundred years ago?"

"No, it hadn't." They were back at the safe again. Polanski reached in and pulled out a heavy metal disc that Cara guessed was the base plate for the tube.

"Can you get the bag and the shell? You probably want to be careful with that."

"What's in the bag?"

"The sights and the remote control unit. The shell will definitely explode if you drop it, so treat it like a holy relic, huh?"

"You're putting a lot of trust in me."

He glanced at Cara but said nothing. He lugged the base plate over to the sphere, with Sandra cradling the bomb behind him. "This place we're in right now, Alley Shanty, used to be the city of Alexandria. It was part of the original gift of land by the States of Virginia and Maryland to the nation to establish the District of Columbia so that our capital city could be built. That was in 1790. Virginia got its land back later on but that's by the by. Alexandria was a tiny little settlement at the time. Most places were back then. Now it's just another suburb in the mighty Washington Metropolitan Area." They gently placed the final parts of the mortar in the plastic bubble.

Sandra looked at it and then at Polanski. "You know that,

if you have a rough landing—and you will—this contraption is going to be torn to shreds by all that heavy metal."

"Can't be helped," Polanski said.

Cara felt a frisson of shock as she realized what a torn sphere would mean for the return journey. Polanski intended to die on this lob.

"You could pad it," Sandra said.

"What's the point? When I get back here, I'll only have a few minutes before the backwash hits."

"I can tune that to some extent. I could get you ten, maybe more."

Even though Polanski was the enemy, Cara could see why her mum didn't want to let him just kill himself. The idea was horrible.

"Could you get me fifteen?" he asked.

Sandra seemed doubtful. "Maybe. I could trade it off for time at the target."

Whatever brief hopes he'd entertained, Cara could see that they evaporated instantly. "Padding would add mass," he said, dismissing the idea. "And I need the full twelve minutes."

Sandra considered a moment. "So… A total of about fifteen minutes before the backwash hits, eh? If I drove like a madwoman, I could get quite a long way in that time. How far do I need, exactly?"

"Fifteen miles, maybe. That's what Matthew reckoned."

"To cause a splash with a fifteen-mile radius you need to do a bit more than kill some distant ancestor of yours. Even in 1736."

"In 1735," Polanski said, continuing his history lesson, "Lawrence Washington had a house built on a family property called Mount Vernon. He moved his young family there the next year, including his four-year-old son, George."

"Jesus."

"Mount Vernon is about eight miles from here. Well within the range of my Venezuelan mortar with its rocket-propelled shell."

"Even so, the chances of killing a particular person… even if you scored a direct hit on the house…"

"That's why I had a very special warhead made. In the late Twentieth Century, the Brits came up with a particularly nasty range of nerve gasses called the "V" range. Of these, VX was by far the worst. Not only is it extremely lethal, even to the touch, but it persists in the environment for a long, long time. The US army actually deployed munitions containing VX— landmines, missiles, airplane spray tanks—and my people happened to come into possession of a small stockpile. So I don't have to hit little George directly with that thing, If he's anywhere in the neighbourhood—or if he visits even years later—he's dead."

"Christ Almighty. You're going to kill George Washington, before the War of Independence, before the founding of the United States. And you think the radius of the of the backwash will be just fifteen miles?" She jumped off the platform and ran to the control console.

"What is it, Mum?" Cara asked. Her mother looked anxious as she worked the interface field of the computer.

"I don't know yet. I just need to do some calculations."

Polanski came over and joined them. "It doesn't matter how big it is, as long as it covers DC itself."

"Do you know how many millions of people are in that radius? At least three million. But I think Matthew is talking a load of bollocks. I think fifteen miles is the minimum likely radius. I think we could be looking at the biggest damned timesplash ever."

"Mum?" Cara felt the fear rolling over her like cold air. Her mother had rarely spoken about timesplashes. It was a topic that, by silent agreement, was taboo in their household. Even though time travel was Sandra's business, avoiding the creation of a timesplash was at the core of her mother's expertise. Those few times that Sandra had opened up about her past had filled Cara with dread. It was clear to her, even as a very young child, that nothing in this world scared her mother the way a timesplash did. And when the strongest, bravest, smartest person you know—the person you rely upon for your own security, for your very survival—fears something so much, it becomes your own dread, your own bogeyman.

There must have been something in Cara's tone, because Sandra dragged her attention from the computer display to look at her. For a moment their gazes met and Cara saw her own fear reflected in her mother's eyes. It sent a shudder through her. The splash was going to be big, the backwash terrible. It wasn't the first time in the past few hours that Cara thought, "I'm going to die," but it was the first time she also thought, "and no-one can save me."

And then she saw her mother's expression harden, saw again that fierce determination she had seen at Duvalle's mansion. A spark of hope kindled into flame. Her mum was going to do something. She could see it. Her mum wouldn't let anybody hurt her. Relief and gratitude surged inside her and forced a sob from deep within. Her mother gave her a quick smile and turned to Polanski.

"All right. I've got your parameters. And, frankly, why should I care how many of your own people you kill? I need to work now. Cara stays with me. Fill the place with your armed acolytes if you like, but Cara stays."

Polanski shrugged and walked away. He seemed distracted and strangely emotionless. Aware that the man planned to kill himself in a few hours, Cara really didn't know how he should behave. How would she feel if she were going to make the same sacrifice? Could she kill herself for the sake of her country? It was creepy and disturbing. For the millionth time, she wished she and her mum were back home and away from all these crazy, horrible people.

* * * *

Jay checked the map on his commplant again and again, but it was of little help to him in the Shanty. His clothes were wet and caked in mud and the chill of the autumn morning was seeping into his bones. Even in this slum where scarecrow ghosts haunted the tumbledown dwellings, he was stared at and shunned.

He clutched his aching shoulder and limped from the pain in a twisted knee. He had no money and no comms. His only hope of finding his way out of there was by dead-reckoning based on maps no-one bothered to update any more. He avoided the gangs of men and youths who hung about in broken-down shanties, on street corners, and around the husks of rusted vehicles. Nobody seemed to have work to go to and, from the territory markings and body art, he supposed that gang membership was the norm. As much as Jay sympathized with their condition, he did not want to help them through their purposeless days by providing a few minutes of idle entertainment. He still had the gun, of course, but it was cold comfort. He didn't want to use it to defend himself against some uneducated kid, someone who didn't know any better than to try to shake the ennui by pushing around a derelict stranger for the amusement of his friends.

When the challenge came—"Hey, gimp!"—Jay screwed up his eyes, clenched his jaw, and pressed on, hoping against hope that whoever it was would be too lazy to do anything but shout.

"Hey, I'm talkin' to you, gimpy."

Jay kept moving. He heard footsteps splashing in the mud nearby. A young man ran in front of him, blocking his path. Jay looked at him, dreading what he might have to do. His challenger was a boy, really, seventeen perhaps, short and broad, with a shaved head and very bad teeth. Despite the cold, the boy wore only jeans and a khaki vest. Up one side of his face and down one arm he had poorly-executed tattoos—words and symbols, snakes and chains, a prominent crucifix with a Death's Head impaled by it.

Jay heard more footsteps coming up behind him. Two sets. "Maybe you can help me," he said to the boy.

"Hey," the boy said in a voice intended for his gathering friends to hear. "Gimpy wants a handout."

Jay raised his own voice. "I am Detective Chief Inspector Jay Kennedy of Europol and I'm here working with the FBI." Well, that would either get him killed or scare the shit out of everybody. From the way the boy's face fell and his lips twitched, Jay couldn't be sure. He took a step towards the boy and the lad's head twitched sideways in a kind of flinch, but he kept his eyes on Jay through narrowed lids. The footsteps behind Jay had stopped.

"What's your name, boy?"

"Fuck you, I ain't tellin' you my name."

He sounded surly but uncertain. Jay pressed his advantage. "You'd do best to cooperate fully. I need a compad. Do you have one?"

"What the fuck you think I'd do with a compad, call my stockbroker?"

Jay heard a snigger from behind. Not so good. He took another step forward. The boy looked nervous but didn't retreat. "Then tell me how to get out of this shithole before I take you in for being a moron in a public place."

"Who're you callin' a moron? I bet you ain't even a Fed anyway."

Jay spoke louder, so that everybody around him could hear. "Keep talking like that and you're going to bring down a whole mountain of trouble on your pointy little head. And not just yours. I will make sure your friends get it, and your family, and this whole stinking neighbourhood." What was the good of being a cop in a police state if you couldn't throw your weight around a bit? "Do you really want to piss me off, boy? Do you really want an FBI tactical unit in here rounding up this nest of atheists and blasphemers?"

Jay heard the footsteps behind him again, only this time they were retreating. The boy noticed it too. "Hey! Where the fuck do you think you're going? He's not a Fed. He's just some fucking…" But the young man's imagination seemed to fail him in explaining what Jay might actually be.

Jay lowered his voice again. "Look, kid, just tell me how to get to somewhere where I can find a phone and a taxi and I'll forget the whole thing. You're on your own, now. No-one's going to risk helping you. You turn this into a fight and everybody you know is going to blame you for the consequences. I'm only guessing, but I suppose you know one or two people who would kill you for bringing them that kind of trouble."

Jay saw the boy look around him. People were watching. Nobody was smiling. When he looked again at Jay, he was visibly shaken. Jay supposed the lad was very unhappy to be standing out there all alone. Yet he was still unwilling to back down.

"I want those directions," Jay said so that only the boy could hear. He had begun to feel sorry for the kid. It wasn't his fault he lived in this miserable excuse for a society. "Here's what's going to happen. I'm going to point a gun at your head." The boy's eyes widened. "But it's OK, I won't shoot you. You'll just back off, call me a couple of names, and I'll walk on by. You'll look like a brave little punk, and I won't have to come back here with my friends. OK?"

The boy didn't speak for a moment. Then he made his decision. "You go on the way you're headed 'bout three blocks. Then turn left and keep goin' 'til you hit the fence. You'll see the gate."

"Thank you." Jay pulled his gun and pointed it at the boy's head. The boy raised his hands and the two of them circled around each other until they had swapped places in the road.

"Don't you come 'round here again, Fed," the boy shouted in his face. "I'll be ready for you next time." Jay turned and walked away, keeping the gun in his hand, just in case. "That's right. Get back to DC, cop. Back to Fucking Bastards Incorporated. Faith Before Intelligence, right?"

Jay tightened his jaw. Damn, the boy was overdoing it. Still, he kept walking, and nobody followed him.

He found the gate without difficulty and without further challenge. Another fifteen minutes' walk brought him to a strip mall where he surprised a pair of Sons of Joshua eating stew in a dingy café. They told him to clear off and threatened him with their night sticks until he did a "take me to the FBI right now or I'll have the pair of you executed" routine on them. It worked so well that they got him a bowl of stew and a coffee to have while he waited for the black SUV sent by an astonished Special Agent Simmons.

Chapter 24

Cara

The lob was set to happen at noon and Sandra's commplant showed that she had less than four hours. She worked steadily at the command console to fix up the sloppy, indecipherable code. Sometimes she would spot a physical cause for noise in one of the signals and dive into the rig itself to pull out some component, clean a contact, or tighten a screw. It was a hopeless task, especially given the time available. The equipment was old and mismatched and much of it had begun its life as cheap, low-quality hardware. But Sandra worked through the diagnosis and tune-up of the rig and its mare's nest of control software with the care and rigour she'd spent more than a decade acquiring. When this rig lobbed Polanski back into the timestream, it would do so with as much efficiency and effectiveness as she could squeeze out of it.

Not that it would do Polanski any good. She would be sending him to the year 1796, not 1736, and the would-be martyr could bomb Mount Vernon to smithereens for all she cared, because George Washington would be dead by then. Whatever backwash Polanski created by poisoning Mount

Vernon in the mid-1790s would be nothing compared to the one he hoped to create by eradicating Washington's legacy. The backwash might not even hit the Shanty. Most likely it wouldn't. People might die—but possibly just tens, or hundreds of people, not the hundreds of thousands or millions that Polanski planned to kill.

Most importantly, Cara would be safe. In which case, Sandra could be generous and spare Polanski's life by making the rig work well enough not to shred him.

She looked across at her daughter. She now saw so much of Jay in her. Somehow the strain of this terrible adventure had brought it out in her, or perhaps Sandra had not noticed it so strongly before. Like Jay—like Sandra too, of course—Cara was tall and willowy. She was beautiful too. So beautiful it made Sandra's heart ache. But her daughter's beauty was not the same as her own at that age. Her own looks had been the sort that every man wanted to possess, the kind of looks that could get you anything and anyone you wanted. The kind of beauty that had given Sandra enormous power. The kind of beauty that was a curse. It had led her into the clutches of powerful, dangerous men who had used and abused her. She had thought at the time that it was a fair deal: she got what she wanted and they got her. But she had been a child, and a disturbed one at that. The deals she'd made were never fair and the things she got from them had never been worth having.

So often these days, Sandra examined her daughter for that insidious self-destructiveness that she herself had possessed as a teenager. She was terrified she would find it, she looked and looked. And now she saw things so clearly. Cara wasn't like Sandra at all, she was like Jay—kind, sweet, serious, reliable Jay. She was generous and loving and morally strong, like her father. Easy-going, dependable, loving, and, when necessary, even courageous...

But thank goodness she had her mother's brains.

"How are you doing?" Sandra asked.

Cara looked up from whatever reverie she was in and gave her mother a small smile. "I'm fine. How are you?"

"It's still four hours to the lob. Do you want to get some sleep?"

"I don't think I could."

For a moment they simply looked at one another. Sandra could have wept for all the trust and love she saw in that sweet face.

"Honey," she said, "I never asked how you got on with Jay." Cara gave a shrug.

"Did you get much chance to talk?" Sandra pressed.

"Yeah, I suppose. He's all right."

As much as she loved her daughter, this process of having to extract information in small, vague drips, was something she would not miss when Cara finally grew out of her teens. "I bet he was surprised to see you."

"He didn't freak or anything. Not much. He's got a nice flat."

"Yes? Near where he works, I bet. Was there a Mrs. Jay Kennedy?" She hadn't meant to ask that, although, to be honest, it was something she'd often wondered about over the years.

Cara looked scandalized. "Mum! You're not thinking of getting back with him after all this time. That would be so... weird."

"No!" Sandra was equally scandalized. And then it struck her that, if the slightest possibility of such a thing existed, it would invalidate all the choices she had made since the day she discovered she was pregnant with Cara. All those years she had denied Jay the knowledge of his daughter, all those men and potential women friends she'd spurned so that she could keep Cara out of sight and safe from her enemies, it would all seem like cruelty and irrational self-denial if she were to get together with Jay again. Yet here was the possibility. The worst had happened. If she and Cara and Jay survived, a new kind of life might need to be negotiated. Of course, there was also a major obstacle to any kind of reconciliation. "He must really hate me," Sandra said.

"He seemed OK with it."

Sandra doubted that was the case. Her daughter probably didn't know how to read Jay's "brave face".

"Do you hate me, now you've met him and you've—you know—seen what you've been missing? Do you think I should have let him know about you?"

She waited in an agony of hope while Cara chewed it over. "He said he might not be a cop any more. soon."

It wasn't the exoneration Sandra had wanted. "Because of you?"

"I don't think so." She suddenly brightened. "You were right about him dropping everything and coming after you. It must be nice to inspire such devotion in men."

Sandra shook her head, feeling leaden. "No, not really. Sometimes it's hard to cope with the guilt."

She puffed out her cheeks and blew out a big sigh as she sank back into her chair. She didn't want to go on with the conversation. She should never have started it. It was a distraction, and it hurt. On the other hand, she didn't want Cara to just sit there and fret for the next four hours.

"Tell you what. Why don't you tell me everything that happened to you from the minute you heard I was missing, while I get on with untangling this spaghetti code?"

So Cara began telling the story, and Sandra listened with half an ear. At one point, she almost interrupted to say, "I think your father was the only man who ever really loved me," but she stopped herself and let Cara talk on.

* * * *

"I could have killed him when he dropped the gun and that thug charged at him." Cara was now laughing toward the end of her story. Sandra could tell that her daughter was proud of Jay's clumsy heroics. Her affectionate tone filled her with warmth. If Jay had helped raise Cara, they'd probably have been very close. Sandra might even have been jealous of their special bond. It was a curious idea, and not an unpleasant one. For a mad moment, she wished the machine she was working on could actually change the past. She wished that she might go back to the day in the institute when they told her she was pregnant, the day she had wrapped her arms around herself and thought, *Oh God, how can I keep my baby safe?*

Sandra realized Cara had stopped speaking. "Honey?" Her daughter's eyes were wide and her gaze fixed at a point on the floor. She looked like she was about to cry. "What is it?"

Cara licked her lips in a quick, nervous gesture and frowned. "It's that man. The one that Jay shot. A load of people started shouting and firing their guns, and Jay had to run for it. The bloke who'd been untying me ran after him too. But they left the wounded man on the floor in the room with me. I was tied up and I couldn't do anything." She seemed to be struggling with her words. "Jay shot him in the hip, and he was bleeding and bleeding. He must have hit an artery or something because there was just tons of blood, and the bloke sort of squirmed about in it, getting weaker and weaker. I screamed and screamed for help, but no-one came until it was too late. And then a stupid old woman came and she didn't know what to do. But he was dead by then, anyway."

Sandra went to her daughter and wrapped her arms around her.

"I know he was going to hurt Jay," Cara went on. "I know it's us or them. Only…"

"I know, darling. I know."

Footsteps marched into the room. Sandra looked up to see Polanski and two armed men crossing the floor towards them. There had already been three guards in the room. Now there were five. Polanski was growing more paranoid as the moment for the lob approached.

"Have you finished the work?" His tone was gruff and challenging.

"Hello, *Mein Führer*," Sandra replied, stepping away from Cara. "Come to see how the final solution is progressing?"

One of Polanski's bodyguards went straight to Cara and put a gun against her head. Polanski was taking no chances.

"Funny you should mention that," said Polanski. "Do you know there were six million Jews living in America when the Lord's True Path Party took power? Would you like to guess how many there are now? Can't guess? Well, it's zero. That's the official figure. There was a period of enforced conversions—just like they used to have in Europe under the Inquisition. Then came the voluntary repatriations. You might have seen the news pictures when you were a child? Huge cruise ships, massively overcrowded, sailing to the Middle East to dump them where Israel used to be. The rest, the ones whose 'conversions' didn't take, were moved to the labour camps and were no longer counted on official censuses. It happened to the Muslims too—only in smaller numbers, of course—and to the Hindus, the Buddhists, every non-Christian religion."

He was pacing up and down like a caged animal. "The Idolators—Catholics, you probably call them—were a special case. They were allowed to remain free and unmolested for a limited period, to enable their gradual re-education. They weren't allowed to practice their religion, of course, because it was blasphemous. They proved very stubborn, and it looked like the Jewish thing was about to start up all over again, but the Pope gave them special dispensation to worship according to the dictates of the Lord's True Path without their souls being damned to Hell, and that seemed to solve the problem."

Sandra thought the whole lot of them should be under psychiatric care. "What's your point, Napoleon? You think killing millions of people for the sake of your revolution is somehow better than killing them for the sake of religion? Is that it?"

He stopped pacing, rigid with rage. "I thought you'd understand. I thought you might have some feeling of compassion for all those people out there."

"What the hell do you care what I think? I'm just your instrument, aren't I? Another living tool to be picked up or tossed aside depending on whether you can use me. Like all these poor deluded bastards playing soldier for you."

Polanski turned his back on her, apparently struggling to control himself. It dawned on Sandra why he kept trying to explain himself. It was because he liked her. He thought she was OK. An educated, reasonable person, the kind of person he might expect his future America to be peopled with. And her relentless condemnation of him showed him how that future America would see him—dedicated and self-sacrificing, perhaps, but hideously misguided, monstrously callous, criminally insane, exactly the kind of demonic figure he did not want to become.

Well, tough.

"Did you just drop by to give me another lecture on how enlightened you are, or did you want something?"

He turned back to face her, rigidly self-controlled, and stepped up to the console. "Show me the lob parameters. Convince me everything's exactly the way it should be."

Sandra was prepared for this. She opened displays, pulled up data, explained what everything did. Every number Polanski saw was consistent with the lob he wanted, even the date of the splashtarget. It took a long time. He made her go over it again and again until he understood how the many variables related to one another.

"Those variances are still large," he said, scowling.

"I've still got a couple of hours. They'll be better."

"I will check."

"You do that."

He stomped out as abruptly as he had stomped in, his bodyguards in tow.

* * * *

"I didn't know you could do all this."

"What?"

"Build a time machine."

Sandra smiled weakly and then pushed back from the console. She squeezed her eyes shut, exhausted. When she moved her head the world had a noticeable lag in catching up. She'd had a few hours sleep the night before last and had been on a physical and emotional roller coaster ever since. The past few hours of programming and troubleshooting the rig had required the last dregs of her energy.

"I didn't know you were such a badass either."

"You know I'm in the karate club at the uni."

"Yeah, but I thought that was like your "keep fit" class, you know how Sonja's mum goes to pilates twice a week? I didn't know you could, like, kill great big men with your bare hands."

Sandra gave a wry grin. "It comes in handy once every sixteen years or so."

"But the time machine stuff…"

"They're called displacement rigs. No-one calls them time machines."

"You always told me you were a technician in the Direct History group. You always made it sound really boring, like you were the one who plugged the computers together for the bigwigs."

It was true. Just another piece of misdirection in Sandra's grand plan to keep the wool pulled over everybody's eyes. "Yeah, well. I didn't want you telling all your friends your mum was a cool teknik. I'd have told you more if you'd asked. Fortunately, you never showed any interest in what I did."

Cara's frown suggested she didn't much like that idea. "It's like I don't really know you at all. I mean, you told me about being an orphan and all, and about the foster homes, and how you fell in with a bad crowd, and that, but you never told me you were the one who saved London."

"Who told you that load of old nonsense?"

"Jay did. He said you stopped a brick called Sniper from killing Lenin in the British Museum in 1902. I mean, holy crap, Mum. It's like I've lived with a stranger all my life."

Sandra rubbed tired eyes and ran her fingers through her tangled hair. "We should probably talk about this later, honey. It's nearly time for the lob and this conversation is going to take a while, I think. Look, I promise you, the mother you think you know... that's me. My job is pretty mundane most of the time, I don't kick the arses of big tough guys except in the dojo during competition fights—and, most of the time, they kick mine, I assure you—and if I did some stupid, dangerous things when I was a kid, believe me, none of them were the least bit glamorous and I regret just about everything."

Cara opened her mouth to argue but gave up and flopped back in her chair. "All right. Later. If there even is a later."

"There will be. Trust me. I—"

Footsteps drummed in the corridor and the door burst open. Polanski and his bodyguard marched in. There were more of them this time. Two went straight to Cara and pointed guns at her. Another two went to Sandra. They grabbed her by the arms, yanking her out of her chair, dragging her away from the control desk.

"What the hell are you doing, Polanski? You know you can't operate that thing without me."

"Shut up."

There were more people at the door. They carried in a man whose head was swathed in bandages and whose left arm was splinted. All that could be seen of his face were eyes so bruised that one was closed and the other barely open. She saw the good eye swivel towards her. The man seemed unable to walk, and his two assistants had to place him in the chair

Sandra had just vacated. Carefully, they pushed it up to the desk so that his one good arm could be lifted to rest near the sensor field.

"Matthew?" she asked, although it had to be him.

"Yo, bitch," he said, through a jaw bandaged shut.

Chapter 25

Waiting

The FBI treated Jay with exaggerated politeness, even though he plainly saw the suppressed anger in everyone he met. After his initial call to Special Agent Simmons, he'd heard nothing from the man. Given the way he was being treated, Jay assumed Simmons was in big trouble for letting him slip away. He felt sorry for his former minder, and several times tried to explain to people that it wasn't Simmons' fault.

They had him in an interview room and the wooden chair he sat on was becoming increasingly uncomfortable. He thanked the stars they'd let him go to the hotel to shower and change before bringing him in, otherwise he'd still be stewing in the mud and effluent of the Shanty which had penetrated every fibre of his clothing. People had come in to ask him questions. Lots of people. To every one of them he repeated, with as much urgency as he could, that Polanski was planning a timesplash, that it was going to be big, that they'd better evacuate the city, that they should mobilize everything they could and stop him.

He was hoarse from talking, and he'd had enough.

He went to stand in front of the two-way mirror—an

apparatus he'd only ever seen in very old 2D movies. "I want to see the Director now," he said to whoever was listening. "I want to speak to the European Ambassador, and I insist on calling my superiors in Brussels." He had a vague notion that the ambassador might have some means of airlifting herself out of harm's way. If so, he wanted to be on that flight—with Sandra and Cara. "I am a representative of the European Union and I insist on being treated with appropriate respect." Which Jay thought sounded a lot better than, "I'm just a police officer of no particular status who got sent here against his will and who would very much like to be somewhere else before the Apocalypse starts."

Nothing happened. He waited a few seconds then banged on the glass and repeated his message, trying to sound as much like an outraged visiting dignitary as he could.

Again, nothing happened, so he went to sit down on the bruising chair to consider his next move. After a few minutes, the door opened and Deputy Director English came in with another man. The man went to stand quietly against the wall while the Deputy Director eased himself into the chair opposite Jay.

"I'm terribly sorry, Chief Inspector, but the Director is busy at the moment. As you can imagine, the Bureau is taking your new intelligence very seriously and action is being planned even as we speak." He punctuated the news with a small smile that seemed completely disconnected from his words. "Arrangements are being made for you to call your people, and the European Ambassador is being located."

Jay was surprised—astonished, in fact—but tried not to seem it. "Thank you. And the evacuation? Has it begun?"

"There will be no evacuation. We wish to avoid panic." The deputy director raised his voice to override Jay's protests.

"It is considered far better that we attack Polanski's compound and prevent him from using his time travel machine. You will accompany us on the raid, I hope. You're the only person who knows exactly where this equipment is." He hesitated. "You will be pleased to hear that the Director has vetoed an earlier plan to send in helicopter gunships to destroy the compound." English, however, did not look pleased. "He believes there will be some advantage to seizing the time travel device and letting our technicians examine the way your… ah… Miss Malone has configured it for this 'long lob' you say they are planning."

Jay suppressed his objections. It was better in the short term that the FBI got hold of Sandra's work than that they blew her and Cara to pieces. As least the damned rig might help keep them alive.

"It's not really a compound as such," Jay said. He didn't really know what a compound was given the context, but English made it sound like some sort of fortified stronghold. "It's just another shanty, built out of odds and ends. A strong wind would blow it over. Frequently does, I gather."

"Good. That makes things easier."

"And it's full of women and children. People living there. It's their home."

English looked grim. "We're used to terrorists like Polanski hiding behind human shields. Don't worry, we know how to deal with the situation." He gave Jay an extended scrutiny. "So we can count on you joining us for the assault?"

"Of course. When do we leave?" He started to rise but English smiled again. "Oh, not for some time yet. These things take a while to organize, you understand."

* * * *

The Deputy Director took Jay to his own office to let him use the phone. Along the way, they passed a small group of men going in the opposite direction. They were all FBI agents, except for a very short man in a cowboy hat that he pulled down over his face as he went by.

Jay stared after him and English asked, "Do you know that man?"

"O'Dell? Yes, we met. What's he in for?"

English gave his disconnected smile. "Mr. O'Dell often drops in to supply us with information. After the death of the Reverend Duvalle, he came forward with some very interesting intel about the possible involvement of a terrorist group known as The Friends of Democracy. He's been tracking them for us for some time." A small frown crossed English's face as the implications of Jay recognizing O'Dell finally sank in. "Where did you say you met him?"

"In the Shanty. Some kind of local crime boss, isn't he?"

By then, English was looking very unhappy. "Yes, the kind of man who would know everything that goes on in his own territory. Like that Polanski had his headquarters there."

They reached English's office and the Deputy Director hastily showed him in. "Make yourself at home. The phone's on the desk. Would you excuse me a moment? There's something I need to attend to." He hurried off in the direction O'Dell had gone.

The office was large, but not as large or well-appointed as the Director's. Jay found the "phone" as promised—a compad sitting in a docking station. He started fiddling with it, trying to find directory inquiries. To his surprise, a man's face appeared in its tiny screen.

"Switchboard," the operator said.

"Sorry?"

"How may I connect you?"

"Oh. Thank you." He gave Kapellhof's name and location.

"Thank you, sir. Just one moment." The screen showed a short repeating animation of a country scene while Vivaldi thrummed and twittered over it. Jay listened to the music for a while wondering what to do. He'd just came to the conclusion that the device had malfunctioned when Kapellhof's face appeared.

"Jay?"

"Yes, sir."

"You just caught me. I was on my way out."

"What? Oh, er, sorry."

"You haven't reported for nearly two days and now this. Well?"

"I found Polanski."

"You found him? You're there as an adviser. What about the FBI?"

"Well… They know where he is now."

"And the woman? Malone? Is she alive?"

"Yes, sir. Well, she was a few hours ago. Polanski's got her again."

"Again?"

"It's a long story. He's got my daughter too. The thing is, sir, he's planning a timesplash."

"We knew that all along, didn't we? When and where?"

"That's just it. It's going to happen here in Washington, and it could happen any minute now."

"What?" If Kapellhof had been just a little distracted, Jay now had his full attention. "Good God. And the FBI is fully aware? They know everything you know?" He seemed to require reassurance.

"Yes, sir. They have a raid planned on Polanski's

headquarters. It's about ten kilometres away. I'm going with them to see if I can't get Ms. Malone and my daughter out of there."

To Kapellhof's credit, he didn't try to order Jay not to go. "How's the evacuation going? It must be chaos over there."

"No evacuation. They're trusting that they can stop Polanski before the lob starts."

"But surely…"

"They've got God on their side. That's probably what they're thinking. They've no doubt sent a task force of crack chaplains to the nearest church to pray for a good outcome."

"Are you all right, Jay?"

"Just feeling a bit vulnerable, sir. Look, if I manage to get Sandra and Cara away, is there anywhere I could take them where we could be extracted?"

"Extracted? I work for Europol, not the SAS."

"An airport? A dock? Even some place we could hide out for a while?" Jay was well aware that the FBI would be listening in on the call, but he needed somewhere safe to head for so that the three of them stood a chance of getting out of the U.S. If Polanski's splash happened, it wouldn't matter if anyone in Washington knew where they were heading— because Washington wouldn't exist any more. And, if Polanski was right and his splash started a revolution, America would not be a safe place for anybody.

Kapellhof regarded him in silence then said, "Remember that case we worked with the French police a couple of years ago?" Jay nodded. A splashteam in Paris had been using an American subsidiary of a French mining company to smuggle F2 generators from South America to a group in Toronto. "We did them a big favour, keeping their involvement quiet. I'll make a few calls. You know where their North American head office is, don't you?" Kapellhof had also seen the need for silence. "Well, go there. I'm sure you will be well received."

Jay wanted to say more but this was not the time.

There was a long silence then Kapellhof said, "Have you thought about your future yet, Jay? What you'd like to do next?"

The idea that he might have a future beyond the next few minutes or hours seemed almost laughable. "I haven't really had time to think about that yet, sir."

Kapellhof pursed his lips and nodded, which might have been a sympathetic acknowledgement, or it might just have meant that he expected no better from Jay. "I will call the commissioner and have him call the minister, get him to remind the Yanks that we'd like you and Ms. Malone back in one piece if possible. Is there anything else I can do for you?"

Jay slowly shook his head. "Thank you, sir."

As soon as he hung up, the office door opened and an FBI man poked his head in. *Coincidence?* "Deputy Director English and the European Ambassador are waiting for you in meeting room one, Chief Inspector."

* * * *

Ambassador Borghese was a rather svelte, fifty-something, Italian woman who made Deputy Director English look a little shabby and uncomfortable. She turned sharp, appraising eyes on Jay as he smiled deferentially and bumbled into the room, feeling a little shabby and uncomfortable himself. She rose and shook hands with him, making English rise too. It struck Jay that the EU might have sent a female ambassador here on purpose, just to discomfit everybody she dealt with.

"You wished to see me, Chief Inspector?" A raised eyebrow gave her gaze an ironic tinge. *I am going to play along*, it seemed to say, *but I find myself a trifle amused that I should be summoned by such an insignificant person as yourself.* She turned her aristocratic smile on English. "Apparently, it is a matter of extreme importance." Her tone said that she had already grown to doubt it.

Jay did not blame her at all. In truth, he had not expected the FBI to drag an ambassador across town for him, and he'd mainly demanded to see her to make himself sound important and to create as much fuss as possible. However, now she was here, he could at least warn her—and maybe try to line up some kind of escape route.

"Madam Ambassador," Jay began, at which point she sat down and so did English. Finding himself alone on his feet, Jay pulled over a chair and also sat. "You and your staff are in extreme danger."

Her eloquent eyebrows arched into a frown, which she turned on English. "Danger?"

Jay pressed on. "There is a terrorist in this town—"

"A terrorist? Has there been a threat to the embassy?" she asked English. "The threat is to the whole city," Jay said, beginning to feel a certain irritation with this pompous woman. At least he had her attention now. "Zadrach Polanski is about to create a timesplash big enough to wipe out the whole of the Washington metropolitan area."

"But that's millions of people," the Ambassador said, forgetting to aim it at English.

The Deputy Director jumped in. "The danger is minimal, I assure you. I'm assembling a team right now. Polanski will never be allowed to unleash this terrible weapon."

"Then why am I here?" Ambassador Borghese asked.

"Because the threat is imminent," said Jay before English could reply. "It could happen at any moment. I'm sure you have emergency procedures in case of terrorist attacks. I suggest you invoke them right now. Get yourself and your people out of Washington. Polanski will probably strike at the Capitol, or the White House, or somewhere else very central. If Beijing and Mexico City are any guide to what we can expect, you need to be fifteen kilometres from the centre when the backwash hits. Twenty would be better."

"Beijing and…" She turned to English, aghast. "Is this true?"

"The Chief Inspector has recently been a captive of the terrorists," English said. "He is still a little overwrought." He turned to Jay. "I'm sure, when you get yourself some sleep, things won't seem so bad."

"What?" Jay couldn't believe what he was hearing. "With all due respect, Deputy Director—" He stopped himself saying the many things that were on the tip of his tongue and instead tried to focus on what really mattered. "You really are planning an assault on Polanski's headquarters? That isn't just you trying to humour. me?"

"Of course, of course. But, really, there's no need to go alarming people. Our analysts believe we have days, if not weeks before Polanski could get your… ah… Miss Malone to build him a time travel machine."

"Your analysts? Your analysts?" For a moment Jay was speechless. "The same analysts who thought Polanski was building a dirty bomb? Those analysts? And what do these morons use for intelligence? Star charts? The Book of Revelation?"

"Chief Inspector!" the Ambassador snapped. "Do I have to remind you that you are a guest of the FBI and a representative of your own department?"

Jay opened his mouth to tell the stupid woman what place diplomatic protocol had in the current proceedings but decided not to waste any more time. "You need to get yourself and your staff out of Washington right now. The rig they've built is complete and it's ready to go. You," he turned to English. "When is this raid of yours planned for? Tell me."

"Chief Inspector, I really think—" English began.

"And I really think that if anyone survives to tell the tale, yours will be the name of the bureaucrat who screwed around while terrorists blew up his nation's capital. Now, when is that raid?"

English sighed and looked at his watch—a gesture Jay had never seen before, except in old vids. "We leave in one hour. We attack Polanski's compound at twelve noon. Are you happy now?"

"No!" There seemed to be no getting through to the man. "We should go right now. Right now."

The Deputy Director's irritation finally got the better of him, despite the Ambassador's presence. "Chief Inspector, I have tried to be patient with you, and to accommodate your wishes. However, you have been nothing but a burden on this investigation since the moment you arrived. My report to your superiors will reflect this." Perhaps he saw Jay preparing to jump in with an objection because he added, "Yes, you stumbled on Polanski and for that we are very grateful. However, that means your work here is done. We'd like your assistance with the raid but, after that, you're on the next flight home. Understood?"

Jay nodded. "If there's a working airport anywhere around DC in two hour's time, I will be more than happy to be there."

English stood up. The meeting was over. "Chief Inspector, there is an agent outside who will take you through the preparations for the raid. Do not try to run away again. Madam Ambassador, it was an honour. to meet you. Now, if you will excuse me…" All smiles, he shook hands with Ambassador Borghese and left the room. He was replaced immediately by another FBI man there to escort the ambassador out.

Before she went, Ambassador Borghese looked down her long nose at Jay and said, "It's a pity you did not put more effort into dealing professionally with your American counterparts. I am personally very disappointed."

Jay was so far beyond amazed at the way the meeting had gone that he didn't react at all. Wearily, he said, "You need to evacuate the embassy and warn anyone else who will listen to get away from Washington. Don't be fooled by the complacency you see in this building. These people are all high priests of the church of damned fools. Maybe they trust that God won't turn the city into a mass of twisted metal and powdered rubble."

"Trust in God is nothing to sneer at, Chief Inspector. I myself am a devout Catholic."

Jay threw up his hands. "Of course you are. Tell me, is it still a mortal sin if you commit suicide through sheer stupidity? Or how about murdering all your colleagues through wilful ignorance, will that send you to Hell? Think about it."

She was already marching to the door, pretending not to hear him, but she stopped on her way out. "It's Chief Inspector Jason Kennedy, isn't it? I must get it right so that I can mention you to the Minister when we next speak."

"Better call him right now, then," Jay shouted after her

retreating footsteps. "Because the clock's ticking."

He flopped into the nearest chair and closed his eyes. I'd better hope Washington does go up in flames now, he told himself, because otherwise that's the end of my career in the police.

And yet, it didn't really matter. All that mattered was saving Sandra and his daughter. After that, he didn't care. He'd given his life to the pursuit of timesplashers ever since his friend had died in a backwash eighteen years ago. He'd served in MI5 and then in the Temporal Crimes Unit at Europol. But the TCU had done its job and was closing down. The bricks that had plagued Europe two decades ago were behind bars, lying low, or dead. The technology was still out there—there was no way to put that genie back in its bottle—but it was mostly in the hands of governments and their oppositions now. It had all moved up to a level beyond Jay's expertise. And, truth be told, beyond where he cared any more.

With the bricks shut down, Jay's personal quest was over. It had been over years ago, really. And now he was here, sitting alone in a doomed city, waiting for the modern-day equivalent of the Inquisition to rescue the only two people on Earth—apart from his mother—who mattered at all to him; the woman he'd once loved with a brief, adolescent passion, and a girl he barely knew but who had a confusing genetic claim to his devotion.

In a wild moment of fantasy, he imagined them together, in an old farmhouse in Provence, perhaps, eating cheese and olives and drinking a cheap local wine out of tumblers, laughing in the Mediterranean sunshine as they grew intimate and comfortable with one another.

"Sir?"

It was his new minder at the door. Jay waved a delaying hand at him and tried to recapture the image of his daydream, with no success. More likely, his future was in a flat in London, working for the Metropolitan Police, and signing up for an online dating service when the loneliness became too unbearable.

If he survived beyond today.

He stood up and joined his minder.

"There's a briefing in five minutes for the assault team, sir." Jay nodded and let himself be led away.

Chapter 26

Polanski

Polanski made sure that Sandra and her daughter were soundly tied and well guarded, and that Matthew was able to operate the control computers with his uninjured hand, before going to see Peter.

The young man was propped up in bed with pillows but was still unable to move much. The woman who had been nursing him got up and left the room as Polanski came in. Peter's eyes met Polanski's and the boy smiled.

Polanski smiled back, although it was hard. "How are you feeling, Peter?" He didn't really need to ask since he'd been getting regular updates after that damned woman laid out the big lug.

"I've been better. What hit me? Must have been a train at least, way I'm feeling."

"Does the name Sandra Malone mean anything to you?"

"Sure, she's on your list for snatching a teknik over in Europe. Hey, you're still gonna take me, right? I'll be out of here in no time, you'll see."

"Don't excite yourself. I ain't going nowhere without you. You just try and get some rest and you'll be fine in no time."

Peter settled back in his pillows as if even that brief conversation had exhausted him. "I don't feel right, Zak. You always said my head's got rocks in it. I think maybe you were right after all."

Polanski took a seat beside the bed and put a hand on the boy's beefy shoulder. "I've said and done a lot of things I regret now, Peter. Number one is putting that woman's name on the list."

"Well, take her off, Zak. Ain't no harm done. Plenty more names to go after." Polanski shook his head. "Here we are sitting on the most powerful time machine in the whole country and we can't go back and change just one tiny thing. Now that's what I call irony. I can almost hear God slapping His thigh and laughing His head off."

"God ain't cruel, Zak. He's more like to weep over our misfortunes than laugh."

Polanski felt the admonition like a hand clutching his heart. "I'm sorry. I don't mean to talk like that, but I've got a lot of grief weighing on my soul today. I just don't know how I'm going to carry a load like that and still do what I have to do."

Peter tried to get up, but Polanski easily held him in place with a gentle pressure from his hand. "Whatever you need, Zak. You know I'll do anything for you."

"I know. I know." His throat closed on a sob and choked off any more talk for the moment. When he was able, he said, "I haven't looked out for you right, Peter. I should have watched you better, worried more about how you were doing. I've been so wrapped up in getting things done."

Peter reached out for Polanski's arm and held it weakly. "You been like a father to me, Zak. You always looked out for me."

"Hush now. You try and get some rest. I'll just sit here with you."

He turned away so that Peter wouldn't see the tears flowing down his cheeks.

Some father, he thought. Some friend. Taking the boy to Europe had been a bad idea, although Polanski hadn't known it at the time. Looking back, he could see it had started in Liverpool. They'd walked from the docks to Lime Street Station and Peter had been big-eyed and excited at first. The streets were full of cars—not old wrecks either, but smart ultramodern models—and the buildings were clean and bright, with shop fronts full of amazing luxury goods. And the people... The people were healthy and clean and dressed in beautiful clothes. Polanski didn't see a single invalid, not so much as a harelip or a pock-marked face.

"They don't have polio here," Polanski explained when Peter marvelled at it. "Or TB, or smallpox. People can afford vaccinations and decent health care." When his companion didn't reply, he said, "This is what we're fighting for, Peter. America was like this once. Better than this. It will be again."

Even so, as he walked through the streets—sidewalks that weren't cracked and crumbling, pavements without a single pothole—he couldn't help thinking they'd stepped off the ship into a futuristic utopia. They'd both flinched and laughed at themselves when the first 3D holo-ads had popped out of the air to beckon them into a shop, and they'd both gaped at the first telepresence bot they saw travelling among the other pedestrians and chatting to a human friend. People seemed happier, faces were open and curious, not closed and anxious. The atmosphere filled Polanski with a renewed urgency and determination. It was only on reflection that he realized how silent and withdrawn Peter had become.

They'd met friends at the station. England was full of people who wanted to help restore democracy to the U.S. Some of them did more than just talk about it. They promised to get Polanski and Peter to London where they could spend a day or two preparing for their task, and then they would provide the van for them to travel up to Norwich. They arranged for the flight to the Netherlands too, for after the abduction.

"What do you think of the girls?" he'd asked Peter in London, nudging him and grinning. He'd seen his young friend ogling the women for the past couple of days.

"They all look like whores," the young man said. "Or worse."

"They can look like they want here," Polanski said, at the time not seeing the boy's surliness as anything more than embarrassment. "They're free. Imagine that, Peter. Free to be what they want and do what they want. No-one to call them names, or beat them up, or rape them, or kill them for not doing what they're told." It was a dizzying prospect. It filled Polanski with awe.

Peter said, "I don't get it. If they're so free, why do they want to look like whores?"

And Polanski had laughed, thinking it was a joke.

"Zak?" Polanski turned back to his friend on the bed. "What hit me? I mean, something sure hit me hard. I feel like my insides are all hollowed out."

"Don't worry about it. You'll be fine in a couple of days. Just try to rest."

What else could he tell him? That he'd been kicked in the head by a girl he didn't even remember meeting? That, even if Polanski told Peter who she was, he'd have forgotten again in half an hour? That he was most likely dying of brain injuries, but the medical care that might save him was reserved for the super-rich? That none of it mattered a whole lot since the lob was just a little over an hour away and everyone for many miles around would be dead soon?

"Peter, would you mind if I just got down on my knees here and said a little prayer for your safe deliverance? You wouldn't be embarrassed?"

"I ain't dying am I, Zak?"

Polanski made himself smile. "I just want to put in a word for you with the Big Guy. Our medics are doing what they can, but it might help just to say a couple of words."

"Can't hurt, I suppose."

Polanski knelt beside the bed and clasped his hands together.

"Zak?"

He opened his eyes and looked into Peter's troubled face.

"I can't remember getting here. We was over in Boston making plans for the trip. Then suddenly I'm on my back in the Shanty."

"A knock on the head can do that sometimes."

"Yeah. I guess. You'll wait for me, won't you? You won't go to England without me?"

"Don't worry. I ain't going to leave this building without you right there with me."

A smile flickered in the boy's face. "I sure was lucky the day I met you, Zak. You can thank God for me when you start your prayers. OK?"

Polanski nodded and bowed his head.

* * * *

"We need a word."

The little group of men blocked Polanski's way, filling the narrow corridor between rooms. As soon as he saw them, he knew it was trouble.

"What's up, Jed?"

The man looked scared as hell to be confronting Polanski but, for some reason, he was the spokesman for this little delegation and backing down now was not an option.

"We need to talk about this timesplash thing."

Polanski took his time and looked at the faces of the men. These were not hotheads or crazies. They were people he knew and trusted. At the back of the group was Ira Frohock. Ira was an ambitious man, and fancied himself as a future leader of the country. But Polanski had other ideas. The people he had in mind to found the new Republic were all safe and far from Washington. If anyone had put these guys up to it, Ira was the man.

"So talk," he told Jed. "But can we keep our voices low? Out of respect for Peter."

Jed glanced back the way Polanski had come. "Right. How is he?"

"He just died, Jed. Thanks for asking."

The man started as if he'd been slapped. "I don't mean to show no disrespect, not at a time like this, Zak."

Polanski was bone weary. And he didn't have time for any of this. "What's this all about?" He locked eyes with Frohock. "Ira? You got anything to say?"

"Why don't you hear Jed out?" Frohock said in his deep, slow voice.

More games. He turned to the spokesman. "All right, Jed, spit it out. I'm on a timetable here."

Jed swallowed, licked his lips, and plunged in. "People been overhearing things, Zak, about the timesplash. That foreign bitch who killed Peter, she's said things that don't square with things we been told."

"What kind of things, Jed?"

"Things about how big this splash thing is going to be. Shoot, Zak, you always made it sound like we got plenty of time to get clear. You always said it was aimed at the folks in DC. They was the ones who'd get their asses kicked, not our own people. Now there's talk of destruction out past the Beltway, maybe the whole Metro Area. How're people going to get clear, Zak, if they've only got an hour from when you set off?"

"Who's spreading these tales, Jed?"

"I—I don't want to get anybody in trouble." The question seemed to have thrown him, but he rallied. "Everybody here's heard the talk, Zak. That's why we come to ask you about it."

People nodded. The point was made. Now they were waiting for Polanski to speak. He took the opportunity to look into their faces one more time. It might be the last time he'd see most of them. He could tell them the truth now and there would be a chance for them to save themselves and their families. The temptation was powerful, almost too much to resist. But he needed everyone to stay put so that nobody in the Government got spooked and ran. Even if that meant he was talking to a bunch of dead men.

He took a long, deep breath. "The lob's in less than an hour. Soon as it starts, I don't need anyone to guard the place or keep things looking normal. It's going to take an hour for me to go back and do what I have to do and then it will be another fifteen minutes after I get back before the backwash hits. That's an hour and fifteen minutes you've got to get out of here. Me? I've got just fifteen minutes. Think about that.

Fifteen minutes. Would I leave myself just fifteen minutes if I didn't think there was a chance I'd make it?"

"Seems to me," Frohock said from the back, "that you might just be willing to sacrifice yourself, thinking that's what had to be done."

Polanski could have strangled the man. "Damn right I'm willing to sacrifice myself. I reckon there ain't a single man or woman in this whole place wouldn't lay down their lives in a heartbeat for freedom. There's not a true American patriot anywhere in this whole beautiful country who wouldn't gladly give his life to set our people free. Am I right?" People nodded and muttered their agreement.

"Did I ever tell you there wouldn't be risks? Did I ever tell you the path to freedom would be easy? Don't we all live with the knowledge, every day of our lives, that the Feds and the SOBs and every armed thug on the Government payroll might come crashing in here with their tanks and their guns and kill every last one of us? Don't we? And does it scare us? Hell yes! And does it stop us dreaming of freedom and working for freedom? Hell no!"

He could see he had them stirred. He could see they were good people. If they thought about it the right way, they'd gladly do the right thing—the only thing that would shake this country loose of its chains.

"Listen," he said. "I know there's been some wild talk. I know that foreign hell-cat has got people feeling edgy with her crazy prophecies of doom. I know we're standing on the verge of a revolution, a civil war no less. It's enough to rattle the nerves of the bravest of men. But I also know that no-one here is a coward. Every man who has come this far with me has already proven his mettle a dozen times over. So this is what I say, if anyone wants to head on out of here, to go now and make sure you're safe, you just go right ahead and leave us. I won't think you any the worse for it. Nobody will. You won't hear a single reproach from me. If that's what you want, you go right ahead."

There was a silence. Once more, he scanned their faces. "I'm staying," one man said.

"Me too," said another, then another, until they were all clamouring to let him know their resolve. He smiled and thanked them. They shook his hand and patted his back and stood aside to let him through. He noticed Frohock had gone. The would-be leader had slipped quietly away while Polanski had been speaking. It was no big deal. There was nothing he could do about it now anyway.

* * * *

"Well?"

Matthew raised his head to look Polanski in the eye. The teknik was sagging, his head wobbling a little, his breath laboured and uneven. When he spoke, his words were forced out between teeth clamped together by a too-hasty repair to his broken jaw.

"You were right. The bitch screwed with the parameters. Disguised the real settings. She planned to send you to 1796."

Polanski looked across at Sandra. Even bound hand and foot to a chair and wearing tattered clothing, the woman was stunningly beautiful. The look she returned was serene and dignified, even though she must have heard what Matthew said, must now know her last attempt to thwart him had failed. It was impossible to look at her without feeling admiration, and, he had to admit, desire. If she'd worked with him, if she'd seen the necessity of what he had to do, perhaps they would have found a way to bring him back safely. He had known for a long time now the impossibility of building the country he dreamed of with the death of so many on his conscience. He would be a monster and monsters could not also be saviours. Yet, with a woman like that at his side, what miracles of redemption might not have been possible?

He looked away sharply, ashamed of himself. For her to have helped him, she would have needed to be a completely different person. Not his Eva Braun but his Evita Perón.

"Check it again," he told Matthew. "Look deeper. She's got something else in there, something you haven't found yet."

Matthew looked at him, breathing heavily for a few seconds. "I can't do any more."

"You must."

"I'm fucking dying here."

Polanski leaned in close so only Matthew could hear him. "If you want that ride out of DC, you will do exactly what I tell you. So stop wasting your energy arguing with me, find whatever else she's hidden in there, and fix it."

He turned away from Matthew's malevolent eyes and stepped across to the platform where the plastic sphere stood. It seemed to Polanski that he was already inside a bubble, its walls perfectly clear but impenetrable. They all watched him, all the people he'd condemned; cool, judgemental Sandra; the bored, watchful guards; the child, nervous as a thoroughbred colt.

There was no ride arranged for Matthew, or for anybody. After the attack on Peter, he'd sent two men to disable every vehicle his followers owned. His last words in this life would be lies, bullying commands, evasions, and covert betrayals, but he would not let a crowd of fleeing, hysterical cowards give the Government even one hour's warning.

And that woman was going to die.

There were forty minutes to go. Was there really a point in waiting? He could go now, step onto the platform, push the hatch closed, and give Matthew the nod. He longed for the moment when he could act, for the waiting to be over. But he stayed still and studied the sphere. Forty more minutes. He must wait. He must give Matthew a chance to be sure the woman had not further sabotaged the lob.

It was good that Peter had gone before him. It was good the boy would not be driving through the city when the backwash hit, fighting for his life as the roads buckled and the buildings fell. It was good, truth be told, that Polanski would not have Peter's survival on his conscience. It had been weak of him to create a chance for the boy. It was better to be fair and play no favourites. Who was he to say Peter should live while the rest should die? Far from being the villain, that damned woman had been an unwitting instrument of God, saving Polanski's soul from the blemish of that one inexcusable act of compassion.

Without realizing it, he had sunk to his knees and bowed his head in prayer once again.

Chapter 27

Countdown

"Forever and ever, Amen."

The briefing was without doubt the strangest Jay had ever attended. Certainly, beginning and ending a pre-raid briefing with a prayer was unusual. The Deputy Director had moved straight from the prayer to a short sermon on the theme of discovering the will of God, quoting extensively from the Psalms. Jay had that old down-the-rabbit-hole feeling for a while, until he realized the sermon was probably the FBI's equivalent of a pep talk before the big raid.

The meat of the briefing was recognizable enough, though. Aerial photographs of the Shanty were projected on the wall. Graphical overlays appeared, indicating where cordons would be set, and where and when various armored and infantry units would penetrate the scruffy maze of streets. There would be air cover from a small fleet of drones, and an artillery unit with mobile missile batteries would set up outside the Shanty in case the "compound" had to be pounded to splinters in a hurry. But the main assault would be led by mobile light armour. with armored personnel carriers to take nearly a thousand troops into the "battle zone."

These guys were not messing about. Polanski's ragtag mob—probably no more than a couple of hundred if you counted the women and children—armed with Brazilian AK-45s and an assortment of antiques, didn't stand a chance. It made Jay increasingly concerned as to how he was going to get Sandra and Cara out safely. Although the Deputy Director flashed up photos of both of the "civilian hostages," Jay was less than happy with the comment that the women should be rescued, "if conditions permit their safe extraction."

When English asked for questions, Jay was back in the rabbit hole. A debate broke out over some fine point of the Church's theology, which seemed to exempt the FBI from all sins associated with inflicting pain and death, versus another which required that the prosecution of God's work should involve as little suffering as was necessary. Biblical quotations came thick and fast from both sides. It went on until English called them to order. He was smiling, as were many others, clearly enjoying the debate. He said they'd just have to take their best shots and let God decide where the bullets fell, which got a good laugh and even a ripple of applause.

The final prayer was said with full solemnity, however, after which Jay was taken down to the armoury. He was told to put on a jump suit and body armour. and to collect his weapon. Everyone else was handed assault rifles and buzz guns, pistols, knives and clubs, but Jay was given a stunner. He didn't argue. Back home, police raids like this would be undertaken exclusively with stun weapons. They were accurate and effective and left the bad guys alive to face interrogation and trial. Leaving anyone alive at all was clearly not a priority for his FBI colleagues. "You know how to work one of these, sir?" his minder asked, handing over the weapon. "Just point it and pull the trigger. Recharges in no time. No recoil or nothing."

"I've used one before."

"It's got a targeting spot just like a real gun," the minder went on, oblivious. "Put that on the perp—it don't really matter where—and squeeze off the shot. It's got settings on the back, see?" He showed Jay a little dial that had three settings, illustrated by little pictures. The lowest setting was a man's silhouette, arms and legs twisted, with sparks coming off it. The middle setting was a man flat on the ground with what could have been wisps of smoke coming off him. The final setting was a skull and crossbones. The dial was turned to the skull.

"You can kill people with this?" Jay asked, shocked.

His minder was equally shocked. "Sure. We wouldn't send you out there with no kind of protection, sir."

"No, of course not." Jay surreptitiously turned the dial down to the minimum setting. He dropped the stunner into its shoulder holster and hoped he wouldn't need to use it.

They took a lift down to a sub-basement where the vehicles were waiting. Row upon row of armored personnel carriers, painted light grey, with "FBI" on the sides and a black crucifix on the front, stood in the artificial light. Each one was the height of a small lorry, and considerably wider and heavier. Each had eight massive wheels that raised the vehicle high above the road and revealed the smooth "keel" of its armored belly, designed to deflect explosions from beneath. The driver's windows were armored glass slits in the solid, chiselled snout. On the roof, accessed by a hatch, was a machine gun turret. A couple of big, black command and control trucks waited like sharks to lead away their swarm of remora fish. Agents bustled everywhere, finding their allocated vehicles and clattering in through the back doors.

"The tanks and guns are on their way from the barracks," the minder explained, although this had been mentioned at the briefing. "Same with the missile launchers. The drones will come in from Andrews Air Force Base."

"People seem to be in high spirits," Jay said.

"Yes, sir. We've been waiting to get Polanski in our sights for a very long time."

"There's not much chance of him being taken alive, is there?"

His minder looked at him and frowned. "There ain't a man in this building who don't know his duty in that respect, sir," he said, ambiguously.

The APC they put Jay in reminded him of old times—sitting in similar steel boxes, in uncomfortable body armour, in cities all over Europe. The smell of excited, nervous people and the thump of boots on steel floors was as familiar to Jay as his own quickening heart rate and the tension in his muscles.

"Nobody mentioned sweepers," he said to his minder, sitting next to him. On any raid he'd ever been on before, it was standard procedure to send the battle droids in first to bear the brunt of the opponent's fire and to soften up whatever defences they'd laid.

"What's that?" his minder asked, inadvertently explaining their absence.

It had been years since Jay had travelled with the foot soldiers on an outing like this. These days, he was either in the command and control vehicle, or he stayed back at the local police HQ and helped direct the action from there. The Deputy Director clearly wanted to keep him out of the decision-making loop and, probably, out of earshot. Sticking him in a van filled with troopers had the additional benefit that a whole bunch of armed men could keep an eye on him.

Angry at the idea, he got up and went to the front, stepping between booted feet in the vehicle's narrow aisle.

"I'm going to sit up here with the driver," he called back to his minder, climbing into the still-vacant passenger seat. It was a small act of rebellion and it also gave him slightly more freedom of movement in case he might need it at the other end.

"You'll be safer back here, sir."

"I'll be fine."

His minder was out of his seat, crouching in the aisle. "That's the navigator position, sir."

"Yeah, I know. Relax. I can follow the van in front as well as the next guy. I want a ringside seat for this little show." He looked back at the rest of the troops, all staring at him, and shouted, "We're going to kick Polanski's arse, right?" There was a loud chorus of agreement. He turned back to his minder. "So why don't you just sit down and let me enjoy it? I'll be happy to mention your cooperative attitude next time I speak to the Director, OK? Besides, it's a more comfortable ride in the front. You want me to be comfortable, don't you?"

Shaking his head in frustration, the minder sat down again. Grinning happily, Jay settled into his new seat.

* * * *

If glaring at the back of someone's neck could kill, Sandra would have sent Matthew to meet his maker long ago. In lieu of murder-by-telepathy, she had to make do with teasing the little shit relentlessly.

"Found it yet?" she'd shout, or, "Too clever for you, was I?"

Mostly, Matthew would ignore her, but now and then his temper would get the better of him and he'd shout back, "Will someone shut that fucking bitch up?" This would prompt one of the guards to shove her and say, "Shut up, bitch." No-one seemed to think of gagging her. With Polanski out of the room, his Merry Men appeared to lack any kind of initiative. Nevertheless, she kept a sufficient gap between taunts to avoid the idea from occurring to one of the bright sparks around her.

The problem was that there was no booby trap. Disguising the true date of the splashtarget was all she'd had time for before they'd dragged Matthew back into the room. Now all she could think of to do was to get the teknik so wound up about things that he'd recommend Polanski should abort the lob, or at least postpone it. Matthew's breathing was laboured and the man seemed ready to fall off his chair. There was a small chance that she could add enough to his stress level that he would finally keel over and Polanski would have to ask her to work the console.

She had struggled against her ties to the point where her guard had slapped her about a bit and pushed his gun in her face. There was no way she'd get free with him watching all the time. However, she had at least discovered that the wooden chair she was tied to was rickety enough to fall apart if she could give it a hard enough knock. But that wasn't much use either, unless she had both the opportunity to throw herself about the room and the time to untangle herself from the wreckage. She needed a distraction but, so far, she hadn't worked out how to get one.

For the thousandth time she regretted not having broken both Matthew's arms, or, better still, to have killed him when she had the chance. Next time, she would not be so humane.

And, always in her mind, gnawing at her reason, was the knowledge that Cara was sitting there beside her, silent, frightened, trusting.

The lob, of course, would be a distraction. A chance for her to get away. If nothing else, Matthew would kick up a fuss, demanding that they carry him off to safety. She didn't suppose they would. But she didn't have time to wait for the lob. She had to get away now, steal a car, and drive fast if she stood any chance of avoiding the backwash. She had about twenty minutes before the lob started, which meant there was about an hour and a half before the backwash hit. She realized she was straining against the ropes and forced herself to relax. She felt exhausted enough as it was without tiring herself further. She was hungry too, and dying for a pee. A turgid wave of old, tired anger rose inside her.

"You're all going to die, you stupid bastards!" she yelled. "Matthew's an arsehole. He has no idea what he's doing. The Shanty, DC, the whole Eastern Seaboard for all I know, is going to be rubble in about ninety minutes. You should shut that rig down now and smash the fucking thing. Polanski doesn't care—"

The guard hit her so hard across the back of the head that lights flashed across her vision. She heard Cara scream as the floor rushed up and smacked her in the head again. Cara was shouting, "Mum! Mum!" Sandra tried to reassure her, to say she was OK, but she couldn't get her voice to work properly. She lay on her side on the floor. Apart from Cara's sobbing and pleading for someone to help, there was silence. The heaving spinning tilt of the floor made her feel sick and she retched a puddle of thin bile that stank and made her heave again. *Lucky my stomach's empty*, she thought and retched again.

"Mum! Please say something," she heard Cara say, crazy with fear. "Why won't anybody help her?"

"I'm all right, darling," she said and this time she heard herself say it.

"No she's not," Cara said. "Get her up. She needs a doctor."

"Taste of her own medicine," said Matthew, through his bandaged-shut jaw.

Sandra had to admit the justice of what he said. She closed her eyes but it didn't stop the room spinning.

"Please, please help her," Cara said.

"Leave the bitch where she is," said Matthew.

Sandra, on the whole, favoured Matthew's point of view. Her puke stank and the floor was hard but the whole damned Shanty stank and she felt that, if she lost contact with the floor, she might just drift loose and float away like a balloon.

"What in God's name is going on here?"

Sandra cracked open an eye and saw Polanski's legs planted solidly on the heaving floor.

"She was mouthing off so I hit her," someone said.

Polanski bellowed back at the man, "Get out of here before I have you shot, you idiot. Get her off the floor."

"I'm fine," Sandra said, not wanting a fuss. She felt men grabbing her chair, taking her weight. They heaved her upright and set the chair back on its legs. The room whirled end over end and she threw up again.

"He hit her with his gun," Cara said. "She needs to go to a hospital."

"It's too late for that." Polanski's voice was firm, but not harsh. Sandra felt fingers on her chin as he lifted her head up.

Polanski's face swam in front of hers. "I'm sorry," he said, quite gently. "You'll probably be all right, given time."

"Time," she said. It was a cruel joke. An urgent thought pushed its way up to the surface, and she made herself focus on it. "Let my daughter go," she said.

He gazed steadily into her eyes but his face kept sliding away. He looked as if he really wanted to set Cara free. Even though she knew that he wouldn't, for a moment she felt a glimmer of hope.

"No! I'm not leaving you," Cara said.

Polanski blinked, let go of Sandra's chin, and stood up, wiping his hand on his trousers.

Sandra closed her eyes again and let her head fall forward. It was the end. If they untied her right now, she couldn't even stand up, let alone fight them. She heard Polanski speaking to Matthew.

"Nothing," said the teknik. "I couldn't find anything."

"Then we go ahead with the lob. Are you ready?"

"Sure. Starting the timer at…" There was a slight hesitation as he set the clock. "…ten minutes. Bricks to the stage, please."

"What?"

"Nothing. It's just something from the old days."

Sandra could almost see it, beautiful young men in their splashgear, strong and bursting with energy, the lights on them, the music pounding and the crowd screaming their adoration. There had been good times, innocent times… Well, maybe not good, or innocent, but better than this.

"Is this the revolution you wanted?" Cara shouted.

Sandra snapped out of her daze and turned to look at her daughter. Cara was flushed and angry, her lovely face wet with tears. Her words were directed at Polanski who was now standing on the platform, one hand resting on the loose plastic sheeting of the sphere.

"Is this the America you wanted to build?" Cara said. "A place where women are kidnapped and beaten? Where children are tied up and left to die? Where your friends and followers are just used up and thrown away? Is that what you want?" Sandra felt a sob in her throat. How did her little girl get to be such a brave, fierce woman?

"Are you listening to me, Polanski? Are you listening to anyone except the voices in your head? Because you're not Joan of Arc."

Polanski turned to face her and Sandra caught her breath at the look on his face.

"You're not even—"

"No!" Sandra said with all the strength she had. Cara looked at her, confused. "Darling, no more. He'll kill you. So just... No more, eh?"

She saw the pain and pity in her daughter's face. She saw her struggling not to cry as she said, "I don't know what to do."

Again, a sob almost choked her. "I love you, Cara."

Whatever Cara might have said in reply was lost as the girl broke down into helpless tears. Sandra turned her gaze slowly towards Polanski. He was standing on the platform, watching them with a zombie stare.

* * * *

Polanski turned away from the sobbing child and her glaring mother. They didn't matter any more. There was only one thing left to do in this life. After that... Well, he would face the judgement that was coming, confident that he had done all that he could.

He pushed his shoulders through the narrow hatch and climbed inside the clear plastic sphere. As he put his boot onto it, he hoped once more that the material was as tough as the engineers said it was. Just one small hole, anywhere, would end his dreams of a new Republic forever. He would suffocate and freeze in the void and his frozen corpse would be returned to the Shanty as a lesson in hubris.

He sat on the padded seat and pushed the hatch closed. It did not fasten, but the internal pressure would hold it closed and sealed throughout the trip. He hoped.

He picked up the mortar tube, the bipod legs, the heavy base, the mortar shell, the sights, the remote control unit, and he clutched them. He must not let them fly loose. If the landing was bad, they might break his bones, crush his skull. He practised wrapping his legs around the tube and the bipod. That's how he would hold them when he landed.

"One minute to lob," Matthew called out. The teknik sounded calm, like he'd done it a hundred times before. Polanski was not calm. His heart was thudding and his palms were sweating. He'd been in plenty of operations against the Government and its lackeys. He'd planted bombs, staged ambushes, robbed banks, assassinated Church leaders. He knew the symptoms of fear well. Only this time was worse. Could you die of fear? he wondered. Could your heart beat so hard it just burst?

"Thirty seconds to lob."

Thirty seconds? How had the countdown happened so fast? He held his heap of deadly weapons closer, even though he knew there was no need for it yet. He held his breath in a frightened anticipation of all his air being sucked away as the sphere ripped apart. He closed his eyes and prayed to God to let him live, to succeed, to make the splash whose ripples would be felt from sea to shining sea.

"Eight. Seven. Six."

What? So soon?

"Four. Three. See you in Hell motherfu—"

The light went out. The sphere inflated with a slap.

Chapter 28

Assault

There was already a contingent of the Sons of Joshua waiting. They blocked the Shanty gates on Jefferson Davis Highway to prevent anyone from entering or leaving. At the sight of the FBI convoy, they pulled aside the barricades. Jay could see expressions of grim satisfaction, sometimes outright jubilation, on the faces of the militiamen as his APC ground slowly past them. It wasn't just because Polanski was about to be killed or captured. He could tell from the chatter inside the vehicle that any chance to stick it to the godless scumbags in the Shanty was something the law enforcement agencies relished.

Jay checked the time. It was exactly noon and the assault was running late. Steering the big C-and-C trucks through the narrow Shanty streets was slowing things down even further. The structures were so flimsy that whenever one of the trucks clipped the corner of a building—which happened often—walls came down and roofs collapsed.

An outer and an inner cordon were being established within the Shanty to encircle Polanski's headquarters. The C-and-C trucks stayed at the outer cordon, while the mounted guns, the light tanks, and most of the APCs went on to the inner one. Jay's vehicle stayed back. It was almost ten minutes past twelve when it pulled up alongside the Deputy Director's truck and everybody got out.

Jay marched over to the command centre and tried to get in. Two agents at the door blocked him.

"The Deputy Director needs me in there to help direct the assault," he insisted, making enough noise to be heard inside.

His minder hurried up behind him. "I'm sorry, sir, but the Deputy Director asks if you wouldn't mind waiting out here for a while. The inner cordon won't be set up for at least another ten minutes. Can I get you a coffee? The mess truck's just arrived."

"Does no-one here understand the urgency of this mission?" He kept his voice loud so English could hear him. "We don't have time to do this by the book." A light drizzle began to fall. With a frustrated sigh, he stepped away from the two guards. To his minder, he said, "White with no sugar, please. I'm going to sit in the APC, out of the rain."

He climbed in the back and shut the door after him. He was all alone in the vehicle, which seemed much bigger without a dozen armored bodies inside it. He sat down and pulled off his helmet. The engine was still running, and the lights and heating were still on, so at least it was warm. He didn't know what a Washington DC autumn was like in the days before climate change, but if this one was anything to go by, cold and wet was now the norm.

It was hard to sit still. His body crawled and itched with the need to be moving, to get to the rig, to stop the lob. It could be happening right now. Hell, it could already have happened. While English arsed about lining up his soldiers like some kind of wargaming nerd, Polanski might already have unleashed a splash that would sweep them all from the board like the hand of God. *Which would be kind of ironic*, Jay thought.

If he'd been in charge, he would have sent in a small force of commandos. Polanski's defences were pathetic. Half-a-dozen well-trained men could have fought their way to the lob site and blown up the rig with minimal preparation. They could have done it hours ago. Hell, one man could have done it. He should have done it himself instead of going to the FBI. That was a stupid mistake. He should have just—

He should do it now. *Don't think about it*, he told himself as arguments and potential problems began to pop into his thoughts. *Just fucking do it.*

He put his helmet back on and rushed to the front of the APC. This time he climbed into the driver's seat. He'd seen how the thing was driven. There was nothing to it. It was even an automatic transmission. He revved it up, put it into drive, and hit the accelerator. Through the armored glass slit, he saw his minder, a coffee in each hand, leap out of the vehicle's way, his face a picture of shock and surprise. Jay threw the wheel around and skidded onto the muddy road, glad to find the APC a lot more stable than it looked.

"Jay", the Voice of Reason said into his ear. "You know that, however this goes, someone is going to end up shooting you."

"Shut up," he said out loud. "Or come up with a better idea." Hearing only silence, he floored the accelerator.

* * * *

Sandra and Cara were alone. Well, almost. Matthew was still at the control desk but he had slumped forward and seemed to be unconscious. The last thing Sandra remembered was Polanski winking out of existence and her guard bending down to her ear to say, "Enjoy the rest of your life, whore," before leaving with the others.

After that, she must have passed out.

"Cara?" Her daughter was lying on the floor, still tied to her chair, making no noise except when she took a deep, sobbing breath.

At the sound of Sandra's voice, she looked up sharply and said, "Mum? Oh God, Mum! I thought you weren't going to wake up again. I thought..."

"What are you doing down there?" Her head felt much clearer now, most of the wooziness having been replaced by sharp pain. The nausea had gone too.

"I tried to, you know, throw myself about a bit and break the chair, but I just sort of toppled over and then I couldn't do anything." She gave a short laugh, which quickly died. "Are you...? I mean, do you feel all right?"

Sandra could have cried upon hearing all the hope in her daughter's voice. "Much better, now." She checked her commplant for the time. "Christ, we've got to get out of here." There was still a chance. They had an hour to get away from the centre of the splash. If she could get free, find a car, drive like a maniac... An hour would give them, what, thirty kilometres dodging through city traffic, running all the lights? It could be done.

First the chair, then. Running backwards into a wall to break the chair would be ideal, but she couldn't run, or walk, or even shuffle much. Each of her legs was tied to one of the front legs of the chair. Each of her arms was tied to one of the back legs. She could lean forwards, maybe, get her balance and then try to walk the chair over to a table with tools on it. If she could get a tool with an edge to it, she might be able to cut the rope. Despair filled her chest and made it hard to breathe. It was such a long way to go, tied up like that. It would be so hard to keep herself from falling flat on her face, and, if she got a tool, it would be a long, hard job to cut the rope. Even if she could do it without braining herself or slitting her wrist, it would take so long. Ten minutes. Maybe more. They didn't have ten minutes.

Nevertheless…

She rocked forward, trying to shift her weight over her feet. The chair didn't budge.

"Mum, be careful!"

"Says the girl on the floor."

She tried again, harder. The back legs came up with a sickening feeling of toppling helplessly forward, but she was nowhere near the balancing point and the chair rocked back with a thump. Her heart was pounding, partly from the effort, but mostly because she knew she wasn't going to make it. She'd felt dizziness and nausea as she tilted forward. She almost certainly had a concussion. Teetering a few meters tied to a chair was probably as far beyond her as crossing Niagara Falls on a tightrope. If only there was a way to get Cara off the floor.

Or to untie her.

Her daughter was tied up the same way Sandra was. She could see quite clearly the knot that held Cara's uppermost hand to the back leg of her chair. If Sandra could get her own hand near that knot, she could untie it relatively easily. All she had to do was shuffle her chair close to Cara's. She could probably reach the knot with her fingers. She began working her way towards her daughter, explaining what she was trying to do as she went.

"God, Mum, you're a genius! I knew if you woke up, you'd get us out." A man's voice said, "Stop it, please. I think I'm going to be sick."

Sandra looked to see Matthew propped against the control desk, swaying unsteadily. In his good hand, he held a gun.

"Persistent bugger aren't you?" he said. "But there's no escaping this time. Those bastards wouldn't take me with them. They said I'd slow them down. But I had the last laugh because someone fucked with the cars. They're all useless." He gave a short, bitter laugh. "So there's no way out of here. No escape." He wagged the gun at Sandra like an admonitory finger. "Not for you. Not for me. Not for anybody." He raised the gun and aimed it at Cara's chest, keeping his puffy, slitted eyes fixed on Sandra. "But you, bitch, you really need to suffer some more." The mouth within the swaddling bandages was smiling.

* * * *

A woman fell off her bicycle and rolled aside. Jay heard the bike crunch beneath the massive wheels of the APC. He prayed there were no bones crunching along with it. But he did not slow down.

"Chief Inspector, what are you doing?" It was English's voice coming from a speaker somewhere. Jay looked for a microphone but couldn't see one.

"Can you hear me?" he said but no reply came. The APC grazed the side of a building, shattering the structure with a tearing screech. He stopped scanning the dashboard and focused on keeping the speeding machine on the road.

"If you're thinking of approaching the compound on your own, I suggest you abandon the idea. The road ahead of you is blocked and my men will stop you if they have to."

"Shit."

He could see the FBI up ahead, two APCs across the road, and armed men everywhere. It would be suicide to attempt to crash through. He turned the wheel hard and ploughed straight into the nearest building. It offered almost no resistance as he crashed through insubstantial inner walls, the APC bouncing over beds and furniture. He hit the ceiling with every bounce and the APC shuddered as the machine gun on the roof was ripped off its mounting. A large wardrobe loomed ahead and was smashed to splinters as he charged through it, into a flimsy wall, and out into the street again. He pointed the vehicle in the direction of Polanski's HQ and gunned it. He doubted that English would be very happy that he'd avoided his trap so easily.

As he passed a point parallel to the roadblock, a handful of FBI agents came rushing into the street in their black armour. and helmets. They opened fire with automatic weapons and bullets pinged off the vehicle's sides. He was past them in a moment but had time to notice one man shouldering a rocket-propelled grenade launcher. Swearing, he threw the APC into the nearest building, tunnelling through it like a thirty-ton mole. A massive explosion hit him from behind as the grenade slammed into the building and detonated. He burst out into another street in a shower of debris and flame. Having completely lost his bearings, he took the first turn that led away from the men with guns and hoped it was right.

He barrelled along, trying to put distance between himself and any pursuit. He took another turn and another and found himself in a street full of running people. There were scores of them—men, women, and children—all carrying bundles and overstuffed bags, all running the same way as he was going. He searched for a horn but didn't find it. He kept going, making them jump out of his way. Then he realized what he was seeing: Polanski's people, fleeing the lob site.

He slammed on the brakes and threw the APC around. The heavy vehicle skidded in the mud, sliding into a three-quarter turn before it stopped, rocking on its springs. He slapped down the accelerator pedal again before he had a chance to dwell on how close he had come to rolling it, and the APC took off, barging into another rickety dwelling as he fought with the wheel to get it back on course. Now he was driving straight into the oncoming crowds and trying desperately not to kill anyone.

The lob's happened, he realized. *Jesus Christ, the lob's already happened!*

And there it was, Polanski's HQ. People were still coming out of it. It can't have been long ago. They'd have started leaving as soon as it happened, he thought, slowing to a halt outside the building. There's still time.

He became aware of a commotion building around him. People were pointing and shouting, not at him but into the sky. He stretched across the seats and peered through the side slit to see what it was.

Oh crap! He dragged himself back behind the wheel and hit the gas again. Outside, a drone was turning in the sky like a giant eagle, swooping towards its prey. The APC lurched into motion, bounding across the street towards Polanski's headquarters. A couple of men with guns started firing at him, bravely barring his way. He shouted ineffectually at them and kept going. In his mind's eye, he saw the little puffs of smoke from beneath the drone's wings as two small missiles pushed ahead of the robot aircraft, two missiles accelerating away from it at high speed, tipping their noses down towards the fat, lumbering APC as it scampered for the shelter of the ramshackle shanty.

* * * *

"I'm really glad you're awake," Sandra told Matthew. "I thought you were dead. Don't worry, I'm not going without you."

She felt rather than saw his finger tightening on the trigger.

"Set us loose and we'll get you to safety," she said quickly. "Kill either one of us and the other will leave you here to die."

He snorted with surprise. "You are incredible," he said. "Absolutely in-fucking-credible."

"You think I'm lying? Cara, have I ever not kept my word about anything?"

"There was that time you said I could go to Susan's party and then you—"

"About anything important?"

"Well, I suppose not."

Sandra glared at her and turned back to Matthew. "I give you my solemn word. I will get you out of here if you set us free."

"Really? Your solemn word? Well, in that case…"

"You're such a fucking arsehole. You'd rather die for sure than take a chance on surviving?"

"If she doesn't keep her word, I'll never speak to her again."

They both turned to look at Cara. She'd spoken with such complete conviction that even Sandra believed it.

"Do you want to die? Is it worth it for some petty bit of vengeance?"

"She broke my fucking jaw," he said and it sounded so childish and petulant that even he must have heard it because, with a lot of cursing, he limped and hobbled across the room to Cara. He put the gun on the floor and, struggling with his one hand, untied her. She, in turn, untied Sandra while Matthew snatched up the gun and hobbled away from them.

"All right, I'm trusting you. What's the plan?"

Sandra rubbed the blood back into her limbs. "First we get out of this building. Then we find a car. One that hasn't been sabotaged. Give me the gun."

"No way."

"You're going to have your good arm around my shoulders. If anyone tries to stop us, I'll need the weapon." She held out her hand. "We don't have much time."

He hesitated for only a moment. "Ah, what the fuck." He tossed her the gun and she caught it. To his evident relief, she did not shoot him.

"Now," she said and froze.

A rattle of gunfire came from outside. They barely had the chance to exchange questioning glances when the ground shook and the building rattled. *A bomb.* Sandra turned to throw herself on Cara who was standing, rigid and wide-eyed behind her. Before she could take one step, the wall behind Matthew blew in and a cloud of smoke and heat blasted in to envelop him. A shock wave hit her from behind and threw her into Cara. They both tumbled to the ground, tangled together.

When she could turn again, Sandra saw a massive flame-scarred military vehicle with a black crucifix come smashing though the half-demolished building, braking hard as it slewed to a stop right in front of her. She scrabbled in the rubble and smoke for the gun she'd dropped, touching its cold steel just as an FBI agent in full body armour. leapt from the cab and rushed towards her. Without hesitation, she fired two rounds into his chest.

Chapter 29

Timesplash

One summer night in Ohio, Polanski had been on the run from a local cop. It had been a betrayal, one of several he had experienced in his life. Sometimes the cops were OK. They hated the SOBs and they feared the FBI as much as anyone. Cops had helped him get away before, but not this one. This one was mean and smart and had chased Polanski across three counties. Yet that summer night was one of Polanski's fondest memories. He had taken a moment to rest on his back, with the cool grass beneath him and a warm breeze on his skin. Above him, a perfectly clear, moonless sky was painted with the glory of the Milky Way. Thousands upon thousands of stars filled every inch of the heavens in such profusion that he was overwhelmed by the wild extravagance of it. And, as he lay there, his arms and legs spread in complete surrender to the moment, the illusion of up and down left him and he experienced the world as it truly was. Just for a short moment, gravity held his body to the surface of a staggeringly huge sphere and he was looking across at a galaxy of unimaginable scale, filled to bursting with stars.

It was the closest Polanski had ever come to a true religious experience. In that brief but timeless episode, he felt an all-consuming awe at the wonder of God's Creation. He believed he had been given a tiny glimpse of how God Himself might see His Universe, and he held that gift close to his heart always.

Yet there, clutching the hard, cold components of his mortar, drifting weightlessly within a plastic bubble, a bubble itself drifting—or flying, or keeping perfectly still, he could not tell—in an infinite black void, he believed God was showing him another aspect of His Creation. The world of Man was filled with light, glorious suns lighting up the darkness like a host of Angels. But this place—the pseudospatial void—had nothing. It was nothing. As if God Himself, spooked by its emptiness, hesitated to say the words, *fiat lux.*

He should have brought a flashlight with him. He should have brought a luminous watch. He had no idea how long he had been in in this weightless nothing, bumping against the wet, cold plastic walls of the sphere, clutching his tubes and rods until his arms ached, listening to the soft, unvarying whine of the air conditioner. It could have been hours. That damned woman might have sabotaged the lob after all and he might be stuck forever in this Limbo, or until his air ran out, or the heater failed. He had counted his heartbeats into the hundreds, but his heart was beating fast and his counting was uncertain. He had given up in the end and waited, sometimes squeezing his eyes tight shut, just so he could see something, anything.

If he was truly travelling, he had no sense of it. He'd asked Matthew to explain it once, but the teknik had spouted jargon—psuedometatemporal gobbledygook. He should have asked Sandra. He had a feeling she could have taught him to understand what happened in a lob. But maybe understanding wouldn't help. He was a goldfish in a bowl, set inside a block of frozen obsidian. That was all that made sense.

The light, when it came, blazed like headlamps straight into his eyes. Blinded and shocked, he floated yet for another instant, then the ground hit the sphere, and the tubes and rods and plates in his grip smashed into his body and his face, cutting and bruising him. He held on tighter, and flew and whirled helplessly. The metal parts battered his arms and chest and slipped away from him, clanking together and beating against him. All he had left was the mortar shell, and he tucked it into his belly and curled around it. He hit the ground with his shoulder and then the bipod hit his head, causing a flash of pain brighter than the dazzling daylight. All he could think was, *Don't let it be broken. Don't let it be bent.*

He lay in a tangle of plastic sheet and twisted wire. Carefully, he set the shell beside him and sat up. It felt as if he had tumbled into a rocky ravine, and yet he was on the gentlest of grassy slopes. Even so, the sphere was wrecked and torn. The tiny part of him that had hoped he might go home felt the desolation of the new reality. In less than twelve minutes, he would be pulled back into that Godforsaken void to die there. His frozen corpse shattering on impact when it arrived home.

So be it.

He did a quick inventory of the mortar parts. The shell, sight, remote, and the bipod were all with him, but the tube was a few yards away, up the slope, and the base was even farther. It looked as if the heavy base had torn through the sphere first, followed by the tube, a fact which had probably saved him from serious injury or death. At least, in the short term.

He got to his feet. Blood trickled into his left eye from a cut on his forehead. He had many other cuts and bruises and his right knee hurt when he bent it, but, all in all, he was fine and able to carry out his mission. He stopped for a moment and put his hands together.

"Thank you, Lord," he said. "I know you had the perfect opportunity to stop me right there, and I hope I can take the fact that you didn't as a sign of permission for what I'm about to do. Amen."

When he lowered his hands, he noticed that they seemed to leave shimmering vortices in the air around them. He touched the cut above his eye and wondered how much damage had actually been done to his head.

He began to gather up the mortar parts, taking them to relatively flat ground nearby. He soon realized that the shimmering was not in his eyes, but was connected to everything he moved. The ground shimmered beneath the mortar parts, his footprints shimmered in the grass, his body left a trail of shimmering air as he limped from place to place.

He was off to a slow start in assembling the mortar and aligning it with Mount Vernon. At first, his hands were shaking, slowing him as he fitted piece to piece and tightened nuts. Beyond these merely physical impediments, he found the world of 1736 so different from 2066, that he was constantly distracted by it. He could not see the settlement of Alexandria at all from where he worked. He would dearly have loved to wander about and find it. The field he was in was broad and peaceful. A couple of dozen cattle grazed at the edge of the surrounding forest. He could not be certain, but one of them appeared to be twitching, moving back and forth in an unnatural way. He had no time to stare at it to be sure. The main thought that preoccupied him was the idea that all of America had been like this little corner of Virginia back then. The air was clean, the rivers pure, and the only tyranny that of the English lawmakers and tax collectors—which seemed benign compared to the iron fist of his own government. And, when the boy he had come here to kill had grown into the great leader he was destined to be, even that tyranny would be set aside. Then, for nearly two hundred years, the American people would be free.

And they will be again, he promised himself as he made the final adjustment to the mortar's angle. All the calculations had been done beforehand. He just needed to point the tube to the right compass bearing and set its angle to get the correct range. He turned on the remote and checked his watch. Three minutes left. He had taken longer than usual to set up, but that was OK. He still had plenty of time.

"Greetings, friend."

His heart lurched and he whipped around. A man in tan moleskin breeches and a voluminous linen shirt was striding towards him. His thigh-length waistcoat was undone and a black coat was slung over his shoulder. On seeing Polanski's shocked reaction, the man slowed and stopped. He wasn't armed, Polanski noted.

"Why, man, you're bleeding," the newcomer said.

The man looked concerned, not aggressive. Polanski didn't know what to do. "The worst thing that could happen," Matthew had told him, "is that you bump into one of the locals." And here it was. The worst case scenario. "If you see one," the teknik had said, "try to keep out of sight, or just pick up your stuff and go somewhere else." But he couldn't do that. It was too late. The shell needed forty seconds of flight time and Polanski needed to guide it on the final part of its trajectory. That gave him—he glanced at his watch—ninety seconds to do something.

The stranger, who had been studying the mortar, switched his attention to Polanski's wrist. "Is that a pocket watch, strapped to your arm?" An aura appeared around him as he spoke, just like the shimmering of the grass and the air, but more intense. It seemed as if the man were vibrating too, slightly, yet so fast that it blurred his features just a little.

"I'm afraid I'm busy just now, er, friend," Polanski said. "If you can wait one minute, I'll be pleased to talk all you want." Moving slowly, so as not to alarm the stranger, he picked up the mortar shell and raised it above the open end of the tube. All he had to do was drop it. When it hit the base of the tube, its charge would ignite and it would be away.

The stranger took a step forward. So much for not alarming him. "Good Lord, that is some kind of can-can-can-on-on, if I am not not not not mistakenn-n-n-n-n." The stranger twitched back and forth as he spoke. It was horrible and fascinating at the same time. Transfixed, Polanski stared at the man as he held the shell above the tube. "Who are you and w-w-w-w-what are you do-do-do-do-do" The man now seemed stuck on that one syllable, repeating the sound, repeating the same movements of his mouth, the little movement of his head. Stuck in a behavioural loop, Polanski thought, as if he might never move on from that moment.

And yet everything else around them continued normally. The trees nodded in the breeze. The cattle went about their business—except for that one he had noticed earlier. Insects buzzed and flitted. Only this stranger in his buckled shoes and tricorn hat was stuck in his own private loop. "Do-do-do-do-do-do—" Like a machine. And still Polanski's hand held the shell.

At the stranger's feet, in their buckled shoes and white stockings, a new motion began. The grass waved. It rose and fell in little ripples. As he watched, the ripples moved out from the stranger's feet, little concentric circles, spreading further all the time, now a yard in diameter, now two. A timesplash was beginning, simply because this man from three hundred years ago had seen Polanski and his peculiar equipment.

When the rippling ground touched Polanski's foot, he snapped out of his trance with a gasp. Time was slipping away. Worse still, the moving undulations were just a couple of feet from the mortar. If they reached it and unsettled it, there was no time to get it back on target. He dropped the shell and ducked down, covering his ears. The percussion was almost instantaneous and he felt the warmth of the blast on his hands and neck. Quickly, he looked up to see the projectile streaking away into the sky. The air in its wake crackled and shone, not from the little rocket engine, but in some kind of temporal protest at being forced into the wrong place at the wrong time. It was pretty. A contrail of rainbows. "You'll be so far back," Matthew said in his mind, "that the Universe is going to resent every moment you're there."

Suddenly, he toppled and fell onto all fours. The ground pulsed beneath him. The timesplash around the stranger was worsening. Polanski staggered to his feet and got clear of the widening disturbance. He ran about twenty yards down the slope before he felt safe. Cracks were appearing in the ground and he could no longer be sure of sizes and distances.

He turned to look at the stranger again and, as he did, the remote in his hand bleeped to warn him of the shell's proximity to the target. He peered into its little screen and saw the image from the missile's nose camera. The display showed the estimated point of impact with an oval around it indicating the possible error margin. It was hard to understand what he saw, even though he had practised this very operation half-a-dozen times. At first the aerial view just seemed to show empty countryside, fields and forests. Then he could see buildings—a house, barns, stables. A timer gave the countdown to impact. The digits were flying. He had almost no time. With a trembling finger, he touched the estimated point of impact and dragged it onto the house. It would not go all the way to the centre of the building, and instead stopped in one corner. He had left it too late, the projectile's limited manoeuvring capability could not change its trajectory as much as he wanted.

He watched without breathing as the last few seconds tumbled off the readout. The image of the house grew larger, the point of impact shifted about on the roof by small amounts, the oval of uncertainty began to contract around it. Everything accelerated until the oval snapped closed around the impact point and the image went blank.

Immediately, Polanski was thrown to the ground. The earth heaved. The sky darkened and the world seemed to fold. In the direction of Mount Vernon, the forest melted into itself then shrank away from him like an ebbing tide. He tried to stand but the ground had moved away from his feet. "Do-do-do-do-do-do—" the stranger said nearby with deafening loudness. Polanski turned in fright and saw the world tear itself in two, scattering cattle and trees.

"It worked!" he yelled, elated and terrified.

Something seemed to bore under the ground towards him, growing bigger and more fearsome as it came. It passed under him, the size of a train, tossing him into the air with a bone-jarring force. He twisted and spun helplessly above a world monstrous with violence. The ground rushed up at him, faster than it should.

The light disappeared.

Chapter 30

Flight

"O-o-o-o-owwww!" the FBI man complained. He staggered back, holding his chest where the bullets had struck, and fell onto his backside. "What did you do that for? It really hurt."

Sandra gaped. She knew that voice. "Jay?"

"Dad!" Cara shouted, and ran past Sandra to help him up.

Jay pulled off his helmet and received his daughter with a big hug and a lot of wincing.

"I thought you were the Feds," Sandra said.

"What, and you always shoot policemen on sight? I thought you'd got over that."

Sandra looked at him in amazement. He had the same long, lean body, the same dear face, only now he was a man, not a boy. He'd aged well. Cara was hanging onto him, beaming. When Jay looked at her and smiled back, Sandra's heart gave a little kick. But this was no time for working out what her feelings were at seeing them together.

"How fast can that thing go?" she asked, shoving the gun into her waistband and running to the APC.

"It's lovely to see you too," Jay replied, but hurried Cara into motion. "How long have we got?"

"About forty-five minutes."

She went to the passenger door and climbed in. From there she could see the burnt, mangled remains of Matthew. She turned her face away. Jay was handing Cara in through the driver's side. He climbed in after her, asking, "How far away do we need to get?"

"Go north," she told him, and he slammed his door shut and then stopped moving. "What are you doing?"

"Checking the direction on my commplant."

"North's that way," she said, pointing towards the F2 generators across the room. "Do you want me to drive?"

"No thank you, I'll be fine."

He gunned the engine, took off the brake and swung the wheel. The heavy machine lurched into action, swerving through a hardboard wall and into the dim bowels of the building. Cara squealed and hurried to find herself a seat in the back where she could strap herself in.

"How far do we need to get?" Jay repeated.

"I don't know. A long way. The crazy bastard went back to kill George Washington." Jay said nothing, perhaps saving his attention for the job of bulldozing his way through people's kitchens and living rooms. "It's three hundred and thirty years back. He might not make it. Every little thing he does back there could start a splash that would stop him."

"He seems the determined sort," Jay said.

They burst through a wall into a confusion of trucks and armed FBI officers in the street. Bullets hit them like a sudden hailstorm. Sandra winced and looked back at Cara.

"It's all right," Jay said. "Bullets won't get through. But they've got RPGs, and artillery, and drones. Nothing too sophisticated, though."

Sandra looked around at the steel walls enclosing her and

her precious daughter. It wouldn't take anything sophisticated to blow this rolling death trap to pieces. When she looked forward again, it was just in time to see them plunge into the wall of a building. She let out an involuntary cry of alarm before she realized they'd already demolished the wall and were through it with barely a bump. "You'll get used to that," Jay said as he drove the APC through someone's empty bedroom. A great explosion slammed into the side of them like a truck, blasting the walls and ceiling all around them.

"RPG," Jay said, flinching as the roof landed on top of them. "What the hell did you do to piss them off so much?" Sandra asked.

"They're just a bit over-sensitive." Jay crashed through an outer wall and they were in a street once more, even though it was so narrow that the APC could barely squeeze through without knocking down porches and flattening parked bicycles.

"They probably think we've got Polanski with us," Cara said, and Sandra and Jay both looked back at her.

"Shit. She's right," Jay said, eyes back on the road.

"What the hell would we want with him?" Sandra wanted to know.

Jay cut a corner, taking out a little hut with a barber's pole outside. "They'll just jump to that conclusion because they can't find him anywhere. Paranoia seems to be part of what they feed them at Quantico these days."

"Have you tried telling them? This thing's got a radio, right?"

"Probably. I couldn't find the microphone."

Sandra wondered if he was joking and decided he wasn't. She reached forward and unhooked the fist-sized mike from the dash.

"I was a bit preoccupied," he said, taking it from her. He held down the send button. "This is Jay Kennedy. Patch me through to Deputy Director English."

In seconds English's voice was growling out of the speakers. "Chief Inspector Kennedy, I want you to pull over right now and wait for my officers to arrive."

"I'm sorry but I can't do that. I have my daughter and Ms. Malone in here with me and I have to get them as far from the lob site as possible before the backwash hits. I suggest you and your men evacuate the area immediately and head North. Do you copy?"

"If you don't surrender right now, I will blow you and your passengers to pieces. Do *you* copy?"

Sandra saw Jay's jaw muscles tighten. "English, you are a fool. The backwash arrives in—"

"Thirty-nine minutes," Sandra said.

"—thirty-nine minutes, so you've got that long to get your sorry bunch of crusaders fifteen kilometres away from here."

"Thirty," Sandra corrected him. "Thirty?"

She could see him doing the calculation that they would need to average sixty kilometres an hour. His face turned white. "At least thirty, Jay. It could be much worse than that. I just don't know. It's George Washington, and it's deeper than any target of that significance has ever been."

English was threatening them with all kinds of things over the radio so Sandra leaned across and turned it off, acutely aware of invading Jay's private space.

"Dad?"

"Yes, love?"

"There's a little aeroplane following us."

Sandra turned to find Cara crouching by the rear hatch, peering up into the sky.

"Spy drone?" Sandra asked.

"The last one wasn't," Jay said. "Cara, if you see little puffs of smoke from its wings, give me a shout." He turned to Sandra. "I should drive inside the shanties for cover, but it slows us down."

"I'll go and keep watch," Sandra said and climbed into the back. "Cara, you get strapped in. I'll take over." The inside of the van whirled and she fell sideways into a seat and then onto the floor.

She heard Cara shout, "Dad!" as she felt her daughter's hands trying to turn her over.

"I'm all right," she said, struggling to sit up.

"What's the matter?" Jay asked. The APC swerved off the road and into the side of a building. Then they were bouncing and grinding their way through someone's home. "Sorry," he said.

Sandra realized Jay had taken cover because no-one was watching the drone.

She felt guilty, but it was hard to think straight.

"One of Polanski's thugs hit her on the head," Cara called to her father. "She hasn't been right since."

"Concussion?" Jay asked.

"Probably," Sandra replied, hoping that's all it was. "Go and buckle up," she told Cara. "I'm all right now." She managed to stand and then went back to the door, hanging on tight as the APC jounced across the rough internal terrain of armchairs and refrigerators. All the movement set her head swimming. Jay must have been watching because he swung the vehicle back onto the road. "Got it," she called, spotting the drone a hundred meters in the air and maybe two hundred meters behind them. Even as she said it, the aircraft dived.

The APC swerved back into the shanties.

"Jay," Sandra called to him. "You can't keep driving through peoples homes. You'll kill someone. Also—"

The front of the APC lifted as they came to a screeching halt. Sandra was thrown up the aisle almost to the front. Cara let out a shout.

"Also, you can't count on every pillar and pole in these places being as flimsy as the one's we've hit so far," she finished.

"Mum, are you all right?" Cara asked. Sandra patted her daughter's leg and pulled herself off the floor. "What did we hit?"

"Looks like some kind of pillar or pole," said Jay, drily. "The back wheels are still on the ground. This thing's got eight-wheel drive." He put the vehicle in reverse and it began juddering its way down the heavy beam it had struck. "The roof's on top of us," he said, peering up through the window slit. "Maybe a whole second story. I might need to go back and forth a bit to shake it all loose."

The APC jumped as a powerful explosion hit it. Sandra found herself back on the floor again.

"Everybody OK?" Jay called and, without waiting for a reply, raced the engine and set the vehicle scrabbling for traction through burning rubble. "Good news is, the missile blew the building off the top of us." The APC's big wheels finally got a grip and it shot off through the wreckage.

"Give me that damned thing," Sandra said, climbing forward and grabbing the mike from the dash. "English!" she shouted into it.

Moments later, Deputy Director English was back on the line.

"English you fucking moron, we have not got Polanski

with us. It's just me, Jay, and Cara and we're evacuating the disaster area. So stop fucking trying to kill us, arsehole."

"Do you know who you're talking to, young lady?"

"If you're still within the backwash radius, I'm talking to a dead man. Polanski's going to turn up at the lob site in about twenty minutes, probably dead. He'll have a canister of a nerve gas called VX with him, which might well have already opened, in which case, it will spread explosively through the area, killing everyone it touches. After that, the backwash will hit and, if Polanski was successful, you'll be standing near ground zero in the single most destructive event humankind has ever devised. And all you can think of doing is to chase me and my child with drones? Are you out of your fucking mind? Get out of there and run. Run for your miserable life."

There was a long pause before English said, "What about the plutonium?"

Sandra threw the mike into Jay's lap, too angry to speak to the ridiculous man. Jay picked it up and said, "Deputy Director, I've no idea who's got the plutonium you lost, but it's not Polanski. He's using nerve gas to kill George Washington. The plutonium is a red herring. Now, please, evacuate as many people as you can. Call ahead to DC, get them moving north. You might still save some people, even if you can't save yourself."

Sandra looked crossly at Jay and took the mike off him. "If you start a mass evacuation from DC, we'll get stuck in it, you idiot."

He snatched the mike back, scowling at her. "She's your daughter too," Sandra said.

English didn't reply for a long time. Sandra assumed he was taking advice from some other morons. When he spoke again, he sounded shaken, as if the truth had finally dawned on him. "I've called off the drones," he said. "And I'll make a few calls." He hung up.

"Great," Sandra said, for Jay's benefit. She was angry with him, even though she knew it was the right thing to do. "At least you'll die knowing you were totally noble to the end."

"I'm sorry," he said, and he did sound sorry, curse him. But sorry wasn't going to keep Cara alive when they hit the traffic chaos in DC.

She kicked at the dash in a frenzy of agitation. "All right! All right! It was the right thing." She subsided into her seat, fuming. She felt Jay and Cara watching her but wouldn't look at them. Wanting to keep Cara safe was the right thing, too.

"At least we can use the roads now," Jay said.

They had turned onto what was, for the Shanty, a broad thoroughfare, and the APC's speed was creeping up at last. Sandra studied the instruments. One of them seemed to show their current speed, sixty miles an hour.

"What's that in real money?" she asked, tapping the display. "I dunno. Ninety kilometres an hour? A bit over?"

"And it's the best we can do?"

He nodded, frowning at something ahead on the road. "Bugger," he said. "It's the roadblock at the main gate."

Sandra studied the obstacle. A dozen or so cars and vans, a horse-drawn cart, and some bicycle rickshaws were lining up to get out of the Shanty. SOBs were hanging about in large numbers. Beyond the roadblock, a motley collection of military vehicles with FBI markings—including a couple of APCs—were parked across the road. The actual roadblock was a couple of red and white striped poles between wooden trestles.

Jay began to slow down.

"No," Sandra said. "Keep up the speed. In fact, sound

354

your horn. We look like the Feds, remember. They won't know what to do until we're right on top of them."

Jay speeded up again. "I can't see a horn," he grumbled, studying the dashboard. "Why can't they just have driverless cars like anybody civilized?"

Sandra hung over his shoulder and searched too. She found a button on the steering wheel with a little horn glyph on it. "That one," she said, pointing. Her breasts pressed against Jay's shoulder as she leaned forward and she saw him glance quickly down at the point of contact before reaching out to push the button. The horn blared and Sandra retreated to her seat, confused and embarrassed. Outside, every head turned to look at them. Jay hammered on the horn again.

"What's that?" Sandra asked. They were so close now they could see the puzzled expressions on the faces of the men in the gun emplacements beside the barrier.

"Bit busy to look," Jay said, swinging across the road to get a good line between the queuing vehicles on one side and the small army on the other.

"It's a small truck with what looks like an F2 generator on the back and a couple of movie projectors on a rotating platform."

"Sounds like a radar-guided laser canon," said Jay, swinging through the gap and smashing the barrier to pieces as they hit it. "Please tell me it's not tracking us."

She turned to keep the truck in sight. "Oh, it's tracking us all right."

She felt his hand on the back of her neck as he yanked her towards him, away from the window, yelling, "Get down!" At the same moment, a bright light and a hissing, spitting noise came from the back of the APC and then another came from the front. A tiny rain of molten metal splashed down from the hole that had just appeared above Sandra's head. Jay threw the APC to the right and the hole turned into a line that burned its way above their heads. In the smoke it made, Sandra could see the thin line of the beam that was slicing through their armour.

Then it stopped. The APC, turning hard left, skidded sideways for an instant before its rear end hit something boneshakingly solid and Jay got it back under control. Sandra looked outside again and was shocked to find they were weaving through the parked military vehicles. The object they'd hit was a tank. The words, "Are you nuts?" sprang to her lips but she bit them down. This was the perfect shelter. Probably the only shelter for miles that the laser gunner wouldn't cut through to get at them.

"Remember you said they didn't have anything sophisticated?" she grumbled.

"Yeah, well, I hadn't noticed the ten megawatt laser."

"What's the range on one of those things?"

"Ten or twelve kilometres."

"Well let's hope it doesn't come after us, then."

It didn't. Sandra could only assume that someone at the blockade had finally got through to English and he'd told them to stand down.

Clearing the last FBI vehicle, Jay put his foot down once more and they motored along the ill-maintained concrete of U.S. Route 1 at top speed. Sandra checked her commplant. Thirty minutes left, give or take, with the whole of DC still to cross and no guarantee they would be safe even then. She sat back in her seat and rubbed her face with her hands. She could not remember ever being so tired.

"How's your chest?" she asked Jay.

He gave her a sideways look. "You'll be happy to know

the FBI give their agents decent-quality armour."

"Yeah, I thought you were making a lot of fuss about nothing."

"Apology accepted. How's the head?"

"Nothing a week in intensive care won't cure."

"It's funny how our little get-togethers always end in the ICU."

Sandra fell silent. She wanted to say, "Yes, that's why I've kept Cara away from you all her life." But that would have been unfair. Jay was only there to save her. It was Sandra and her chequered past that had led them all into this mess, not Jay. On the other hand, if he hadn't been so stupid as to bring Cara along, Sandra might have been home and free by now.

She brushed idly at the tiny specks of molten steel that had embedded themselves in the back of her hands and her clothes. Jay had done well to get them out of that one. She had a memory of him as a bumbling, gangly youth, a nice person, the nicest she had ever known, but just a bit on the inept side. It seemed that sixteen years of police work had changed him. He'd certainly filled out a lot. He looked good. His soft, gentle eyes looked so much better in a face that had more character in it. She remembered how sweet he'd been when he'd declared his love for her. In the tough, violent world she lived in then, sweet was probably the only approach to which she had no resistance. He had quite overwhelmed her, and his lovemaking had been deliciously tentative and delicate. For a while back then, she had thought herself in love. Until Cara came along and her priorities changed.

Chapter 31

Backwash

"You've woken her up." Cara sounded as if it had been reckless negligence on Jay's part.

He gritted his teeth and drove the APC up onto the pavement. People ahead screamed and ran for their lives. "Well, pardon me for trying to save everybody's lives. Next time we hit a red light, I'll just stop and wait for all the bicycles to go by, shall I?"

"God, are you always so whiny?"

"Yes he is," said Sandra, rubbing at her eyes. "But don't worry, love, he grows on you. What's going on?"

"We hit traffic," Jay said. He gave Sandra a quick, worried glance. It was all he could spare.

"I fell asleep," she said, seeming as surprised as he and Cara and been. "Where are we?"

"We just crossed the 14th Street Bridge."

"Do you know where we're going?"

"North on 14th. You said to go north."

"Dad's got maps of DC in his commmplant," Cara said. "I've been navigating."

Sandra reached behind her. "Give me a copy."

Cara stretched out her hand and held her mother's, creating a connection between their bodies' natural electromagnetic fields. Their commplants connected across the merged field and transferred the data. It took only a moment. Then it took another moment for Cara to explain to Sandra where they were. Meanwhile, Jay had driven the APC back on the road and was weaving through the traffic. So far, no cops were chasing him, but he expected them any moment.

"This is not good, Jay," Sandra told him. "Have you seen the time?"

He had no time to reply. He threw the APC across two lanes to avoid a hold-up, barging a delivery van off the road.

"This thing should have flashing lights and a klaxon, like a fire engine," he grumbled. The thought had occurred to him a dozen times in the past few minutes. Most drivers got out of the way when they saw the APC behind them—probably the big black crucifix on the front was more of an incentive than the fear of being rammed from behind—but some people were just plain stupid.

"Jay, we've only got seven minutes. We'll still be in the city when it hits."

"At least there's no evacuation going on, just normal traffic. The bastards kept it to themselves after all." He pushed down on the accelerator but it was already fully depressed. "I'm going as fast as I can."

She must have heard the desperation in his voice, or seen the sweat on his forehead, because her own tone was kind and sympathetic. "I know you are." He glanced quickly at her again. "If we don't make it, it won't be for lack of trying. I know that. Now let's see if we can't get off this main road, eh? Take the next right."

He barely made the turn. For the next couple of minutes, he found himself steering a complex route through back streets and alleys, plunging across streams of traffic at crossroads, and, at one point, pushing a parked car ten meters along a narrow road because there was no other way through. After that, however, they were on a long, straight road with very light traffic and were making good speed again.

"Five minutes until it happens," Sandra said but Jay's right leg was already aching from pushing the pedal as far down as it would go. He thought again about swapping the heavy vehicle for something faster, but again rejected the idea. The APC's armour. might soon be all that stood between them and chaos.

"What will it be like?" Cara asked. It was the thought on all of their minds.

"We're a long way from the centre already," Jay said, evading the question.

The road climbed a little and he saw the dome of the Capitol building in his rear view mirror. Even Polanski had expected the backwash to reach this far, but Jay trusted Sandra's more pessimistic estimate.

"It's going to be scary," Sandra said, answering Cara's question. "At least as scary as anything we've seen yet. But we'll get through it. Jay and I have done this before—more than once—and we can do it again."

"Can't we just hide somewhere until it passes? Underground, maybe?" The fear in Cara's voice was heartbreaking even to Jay. He didn't know how Sandra could stand it.

"I'm sorry, darling, there's nowhere to hide. A backwash distorts spacetime itself. It messes with causality."

"I—I don't even know what any of that means," Cara said.

"Neither do I," said Jay. "But I know it gets very weird. Things are distorted, time runs at different speeds, sometimes backwards even, but it's all broken and fragmented. At low levels, it's like a mild hallucinogenic—which you wouldn't know anything about, of course—but at high levels…"

"But we're going to be all right," Sandra said, firmly, poking Jay in the arm.

There followed a frantic period of turns and twists as they negotiated a maze of streets to another long, clear road. As Jay skidded the APC onto it, a police siren whooped into life behind them.

"Two minutes," Sandra said.

Jay took a long, deep breath, feeling his pulse quicken. Driving at high speed through Washington, with the constant whistling and blast of cold air from the slot the laser had cut, and the fear that he might not get Sandra and Cara to safety, had frayed his nerves to the point where his mind was crying out for a break. Yet he knew that in two minutes, those things would be the least of his troubles. He certainly did not need the Washington police force hassling him too.

"Shame these things don't have guns on the roof," Sandra said.

"It had one when I set off," said Jay. "But we lost it in the Shanty."

The APC bounced over yet another giant pothole and Jay's teeth clacked together. He took a quick look at the wing mirror. There were two cop cars behind him and a third swinging into the road to join them. They weren't Washington PD at all, but had the Sons of Joshua logo on their bonnets. Well, that was good. He'd feel so much better about having to sideswipe a bunch of SOBs than if they were regular cops. He looked again and they were all much closer.

"One minute," Sandra said. "Maybe you should slow down."

"When I have to. Distance is our only hope."

"We're twenty-five kilometres from Mount Vernon." Her voice was edgy and taught. "Everybody check your seatbelts, and hold on."

Jay recalled that there was a complicated formula for calculating how quickly a backwash propagated from its centre. Something about a spherical wavefront coming up from the timesplash, its speed proportional to how far it had travelled through time and the intensity of the splash. There was other stuff in there too. The wavefront was an eleven-dimensional sphere, or something, but only the first four dimensions were what mattered. He should have paid more attention, he supposed, but he knew it wouldn't have made any difference, either to his comprehension, or to how dead he was going to be soon.

A sudden roar brought him fully back into the moment. Sandra had opened a hatch set into her door. "What the hell are you doing?" She didn't answer him but pulled the gun from her waistband, stuck it out of the hatch, and fired three shots. He heard tires squealing outside as she ducked back in and slammed the hatch.

"They were about to take a shot at our wheels. That'll keep them away for a while."

"Jesus."

"It's happening," she said and braced herself against the dash. "It won't be long. Less than thirty seconds. Hold on, Cara."

He kept driving hard and fast. Every meter farther from

the centre would help. He would be hundreds of meters farther on by the time it happened.

* * * *

The first thing he noticed was how the road began to slope upwards. They were accelerating up the slope so fast that he was pressed down in his seat. Sandra shouted something that could have been, "Gravity!" but her voice was low and distorted. Buildings at the side of the road began to collapse. Pieces fell from walls and rocketed to the ground at unnatural speeds. The downward pressure was crushing him. He had to slow down. This rate of ascent was crippling. But slowing down had no effect. And then he understood what Sandra was trying to tell him. The local gravitational force was increasing. He pushed down on the accelerator pedal. He heard Cara scream from behind him. They were going to be crushed to death under their own weight.

With a sickening lurch the APC bounced so high, its wheels momentarily left the road. What he had felt had been just a patch of high gravity, and they were finally through it. He almost laughed, the relief was so intense. Sandra unbuckled and went back to sit next to Cara. She was moving too fast. A temporal distortion. He groaned, already yearning for release. But the nightmare was just beginning.

One of the SOB patrol cars shot past him, racing up the road at panicky speed. It didn't get far before a crack opened ahead of it and the car drove straight into it. It wasn't a wide crack, but enough for the car's front wheels and axle to drop into it and snag there. A cloud of sparks erupted from the car's front as its nose bit the concrete. Then it flipped into the air and somersaulted down the road.

Jay hit the brakes but there was no chance of stopping. The APC hit the crack but its giant wheels were big enough to straddle the narrow chasm. It thudded into the hole and bounced out again, slowing almost to a stop. Heart racing, Jay hit the accelerator again. He couldn't afford to come to rest with his wheels in that gap. Another jarring drop as more wheels hit, but the all-wheel drive saved them, and dragged the vehicle back onto the road.

Clinging to the steering wheel so hard his knuckles went white, Jay built up speed again. He went through a junction and saw that the lights were out. Probably the power was down throughout the city. A row of townhouses to his right buckled and collapsed into the road as if their brickwork was turning to dust. A row of shops ahead was ripped to fragments by a massive explosion. A huge fireball rose into the air from the ruins.

"Directions," he shouted back at Sandra. "It doesn't matter. Keep going north."

His wheels crunched over the debris from the shops and the stink of burning filled the cab. "There's a T-junction ahead."

"Go right then left," she said.

"You just made that up."

Sandra didn't answer.

"Find me a park," he said. "A what?"

"A park."

"You want to feed the ducks?"

"Christ!"

He spun the wheel as the road ahead began to ripple like water. He had to get right up on the pavement to be clear of it. The APC rang like a drum as bricks and tiles rained down from the adjacent buildings onto its roof. He gunned the engine, pushing on, fighting the urge to just stop and cower.

Then everything moved into slow motion.

He asked Sandra again for directions but she merely blinked at him in slomo, her face slowly creasing into a confused frown. To her, he knew, he must be twittering unintelligibly. Cara, also regarding him as if he'd gone mad, turned to her mother and began growling out a question that he had no time to listen to. However slow things seemed to him, the APC was still racing along the street, and buildings were still about to fall on top of it.

The rippling, liquid road beside him seemed more solid now, but he saw that a cyclist—caught in the ripples—was slowly sinking, now to his wheel hubs, now to his thighs. Another falling brick hit the roof and the sound was like rolling thunder. Slowly, slowly, the APC inched its way past the danger.

People everywhere had run out into the street, no doubt trying to escape their crumbling homes. Jay watched them with a terrible fascination as they slowly ran from one deadly danger to another, their faces contorted with fear as they screamed and shouted or looked wildly about them at a world gone mad. He saw a woman run from her home straight into the liquefied road, sliding down into it as if into thick quicksand. He saw a man and his young son standing together as a pile of bricks drifted down from the sky to crush them. An old lady, limping up the street towards him, waving her arms to flag him down, collided slowly with a young man running away from the APC. Then they spun together, whirled off their feet like a couple in a graceful ice ballet. The APC bore down on them with relentless inevitability. Jay grabbed the wheel to turn it, but had plenty of time to think about the cost of plunging Sandra and Cara into that concrete quagmire. His arms locked. He couldn't turn the wheel. As the APC slowly ground its way over the two people, he screwed up his eyes and put his head on his hands.

When he looked up again, he had passed the danger and could get them back onto the road. He turned the wheel but it was stiff and unyielding. He put more effort into it and it slowly turned, the APC responding with the extreme sluggishness of a supertanker. He shouted out an inarticulate cry of relief, realizing that he could never have avoided killing those people, even if he had tried. The APC would not have responded in time, but it would have pitched them all to their deaths in the liquefied road.

"...running faster for him," he heard Sandra explaining to Cara, as everything snapped back to its proper speed. The steering wheel was no longer sluggish and whirled in his grasp, sending the APC into a tight turn on the road. Too tight. The houses at the other side of the street swung into view. He wrenched the wheel back the other way, stamping on the brake, feeling the world tilt as they went up onto four wheels. The APC turned away from the wall it was heading towards and fell back onto eight wheels with a crash. Jay was thrown almost out of his seat but hung on as the vehicle juddered to a halt.

He swivelled around to check on Sandra and Cara and found them clinging to one another, staring back at him. One by one, they each began to breathe again.

Jay restarted the stalled engine and got them moving. "I need the nearest park," he told Sandra. "A football stadium, or an airport would do, but I need lots of open ground, OK? Shit!"

A massive wave was heading up the road behind them. A

tsunami travelling through the earth itself, five meters high, throwing everything—roads, houses, street lamps, vehicles, and people—to its crest and beyond. There would be no surviving it. Everything it passed beneath was smashed to dust before it reached the crest. Jay stood on the accelerator and willed the straining APC to go faster.

"What is it?" Sandra asked.

"You don't want to know."

"I think I do."

"Well, Cara doesn't."

"Yes, I do."

"Well, I don't."

Sandra climbed out of her seat, despite the jolting, veering progress of the APC as Jay steered it over and around the debris on the road, and went to the rear window to see for herself. She staggered back to her seat and sat down again without a word.

"Well?" Cara demanded. What is it?"

"You don't want to know," she said.

"We're outpacing it for now," Jay called back to them. "But if we have to—Bugger!"

A tall building ahead was falling into the road, or rather, sliding into the road as if it were made of molten cheese. He slammed on the brakes and hauled at the wheel, throwing the APC round a right-hand corner and into a side street. The back of the vehicle swung out in a dramatic skid despite the all-wheel drive. At the first opportunity, he turned left again, horribly aware of how the advancing wave must have gained on them.

Sandra climbed into the passenger seat beside him. "You can keep going up here for about ten blocks then you need to take another right," she said. Her confident tone sent relief flooding through him.

"I can outrun it on the straight," he said, "but if we need to do too much manoeuvring it'll catch us."

He saw she was watching the tidal wave of earth in the wing mirror.

"It's getting smaller," she said. "It might be nothing to worry about in a minute or so." A minute sounded like an impossible time to keep up that speed given the state of the roads. Jay's shoulders were on fire from the tension of this nightmare drive. They needed to slow down before he ran into something he couldn't avoid, yet he had to keep moving away from the centre.

"Have you found that park, yet?" He sounded snappish, even to himself, but he couldn't help it. His nerves were shot and he was exhausted.

Now on a new street, Jay saw bodies strewn across the road as if tossed there by some giant hand. Most of the buildings were on fire, but, whatever had caused such destruction appeared to have passed on. Sandra called the next turn and he swung into it, almost colliding with a car travelling fast in the opposite direction. In his mirror, he saw the car and its white-faced occupants turn towards the wave.

According to Sandra's directions, a turn was coming up that would take them away from the wave and Jay slowed for it.

"Not this one," Sandra shouted. "The next."

He swore to himself and revved the engine. They couldn't afford to waste precious seconds like that. "You've got to tell me what's coming up," he complained.

"There," she shouted, pointing. "Left, left, left!"

They almost missed it. The APC mounted the pavement and grazed the wall of a building before Jay could wrestle it back onto the road. He felt the urge to shout at her for almost getting them killed, but he fought it down. Shouting would feel great, but if anything could make matters worse right now, having a screaming match with Sandra would be it. He could see the wave in his mirror again. It was demolishing the street they'd just turned out of. So close! There was no more leeway. No more manoeuvres. But Sandra was right, the wave was much smaller, maybe just three meters high now. It was still pulverizing everything it passed beneath, but, maybe in another minute or so…

A bolt of lightning cracked through the air ahead of them, striking the road and blinding Jay. He hadn't been watching the sky and now all he saw when he looked was a broad red afterimage. "Damned heap of junk!" he shouted at the APC. "You couldn't even have reactive glass?"

"Are you all right?" Sandra asked.

"No, I'm—"

They all flinched as another lightning strike hit the ground beside them.

"I can't see a bloody thing," Jay said, blinking and squinting at the road ahead. Even so, he did not slow down, still feeling the presence of the wave behind them. In fact, now that it was so near, he could literally feel the ground rumbling and, as his vision cleared, he saw debris dancing on the road as everything shook. Cracks formed in buildings and houses, and they began to crumble as if in anticipation of the climactic shock racing to meet them.

"Mum!"

Jay turned to see Sandra and gasped to find her fifty meters away at the far side of the cab. The whole street had stretched wide, distorted in just one dimension. But Jay had hardly had time to wonder what the hell to do about it when the world snapped back to normal.

"Two blocks on," Sandra said, as if nothing had happened, "the road divides. Take the left fork."

He was panting and it took him a moment to realize what she'd said. "Right. Left. Got it."

He passed another area of melted buildings and kept the APC's wheels out of the pink and grey goo as if it might be contagious. He shot into the left fork at a reckless speed, terrified that they were now vectoring sideways to the wave, meaning it would catch them that little bit sooner.

"That's your park, up ahead," Sandra said. He could see where the houses stopped and a low fence began. There were trees and green grass. His thudding heart didn't slow, but some almost-numb part of his brain gave a little yelp of joy.

"There was a report done a few years ago," he said. "On civil defence procedures in case of a level five backwash." A bird, hanging in the air, frozen in time, hit the front of the APC like a sledgehammer blow. "Huh," he said.

"The report?" Sandra said, urging him on.

The park entrance was broad and opened into a gravelled car park. The turn would be sharp and the surface tricky. "Hold on tight, everyone." He took the straightest line he could into the turn, demolishing a small brick pillar on one side and a traffic sign on the other, and bouncing up over the curb. The APC slid on the gravel but Jay kept powering it forward—across the car park, through a bed of roses, across a path, another flowerbed and onto a neat lawn. The wave was just seconds behind him, still advancing in a wall of dust and devastation. Ahead, he saw a wide open field and steered towards it.

"They came to the conclusion that there was nowhere safe to hide from a backwash, but fatalities were significantly lower in broad, open spaces." He raised his voice. "When I stop, you'll have three seconds to get out of the APC and as far away from it as possible. Cara, get to the back hatch. Get your hand on the lever. Be ready to open it." He looked over his shoulder to make sure she was doing it. "All right? Here goes!"

He pushed hard on the brake and swung the tail around. The APC skittered across the grass and bounced to a halt. He threw open his door, jumped out and ran.

* * * *

The wave was less than two meters high when it hit them, hurling each of them and the APC into the air as it surged beneath them. The APC came down on its roof and Jay came down on his ass. For a moment, he was too stunned to move, and then he ran for Cara. She was on her back, winded but unhurt. He got her to sit up and then they both looked around for Sandra. They found her sprawled across the churned-up ground, out cold but still alive.

For the next half hour, they huddled around Sandra's unconscious body while the city tore itself to pieces. Another wave came through, but it was only half a meter high and did no farther harm. Away to the south, they saw strange, writhing distortions in the air and felt occasional tremors. The whole city was on fire and, at one point, a group of trees in the park sank into the ground and disappeared.

When it was over, Jay went in search of a car and came back with a battered Ford Greenie.

"It's got a full charge," he told Cara as they lifted Sandra into the back. "That's enough to get us to Toronto." Cara had not stopped crying since they found Sandra but she nodded her acknowledgement.

"Do you think you can navigate?" he asked. She looked a little desperate at the prospect so he said, "Don't worry. I'll get us there."

Chapter 32

Birthday Party

Jay went direct from Brussels to London through the new CT2 tunnel. At Liverpool Street Station he swapped the smooth-gliding luxury of the high-speed train for a clanking three-carriage metropolitan unit that would take him up to Norwich. On the way he watched newsfeeds on his commplant about the ferocious civil war that was raging in the U.S..

The rebels, armed and assisted by the South American Alliance, had taken control of most major cities in the North and West, but the South and the old Bible Belt were holding out. Texas had thrown its hat in the ring for the rebels and was now fighting its own war with all the States. Canada had declared itself neutral, although there were accusations from the U.S. Government, speaking from its new administrative centre in Atlanta, that the Canadians were giving support to rebel groups in refugee camps north of the border.

China was expected to declare itself for the Lord's True Path Party after a speech in Beijing on the subject of how stability and the rule of law were the overriding principles in international affairs. Europe was still holding back, refusing to commit itself.

But it's early days yet, Jay thought. It was only three weeks since Washington had been turned into a mass grave for nearly three million people. He supposed that Zadrach Polanski would be pleased with how much he had achieved.

When Jay got off the train, Sandra and Cara were on the platform to meet him. It was a bright November morning, cold and fresh, and Jay felt his spirits lifting as he breathed in the air of England for the first time in a great many years. Sandra looked stunning in a clinging Jersey dress, but Sandra would have looked stunning in a sack. Beside her, Cara was beaming and waving to him with both arms.

They took a cab out to Sandra's home near the university and had lunch in the garden of a pub nearby. When they'd eaten, Jay handed Cara a small package and said, "Happy birthday, sweet sixteen."

Her face lit up and she took it from him but hesitated before unwrapping it. She gave him a sly look. "Oh God. I don't know what kind of present-giver you are. This could be epically awful."

Jay shrugged. "My usual standard is catastrophically embarrassing, so anything less than that is a win, right?"

She grinned and tore it open. "Oh. My. God." she said and showed it to Sandra. "It's the new Fairy Tales of the Adjustment headworm!"

"I don't even know what that is," Sandra said, laughing.

Cara ran round the table to give Jay a hug. "Do you mind if I try it out now, Mum? Just a quick go?"

Sandra looked at Jay and he shrugged his approval. "All right but just for five minutes. It's very antisocial."

Cara laughed as if her mother had made a joke. Then she

sat down again, took the sensor ring out of the packet and fixed it around her forehead. She flashed Jay a quick grin and then appeared to fall asleep sitting up.

"She seems to have got over it quickly enough," he said.

Sandra gave a wan smile. "She has good days and bad days. We both do. Between us, I don't think we've had a full night's sleep since we got home."

Jay nodded. He knew all about not sleeping. "Is she seeing anyone?"

"What, you mean dating?"

"I meant a therapist, but… is she? Dating?"

Sandra laughed. "She's a beautiful girl. She's had boyfriends off and on since she was twelve. Nothing serious though. She's a very level-headed young lady."

"She must get that from me."

They fell silent until Sandra asked, "Did you sort out what you'll be doing next? Has the Temporal Crimes Unit closed for good now?"

Jay sighed. He'd spent the last fortnight running between Brussels and Berlin working on this very problem. "The TCU closes officially on Friday, but there's no-one there any more, so I guess it's gone."

"Have you been to see your old boss, Jacques? He must be sad to see his baby laid to rest."

"He is. He sends you his regards."

"Poor old Jacques."

"Nah, he's happy as a sandpiper. Lovely apartment in Paris with his beloved Marie."

"I haven't been back to the university yet," she said. "I don't think I can." Jay watched her and waited for more. "Olivia says I should take a couple of months off and not make any decisions but I've already decided."

"Seems to me you worked damned hard to build a career there."

"I never told you, did I, that I met myself on that lob I took in Alley Shanty. It was weird—about as weird as it gets, really—and sad."

"Sad?"

"I knew I'd been spun off as a temporary diversion of the timestream. I knew I'd been given a life that would last just a few hours."

"Like a mayfly."

"It was horrible." She drifted into a reverie until Jay called her back.

"I saw right through me," she said. "It was like having a mirror that would only tell you the truth about yourself." She shuddered. "So, no, I don't think I want to have anything to do with timesplashing any more. It was… just more insanity, from the same old place."

Jay watched this beautiful woman speaking about herself and found it hard to connect her to the girl he had known sixteen years ago.

* * * *

There was a pile of presents and a cake with candles waiting when they got back to Sandra's house. Cara blew them out in one go and made a wish.

"What did you wish for?" Jay asked.

"If I tell you it won't come true."

"You should tell people what your hopes and dreams are," he said, channelling his mother. "It gives you a bigger incentive to make them happen."

She laughed. "What a wise Daddy I've got." Her eyes

flicked towards her mother and then back again, her smile faltering. "Well, some things are just out of my control. I'm forced to rely on the cake gods."

Olivia came to visit and greeted Jay like a long lost friend, much to his embarrassment. She then made it worse by telling him what a hero he was for bringing her lovely girls back home safely. She'd brought champagne and they toasted to everyone's safe return. Then to Cara's sixteenth birthday. Then they toasted to the revolution going on in the States and wished it luck.

Towards evening, a group of girls called Cara on her commplant and she went to her room to don an immersion helmet and join them, continuing the celebration at a much higher volume. Jay was completely astonished by this, but Sandra and Olivia seemed to think it was all perfectly normal. Sandra went to the kitchen to clear up and Olivia buttonholed Jay, telling him he had to make Sandra stay at the university.

"It's important work," she told him. "And I'd be completely lost without Sandra."

"I don't think it's up to me to advise—"

"Oh, of course it is! She still loves you, you know. Never says anything, but I know."

Jay got her off the subject and onto her research. After a while he just needed to nod and make listening noises. It turned out that the images brought back from Queen Boudica's attack on Camelodenum were rather disappointing, but the historians were chewing it over and now thought they understood where they had gone wrong. When Sandra came back they carried on talking about Celtic England until Olivia jumped up as if she'd remembered something and said she had to go.

"Have a nice time, you two," she said from the doorstep, her voice heavy with innuendo.

"I hate leaving her," Sandra said once the door was shut. "She was my lifeline for so many years."

"Like Jacques was mine. Look, I should probably get going to the hotel. I don't want to lose my booking."

"Call and reassure them. We haven't really talked since the hospital in Toronto."

He reluctantly made the call and sat down again.

The doctors in the hospital had treated Sandra for a severe concussion, stitched up the gash in her scalp, and insisted on three days of bed rest and observation before they'd let her fly home. On the day they discharged her she had taken Jay's hand and said, "I'm sorry, Jay."

"For what?" he'd replied, stupid as ever.

"For keeping Cara a secret from you. I—I was so scared."

"Too scared to trust me to do the right thing."

He hadn't meant to speak so harshly, but there it was, hanging between them.

She said, "I hardly knew you. I just thought—"

"I loved you."

"What?"

"I loved you. With all my heart. Utterly. I trusted you to finish your treatment and come to me. I waited for you, Sandra. I waited for you for bloody years. Christ help me, I think I was still waiting for you when Cara showed up." For just a moment, the lid came off all the pain and anger and a little of it spurted out. "How could you do that to me? How could you not even tell me, give me a chance to see my daughter grow up?"

He hadn't waited for an answer but had walked out of the room, leaving Sandra looking as if he'd just slapped her.

Now he found it hard to find anything to say to her.

"We're leaving Norwich," Sandra said. "We have to. Olivia and the university got the police involved and the police managed to leak it to the local press. Your people kept it quiet—thank you—and no-one in the States who knew anything about it is still alive. Even so, I don't think it's safe here any more."

Jay didn't want to tell her she was being paranoid. He wasn't sure that she was. He said, "Where will you go? I don't want to lose track of you and Cara again."

She shrugged. "I haven't decided. I don't have very marketable skills, but maybe I'll go to another uni, in a non-time-related department. Maybe in industrial R&D somewhere. It would be nice to have some money for a change."

"I could have been sending you money," he said. "I—I didn't mean…"

She looked down at the carpet and, after a while, looked into his face. She wore an expression he remembered, at once brave and scared and determined. She said, "Jay, maybe what I do next depends on what you do. Maybe where I go depends on where you go."

The lid blew off and his anger erupted. "You piss away sixteen years of my life because you don't trust me to love my own daughter, you hide her away from me because you think I'd rather be chasing villains than being with you both, and now you think we can, what, make a go of it, put the past behind us, let bygones be fucking bygones?" He was on his feet and shouting and he really hadn't meant to. That wasn't the plan at all. He'd just wanted to establish some kind of normal relations, so he could visit Cara, get to know her.

He sat down again, cursing himself, and pressed a palm to

his forehead. He hoped Cara had not heard him.

"Jay?" He looked up. "I'm sorry. I think maybe I made the biggest mistake of my life when I didn't tell you about Cara, and you know I've made some really big ones. The thing is, I don't want to make another one. There's still time for you and Cara to be together—even if it's just for a couple of years before she goes to uni. There's even still time for you and me, if you could just not… hate me so much."

The rush of anger had passed and weariness had replaced it. "I don't hate you, Sandra. I couldn't. However crazy you make me." He hunted about for the words that would explain it while Sandra watched him, puzzled and anxious.

"You're the love of my life, you see. I thought I'd got over it, but, seeing you again just brought it all back. I don't think I'll ever stop loving you."

"So?" she said, hopefully.

"So that's why it could never work. It just all hurts so much. It hurt when I thought you didn't love me enough to be with me back then. But now I know the real reason you didn't come to me was because you thought I was too weak, or stupid to…" He took a steadying breath. "Well, it hurts twice as much. And there's a whole world of pain from having had my daughter stolen from me that I have barely scratched the surface of."

He stood up. There was nothing more to say. Sandra must have understood because she didn't try to stop him. He said, "You'll keep in touch, though? So I can see Cara?"

"Of course," she said and wouldn't stop looking at him.

"Say goodbye to her for me. Tell her I love her and I'll see her again soon."

* * * *

It was late when Jay got back to his hotel. He'd walked around the town. He'd dropped into a couple of pubs. He'd gone to the hotel bar. All of it to avoid this room, this anodyne, anonymous room. He'd been in far too many like it, all of them lonely rooms.

He synced his commplant to a big display on the wall, kicked off his shoes, and lay on the bed. His messages were few, and none of them were particularly interesting, except for one he'd seen several days ago and had not yet replied to.

It was from the Office of the Head of Military Intelligence, European Defence Force, and concerned a conversation he'd had in Berlin last week. Ostensibly, the conversation had been a debrief about his recent experiences in the U.S. He'd spoken with an English woman called Crystal, early fifties—round face, bright eyes—he hadn't asked if it was her first or second name. She told him she'd just established a new Section within EDF Military Intelligence. "A kind of counter-espionage unit," she'd said. "Focusing on the use of temporal displacement technologies by foreign powers. The kind of thing you've been doing domestically for some time now, only this would be on a much bigger scale, with much bigger budgets."

The follow-up message referred to their meeting as an "interview" and stated that she was pleased to offer him the post of Section Head, if he were willing to accept it.

Sitting on the stiff hotel mattress, he thought about it. Berlin wasn't so far away from the UK. He could still see Cara every weekend if he liked. If she wanted that. And what else was he going to do now the TCU had closed down and he'd burned his bridges with Sandra? He needed a new challenge, something he could immerse himself in, lose himself in.

Post-Adjustment Berlin was a beautiful city. As the new *de facto* capital of Europe, it was one of the most vibrant and exciting cities on Earth. The centre of European political, economic and military life, it was a city bursting with opportunity.

A good place for a fresh start, he told himself, his finger hovering over the reply button.

Thank You

Thank you for reading *True Path*, book 2 of the Timesplash series. I really hope you enjoyed it as much as I enjoyed writing it. If so, I'd be grateful if you'd leave a review on one of the book retail sites, your blog, or pasted to a wall on the nearest underpass. The rest of this series is available from your favourite online book store. To stay informed of when new books of mine are about to appear, please visit my website and sign up for my newsletter.

About the Author

I am a science fiction writer living in Queensland, Australia. A former research scientist, IT consultant and award-winning software designer. I now live and write in a quiet corner of the Australian bush with my wife, Christine, and a Tonkinese cat called Minsky.

Other Books By Graham Storrs

Timesplash, my début novel, was a Kindle best-seller. The series, *Timesplash* and its sequels, *True Path* and *Foresight,* was originally published by Pan Macmillan Australia. Both *True Path* and *Foresight* were shortlisted for Australia's première science fiction awards, The Aurealis Awards, as Best Science Fiction Novel.

In addition, I have been writing three series of novels set in my Placid Point universe: the Rik Sylver series, the Canta Libre trilogy, and the Deep Fracture trilogy, set eighty, three hundred, and ten thousand years in the future respectively. They are adventure stories, space opera, first contact novels, tales of the first transhumans, and so much more.

I also have a few stand-alone novels out there. *Heaven is a Place on Earth* is a thriller set in a near future dominated by augmented and virtual reality technologies, with all the opportunities for deception they bring. *Cargo Cult* is a sci-fi comedy in which the most ridiculous things that could plausibly happen, keep happening. *Time and Tyde* is a dark comedy set in the present day, about a man stalked by an amoral jerk from the future, or perhaps a man driven insane by a present-day stalker. Either way, it doesn't turn out well. And *Mindrider* – an urban sci-fi thriller about an alien invasion nobody wants and which even the aliens seem unable to prevent.

You can find links to fuller descriptions of all my novels on my website (grahamstorrs.com). Or just type my name into your favourite online book store and they should all appear.

Contact the Author

I am always happy to hear from readers, so don't be shy. And if you enjoyed this book, don't forget to post your review.

Follow me on Twitter: @graywave

or on Facebook:
facebook.com/GrahamStorrsAuthor

For details of all my novels and short stories, visit
grahamstorrs.com